The Complete Philosophy Collection (Vol. 1)

The Art of War, Meditations, Tao Te Ching, The Book of Five Rings & More Essential Classics on Strategy and Serenity

A Modern Translation

Adapted for the Contemporary Reader

Various Authors

Translated by Tim Zengerink

Table of Contents

Preface - Message to the Reader

What If You Could Help Rebuild the Greatest Library in Human History?

Thousands of years ago, the Library of Alexandria stood as the crown jewel of human achievement — a sanctuary where the collected wisdom of every known civilization was gathered, preserved, and shared freely.

And then, it was lost.

Through fire, conquest, and the slow erosion of time, humanity lost not just books — but ideas, dreams, discoveries, and stories that could have changed the world forever.

Today, the Library of Alexandria lives again — and you are invited to be a part of its restoration.

Our mission is simple yet profound:

To rebuild the greatest library the world has ever known, and to translate all timeless works into every language and dialect, so that no seeker of knowledge is ever left behind again.

By joining our movement to rebuild the modern Library of Alexandria, you become part of an unprecedented mission:

- **Unlimited Access to the Greatest Audiobooks & eBooks Ever Written:**

  Instantly explore thousands of legendary works—Plato, Shakespeare, Jane Austen, Leo Tolstoy, and countless more. All instantly available to read or listen, placing a complete literary universe at your fingertips.

- **Beautiful Paperback & Deluxe Editions at Printing Cost**

  Own any title as an elegant paperback, deluxe hardcover, or stunning collectible boxset—offered to you at true printing cost, delivered straight to your door. Build your personal Library of Alexandria, crafted for beauty, built for durability, and worthy of proud display.

- **Fresh Translations for Modern Readers—in Every Language & Dialect**

  Enjoy timeless masterpieces reimagined in clear, contemporary language—no more outdated phrases or obscure references. Alongside the original versions, we're tirelessly translating these classics into every language and dialect imaginable, ensuring accessibility and understanding across cultures and generations.

- **Join a Global Renaissance of Literature & Knowledge**

  You directly support expanding our library, publishing deluxe editions at true cost, translating works into all global languages, and bringing humanity's greatest stories to people everywhere. By joining today, you're not just preserving a legacy of masterpieces; you set in motion a powerful wave of literary accessibility.

Become a Torchbearer of Knowledge.

Join us for free now at **LibraryofAlexandria.com**

Together, we will ensure that the light of human wisdom never fades again.

With gratitude and a shared love of knowledge,
The Modern Library of Alexandria Team

Visit:

www.libraryofalexandria.com

Or scan the code below:

Introduction

Ancient Strategy, Timeless Serenity:
The Path of Power and Peace

The Complete Philosophy Collection (Vol. 1) assembles seven of the most enduring and influential texts on inner mastery and outer strategy ever written. In this single volume, readers will discover a treasury of insight from East and West, from battlefield wisdom to meditative reflection. These works—The Art of War by Sun Tzu, Meditations by Marcus Aurelius, Tao Te Ching by Lao Tzu, The Book of Five Rings by Miyamoto Musashi, As a Man Thinketh and From Poverty to Power by James Allen, Self-Reliance by Ralph Waldo Emerson, and On the Shortness of Life by Seneca—complement one another in their pursuit of clarity, control, and conscious living.

Though composed across centuries and cultures, these texts converge on common themes: the power of discipline, the necessity of aligning with nature or reason, the imperative to master the mind, and the importance of living deliberately. They are books of war and peace, of combat and contemplation, of solitude and societal engagement. They do not offer passive comfort. They demand inner transformation.

This introduction will explore how each of these works contributes to a shared philosophical project: cultivating strength without arrogance, wisdom without withdrawal, and action without agitation. These authors—generals, emperors, mystics, poets, and moralists—teach not what to think, but how to think. Not what to fear, but how to act. They show us the enduring truth: the greatest victory is mastery over oneself.

East and West, Sword and Spirit:
A Synthesis of Practical Philosophy

At the heart of this collection lies the balance between action and reflection. The Art of War, The Book of Five Rings, and Tao Te Ching emerge from Eastern traditions that emphasize harmony with nature, adaptability, and the paradoxical strength of yielding. They are not books of brute force, but of subtle power. Sun Tzu teaches that the greatest warrior wins without fighting; Musashi reveals that mastery of swordsmanship is also mastery of the self; Lao Tzu shows that true power flows from surrender.

In contrast, the Western contributions—Meditations, Self-Reliance, As a Man Thinketh, and On the Shortness of Life—speak from a tradition of rational introspection, ethical clarity, and moral self-possession. Marcus Aurelius, the Stoic emperor, writes of facing life's burdens with calm and courage. Emerson, the transcendentalist rebel, urges the reader to reject conformity and trust the inner voice. Allen, the prophet of thought-power, shows how our mental habits shape our destiny. Seneca, the Roman moralist, warns against wasting the only resource we truly possess: time.

These traditions are not opposed. They mirror one another across cultural boundaries. Both East and West recognize that strength without reflection becomes tyranny, and that peace without purpose devolves into complacency. What unites these authors is their insistence that wisdom must be lived, not merely learned. Philosophy is not an academic exercise—it is a way of being.

This collection reveals that the warrior and the monk, the general and the mystic, the king and the poet, all share a common path: the disciplined pursuit of excellence, the purification of thought, and the refusal to be mastered by fear, desire, or fate.

The Inner Citadel: Mastery Through Discipline, Purpose, and Thought

Each of the seven works in this volume offers a distinct but compatible approach to the same essential task: the cultivation of an unshakable self.

Sun Tzu's The Art of War is the most concise and influential manual on strategic thinking ever written. It teaches that all conflict—military, political, personal—is won not through brute force, but through clarity, timing, and self-knowledge. Victory begins with understanding the terrain, the enemy, and above all, the self.

Marcus Aurelius's Meditations is a private journal written by an emperor and Stoic philosopher. It reminds us that we are always in control of our attitudes, even if not our circumstances. Marcus urges us to live according to reason and duty, to act with integrity regardless of reward, and to greet death not with fear, but with acceptance.

Lao Tzu's Tao Te Ching is a poetic and paradoxical guide to harmony. Its message is clear: nature does not struggle, and neither should we. The sage follows the Tao—the Way—by letting go, moving like water, and knowing when not to act. Strength lies in softness. Silence is wiser than speech. Power grows from humility.

Miyamoto Musashi's The Book of Five Rings is a text on martial philosophy by Japan's greatest swordsman. But beneath its warrior surface lies a deeper teaching: that one must train relentlessly, remain unattached, and see clearly through the illusions of the world. Musashi's code is about presence, perception, and persistence.

James Allen's paired works—As a Man Thinketh and From Poverty to Power—form the foundation of modern self-help philosophy. Allen teaches that thought is destiny. As the mind is disciplined, so too is life. Negative thinking breeds weakness; right thinking generates strength, peace, and prosperity. These are not empty affirmations—they are calls to conscious mental effort.

Ralph Waldo Emerson's Self-Reliance is an anthem of intellectual rebellion. He challenges us to trust our inner judgment, to resist society's pressures, and to live authentically. Greatness, he insists, is not found in tradition but in the courage to be oneself, even at the price of misunderstanding.

Seneca's On the Shortness of Life is a Stoic meditation on time. He reminds us that life is long enough—if we use it well. But most waste their years in distraction, ambition, or servitude. Wisdom, for Seneca, means learning how to live—not how to delay death, but how to make peace with it through purposeful living.

These teachings are not for the idle or the indifferent. They are for those ready to examine their lives, master their thoughts, and walk with discipline and resolve.

A Philosophy for Living:
Beyond Reading, Toward Practice

This collection is not a museum of ancient wisdom. It is a living guide. Each work was born from real struggle—warfare, illness, exile, leadership, and solitude. These were not armchair philosophers. They lived what they taught. And they left behind not doctrines, but disciplines.

To read these texts is to begin a practice. To challenge your habits. To question your values. To examine what you fear, what you chase, and what you ignore. They ask you to look inward before acting outward. To see clearly before striking. To master yourself before attempting to influence the world.

These texts endure because they speak to the same challenges we face today: distraction, confusion, conformity, powerlessness. Their remedies are timeless: attention, integrity, simplicity, courage.

Whether you seek to lead, to create, to grow, or to endure, this collection offers a foundation. Not of rules, but of principles. Not of certainty, but of clarity. Not of comfort, but of strength.

Welcome to The Complete Philosophy Collection (Vol. 1). May these books become companions on your journey—not only as you read them, but as you live them.

The Art of War

Sun Tzu

Introduction

I. Brief Biography of Sun Tzu

Origins and Early Life

Sun Tzu, originally named Sun Wu, was born around 544 BCE in the state of Qi, which is now part of Shandong, China. The name Sun Tzu, by which he is better known, is a title meaning "Master Sun." Though much of his early life is still unknown, historical evidence suggests he came from a family with strong roots in military strategy and learning. This background likely helped shape his extraordinary skills in warfare and tactics, setting him up for the distinguished career he would later have.

As a young man, Sun Tzu began gaining a reputation for his sharp mind in strategy, though historical records about him are somewhat scarce. The lack of solid information has only made his life more fascinating, with parts of his story seeming like a mix of history and legend. His eventual rise to fame as a general and thinker was based not just on his practical knowledge of warfare, but also his ability to apply general ideas to real-life situations. His famous work, *The Art of War*, would form the foundation of his lasting influence, even though much of his life story has been blended with myths.

Military Career and Rise to Prominence

Sun Tzu's skills in military strategy didn't go unnoticed. He served under King Helü of the state of Wu, a role that gave him the chance to show his expertise on a larger stage. His ability to turn hopeless situations into victories earned him respect across the region. One of the biggest examples of his brilliance was when he defeated the state of Chu, which was much bigger and had more resources. This win highlighted his talent for outsmarting opponents with greater numbers and supplies.

The defeat of Chu was more than just a military win; it strengthened Wu's power and stability during a time when warfare between Chinese states was constant. Sun Tzu's strategies often used psychological tricks and deception, with clever tactics to weaken his enemies' morale before any fighting began. His deep understanding of terrain, human nature, and the use of deception made him stand out among other military minds of his time. These achievements earned him lasting fame and confirmed his place as one of the greatest military strategists in Chinese history.

Creation of The Art of War

It was during this period of political upheaval and near-constant warfare that Sun Tzu is believed to have authored The Art of War. The Warring States period (475–221 BCE) was a time of great instability, with various factions vying for control of China. In this context, Sun Tzu's strategies and insights were not only revolutionary but essential for survival.

Rather than a theoretical treatise, The Art of War is a distilled collection of Sun Tzu's accumulated experiences and the military wisdom passed down from generations before him. The text, composed of concise aphorisms and principles, is a practical guide intended for military leaders facing the challenges of warfare. Sun Tzu's approach to warfare emphasized the importance of strategy over brute force, and many of his insights remain highly applicable even in the modern world. His genius lay in his ability to condense complex concepts into simple, memorable phrases that have stood the test of time.

Even today, The Art of War continues to influence a wide array of fields beyond the battlefield, from business to sports, and remains a touchstone for anyone seeking to understand the nature of conflict and strategy. The timelessness of Sun Tzu's work speaks to his mastery of the art of warfare and his ability to provide wisdom that transcends the ages.

II. Historical Context

Sun Tzu lived during one of the most chaotic times in Chinese history, a period historians call the Spring and Autumn period, which later became the Warring States period (around 771–221 BCE). This era saw the weakening of the Zhou Dynasty's power, leading to constant wars between rival states. Regional leaders fought for control, with alliances constantly shifting and battles happening frequently. The political scene was unstable, and military skill was vital not just for winning but for survival.

As states competed for dominance, warfare was about more than just expanding territories; it was necessary for keeping sovereignty. Even small mistakes could lead to the complete destruction of a state, making military leaders crucial to the survival of nations. It was in this intense environment that Sun Tzu's strategies developed. He created his tactics not only to secure victories but to ensure long-term survival in a world where states were often annexed or destroyed. His strategies responded to a reality where the stakes were incredibly high, offering insights that went beyond war and into the political dynamics of the time.

The fierce competition for power among Chinese states during the Warring States period required new approaches to warfare, focusing on cunning, intelligence, and strategy rather than just raw strength. Sun Tzu's writings came out of this era of near-constant conflict, where he understood that success depended on outsmarting the opponent, not just overpowering them. His methods were designed for a time when a single wrong move could lead to disaster, stressing careful planning and the need for preparation in an unpredictable and dangerous world.

The Role of Warfare in Ancient China

In ancient China, warfare was much more than just battles fought on the field; it was closely connected with politics, philosophy, and governance. Leaders during this time were expected not only to be skilled in battle but also to be strong in diplomacy and statecraft.

Military action was often a tool used to achieve political goals, and leaders had to balance the challenges of internal governance while also preparing for outside threats. Sun Tzu's approach to warfare reflects this larger understanding, as he constantly stressed the importance of planning ahead, being flexible, and understanding both the enemy and one's own forces.

Warfare during this period was all-encompassing. It involved logistics, governance, and diplomacy, areas where military leaders needed to show not only strength but also wisdom. Sun Tzu's strategies, which often focused on winning without fighting, came from this broader view of conflict, where preserving resources and maintaining the stability of the state were as crucial as defeating the enemy. His well-known principle, "The supreme art of war is to subdue the enemy without fighting," demonstrates his understanding of the long-term effects of war. Instead of seeking short-term victories at great costs, he promoted strategies that would protect the state's power while weakening the opponent's will.

During Sun Tzu's era, military leaders were expected to grasp the moral and philosophical sides of warfare. Confucian values influenced Chinese society deeply, shaping how rulers led and how they fought. Leaders were judged not just by their military successes but by their ability to keep order and promote justice. Sun Tzu's work reflects this, as it puts great importance on the qualities of leadership and the ethical aspects of warfare. He supported the idea of a wise and virtuous leader, one who could inspire loyalty among soldiers while staying calm and focused in the chaos of battle.

The political landscape was always changing, with alliances breaking as quickly as they were formed. Espionage, deception, and psychological warfare became key tools for staying ahead. Sun Tzu's contributions to the art of war went beyond just battlefield tactics; they involved understanding the enemy's mind and manipulating both physical and mental conditions to achieve victory. He understood that sometimes the best battle is the one that's won before it even starts.

His insights into psychological manipulation, deception, and moral unity within an army were direct responses to the complex and high-stakes world of ancient Chinese warfare.

In this world of shifting power and constant conflict, Sun Tzu developed his principles not as abstract ideas but as practical tools for survival and dominance. His belief that victory could be achieved in ways other than battle was groundbreaking in a time when brute strength often ruled. His strategies focused on flexibility, intelligence, and the power of unpredictability. By continuously adjusting to changing situations, he believed a general could turn even the most desperate circumstances into opportunities for success. In this way, his work is not only a reflection of his era but a timeless guide for those looking to navigate conflict with wisdom and precision.

III. Philosophical Background

Sun Tzu's ideas didn't develop in isolation; they were influenced by the major philosophical traditions of ancient China, especially Daoism and Confucianism. Daoism, which emphasizes balance, harmony, and non-contention, had a deep impact on his strategic thinking. At its core, Daoism teaches that one should move with the natural flow of the universe, rather than resist it. This belief in flexibility and adaptability is reflected in Sun Tzu's view that a good leader must be flexible in both thought and action, ready to adapt to changing situations instead of sticking rigidly to a set plan. The idea of winning with minimal force—ideally without fighting at all—embodies the Daoist principle of achieving results with the least effort, which is central to The Art of War.

Moreover, Daoism's focus on harmony is seen in Sun Tzu's approach to warfare as an art where the best outcomes are those that avoid conflict altogether. He recognized that forcing a victory often brings about unnecessary destruction and loss, not just in terms of lives but also resources and morale. Instead, he advocated for strategies that involved subtlety, psychological manipulation, and careful planning, all aligned with the natural course of events. Sun

Tzu's famous saying, "The supreme art of war is to subdue the enemy without fighting," reflects Daoist wisdom, where the soft overcomes the hard, and the flexible triumphs over the rigid.

Confucianism also played a key role in shaping Sun Tzu's philosophy. Confucian values like duty, ethical conduct, and governing with moral integrity are present in his view of leadership. In Confucian thought, a leader's role is not just about winning; it includes the well-being of the people and the pursuit of order and justice. Sun Tzu's writings, although focused on military strategy, emphasize that a good general must also be a wise and virtuous leader. This aligns with the Confucian ideal of the "Junzi," or the gentleman, who leads by moral virtue and serves as a role model. Sun Tzu believed that an effective leader earns loyalty and trust, not through fear or force, but through wisdom, fairness, and calm decision-making. The combination of Confucian ethics and Daoist practicality creates a balanced framework for Sun Tzu's strategies, making The Art of War not just a guide to military success but also a blueprint for ethical leadership.

Core Principles of Sun Tzu's Philosophy

The Importance of Strategy Over Force

At the core of Sun Tzu's philosophy is the belief that strategic insight is more valuable than brute strength. He argues that the best victories are those achieved without fighting, highlighting the need for careful planning, foresight, and the use of intelligence rather than relying solely on physical power. For Sun Tzu, a leader's role is to outthink their opponent instead of outfight them. He advocated for a strategic approach that reduces the costs of war, both in terms of human lives and resources. Instead of direct conflict, Sun Tzu advises military leaders to disorient their enemies, target their weaknesses, and use deception to gain an advantage. To him, a well-fought battle is one that ends before it even starts, with the enemy defeated by the unseen forces of superior strategy.

Flexibility and Adaptability in Warfare

One of Sun Tzu's key principles is that rigid plans often lead to failure. Success on the battlefield depends on the ability to adapt and respond to constantly changing conditions. He teaches that no two battles are the same, so no single strategy can work for every situation. Instead, Sun Tzu emphasizes the need for flexibility, urging generals to stay fluid in both thought and action. In his view, the best leaders are those who can read the terrain, understand their troops' morale, anticipate their enemy's moves, and adjust their tactics as needed. By avoiding predictable patterns, a leader can keep their opponents off balance, staying one step ahead.

Flexibility goes beyond just physical movements on the battlefield. It includes mental agility, the ability to think quickly, and the willingness to abandon a failing plan for a better one. Sun Tzu believed that sticking stubbornly to a plan, no matter how well thought out, could lead to disaster if it didn't fit the situation. His philosophy encourages leaders to be like water, adapting to the shape of their environment, changing form as conditions change, and always finding a way to move forward. This principle of adaptability has made The Art of War highly relevant in many areas beyond the military, including business and sports, where the ability to pivot in response to new challenges is often the key to success.

Psychological Warfare

Another core element of Sun Tzu's philosophy is his deep understanding of the human mind, both in terms of the enemy and one's own troops. He places great emphasis on psychological warfare, believing that many battles are won or lost in the mind long before they are fought on the battlefield. A leader who can demoralize the enemy, spread confusion, or instill doubt has already set the stage for victory. Sun Tzu advocates using tactics such as deception, misinformation, and surprise to weaken the enemy's confidence and will to fight. By showing strength when weak or pretending to be disorganized when ready to attack, a leader can manipulate the enemy into making costly errors. To Sun Tzu, deception is not just a tactic—it is the essence of warfare.

Equally important is understanding the psychology of one's own troops. Sun Tzu teaches that a successful leader must know how to keep their forces united and their morale high. Soldiers who trust their commander, believe in their cause, and feel confident in the strategy are far more likely to fight bravely and with determination. Sun Tzu believed that a wise general knows how to inspire and motivate, how to reward loyalty, and how to manage fear and uncertainty within the ranks. In his view, leadership is just as much about fostering the right mindset as it is about military skill.

The Role of Leadership

At the core of Sun Tzu's strategic thought lies Sun Tzu believed that leadership is essential to the success of any endeavor, whether military or otherwise. The qualities of a great leader, in his view, go beyond tactical skill. A leader must possess wisdom, remain calm under pressure, be decisive, and uphold moral integrity. For Sun Tzu, leadership isn't just about giving orders; it's about guiding one's people with a steady hand and clear vision. The ability of a leader to inspire trust and unity among their troops is often the key to determining the outcome of a battle.

In The Art of War, Sun Tzu stresses that a leader must deeply understand human nature and manage both resources and emotions wisely. A good leader knows when to be strict and when to show compassion, when to give rewards and when to administer punishment, always balancing authority with wisdom. The leader's role is to create harmony within the ranks, ensuring that everyone, from the highest officers to the lowest soldiers, works together as a unified team. Sun Tzu believed that leadership was the ultimate factor in determining success, and that no amount of strength or resources could make up for a lack of vision and guidance from the top.

For Sun Tzu, leadership is both an art and a responsibility. It requires not only the skill to create great strategies but also the wisdom to carry them out with compassion and integrity. His insights elevate the role of a leader to that of a moral authority, making it clear that true power comes not from dominance but from understanding and mastering oneself, the situation, and those who follow.

IV. Key Themes and Structure of The Art of War

The Art of Strategy

At the core of The Art of War is the idea that victory is achieved through careful planning and strategic foresight. Instead of depending on brute force or sheer numbers, Sun Tzu highlights the importance of intelligence, preparation, and the thoughtful management of resources. To him, a successful campaign begins long before the actual battle. It requires a leader to evaluate not only their own strengths and weaknesses but also those of their enemy. This involves understanding the terrain, the morale of the troops, and the timing of actions. A well-planned strategy, in Sun Tzu's view, allows one to control the battlefield before the enemy even realizes they are being outmaneuvered.

Sun Tzu explains that strategy is the key to using minimal resources for maximum effect. It's not enough to simply fight well; one must fight smart, knowing when to strike and when to hold back. His focus on strategic thinking teaches that victory often belongs to those who understand when to avoid fighting altogether. For Sun Tzu, the greatest generals are those who can win wars without engaging in combat. His insights encourage readers to look at the bigger picture of their challenges, whether in warfare or life, and to approach them with deliberate, calculated actions rather than reacting on impulse.

The Principle of Deception

One of the most enduring and thought-provoking principles in The Art of War is the role of deception. Sun Tzu's famous statement, "All warfare is based on deception," sums up his belief that a commander's true strength lies in their ability to mislead and outsmart the enemy. Deception isn't just a tactic—it's a fundamental part of strategy, allowing a leader to shape the enemy's perceptions and decisions. By creating a false sense of security or concealing one's true intentions, a skilled leader can manipulate their adversary into making costly errors. Misinformation, fake retreats, and surprise attacks are all tools in the strategist's toolkit.

In Sun Tzu's philosophy, deception is about gaining the upper hand through psychological means. The aim is to make the opponent feel secure where they are weak and vulnerable where they are strong. By hiding one's true strengths and revealing only what is necessary, a general can keep the enemy in a constant state of doubt. This unpredictability, according to Sun Tzu, is essential for achieving success. His teachings on deception go far beyond the battlefield and have proven valuable in many areas of modern life, including business negotiations, competitive sports, and political strategy.

Adaptability and Flexibility

Throughout The Art of War, Sun Tzu consistently emphasizes the importance of adaptability in the face of changing circumstances. A leader who clings to a single plan or strategy, regardless of the evolving situation, is bound to fail. Instead, Sun Tzu advocates for a flexible approach, where a commander can pivot quickly and seize opportunities as they arise. In his view, the ability to adapt is a defining quality of a great general. Sun Tzu compares the ideal leader to water, which conforms to the shape of whatever contains it. Just as water flows around obstacles, a successful commander must move with the ever-changing conditions of warfare.

This principle of adaptability aligns with Sun Tzu's belief that no two battles are alike. The unpredictable nature of conflict requires a mindset open to change, whether in tactics, alliances, or terrain. Leaders must be able to set aside preconceived notions and embrace the fluid nature of their surroundings. Sun Tzu's insight extends beyond military situations to modern leadership challenges, reminding readers that success often depends on staying flexible, innovative, and responsive to new information.

The Role of Morale and Unity

For Sun Tzu, victory is not merely about having the largest army or the most skilled fighters. The morale of the troops and the unity of the command structure are just as vital to success as any weapon or strategy. Soldiers who trust their leader and believe in their cause are much more likely to perform well under pressure than those who are demoralized or divided. Sun Tzu places significant importance on treating soldiers with respect, addressing their needs, and inspiring them with a sense of purpose. A general who can command loyalty and cultivate unity within the ranks is far better prepared to face the challenges of war.

Additionally, Sun Tzu underscores the need for clear and consistent leadership. A general must be decisive and fair, maintaining discipline while also knowing when to show compassion. The bond between a leader and their soldiers is a crucial element in creating a cohesive and effective fighting force. Internal harmony can often be the deciding factor in battle, especially when facing difficult circumstances. Sun Tzu's teachings on morale and unity go beyond the battlefield, offering valuable insights for modern leaders in business, politics, or personal endeavors. They remind us that a team's success often hinges as much on its internal dynamics as it does on external factors.

V. Influence and Legacy of The Art of War

Influence in East Asia

The Art of War has been a foundational text in East Asia for centuries, deeply influencing the philosophies and practices of military leaders, scholars, and political strategists. From China to Japan and Korea, its principles have shaped the ways wars were fought and how empires were governed. In China, where Sun Tzu first developed his strategies, dynasties studied the text to refine their military tactics, using its teachings to defend and expand their territories. Beyond the battlefield, The Art of War guided Chinese governance, diplomacy, and statecraft, serving as a manual for leaders who sought to balance power, strategy, and ethics.

In Japan, The Art of War became prominent during the Samurai era, especially in the development of Bushido, the warrior's code of honor. Japanese military leaders, including figures like Oda Nobunaga and Tokugawa Ieyasu, drew inspiration from Sun Tzu's principles. His teachings on discipline, adaptability, and the importance of psychological warfare resonated deeply with the samurai ethos, further embedding The Art of War into Japan's cultural and military traditions. The text's influence reached beyond warfare, shaping how political leaders approached negotiations and alliances.

Korea also embraced Sun Tzu's strategies, applying them in times of internal conflict and external threats, particularly during struggles with neighboring states. For centuries, Korean scholars and military generals turned to The Art of War when planning defenses and military campaigns, finding in its pages the strategic insight and adaptability needed to navigate complex geopolitical landscapes. Sun Tzu's focus on intelligence, deception, and strategic positioning over brute force made his work a vital resource in East Asia's long history of warfare and statecraft.

Influence in Modern Warfare

As the centuries went by, The Art of War spread beyond East Asia and started to influence military strategies around the world. Its ideas were eventually adopted by Western military leaders and strategists, especially during the 19th and 20th centuries when warfare became more complicated. For example, Napoleon Bonaparte is said to have been greatly influenced by Sun Tzu's teachings. His military campaigns across Europe showed how effective it was to use strategic surprise, careful planning, and taking advantage of the enemy's weaknesses— all key elements of Sun Tzu's approach.

In the 20th century, Sun Tzu's influence could be seen especially in guerrilla warfare tactics. Revolutionary leaders like Mao Zedong in China and Ho Chi Minh in Vietnam used The Art of War's focus on psychological warfare, deception, and asymmetrical tactics to defeat stronger and better-equipped enemies. In Vietnam, during the conflict with the United States, Ho Chi Minh and his generals applied Sun Tzu's strategies very effectively, using the jungle terrain and psychological endurance to weaken their enemy's determination and eventually force their withdrawal.

Today, The Art of War is often studied in military academies alongside other classic works on strategy and tactics. Its ideas have shaped both the theoretical and practical education of military officers around the world. From Sandhurst in the UK to West Point in the United States, Sun Tzu's teachings still provide important lessons about leadership, intelligence gathering, and the moral aspects of warfare. His belief that the best victories are those won without fighting connects well with modern military thinking, where political and economic strategies often work alongside or instead of traditional battles.

Beyond the Battlefield: Business, Sports, and Politics

While The Art of War started as a military guide, its influence has spread far beyond the battlefield. In the business world, leaders and entrepreneurs have used Sun Tzu's principles to navigate competitive markets, secure good deals, and manage teams effectively. The strategic use of resources, understanding the competition, and adapting to changes are all ideas from The Art of War that have been applied to the corporate world. Today, it's common for business executives to look to Sun Tzu for advice on everything from launching new products to negotiating mergers.

Likewise, sports coaches and athletes have found value in Sun Tzu's focus on preparation, adaptability, and mental strength. Competitive sports, like warfare, require knowing your opponent, anticipating their moves, and adjusting strategies as the game goes on. Whether in battle or in sports, the ability to stay calm and outsmart the competition is universally important.

In politics, The Art of War has also left its mark. Leaders use its ideas when approaching diplomacy, forming alliances, and even running election campaigns. Politicians often apply Sun Tzu's tactics to influence public perception, undermine rivals without direct conflict, and take advantage of timing and positioning. The text's focus on intelligence gathering and strategic alliances is especially relevant in modern politics, where behind-the-scenes efforts can determine the outcome of public contests.

A Lasting Legacy

The Art of War remains a timeless resource, providing guidance that transcends time, culture, and discipline. Whether on the battlefield, in the boardroom, or in everyday life, Sun Tzu's strategies have endured because they are rooted in a deep understanding of human nature and the complexities of conflict. His ability to simplify the chaotic and often harsh realities of war into clear, actionable principles continues to inspire leaders across various fields.

As we move further into an age where technology and information play increasingly larger roles in conflict and competition, Sun Tzu's teachings on deception, intelligence, and adaptability feel more relevant than ever. His insights remind us that victory is not always achieved through strength alone, but through careful thought, ethical leadership, and a deep understanding of the human element in every pursuit.

Sun Tzu's influence on both ancient and modern warfare, along with his broader impact on business, politics, and leadership, solidifies The Art of War as one of the most important and lasting texts on strategy. His legacy continues to shape how people approach conflict, competition, and success, offering timeless wisdom that resonates with each generation.

Chapter 1 - Laying Plans

Sun Tzu said: The art of war is critically important to the State. It can be the difference between life and death, leading to either safety or ruin. Therefore, it must always be carefully studied and never ignored.

The art of war is based on five key factors that must be considered in every military decision. These factors are: (1) The Moral Law; (2) Heaven; (3) Earth; (4) The Commander; (5) Method and discipline.

The Moral Law ensures that the people are fully united with their ruler, making them willing to follow him, even risking their lives without fear of danger.

Heaven refers to the natural conditions, like day and night, cold and heat, and the changing of seasons.

Earth involves distances, both large and small, areas of safety and danger, wide open spaces and narrow paths, and the possibilities of survival or death.

The Commander represents the qualities of wisdom, honesty, kindness, courage, and strictness.

Method and discipline cover the organization of the army, the ranks, the roles assigned to each soldier, and the control of supplies and resources.

These five factors must be studied in depth by those who seek to understand the art of war. By mastering them, a ruler can win the loyalty of the people and command a strong, unified army capable of facing any challenge.

The Moral Law creates harmony between the ruler and the people, inspiring them to follow without hesitation, even in the face of great danger.

Heaven includes the cycles of day and night, the changes in temperature, and the timing of seasons. Some interpret this as a reflection of the broader workings of nature, like the balance of forces or natural elements.

Earth includes not just physical distances but also the dangers and safety that different terrains bring, whether they are wide open plains or narrow mountain passes. These elements can determine the chances of survival or death.

The Commander stands for qualities that inspire trust and loyalty—wisdom, honesty, kindness, bravery, and firmness in discipline. These virtues are essential for strong leadership.

Finally, Method and discipline ensure that the army is well-organized, with clear roles and responsibilities, and that resources are well-managed. These elements ensure that the military is prepared for anything and that chaos is avoided during battle.

Method and discipline mean organizing the army into its proper divisions, assigning ranks among the officers, maintaining roads to ensure supplies can reach the army, and controlling military spending.

These five principles should be well-known to every general: the one who knows them will be victorious; the one who does not will fail.

Therefore, in your planning, when trying to understand the military situation, use these principles as the basis of comparison, in this way:

Which of the two rulers follows the Moral Law? (That is, who is in harmony with their people?)

Which of the two generals is more skilled?

Who has the advantage of favorable conditions from Heaven and Earth?

On which side is discipline enforced the most strictly? (There is a story about Ts'ao Ts'ao, a strict disciplinarian who once followed his own rule so closely that he sentenced himself to death for letting his horse damage crops. Instead of execution, he was convinced to cut off his hair as punishment.)

Which army is stronger, both in physical strength and spirit?

Which side has officers and soldiers who are better trained? (Wang Tzŭ once said that without constant practice, officers will hesitate when forming for battle, and without constant practice, the general will be uncertain when a crisis comes.)

Which side has greater consistency in rewarding good actions and punishing bad behavior?

By considering these seven points, I can predict who will win or lose.

The general who listens to my advice and acts on it will win: such a person should be kept in command! The general who ignores my advice and does not act on it will be defeated: such a person should be dismissed!

While you follow my advice for success, also take advantage of any favorable circumstances that go beyond the usual rules.

As circumstances change, you should adjust your plans accordingly. (Sun Tzu, as a practical soldier, rejects rigid reliance on theoretical principles. He warns us not to rely too heavily on abstract rules because, as Chang Yu says, while the basic principles of strategy can be explained clearly, you must adapt to the enemy's actions to secure a favorable position in battle. Before the Battle of Waterloo, Lord Uxbridge, commanding the cavalry, went to the Duke of Wellington to ask about his plans for the next day. He explained that if he suddenly had to take command, he would need to know the plans. The Duke listened quietly and asked, "Who will attack first tomorrow—me or Bonaparte?" Uxbridge answered, "Bonaparte." "Well," replied the Duke, "Bonaparte hasn't told me his plans, and since my strategy depends on his, how can you expect me to tell you mine?")

All warfare is based on deception. (This wise and profound statement is acknowledged by all soldiers. Col. Henderson notes that

Wellington, known for many military qualities, was especially skilled in hiding his movements and deceiving both friend and foe.)

When we are able to attack, we must make it seem as though we are not ready; when using our forces, we must appear inactive; when we are near, we must make the enemy believe we are far away; and when we are far away, we must make him believe we are close by.

Lure the enemy with baits. Pretend to be in disarray, and then crush him. (Most commentators, except Chang Yu, interpret this as "when he is disorganized, crush him," but it's more natural to understand this as another example of how deception works in war.)

If the enemy is well-prepared at all points, be ready for him. If he is stronger, avoid him.

If your opponent has a bad temper, provoke him. Pretend to be weak so that he becomes overconfident. (Wang Tzŭ, as quoted by Tu Yu, compares this tactic to how a cat plays with a mouse, pretending to be weak before suddenly striking.)

If the enemy is resting, don't let him have peace. (This likely means to keep up pressure on the enemy, although Mei Yao-ch'en suggests it could mean "while we rest, let the enemy exhaust himself." The Yu Lan interprets it as "lure him on and tire him out.")

If his forces are united, divide them. (Many commentators offer an alternative explanation: "If the ruler and his subjects are in harmony, cause division between them.")

Attack the enemy where he is unprepared; appear in places where you are not expected.

These military strategies that lead to victory must not be revealed in advance.

A general who wins a battle makes many calculations in his temple before the battle begins. (Chang Yu notes that in ancient times, a temple was set aside for a general about to lead an army, where he could carefully plan his campaign.)

On the other hand, a general who loses a battle makes few calculations ahead of time. Thus, many calculations lead to victory, while few calculations lead to defeat. How much worse it is when no calculations are made at all! It is through understanding this that I can predict who is likely to win or lose.

Chapter 2 - Waging War

[Ts'ao Kung comments: "He who wishes to fight must first calculate the cost," which prepares us for the realization that this chapter is not primarily about what we might expect from its title, but is instead focused on the planning of resources and strategies.

Sun Tzu said: In warfare, when there are in the field a thousand swift chariots, an equal number of heavy chariots, and a hundred thousand soldiers clad in armor (the swift chariots were lightly built and, according to Chang Yu, were used for attack; the heavy chariots were stronger and designed for defense. Li Ch'uan suggests that the heavy chariots were also light, but this seems unlikely. It's interesting to note the similarities between early Chinese warfare and that of the Homeric Greeks. In both cases, the war chariot was central to military formation, surrounded by groups of foot soldiers. As for the numbers here, it is said that each swift chariot was accompanied by 75 footmen, and each heavy chariot by 25 footmen, dividing the army into a thousand battalions, each consisting of two chariots and a hundred men), with provisions sufficient to sustain them for a thousand li (2.78 modern li make up a mile, though the length may have varied somewhat since Sun Tzu's time), the total daily expenditure, both at home and at the front—including the entertainment of guests, small items like glue and paint, and the sums spent on chariots and armor—will amount to a thousand ounces of silver per day. This is the cost of maintaining an army of 100,000 men.

When you engage in actual combat, if victory is slow to come, the soldiers' weapons will grow dull, and their enthusiasm will fade. If you lay siege to a town, you will drain your strength.

Additionally, if the campaign is prolonged, the state's resources will not be able to bear the strain.

Now, when your weapons are dulled, your enthusiasm has waned, your strength is drained, and your resources are depleted, other leaders will rise to exploit your vulnerability. At that point, no one, no matter how wise, will be able to prevent the inevitable consequences.

Thus, while we have heard of foolish haste in war, cleverness has never been associated with long delays. (This brief and challenging sentence has puzzled commentators. Ts'ao Kung, Li Ch'uan, Meng Shih, Tu Yu, Tu Mu, and Mei Yao-ch'en all comment that a general, though typically unwise, might still win by sheer speed. Ho Shih adds that while haste may be foolish, it at least saves energy and resources, whereas prolonged campaigns, even if skillful, lead to disaster. Wang Hsi avoids the difficulty by saying that lengthy operations age the army, drain wealth, empty the treasury, and bring suffering to the people; true cleverness avoids these pitfalls. Chang Yu argues that as long as victory is possible, even hasty actions are preferable to overly cautious delays. However, Sun Tzu does not explicitly suggest that ill-considered haste is better than well-thought-out but prolonged strategies. Instead, his point is more cautious: while speed may sometimes be unwise, delays are always foolish, if only because they lead to national impoverishment. When considering Sun Tzu's point, the example of Fabius Cunctator inevitably comes to mind. Fabius deliberately measured the endurance of Rome against Hannibal's isolated army, reasoning that Hannibal would suffer more in a prolonged campaign in foreign territory. However, whether Fabius' strategy would have worked in the long run is debatable. Though the reversal of his approach led to the disaster at Cannae, this only suggests a negative presumption in favor of his tactics.)

Only someone who fully understands the horrors of war can fully comprehend the value of conducting it in a profitable manner. (That is, with speed. Only those who recognize the devastating consequences of a long war can truly grasp the supreme importance of bringing it to a swift conclusion. Although only two commentators favor this interpretation, it fits the logic of the context better than the alternative rendering, "He who does not know the evils of war cannot appreciate its benefits," which is clearly pointless.)

The skillful commander does not call for a second levy, nor are his supply wagons loaded more than twice. (Once war begins, he will not waste valuable time waiting for reinforcements, nor will he retreat to gather fresh supplies, but will instead cross the enemy's border without delay. While this may seem like a bold strategy, history's greatest military leaders, from Julius Caesar to Napoleon Bonaparte, have all emphasized the importance of time—that is, being slightly ahead of the enemy—over numerical superiority or careful logistical calculations.)

Bring war materials from home, but rely on the enemy for provisions. In this way, the army will always have enough food to meet its needs. (The Chinese word translated here as "war material" literally means "things to be used" and is understood in the broadest sense. It includes everything needed by the army, except for food.)

When the state treasury is poor, the army must be supported by contributions from far-off places. Relying on distant sources to sustain the army leads to impoverishment of the people.

The beginning of this sentence does not connect smoothly with the next, though it is clearly meant to do so. The arrangement is so awkward that it suggests some corruption in the text. It rarely occurs to Chinese commentators that an amendment might be needed to clarify the meaning, so they offer no help here. The Chinese words Sun Tzu used to indicate the cause of the people's impoverishment refer to a system where farmers sent their corn directly to the army. But why would it fall to them to maintain the army in this way, unless the State or Government was too poor to do so?

On the other hand, the presence of an army nearby causes prices to rise, and high prices lead to the people's wealth being drained. (Wang Hsi says that prices increase even before the army leaves its own territory. Ts'ao Kung believes this applies to an army that has already crossed the frontier.)

When the people's wealth is drained, the farmers will suffer from heavy demands placed upon them.

As their wealth is lost and their strength is exhausted, the homes of the people will be left bare, and three-tenths of their income will be consumed. (Tu Mu and Wang Hsi argue that the people are actually deprived of seven-tenths of their income, but this is difficult to extract from the text. Ho Shih adds a characteristic note: "The people are the essential part of the State, and food is their heaven, so is it not right that those in authority should take care to protect both?")

Meanwhile, government expenses for damaged chariots, worn-out horses, breastplates, helmets, bows and arrows, spears and shields, protective coverings, oxen for transportation, and heavy wagons will consume four-tenths of the total revenue.

Thus, a wise general makes it a priority to forage from the enemy. One cartload of the enemy's provisions is worth twenty of one's own, and similarly, a single picul of their supplies is worth twenty from one's own stores. (This is because twenty cartloads of provisions will be consumed during the transportation of one cartload to the front. A picul is a unit of measure equal to 133.3 pounds, or 65.5 kilograms.)

Now, to defeat the enemy, our soldiers must be stirred to anger; and to gain any benefit from defeating the enemy, they must receive rewards. (Tu Mu explains: "Rewards are necessary so the soldiers understand the benefit of beating the enemy. When spoils are captured from the enemy, they should be distributed as rewards, so that all the men will have a strong desire to fight, each for his own gain.")

Therefore, in chariot warfare, when ten or more chariots are captured, the soldiers who take the first one should be rewarded. Our flags should be substituted for the enemy's, and the captured chariots should be integrated and used alongside our own. Captured enemy soldiers should be treated kindly and kept.

This is called using the enemy's resources to strengthen one's own forces.

In war, your main objective should always be victory, not prolonged campaigns. (As Ho Shih remarks: "War is not something to be treated lightly." Sun Tzu reiterates here the central lesson of this chapter.)

Thus, it is clear that the leader of armies holds the fate of the people in his hands, and it is his actions that determine whether the nation will be at peace or in danger.

Chapter 3 - Attack By Stratagem

Sun Tzu said: In the practical art of war, the best course of action is to take the enemy's country whole and intact; to shatter and destroy it is not as good. Likewise, it is better to capture an entire army than to destroy it, better to capture an entire regiment, detachment, or company than to destroy them. (According to Ssu-ma Fa, an army corps consisted of 12,500 men; Ts'ao Kung says a regiment contained 500 men, a detachment could consist of any number between 100 and 500, and a company could range from 5 to 100 men. However, Chang Yu gives the exact figures of 100 for a detachment and 5 for a company.)

Therefore, to fight and win in all your battles is not the highest excellence; the highest excellence consists in breaking the enemy's resistance without having to fight. (Once again, no modern strategist would disagree with these words. Moltke's greatest victory, the surrender of the enormous French army at Sedan, was achieved virtually without bloodshed.)

Thus, the highest form of generalship is to thwart the enemy's plans. (Perhaps the word "thwart" does not fully capture the meaning of the original Chinese, which implies not merely defending by countering each of the enemy's strategies, but actively attacking. Ho

Shih explains this clearly in his note: "When the enemy plans to attack us, we must anticipate him by launching our attack first.")

The next best course is to prevent the enemy's forces from combining. (This involves isolating him from his allies. We must remember that Sun Tzu is referring to the many states or principalities into which China was divided in his time.)

After that, the next best option is to attack the enemy's army in the field. (That is, when his forces are already gathered and at full strength.)

The worst course of action is to besiege walled cities.

The rule is not to attack cities with walls unless it is absolutely necessary.

(Another good piece of military advice. If the Boers had followed this in 1899 and not spread their forces thin around places like Kimberley, Mafeking, or even Ladysmith, they likely would have had the upper hand before the British were really ready to fight back.)

Building mantlets, movable shelters, and other war tools will take up three whole months.

(It's not completely clear what the Chinese term translated as "mantlets" really meant. Ts'ao Kung says they were "large shields," but Li Ch'uan gives us a better idea, describing them as protection for soldiers attacking the walls of a city up close. This suggests they might have been like the Roman testudo, a formation where soldiers would use their shields to form a shell. Tu Mu claims they were wheeled vehicles for defense, but Ch'en Hao disagrees. See earlier, II.14. The term also referred to turrets on city walls. The "movable shelters" were more clearly described by various commentators: they were wooden, missile-proof structures with four wheels, covered with raw hides, used in sieges to transport soldiers safely to and from the city walls, often to fill up moats with dirt. Tu Mu adds that nowadays they are called "wooden donkeys.")

Building up ramps against the walls will take another three months.

(These were large mounds or earth ramps built up to the height of the enemy's walls to spot weak points in the defenses and to tear down the fortified turrets mentioned earlier.)

The general, unable to keep his anger in check, will send his men to attack like a swarm of ants.

(This vivid image from Ts'ao Kung comes from the sight of an army of ants climbing up a wall. It means the general, losing patience due to the delay, may order an attack before his war machines are ready.)

As a result, one-third of his men will be killed, and the city will still not be taken. These are the terrible outcomes of a siege.

(We are reminded of the heavy losses suffered by the Japanese in their recent siege of Port Arthur.)

A skilled leader defeats the enemy's troops without ever having to fight; he takes their cities without needing to lay siege; he brings down their kingdom without long, drawn-out battles.

(Chia Lin points out that the leader only removes the government but does not harm individuals. A classic example of this is Wu Wang, who, after ending the Yin dynasty, was celebrated as the "Father and mother of the people.")

With his army fully intact, he will challenge for control of the Empire, and by doing so, without losing a single man, his victory will be complete.

(Because of the double meanings in the Chinese text, the second part of this sentence could also mean: "And thus, since the weapon has not been dulled by overuse, its sharpness remains perfect.")

This is how to conquer through strategy.

In war, if our forces outnumber the enemy ten to one, we surround him; if five to one, we attack him.

(Immediately, without waiting for any further advantages.)

If we are twice as numerous, we split our army into two.

(Tu Mu disagrees with this advice, and at first glance, it seems to go against a basic rule of warfare. However, Ts'ao Kung offers an explanation: "When we are two to one against the enemy, one part of our army can be used in the regular way, and the other can be used for a special maneuver." Chang Yu adds more clarity: "If our army is twice the size of the enemy's, we should split it into two groups—one to face the enemy head-on, and the other to attack from behind. If the enemy responds to the front attack, he can be crushed from behind; if he reacts to the rear attack, he can be defeated from the front." This is what is meant by saying that 'one part may be used in the regular way, and the other for a special maneuver.' Tu Mu doesn't understand that splitting the army is an irregular strategy, just as concentrating the army is the regular strategy, and he is too quick to call this a mistake.)

If we are evenly matched, we can engage in battle.

(Li Ch'uan, supported by Ho Shih, rephrases this as: "If both sides are equal in strength, only a skilled general will choose to fight.")

If we are slightly weaker, we can avoid the enemy.

(The meaning "we can watch the enemy" is an improvement on this, but there isn't much solid backing for this version. Chang Yu reminds us that this advice only holds if other factors are equal. A small difference in numbers can often be balanced out by greater energy and discipline.)

If we are greatly outmatched, we can retreat.

Even though a small force may put up a stubborn fight, in the end, it will be overcome by a larger force.

The general is the foundation of the State: if the foundation is solid in all areas, the State will be strong; if the foundation has weaknesses, the State will be weak.

(As Li Ch'uan puts it briefly: "A gap shows a weakness; if the general's ability is not perfect—if he isn't fully skilled in his role—his army will lack strength.")

There are three ways a ruler can bring disaster to his army:

(1) By ordering the army to advance or retreat without knowing that it cannot follow those orders. This is called crippling the army.

(Li Ch'uan adds: "It's like tying the legs of a racehorse so it can't run." You might think "the ruler" in this case is far away, trying to direct the army from a distance. However, the commentators interpret it the opposite way, quoting T'ai Kung: "A kingdom shouldn't be ruled from the outside, and an army shouldn't be commanded from within." Naturally, during a battle or when close to the enemy, the general shouldn't be right in the middle of his own troops, but should stay a little apart. Otherwise, he might misread the situation and give wrong orders.)

(2) By trying to govern an army in the same way he runs a kingdom, without understanding the conditions within an army, a ruler causes unrest in the soldiers' minds.

(Ts'ao Kung notes: "The military and civil spheres are entirely different; you can't handle an army with soft, delicate treatment." Chang Yu adds: "Humanity and justice are the foundations for governing a state, but not for leading an army. Opportunism and flexibility are military virtues, not civil ones.")

(3) By using officers without making distinctions between them,

(This means the ruler doesn't carefully assign the right person to the right role.)

because he doesn't understand the military principle of adapting to circumstances, he undermines the soldiers' trust.

(I follow Mei Yao-ch'en here. Other commentators refer to the officers employed, not the ruler as in the previous sections. Tu Yu says: "If a general doesn't understand adaptability, he should not be put in charge." Tu Mu quotes: "A skilled leader will employ the wise, the brave, the greedy, and the foolish. The wise man enjoys proving his merit, the brave man seeks to show his courage in action, the greedy man quickly seizes opportunities, and the foolish man fears nothing, even death.")

But when the army is restless and distrustful, conflict will arise from the other feudal princes. This brings chaos into the army and throws away any chance of victory.

From this, we know that there are five key factors for victory: (1) He will win who knows when to fight and when not to fight.

(Chang Yu says: If he can fight, he moves forward and attacks; if he cannot fight, he retreats and defends. Victory is certain for the one who understands when to attack and when to defend.)

(2) He will win who knows how to manage both larger and smaller forces.

(This isn't just about the general's ability to count numbers accurately, as Li Ch'uan and others suggest. Chang Yu explains this better: "By using the art of war, a smaller force can defeat a larger one, and vice versa. The secret is understanding the terrain and seizing the right moment. As Wu Tzŭ says: 'With a larger force, move on easy ground; with a smaller force, seek difficult ground.'")

Chapter 4 - Tactical Dispositions

Ts'ao Kung explains the meaning behind the title of this chapter: "marching and countermarching by the two armies to find out each other's condition." Tu Mu adds: "It is through the positioning of an army that its state can be revealed. Hide your positioning, and your condition remains secret, leading to victory; expose your positioning, and your condition becomes clear, leading to defeat." Wang Hsi comments that a good general "ensures success by adapting his tactics to those of the enemy."

Sun Tzŭ said: The skilled fighters of the past first made sure they could not be defeated, then waited for the right moment to defeat the enemy.

The power to avoid defeat is in our own hands, but the chance to defeat the enemy comes from the enemy himself.

(That is, of course, due to a mistake on the enemy's part.)

Thus, a skilled fighter can always protect himself from defeat,

(Chang Yu explains that this is done by "concealing the positioning of the troops, covering up tracks, and taking constant precautions.")

but he cannot always ensure he will defeat the enemy.

Hence the saying: One may know how to win but still not be able to achieve it.

Protecting oneself from defeat involves defensive tactics, while defeating the enemy involves taking the offensive.

(I keep the meaning found in a similar passage in §§ 1-3, despite the fact that the commentators disagree with me. Their interpretation, "He who cannot conquer takes the defensive," is reasonable, but this version seems clearer.)

Being on the defensive suggests a lack of strength, while attacking shows an abundance of strength.

A general skilled in defense hides in the deepest recesses of the earth;

(Literally, "hides under the ninth earth," a metaphor for complete secrecy and concealment, so the enemy doesn't know his location.)

while a general skilled in attack strikes from the highest heavens.

(Another metaphor, meaning he falls upon his enemy like a sudden thunderbolt, against which there is no time to prepare. Most commentators agree with this interpretation.)

Thus, on one hand, we have the ability to protect ourselves; on the other, the ability to achieve a complete victory.

To see victory only when it is clear to everyone is not the height of excellence.

(As Ts'ao Kung says, "the key is to see the plant before it has sprouted," meaning to foresee the outcome before the action begins. Li Ch'uan mentions the story of Han Hsin, who, before attacking the much larger army of Chao, which was heavily fortified in the city of Ch'eng-an, told his officers, "Gentlemen, we are going to destroy the enemy and will meet again at dinner." His officers didn't take him seriously and gave doubtful replies. But Han Hsin had already devised a clever plan, and as he predicted, he captured the city and crushed his enemy.)

It is also not the height of excellence if you fight and win, and the whole world says, "Well done!"

(True excellence, as Tu Mu says, lies in planning secretly, moving quietly, and outsmarting the enemy's plans so that victory is achieved without a drop of blood being shed. Sun Tzŭ praises achievements that "the world's clumsy thumb and finger cannot grasp.")

Lifting an autumn hair is not a sign of great strength;

("Autumn hair" refers to the fine fur of a hare, which is softest in autumn when it starts growing back. This phrase is commonly used by Chinese writers.)

Seeing the sun and moon is not a sign of sharp vision, and hearing the sound of thunder is not a sign of quick hearing.

(Ho Shih provides examples of true strength, sharp vision, and quick hearing: Wu Huo, who could lift a 250-stone tripod; Li Chu, who could see objects as small as mustard seeds from a hundred paces; and Shih K'uang, a blind musician who could hear a mosquito's footsteps.)

What the ancients called a clever fighter is someone who not only wins, but wins with ease.

(The second part literally means "one who, while conquering, excels in conquering easily." Mei Yao-ch'en explains: "He who only notices the obvious wins his battles with difficulty; but he who sees beneath the surface wins with ease.")

For this reason, his victories bring him neither a reputation for wisdom nor credit for bravery.

(Tu Mu explains this well: "Since his victories are achieved under circumstances that remain hidden, the world at large knows nothing of them, and he gains no reputation for wisdom. Since the enemy surrenders without bloodshed, he gets no credit for bravery.")

He wins his battles by making no mistakes.

(Ch'en Hao says: "He avoids unnecessary marches and pointless attacks." Chang Yu explains the connection: "One who tries to win by brute force, even if skilled in fighting pitched battles, may sometimes be defeated. But one who can foresee the future and understand conditions before they arise will never make a mistake, and thus always win.")

Making no mistakes ensures victory because it means defeating an enemy who is already defeated.

Thus, the skilled fighter places himself in a position where defeat is impossible and never misses the moment to defeat the enemy.

(A "counsel of perfection," as Tu Mu notes. "Position" isn't just about the physical location of troops; it includes all the preparations and arrangements that a wise general makes to ensure the safety of the army.)

In war, the victorious strategist seeks battle only after victory is already assured, while the one destined for defeat fights first and then looks for victory.

(Ho Shih explains this paradox: "In warfare, first make plans that will guarantee victory, then lead your army into battle. If you rely on brute strength alone without first using strategy, victory will no longer be guaranteed.")

The ideal leader follows the moral law and adheres strictly to method and discipline; by doing so, he can control success.

In terms of military methods, there are: first, Measurement; second, Estimation of quantity; third, Calculation; fourth, Balancing of chances; and fifth, Victory.

Measurement depends on the Earth; Estimation of quantity comes from Measurement; Calculation comes from Estimation of quantity; Balancing of chances comes from Calculation; and Victory comes from Balancing of chances.

(It's hard to distinguish the four terms clearly in Chinese. The first seems to refer to surveying and measuring the ground, which allows us to estimate the enemy's strength and make calculations from that information. This leads to a weighing of chances—comparing the enemy's chances with our own. If the scale tips in our favor, victory follows. The difficulty lies in the third term, which some commentators interpret as a calculation of numbers, making it nearly synonymous with the second term. Perhaps the second refers to considering the enemy's general situation, while the third refers to estimating his numerical strength. Tu Mu suggests that once relative strength is known, we can apply cunning strategies. Ho Shih supports this, but with a weaker interpretation, indicating that the third term points to calculating numbers.)

A victorious army facing a defeated one is like a pound's weight against a single grain.

(Literally, "a victorious army is like an i (20 ounces) weighed against a shu (1/24 of an ounce); a defeated army is a shu weighed against an i." This illustrates the huge advantage a disciplined, victorious force has over one demoralized by defeat. Legge, in his note on Mencius, I.2.ix.2, defines the i as 24 Chinese ounces and corrects Chu Hsi's claim that it equals only 20 ounces. However, Li Ch'uan of the T'ang dynasty supports Chu Hsi's figure.)

The rush of a victorious force is like water bursting through a dam into a chasm a thousand fathoms deep. This concludes the section on tactical dispositions.

Chapter 5 - Energy

Sun Tzŭ said: Controlling a large army is based on the same principles as controlling a small group; it is simply a matter of dividing them into smaller units.

(This means splitting the army into regiments, companies, etc., each with its own subordinate officers. Tu Mu reminds us of the famous conversation between Han Hsin and the first Han Emperor. The Emperor asked, "How large an army do you think I could lead?" Han Hsin replied, "No more than 100,000 men, Your Majesty." "And how about you?" asked the Emperor. Han Hsin responded, "Oh, the more, the better.")

Fighting with a large army under your command is no different from fighting with a small one; it's just about using signs and signals to communicate.

To ensure that your entire force can withstand the enemy's attack without breaking, you need to use both direct and indirect maneuvers.

(Now we come to one of the most interesting parts of Sun Tzŭ's teachings: the discussion of cheng (direct) and ch'i (indirect). These two terms are tricky to fully grasp or consistently translate into English, so it's helpful to consider what various commentators have said. Li Ch'uan explains that cheng is a frontal confrontation, while ch'i is a diversion to the side. Chia Lin says: "When facing the enemy, your troops should be arranged in a conventional way, but victory comes from using unconventional maneuvers." Mei Yao-ch'en adds: "Ch'i is active, while cheng is passive; waiting for the right moment is passive, but action itself brings victory." Ho Shih explains: "We must make the enemy think our straightforward attack is secretly planned, and vice versa. Thus, cheng can become ch'i and ch'i can become cheng." He uses the example of Han Hsin, who marched his army toward Lin-chin but suddenly sent a large force across the Yellow River in wooden tubs, catching the enemy off guard. In this case, the march on Lin-chin was cheng, and the surprise maneuver across the river was ch'i."

Chang Yu summarizes these ideas by noting that military writers disagree on the definitions of cheng and ch'i. Wei Liao Tzŭ says, "Direct warfare favors frontal attacks, while indirect warfare favors attacks from behind." Ts'ao Kung says, "Going directly into battle is cheng, while appearing behind the enemy is ch'i." Li Wei-kung adds, "In war, marching straight ahead is cheng; turning movements are ch'i." These writers treat cheng and ch'i as separate and fixed, but they don't realize that the two can blend together and switch, like two sides of a circle. A comment on the T'ang Emperor T'ai Tsung goes deeper: "A ch'i maneuver becomes cheng if we make the enemy believe it is cheng; then our real attack will be ch'i, and vice versa. The secret lies in confusing the enemy so they cannot understand our true intentions."

In simpler terms, any operation is cheng if it draws the enemy's attention, and ch'i if it catches them by surprise. If the enemy recognizes a movement meant to be ch'i, it becomes cheng.)

The impact of your army should be like a grindstone smashing against an egg—this is achieved through understanding weak points and strong ones.

In all battles, the direct method may be used to engage the enemy, but indirect methods are necessary to secure victory.

(Chang Yu explains: "Develop indirect tactics steadily, either by striking at the enemy's flanks or attacking from behind." A brilliant example of indirect tactics deciding a campaign was Lord Roberts' night march around Peiwar Kotal during the second Afghan war.)

Indirect tactics, when applied efficiently, are as limitless as Heaven and Earth, as unceasing as the flow of rivers and streams. Like the sun and moon, they end only to begin again; like the four seasons, they pass and return.

(Tu Yu and Chang Yu see this as referring to the changing use of ch'i and cheng. However, Sun Tzŭ isn't specifically talking about cheng here, unless, as Cheng Yu-hsien suggests, a part of the text about cheng was lost. As mentioned before, ch'i and cheng are so interconnected in military operations that they cannot be considered separately. This passage expresses the almost endless resourcefulness of a great leader.)

There are only five musical notes, yet their combinations create more melodies than can ever be heard.

There are only five primary colors—blue, yellow, red, white, and black—yet their combinations produce more hues than can ever be seen.

There are only five basic tastes—sour, acrid, salty, sweet, and bitter—but their combinations yield more flavors than can ever be tasted.

In battle, there are only two methods of attack—the direct and the indirect—yet their combination creates an infinite number of maneuvers.

The direct and the indirect lead into each other, like a circle that has no end. Who can exhaust the possibilities of their combination?

The advance of troops is like the rush of a torrent, powerful enough to carry stones along its path.

The quality of decision is like the well-timed swoop of a falcon that enables it to strike and destroy its target.

(The Chinese here is tricky, and a certain key word in this context resists the best efforts of translation. Tu Mu defines this word as "the measurement or estimation of distance." But applying this meaning to the falcon, it seems to refer to the instinct of self-restraint, which prevents the bird from swooping down on its prey until the right moment, along with the ability to judge when that moment has come. The analogous quality in soldiers is the important skill of holding back their fire until the exact moment when it will be most effective. When the Victory went into action at Trafalgar, moving at hardly more than a drifting pace, it was under heavy fire for several minutes without returning a single shot. Nelson waited coolly until he was in close range, at which point the broadside he unleashed inflicted devastating damage on the enemy's nearest ships.)

Therefore, the skilled fighter will be fearsome in his attack and prompt in his decision.

(The word "decision" likely refers to the measurement of distance mentioned earlier, holding off until the enemy is close enough to strike. However, I also believe that Sun Tzŭ meant this word figuratively, similar to our own expression "short and sharp." Wang Hsi's note expands on the falcon's method of attack, adding: "This is how the 'psychological moment' should be seized in war.")

Energy may be compared to the bending of a crossbow; decision, to the release of the trigger.

(None of the commentators seem to grasp the true meaning of this simile. The key point is that energy, like the force stored in a bent crossbow, only becomes effective when released by the decision to pull the trigger.)

Amid the turmoil and chaos of battle, there may seem to be disorder, yet there is no real disorder; amid confusion, your formation may appear to lack head or tail, yet it remains unshakable against defeat.

(Mei Yao-ch'en says: "When the subdivisions of the army have been arranged in advance, and the various signals have been agreed upon, the separating, joining, dispersing, and regrouping that occurs during battle may give the appearance of disorder, but true disorder is impossible. Even if your formation seems headless and without direction, your forces will not be routed.")

Simulated disorder requires perfect discipline; simulated fear requires courage; simulated weakness requires strength.

(To make this translation clearer, the sharp paradox of the original needs to be softened. Ts'ao Kung hints at the meaning in his brief note: "These things are all meant to disrupt the enemy's formation and conceal one's true condition." Tu Mu explains it plainly: "If you want to appear confused to lure the enemy, you must first have perfect discipline; if you want to display fear to trap the enemy, you must have great courage; if you want to show weakness to make the enemy overconfident, you must have great strength.")

Hiding order beneath the appearance of disorder is simply a matter of dividing the army into smaller units.

(See earlier, § 1.)

Concealing courage under a display of timidity requires a reservoir of hidden energy.

(The commentators interpret a specific Chinese word here differently than elsewhere in the chapter. Tu Mu says: "When the enemy sees that we are in a favorable position but make no move, they will believe we are truly afraid.")

Masking strength with weakness is accomplished through strategic positioning.

(Chang Yu recounts the story of Kao Tsu, the first Han Emperor. He wanted to attack the Hsiung-nu, so he sent spies to gather intelligence on their condition. However, the Hsiung-nu, anticipating this, hid all their strong soldiers and healthy horses, and only allowed the spies to see old soldiers and weak animals. As a result, all the spies advised the Emperor to attack. Only Lou Ching opposed them, saying: "When two countries prepare for war, they naturally try to show their strength. Since our spies have only seen old and weak forces, this must be a trick, and attacking would be unwise." The Emperor ignored this advice, fell into the trap, and was surrounded at Po-teng.)

Thus, one who is skilled at keeping the enemy on the move uses deceptive appearances, to which the enemy will respond.

(Ts'ao Kung notes: "Create the appearance of weakness and need." Tu Mu adds: "If our forces are stronger than the enemy's, we can pretend to be weak to lure them in; but if we are weaker, we must make the enemy believe we are strong so they stay away. In fact, the enemy's actions should always be based on the signals we choose to give." There is an anecdote about Sun Pin, a descendant of Sun Wu: In 341 B.C., the state of Ch'i was at war with Wei, and Sun Pin was sent to face the general P'ang Chuan, who was his personal enemy. Sun Pin said: "The Ch'i state is known for cowardice, so our enemy will underestimate us. Let's take advantage of this." When their army crossed into Wei territory, Sun Pin ordered 100,000 campfires on the first night, 50,000 on the second night, and only 20,000 on the third night. P'ang Chuan, in pursuit, thought: "I knew these Ch'i soldiers were cowards; their numbers are already less than half." Sun Pin retreated to a narrow pass, knowing that P'ang Chuan would arrive after dark. There, Sun Pin had a tree stripped of its bark and inscribed: "Under this tree, P'ang Chuan will die." As night fell, Sun Pin hid archers nearby, instructing them to shoot when they saw light. When P'ang Chuan arrived, he struck a light to read the inscription on the tree, and was immediately shot down by arrows, throwing his army into confusion. [Tu Mu's version of the story is more dramatic, though the Shih Chi suggests that after the defeat of his army, P'ang Chuan committed suicide in despair.])

He sacrifices something, knowing the enemy will snatch at it.

By offering baits, he keeps the enemy on the move; then, with a group of carefully chosen men, he waits to ambush him.

(With an adjustment suggested by Li Ching, this reads: "He lies in wait with the main body of his troops.")

The clever combatant relies on the effect of combined energy and does not demand too much from individuals.

(Tu Mu explains: "First, he assesses the overall power of his army as a whole; then he takes individual abilities into account and uses each person according to their talents. He does not expect perfection from those who lack it.")

This is why he can select the right men and make use of their combined strength.

When he employs combined energy, his fighters become like rolling logs or stones. A log or stone remains still on level ground but moves when placed on a slope. If it is square, it stops, but if it is round, it rolls down.

(Ts'ao Kung refers to this as "the use of natural or inherent power.")

Thus, the energy generated by skilled fighters is like the momentum of a round stone rolling down a mountain thousands of feet high. This concludes the discussion on energy.

(Tu Mu points out that the main lesson of this chapter is the critical importance of rapid maneuvers and sudden charges in warfare. "With such tactics," he adds, "great results can be achieved with even small forces.")

Chapter 6 - Weak Points and Strong

[Chang Yu tries to explain the sequence of the chapters in this way: "Chapter IV, on Tactical Dispositions, dealt with offense and defense; Chapter V, on Energy, covered direct and indirect methods. The skilled general first familiarizes himself with the theory of attack and defense, and then focuses on direct and indirect methods. He learns how to vary and combine these two methods before moving on to the topic of weak and strong points. The use of direct or indirect methods arises from attack and defense, and recognizing weak and strong points depends on understanding these methods. Therefore, this chapter follows directly after the one on Energy."]

Sun Tzŭ said: Whoever is first to arrive on the battlefield and waits for the enemy will be well-prepared for the fight; whoever arrives second and has to rush into battle will be tired and worn out.

Therefore, the clever combatant imposes his will on the enemy and never allows the enemy to impose his will on him.

(A mark of a great soldier is that he fights on his own terms or not at all.)

By offering advantages, he can lure the enemy to approach; or by causing harm, he can prevent the enemy from drawing near.

(In the first case, he entices with bait; in the second, he strikes a key point the enemy will be forced to defend.)

If the enemy is resting, he can harass him;

(This passage can be cited as evidence against Mei Yao-ch'en's interpretation of I. § 23.)

if the enemy has plenty of food, he can starve him out; if the enemy is quietly encamped, he can force him to move.

Appear at points the enemy must rush to defend; march quickly to places where you are not expected.

An army can cover great distances without suffering if it travels through areas where the enemy is absent.

(Ts'ao Kung summarizes this well: "Emerge from the void—like a surprise attack—and strike at vulnerable spots, avoid defended places, and attack where you are least expected.")

You can be certain of success in your attacks if you only strike at places that are undefended.

(Wang Hsi explains "undefended places" as weak points, meaning areas where the general is lacking in ability, the soldiers lack morale, the walls are not strong enough, precautions are too lax, reinforcements arrive too late, supplies are insufficient, or the defenders are in conflict among themselves.)

You can ensure the safety of your defense if you only hold positions that cannot be attacked.

(That is, where none of the weaknesses mentioned above exist. There's an interesting nuance in interpreting this line. Tu Mu, Ch'en Hao, and Mei Yao-ch'en suggest it means: "To make your defense completely secure, you must even defend places that are unlikely to be attacked," and Tu Mu adds, "How much more so for places that are likely to be attacked." However, this interpretation doesn't balance well with the preceding clause, which is important in the highly antithetical style typical of Chinese writing. Chang Yu seems closer to the point by saying: "The skilled attacker strikes from the topmost heights of heaven [see IV. § 7], making it impossible for the enemy to defend. Thus, the places I will attack are exactly those the enemy cannot defend. The skilled defender hides in the deepest recesses of the earth, making it impossible for the enemy to locate him. Thus, the places I will hold are precisely those the enemy cannot attack.")

Therefore, the general who is skilled in attack confuses the enemy, so they do not know what to defend; the general who is skilled in defense confounds the enemy, so they do not know what to attack.

(An aphorism that sums up the essence of the art of war.)

O divine art of subtlety and secrecy! Through you, we learn to be invisible, through you, we learn to be inaudible;

(Literally, "without form or sound," in reference to the enemy.)

and thus, we hold the enemy's fate in our hands.

You can advance and be absolutely unstoppable if you strike at the enemy's weak points; you can retreat safely and avoid pursuit if your movements are quicker than the enemy's.

If we want to engage in battle, we can force the enemy to fight, even if he is hiding behind a high wall and a deep trench. All we need to do is attack another place that he will be forced to defend.

(Tu Mu explains: "If the enemy is the invader, we can cut off his supply lines and seize the roads he must use to retreat; if we are the invaders, we can aim our attack at the ruler himself." It's clear that Sun Tzŭ, unlike certain generals in later conflicts such as the Boer War, did not believe in frontal assaults.)

If we do not wish to fight, we can prevent the enemy from engaging us, even if our encampment is only outlined on the ground. All we need to do is confuse him with something strange and unexpected.

(This concise phrase is paraphrased by Chia Lin as: "even though we have constructed neither walls nor ditches." Li Ch'uan adds: "we bewilder him with strange and unusual tactics," and Tu Mu illustrates with three anecdotes. One example is Chu-ko Liang, who, when stationed at Yang-p'ing and about to be attacked by Ssu-ma I, unexpectedly struck his flags, silenced his drums, and opened the city gates, showing only a few men sweeping the grounds. This strange move made Ssu-ma I suspect a trap, causing him to withdraw his army. What Sun Tzŭ is advocating here, therefore, is nothing less than the skillful use of "bluff.")

By discovering the enemy's plans while keeping our own concealed, we can concentrate our forces, while the enemy is forced to divide his.

(The conclusion may not seem obvious at first, but Chang Yu, following Mei Yao-ch'en, explains: "If the enemy's plans are visible, we can attack him with a united force; meanwhile, if our plans are kept secret, the enemy will have to split his forces to guard against attacks from multiple directions.")

We can form a single, united force, while the enemy must divide into smaller parts. Thus, we will have a whole army against only fragments of the enemy's force, meaning we will be many against their few.

If we are able to attack an inferior force with a superior one in this way, the enemy will find themselves in great difficulty.

The location where we intend to fight must not be revealed, because this will force the enemy to prepare for possible attacks at several different points.

(Sheridan once explained General Grant's victories by saying that "while his opponents were kept fully occupied wondering what he was going to do, he was focused mainly on what he was going to do.")

With the enemy's forces scattered in many directions, the number of troops we face at any given point will be relatively small.

For if the enemy strengthens his front lines, he will weaken his rear; if he strengthens his rear, he will weaken his front. If he strengthens his left, he will weaken his right, and if he strengthens his right, he will weaken his left. If he sends reinforcements everywhere, he will be weak everywhere.

(Frederick the Great, in his Instructions to his Generals, wrote: "A defensive war tends to lead us into making too many detachments. Generals with little experience try to defend every point, while those who understand their profession focus only on the main objective, allowing small losses to avoid greater ones.")

Numerical weakness arises from having to prepare against possible attacks, while numerical strength comes from forcing the enemy to make such preparations.

(Colonel Henderson described the highest form of generalship as "compelling the enemy to disperse his army, then concentrating a superior force against each fraction in turn.")

If we know the place and time of the coming battle, we can gather our forces from even the greatest distances to fight.

(Sun Tzŭ is referring to the careful calculation of distances and the expert use of strategy that allow a general to divide his army for a long and rapid march, then bring them together at precisely the right place and time to confront the enemy with overwhelming strength. A dramatic example of this in military history is the appearance of Blücher at the critical moment during the Battle of Waterloo.)

But if neither the time nor place of battle is known, then the left wing will be powerless to help the right, the right will be equally unable to help the left, the front will not be able to relieve the rear, and the rear won't be able to support the front. This is even more true if the furthest parts of the army are separated by over a hundred li and the nearest by several li.

(The Chinese text here lacks precision, but the idea is likely that of an army advancing toward a rendezvous in separate columns, each with orders to meet on a specific date. If the general lets the detachments march haphazardly without precise instructions on when and where to meet, the enemy could destroy the army piece by piece. Chang Yu's note clarifies: "If we do not know the enemy's concentration point or the day they plan to engage, our unity will be lost as we prepare for defense, and the positions we hold will be insecure. If we suddenly encounter a strong enemy, we will be forced into battle in a disorganized state, with no mutual support between wings, vanguard, or rear, especially if there is a great distance between the leading and rear divisions of the army.")

Even though, by my estimation, the soldiers of Yüeh outnumber us, that will not give them any advantage in achieving victory. I say, then, that victory can be achieved.

(Unfortunately, this confident claim was not borne out. The long-standing feud between Wu and Yüeh ended in 473 B.C. with the complete defeat of Wu by Kou Chien, and Wu was absorbed into Yüeh. This likely occurred long after Sun Tzŭ's death. Chang Yu is the only commentator to note the apparent contradiction here, which he explains: "In the chapter on Tactical Dispositions, it is said, 'One may know how to conquer without being able to do it,' whereas here, it says that victory can be achieved. The difference is that in the former chapter, discussing offense and defense, it is acknowledged that if the enemy is fully prepared, victory is not guaranteed. But this passage refers specifically to the soldiers of Yüeh, who, according to Sun Tzŭ's calculations, would remain unaware of the time and place of the impending battle. That's why he says here that victory is possible.")

Though the enemy may have greater numbers, we can prevent him from engaging in battle. Devise schemes to uncover his plans and assess the likelihood of their success.

(An alternate reading offered by Chia Lin is: "Know beforehand all strategies that will lead to our success and the enemy's failure.")

Provoke him, and observe the principle behind his activity or inactivity.

(Chang Yu explains that by noting the enemy's emotional reactions—whether joy or anger—when disturbed, we can deduce whether his strategy is to remain passive or take action. He gives the example of Cho-ku Liang, who sent a woman's head-dress as an insulting gift to Ssu-ma I, provoking him to abandon his cautious, passive tactics.)

Force the enemy to reveal himself, so you can discover his weak points.

Carefully compare the enemy's army with your own, so you will know where strength is abundant and where it is lacking.

(See also IV. § 6.)

In making tactical plans, the highest achievement is to keep them hidden.

(The paradox loses some sharpness in translation. Concealment here doesn't necessarily mean literal invisibility (see § 9 above), but rather not showing any signs of what you intend to do—keeping your thoughts and plans completely veiled.)

Hide your dispositions, and you will be protected from the prying eyes of even the most clever spies and the schemes of the wisest minds.

(Tu Mu explains: "Even if the enemy has intelligent and capable officers, they will not be able to make any effective plans against us.")

How victory is brought about using the enemy's own tactics is something the masses cannot understand.

Everyone can see the tactics by which I win, but no one can see the strategy behind that victory.

(That is, people can observe the outward methods used in winning a battle, but they cannot see the long process of planning and the combinations of strategies that precede it.)

Do not simply repeat the tactics that won you a previous victory; instead, let your methods be shaped by the infinite variety of circumstances.

(Wang Hsi wisely notes: "There is only one core principle of victory, but the tactics leading to it are countless." Compare this to Colonel Henderson's view: "The rules of strategy are few and simple, and can be learned in a week. However, knowing them will not teach a person to lead an army like Napoleon any more than knowing grammar will teach someone to write like Gibbon.")

Military tactics are like water; for just as water flows away from high ground and moves quickly downhill,

so in war, the way is to avoid the strong and strike at the weak.

(Like water, which follows the path of least resistance.)

Water shapes its course according to the nature of the ground over which it flows; in the same way, a soldier works out his victory in relation to the enemy he is facing.

Therefore, just as water has no constant shape, so there are no constant conditions in warfare.

He who can adjust his tactics to match the situation and succeed in winning may be called a captain born of heaven.

The five elements (water, fire, wood, metal, earth) are not always equally dominant;

(Wang Hsi notes: "They dominate in turn.")

The four seasons give way to each other in succession.

(Literally, "they do not always remain in the same place.")

There are short days and long days; the moon waxes and wanes.

(See also V. § 6. The point here is to illustrate the ever-changing nature of war by comparing it to the constant shifts in nature. The comparison is not entirely perfect, however, since the regularity of natural phenomena differs from the unpredictability of war.)

Chapter 7 - Manoeuvering

Sun Tzŭ said: In war, the general receives his orders from the sovereign.

After gathering an army and concentrating his forces, he must blend and harmonize the various elements within it before setting up camp.

(Chang Yu explains: "This refers to creating harmony and trust between the higher and lower ranks before going to battle." He also quotes Wu Tzü: "Without harmony in the State, no military campaign can be undertaken; without harmony in the army, no battle formation can be made." In a historical romance, Sun Tzŭ is portrayed telling Wu Yuan: "In general, those who wage war must resolve all internal issues before attacking an external enemy.")

After that comes tactical maneuvering, which is more difficult than anything else.

(I've slightly adjusted the traditional interpretation of Ts'ao Kung, who says: "From the time we receive the sovereign's instructions until we set up camp opposite the enemy, the tactics are the most challenging." It seems more accurate to say that tactics and maneuvers truly begin after the army has marched out and encamped. Ch'ien Hao's note supports this view: "For recruiting, concentrating, harmonizing, and fortifying an army, there are many established rules. The real challenge comes when we start tactical operations." Tu Yu also remarks that "the greatest difficulty is in seizing favorable positions before the enemy does.")

The difficulty of tactical maneuvering lies in turning the indirect into the direct, and transforming misfortune into advantage.

(This sentence is one of Sun Tzŭ's typically condensed and somewhat cryptic expressions. Ts'ao Kung explains: "Make it seem as though you are far away, then cover the distance quickly and arrive before your opponent." Tu Mu says: "Deceive the enemy so that he becomes relaxed and slow while you advance with utmost speed." Ho Shih offers another perspective: "Even if you have difficult terrain to cross or natural obstacles in your way, this disadvantage can be turned into an advantage through rapid movement." Famous examples include Hannibal's crossing of the Alps, which put Italy at his mercy, and Napoleon's similar feat two thousand years later, resulting in the victory at Marengo.)

Thus, taking a long and circuitous route, while luring the enemy out of position, and although starting later than him, managing to reach the goal before him, demonstrates skill in the art of deviation.

(Tu Mu references the famous march of Chao She in 270 B.C. to relieve the town of O-yu, which was under siege by a Ch'in army. The King of Chao initially sought advice from Lien P'o, who considered the distance too far and the terrain too difficult for a relief mission. However, Chao She, acknowledging the risk, boldly stated: "We will be like two rats fighting in a hole—the braver one will win!" After setting out with his army, Chao She marched only 30 li before stopping to build fortifications for 28 days, ensuring the enemy's spies would report this delay. The Ch'in general, thinking Chao She was unwilling to save a city outside Chao's direct control, relaxed. But as soon as the spies left, Chao She launched a forced march, covering two days and one night, and arrived so swiftly that he seized the advantageous North hill before the enemy knew of his movements. The result was a decisive defeat for the Ch'in, forcing them to abandon the siege and retreat.)

Maneuvering with a disciplined army is advantageous; with an undisciplined multitude, it is most dangerous.

(I adopt the reading of the T'ung Tien, Cheng Yu-hsien, and the T'u Shu for clarity. The commentators using the standard text suggest that maneuvering can be either profitable or dangerous, depending on the general's skill.)

If you march a fully equipped army to seize an advantage, chances are you will be too late. However, sending a flying column for the task often requires sacrificing baggage and supplies.

(Some of the Chinese text is unclear even to the commentators, who paraphrase it. I offer my own translation cautiously, as there seems to be some deeper corruption in the text. Nonetheless, it is apparent that Sun Tzǔ disapproves of undertaking a long march without proper supplies. See § 11 below.)

If you order your soldiers to roll up their coats and make forced marches without stopping day or night, covering twice the usual distance in one go, traveling a hundred li to gain an advantage, the leaders of all your three divisions will end up in the hands of the enemy.

The strongest men will be at the front, while the exhausted ones will fall behind, and following this plan, only one-tenth of your army will reach the destination.

The moral of this, as Ts'ao Kung and others have pointed out, is that you should not march a hundred li to gain a tactical advantage, whether with or without your baggage train. Maneuvers like this should be limited to shorter distances. Stonewall Jackson said: "The hardships of forced marches are often more painful than the dangers of battle." He rarely asked his troops for extraordinary efforts. It was only when he planned a surprise attack or when a rapid retreat was urgently needed that he sacrificed everything for speed.

If you march fifty li to outmaneuver the enemy, the leader of your first division will be lost, and only half of your army will reach the goal.

If you march thirty li for the same purpose, two-thirds of your army will arrive.

From this, we can understand how difficult tactical maneuvers can be.

An army without its baggage train is lost; without provisions, it is lost; without supply bases, it is lost.

I think Sun Tzŭ meant "stores accumulated in depots." But Tu Yu says "fodder and the like," Chang Yu says "goods in general," and Wang Hsi says "fuel, salt, foodstuffs, etc."

We cannot form alliances until we understand the plans of our neighbors.

We are not fit to lead an army on the march unless we are familiar with the terrain—its mountains and forests, its pitfalls and cliffs, its marshes and swamps.

We will not be able to take advantage of natural terrain unless we make use of local guides.

In war, practice deception, and you will succeed. In the tactics of Turenne, deceiving the enemy, especially about the number of his troops, played a very important role.

Only move when there is a real advantage to be gained.

Whether to concentrate or divide your troops must be determined by the circumstances.

Let your speed be as swift as the wind,

(The simile is especially fitting because the wind is not only fast but, as Mei Yao-ch'en notes, "invisible and leaves no trace behind.")

and your formations as dense as a forest.

(Meng Shih's comment comes closer to the meaning: "When marching slowly, order and ranks must be preserved" to guard against surprise attacks. Natural forests don't grow in rows, but they do have the quality of compactness and density.)

When raiding and plundering, be like a raging fire,

(Compare with the Shih Ching: "Fierce as a blazing fire that no one can stop.")

and when holding your position, be as immovable as a mountain.

(This applies when defending a position from which the enemy tries to dislodge you or, as Tu Yu suggests, when the enemy is trying to lure you into a trap.)

Let your plans be as dark and impenetrable as night, and when you strike, hit like a thunderbolt.

(Tu Yu quotes a proverb from T'ai Kung: "You cannot close your ears to thunder or your eyes to lightning—they are too fast." Similarly, an attack should be so swift that it cannot be countered.)

When plundering the countryside, divide the spoils among your men,

(Sun Tzŭ aims to curb the abuses of indiscriminate looting by ensuring that all booty is placed in a common stock and fairly distributed among the troops.)

and when you capture new territory, divide it into allotments for the soldiers.

(Ch'en Hao advises: "Quarter your soldiers on the land and let them sow and cultivate it." By following this principle, harvesting the land they invaded, the Chinese succeeded in carrying out some of their most memorable expeditions, such as Pan Ch'ao's march to the Caspian, and, in more recent times, the campaigns of Fu-k'ang-an and Tso Tsung-t'ang.)

Think carefully and plan before taking any action.

(Chang Yu quotes Wei Liao Tzŭ, saying that we should not leave our camp until we understand the enemy's strength and the intelligence of their general. See the "seven comparisons" mentioned earlier.)

The one who masters the art of deception will win.

(Refer to previous sections for more on this.)

This is the essence of maneuvering.

(These words would naturally end the section, but what follows is an excerpt from an older book on war, which no longer exists but was still known during Sun Tzŭ's time. The style of the passage isn't noticeably different from Sun Tzŭ's own writing, and no commentators question its authenticity.)

The Book of Army Management says:

(It's worth noting that earlier commentators don't provide much information about this book. Mei Yao-ch'en calls it "an ancient military classic," and Wang Hsi refers to it as "an old book on war." Considering the centuries of warfare between different kingdoms in China before Sun Tzŭ's time, it's likely that military wisdom had already been written down in earlier times.)

On the battlefield,

(This is implied but not directly stated in the text.)

spoken commands don't carry far enough, so gongs and drums were introduced. Similarly, normal objects can't be seen clearly in the chaos, which is why banners and flags are used.

Gongs and drums, banners and flags, are used to focus the ears and eyes of the army on a single point.

(Chang Yu explains: "When sight and hearing are concentrated on the same object, the movements of as many as a million soldiers will be as coordinated as those of a single man.")

When the army forms a united body, it becomes impossible for the brave to advance alone or for the cowardly to retreat alone.

(Chuang Yu quotes: "Equally guilty are those who advance without orders and those who retreat without orders." Tu Mu tells a story of Wu Ch'i, who was fighting the Ch'in State. Before the battle began, one of his soldiers, renowned for his daring, went out on his own, captured two enemy heads, and returned to camp. Wu Ch'i had the man executed immediately. When an officer protested, saying, "This man was a good soldier and shouldn't have been beheaded," Wu Ch'i replied, "I know he was a good soldier, but I had him executed because he acted without orders.")

This is the art of managing large masses of men.

In night fighting, use signal fires and drums, and in daytime battles, use flags and banners to influence the ears and eyes of your soldiers.

(Ch'en Hao mentions Li Kuang-pi's night march to Ho-yang with 500 mounted men. They made such an impressive display with torches that the rebel leader Shih Ssu-ming, despite having a large army, didn't dare oppose their passage.)

An entire army can be robbed of its spirit.

(Chang Yu says: "In war, if a spirit of anger can fill the entire army at once, its attack will be unstoppable. The enemy's soldiers will be most eager when they first arrive, so we should not fight right away. Instead, we should wait until their enthusiasm fades before striking. This is how their spirit can be taken from them." Li Ch'uan and others tell a story from the Tso Chuan about Ts'ao Kuei, an advisor to Duke Chuang of Lu. When Lu was attacked by Ch'i, the duke prepared to fight at Ch'ang-cho after hearing the enemy's first drumbeat. Ts'ao said, "Not yet." Only after the enemy's drums sounded a third time did he give the order to attack. The army of Ch'i was defeated. When asked why he delayed, Ts'ao Kuei explained: "In battle, a courageous spirit is everything. The first drumbeat raises this spirit, but with the second it weakens, and by the third it's gone. I attacked when their spirit was gone and ours was at its peak." Wu Tzŭ lists "spirit" as the first of the "four important influences" in war, adding, "The value of an entire army—a mighty host of a million men—depends on one person: such is the power of spirit!")

A commander-in-chief can also lose his presence of mind.

(Chang Yu notes: "Presence of mind is the most vital quality for a general. It enables him to restore order from chaos and give courage to those who are panicking." The great general Li Ching once said, "Attacking does not simply mean assaulting walled cities or striking an army in battle. It also involves shaking the enemy's mental balance.")

A soldier's spirit is at its highest in the morning,

(As long as he has had breakfast, I suppose. At the Battle of the Trebia, the Romans made the mistake of fighting on an empty stomach, while Hannibal's men ate at their leisure. See Livy, XXI, liv. 8, lv. 1 and 8.)

by noon, it starts to fade; and by evening, his only thought is to return to camp.

A wise general, therefore, avoids fighting an army when its spirit is high, but attacks when it is sluggish and ready to retreat. This is the art of studying moods.

To remain disciplined and calm while waiting for disorder and confusion to arise among the enemy: this is the art of maintaining self-possession.

To be close to the goal while the enemy is still far, to wait in comfort while the enemy struggles, to be well-fed while the enemy is hungry: this is the art of conserving strength.

To refrain from attacking an enemy whose banners are in perfect order, or from engaging an army that is calm and confident: this is the art of understanding circumstances.

It is a basic military principle not to advance uphill against the enemy, nor to confront him when he is descending.

Do not chase an enemy who pretends to flee; do not engage soldiers whose spirits are high.

Do not take a bait offered by the enemy.

(Li Ch'uan and Tu Mu, showing a surprising lack of insight, take this literally as food or drink that might be poisoned by the enemy. Ch'en Hao and Chang Yu point out that the saying applies more broadly.)

Do not obstruct an army that is returning home.

(The commentators explain that a soldier whose heart is set on returning home will fight with extreme determination against anyone who tries to stop him, making him too dangerous to oppose. Chang Yu quotes Han Hsin: "Unbeatable is the soldier who desires nothing but to return home." A remarkable story is told of Ts'ao Ts'ao's resourcefulness in San Kuo Chi, chapter 1. In 198 A.D., Ts'ao was besieging Chang Hsiu in Jang, when Liu Piao sent reinforcements to cut off his retreat. Ts'ao was forced to withdraw but found himself trapped between two enemies guarding each exit of a narrow pass. In this desperate situation, he waited until nightfall, dug a tunnel into the mountainside, and set an ambush. Once the entire enemy army had passed, Ts'ao's hidden troops attacked from behind, while he turned to confront them from the front, throwing them into chaos and defeating them. Ts'ao later remarked, "The bandits tried to stop my retreat and forced me into a desperate fight; that's how I knew how to defeat them.")

When you surround an army, leave an opening for escape.

(This doesn't mean you should let the enemy flee. The purpose, as Tu Mu explains, is to make the enemy believe there is a way to escape, preventing them from fighting with the desperation of those with no hope. As Tu Mu adds, "Once they believe they have a way out, you can then crush them.")

Do not press a desperate enemy too hard.

(Ch'en Hao cites the saying: "When birds and beasts are cornered, they will use their claws and teeth." Chang Yu advises: "If your enemy has burned his boats and destroyed his cooking pots, fully committed to the outcome of the battle, you must not push them to the extreme." Ho Shih illustrates this with a story about the general Fu Yen-ch'ing. In 945 A.D., he and his colleague Tu Chung-wei were surrounded by a much larger Khitan army in a barren, desert-like area. Their small Chinese force was suffering due to a lack of water. The wells they dug ran dry, and the soldiers were reduced to squeezing moisture from lumps of mud. Their numbers dwindled rapidly, and Fu Yen-ch'ing declared, "We are desperate men. It is better to die for our country than to be taken captive with our hands tied." A strong wind was blowing from the northeast, filling the air with dense clouds of sand. Tu Chung-wei wanted to wait for the storm to pass before launching their final attack, but another officer, Li Shou-cheng, saw an opportunity and said, "They are many, and we are few, but in this sandstorm, our numbers won't be clear. Victory will go to those who fight hardest, and the wind will be our ally." Fu Yen-ch'ing then led a sudden and unexpected cavalry charge, routing the barbarians and breaking through to safety.)

Chapter 8 - Variation of Tactics

The heading literally means "The Nine Variations," but since Sun Tzŭ doesn't enumerate them specifically and has already stated (V §§ 6-11) that deviations in strategy are practically limitless, we are inclined to agree with Wang Hsi, who explains that "Nine" represents an indefinitely large number. It simply means that in warfare, tactics should be varied to the greatest extent possible. I am unsure how Ts'ao Kung interprets these Nine Variations, but it's suggested they are related to the Nine Situations discussed in chapter XI. This view is also supported by Chang Yu. Another possibility is that something has been lost, which is suggested by the unusual brevity of the chapter.

Sun Tzŭ said: In war, the general receives his commands from the sovereign, assembles his army, and concentrates his forces.

(This is repeated from VII. § 1, where it fits better. It may have been included here simply to provide a start for the chapter.)

When in difficult terrain, do not set up camp. In areas where main roads intersect, join hands with your allies. Do not remain in dangerously isolated positions.

(This situation is not one of the Nine Situations listed in the beginning of chapter XI, but it does appear later on (§ 43). Chang Yu defines it as being located across the border in enemy territory. Li Ch'uan says it refers to land where there are no springs, wells, flocks, or firewood. Chia Lin describes it as a region of gorges, cliffs, and steep terrain with no clear roads forward.)

In situations where you are trapped, rely on strategy. In a desperate position, you must fight.

There are roads that should not be followed,

(Li Ch'uan says this applies especially to narrow passes where ambushes are likely.)

armies that must not be attacked,

(It might be more accurate to say "there are times when an army should not be attacked." Ch'en Hao explains: "When you have an opportunity for a small advantage but cannot achieve a decisive victory, it is better not to attack, to avoid exhausting your troops.")

towns that should not be besieged,

(Compare III. § 4. Ts'ao Kung shares an example from his own experience. While invading Hsu-chou, he bypassed the city of Hua-pi, which lay in his path, and advanced deeper into the country. This strategy paid off with the capture of fourteen key cities. Chang Yu advises: "Do not attack a town that, even if captured, cannot be held or, if left alone, will not pose a threat." Hsun Ying, when urged to attack Pi-yang, responded: "The city is small and well-fortified; even if

I succeed in taking it, it won't be a great achievement, but if I fail, I will be ridiculed." Sieges made up a significant part of warfare in the seventeenth century, but Turenne emphasized the value of marches, countermarches, and maneuvers. He remarked, "It is a great error to waste soldiers on capturing a town when the same effort could win an entire province.")

positions that should not be contested, and commands from the sovereign that should not be obeyed.

(This is difficult for the Chinese, given their strong respect for authority. Wei Liao Tzǔ, as quoted by Tu Mu, states: "Weapons are instruments of evil, conflict opposes virtue, and a military commander stands against civil order." Nonetheless, the reality remains that even the emperor's wishes must yield to military necessity.)

The general who thoroughly understands the advantages that come from varying tactics knows how to manage his troops.

The general who does not grasp these advantages, even if he is well aware of the terrain, will not be able to make effective use of his knowledge.

(Literally, "to get the advantage of the ground," meaning not only securing favorable positions but also making the most of natural advantages in every way possible. Chang Yu explains: "Every kind of terrain has its own natural features and also offers room for variation in plans. How can these natural features be used to their full potential unless topographical knowledge is combined with a flexible mind?")

Thus, a student of war who has not mastered the art of varying his strategies, even if he knows the Five Advantages, will fail to make the best use of his soldiers.

(Chia Lin explains that these Five Advantages refer to obvious and generally beneficial courses of action, such as: "if a road is short, it should be taken; if an army is isolated, it should be attacked; if a town is in a precarious state, it should be besieged; if a position can be stormed, it should be attempted; and if consistent with military operations, the ruler's orders should be obeyed." However, there are circumstances in which these advantages may not be used. For instance, "a certain road may be the shortest route, but if it is filled with natural obstacles or if the enemy has laid an ambush there, it should not be followed. A hostile force may be vulnerable to attack, but if it is desperate and ready to fight to the last, it is better not to strike.")

Therefore, in the wise leader's plans, considerations of both advantage and disadvantage are combined.

("Whether in an advantageous or disadvantageous situation," says Ts'ao Kung, "the opposite state should always be kept in mind.")

If we balance our expectation of advantage with awareness of possible disadvantages, we may successfully accomplish the most important part of our plans.

(Tu Mu comments: "If we want to gain an advantage over the enemy, we must not focus only on that goal. We must also consider the possibility of the enemy inflicting harm on us and include that in our calculations.")

If, on the other hand, we are always ready to seize an advantage even in difficult situations, we can free ourselves from misfortune.

(Tu Mu explains: "If I want to escape from a dangerous position, I must not only consider the enemy's ability to harm me but also my own ability to gain an advantage over them. If my plans balance both considerations, I will succeed in getting out of danger. For example, if I am surrounded by the enemy and only focus on escaping, the weakness of my strategy will encourage the enemy to pursue and crush me. It would be much better to encourage my troops to launch a bold counterattack and use the advantage gained to break free from the enemy's grasp." See the story of Ts'ao Ts'ao in VII. § 35, note.)

Reduce the enemy's leaders by causing harm to them.

(Chia Lin lists several ways to harm the enemy, some of which are quite unique: "Entice away the enemy's best and wisest men, leaving him without good advisors. Plant traitors in his country to disrupt government policies. Stir up intrigue and deceit, sowing discord between the ruler and his ministers. Use cunning tricks to weaken his men and drain his resources. Corrupt his morals with insidious gifts that lead him into indulgence. Unsettle his mind by presenting him with beautiful women." Chang Yu, following Wang Hsi, offers a different interpretation: "Force the enemy into a position where he is bound to suffer harm, and he will eventually submit on his own.")

Create difficulties for them,

(Tu Mu explains that this phrase means to create problems that affect the enemy's "assets"—things like a large army, a rich treasury, harmony among soldiers, and the consistent execution of orders. These are what give us leverage over the enemy.)

and keep them constantly occupied.

(Literally, "make servants of them." Tu Yu says: "Deny them any opportunity to rest.")

Offer deceptive attractions and lure them into rushing to a specific point.

(Meng Shih provides a great example of this idiom: "Make them forget pien (the reasons for acting cautiously) and hasten in our direction.")

The art of war teaches us to depend not on the chance that the enemy will not come, but on our own readiness to meet him; not on the hope that he won't attack, but on the certainty that we have made our position unassailable.

There are five dangerous flaws that may affect a general:

(1) Recklessness, which leads to destruction.

("Bravery without forethought," as Ts'ao Kung puts it, causes a man to fight blindly, like a mad bull. Chang Yu says, "Such an opponent should not be met with brute force but can be lured into an ambush and killed." Wu Tzŭ also points out that too much emphasis is often placed on a general's courage, forgetting that courage is just one of the qualities a general should have. A brave man who fights recklessly, without understanding what is truly advantageous, must be condemned. Ssu-ma Fa adds that "simply rushing to one's death does not guarantee victory.")

(2) Cowardice, which leads to capture.

(Ts'ao Kung explains that the word "cowardice" refers to someone "who is too timid to advance and seize an advantage." Wang Hsi adds that it describes someone who flees at the first sight of danger. Meng Shih gives a more detailed interpretation: "He is focused on surviving at all costs," meaning someone who avoids taking risks. But, as Sun Tzŭ knew, success in war often requires risk. T'ai Kung noted: "He who lets an advantage slip will eventually face real disaster." In 404 A.D., Liu Yu chased the rebel Huan Hsuan up the Yangtsze River. Though Liu Yu's forces were much smaller, Huan Hsuan, fearing the consequences of defeat, prepared a small boat attached to his warship for a quick escape. This lack of resolve destroyed his soldiers' morale. When the loyalists launched a determined attack using fireships, Huan Hsuan's forces were completely routed. They had to burn all their supplies and fled for two days without stopping. Chang Yu also tells a similar story of Chao Ying-ch'i, a general of the Chin State, who kept a boat ready during a battle with the Ch'u army in 597 B.C., so he could escape first if defeated.)

(3) A quick temper, which can be provoked by insults.

(Tu Mu tells the story of Yao Hsing, who in 357 A.D. was opposed by Huang Mei, Teng Ch'iang, and others. Yao Hsing shut himself inside his walls, refusing to engage. Teng Ch'iang, knowing Yao's fiery temper, suggested launching constant attacks to provoke him. He believed that Yao, once angered, would come out to fight. This strategy worked—Yao Hsiang left his defenses, was drawn into a trap as far as San-yuan by the enemy's fake retreat, and was ultimately defeated and killed.)

A delicate sense of honor that is easily wounded by shame is another potential fault.

This doesn't mean that a sense of honor is a flaw in a general. What Sun Tzŭ criticizes is being overly sensitive to slander or criticism, the kind of person who is too easily hurt by insults, even when they are undeserved. Mei Yao-ch'en wisely notes, though it may sound contradictory: "Those who seek glory should not worry too much about public opinion."

The fifth fault is being too concerned for the well-being of his men, which causes unnecessary worry and trouble.

Again, Sun Tzŭ isn't suggesting that a general should neglect the welfare of his soldiers. He simply means that focusing too much on their comfort can lead to poor decisions and lost opportunities. This short-term thinking can ultimately cause greater suffering for the troops in the long run because defeat, or a longer war, will be the result. A misguided sense of pity can lead a general to make choices that go against his better judgment, such as relieving a city under siege or sending reinforcements to a detachment under heavy pressure. In the South African War, it's now accepted that our repeated attempts to relieve Ladysmith were strategic errors that failed to achieve their goal. In the end, it was the general who decided to stop letting sentiment for a small part of the army override the needs of the whole who finally succeeded. I recall an old soldier trying to defend one of our generals, who had notably failed during this war, by saying that he was "so kind to his men." In saying this, though he didn't realize it, he was actually condemning the general according to Sun Tzŭ's principles.

These are the five dangerous flaws in a general, which can ruin the conduct of war.

When an army is defeated and its leader is killed, the cause can almost always be traced back to one of these five flaws. Keep them in mind.

Chapter 9 - The Army on The March

Sun Tzu said: Now we turn to the important task of setting up camp and keeping a close eye on the enemy. When traveling through mountainous areas, it's important to move quickly across the mountains and stay near the valleys.

(This is because the dry, barren highlands can leave your troops without enough food or water. It's better to stay near places where water and grass are plentiful. Wu Tzu, an ancient military strategist, once said, "Don't camp in natural ovens," which means avoiding the entrances of valleys where the heat can become unbearable and where you could easily be trapped. Chang Yu provides a historical example: During the Later Han dynasty, a bandit named Wu-tu Ch'iang hid his troops in the hills. Instead of attacking directly, General Ma Yuan, who was sent to capture him, took control of the areas with water and other supplies. Ch'iang's troops soon ran out of provisions because they hadn't secured the valleys. With no access to resources, they were eventually forced to surrender.)

When choosing a campsite, always pick slightly higher ground.

(This doesn't mean the highest mountain peaks, but rather low hills that give you an advantage over the surrounding area. High ground lets you see the battlefield more easily and makes your camp less vulnerable to surprise attacks.)

It is also important to set up your camp so that it faces the sun.

(Some commentators, like Tu Mu, believed this meant facing south, while others, like Ch'en Hao, thought it meant facing east. Either way, the idea is that facing the sun gives your camp better visibility and warmth, making it more comfortable and easier to defend.)

In mountain warfare, one of the key rules is to never climb uphill to attack the enemy. It's better to hold the high ground and force the enemy to come to you. After crossing a river, always move away from it quickly.

(Ts'ao Kung explained this as a strategy to lure the enemy into crossing the river after you, where they will be more vulnerable. Chang Yu added that moving away from the river ensures that you have the freedom to maneuver, preventing the enemy from blocking your retreat or cutting off your supply lines.)

If the enemy is crossing a river, don't attack them while they're in the middle of the crossing. Wait until half of their forces have crossed, then strike.

(Li Ch'uan refers to Han Hsin's famous victory over Lung Chu at the Wei River as an example of this tactic. Han Hsin's forces built a dam upstream at night and crossed the river to fake a retreat. Lung Chu, thinking Han Hsin's army was retreating in defeat, followed him across the river. At that moment, Han Hsin's troops broke the dam, sending a flood downstream that cut off Lung Chu's army. In the resulting chaos, Han Hsin's forces attacked decisively, killing Lung Chu and routing his army.)

If you're preparing to fight near a river the enemy hasn't crossed yet, don't position your troops too close to the river.

(Doing so could give the enemy the chance to plan a better crossing or force you into a defensive position when you could have set up an ambush instead.)

If you're stationed near a river, make sure to place your boats upstream from the enemy, and always keep your camp facing the sun.

(As mentioned before, being upstream gives you a tactical advantage, allowing you to control the flow of water. This applies whether your forces are on the riverbank or in boats. Facing the sun provides better visibility and can also give you a psychological advantage.)

Never move upstream to meet the enemy.

(Tu Mu warns that, since water flows downward, camping in a lower position is dangerous because the enemy could flood the river or poison the water and send it downstream to your camp. Chu-ko Wu-hou also advised against moving against the current in river warfare, as this would allow the enemy to use the natural flow of the river to their advantage.)

When it comes to river warfare, that's all you need to keep in mind. However, when crossing salt marshes, your only goal should be to get through them as quickly as possible.

(Salt marshes are inhospitable. They have little fresh water, the grass is scarce and not nutritious for animals, and the flat, open terrain leaves your forces vulnerable to attack.)

If you must fight in a salt marsh, camp near a source of fresh water and grass, and position your back against a group of trees.

(Li Ch'uan mentions that trees can signal safer ground, while Tu Mu points out that trees can protect your rear and reduce the chances of a surprise attack from the enemy.)

This concludes the rules for fighting in salt marshes. When fighting on flat, dry land, choose a position that is easy to access, with slightly rising ground on your right and behind you.

(Tu Mu quotes T'ai Kung, who recommended positioning your army with a stream or marsh on the left and a hill on the right. This setup offers natural defenses and strategic advantages.)

By following this rule, you will have danger in front of you and safety behind. This concludes the guidelines for warfare on flat land.

These principles of terrain management are the four essential branches of military strategy: (1) mountains, (2) rivers, (3) marshes, and (4) plains. Understanding these principles helped the Yellow Emperor defeat four kings.

(Some scholars question whether the Yellow Emperor truly defeated four kings, as historical records like the Shih Chi only mention his victories over Yen Ti and Ch'ih Yu. However, the Liu T'ao suggests he fought and won seventy battles, ultimately uniting the empire. Ts'ao Kung speculates that the Yellow Emperor established a feudal system with four princes holding the title of emperor. Meanwhile, Li Ch'uan believes that the art of war began with the Yellow Emperor, who learned it from his wise minister, Feng Hou.)

All armies prefer to occupy high ground rather than low ground because high ground offers advantages for both health and combat. Low ground, on the other hand, is often damp and unhealthy for troops.

(Ts'ao Kung advises generals to prioritize finding fresh water and good pasture for their animals to maintain the health and well-being of their forces.)

When choosing a campsite, look for hard, dry ground. This will help keep your soldiers healthy and reduce the risk of illness.

(Chang Yu adds that dry conditions help prevent diseases from spreading, which can be as dangerous as any enemy.)

Whenever possible, position yourself on the sunny side of a hill or slope, with the incline behind you and to your right. This will benefit your soldiers and allow you to make the best use of the natural terrain.

After heavy rains in higher regions, if you encounter a swollen river covered with foam, you must wait for the water to recede before attempting to cross.

Avoid areas with steep cliffs, narrow passes, or deep gorges with fast-flowing streams. These are natural traps—easy to enter but difficult to escape from. Places surrounded by steep banks or filled with water at the bottom should be avoided at all costs, as they are like natural prisons where you could easily be trapped.

(Dense forests with thick undergrowth, where spears cannot be used, should also be avoided, as well as quagmires and other soft ground that makes it difficult for chariots or horsemen to pass.)

While you should avoid such places, try to lead the enemy into them. If you face the enemy in such terrain, position them so that the natural obstacles are behind them, limiting their ability to maneuver.

If your camp is near hilly terrain, ponds surrounded by tall grasses, or woods with dense undergrowth, these areas must be thoroughly searched, as they are ideal hiding spots for enemy spies or ambushes.

When the enemy is nearby but remains still, it is a sign they are relying on the natural strength of their position. When they are distant and try to provoke a battle, they are likely trying to lure you out of your defensive position and into a trap.

If the enemy's camp seems easy to approach, be cautious—it may be a trap. Movement among trees in a forest is a sign that the enemy is advancing, likely cutting down trees to clear a path for their troops.

Birds suddenly taking flight may indicate an ambush. Startled animals could signal an impending attack.

If dust rises in a high column, it means chariots are approaching. If the dust is lower and spread out, infantry is on the move. Dust that moves in several directions suggests soldiers are gathering firewood, while small amounts of dust moving back and forth indicate the army is setting up camp.

When the enemy uses humble words but increases their preparations, it's a sign they are planning an attack. They may be pretending to be weak to make you feel secure.

If the enemy's camp looks humble but their preparations are intensifying, they are likely preparing for an assault. In one case, an army tried to demoralize its enemy by mutilating prisoners and desecrating graves, but this only strengthened the defenders' resolve. The defenders launched a clever counterattack by sending oxen with burning torches tied to their tails into the enemy's camp, causing chaos and helping them reclaim lost cities.

Aggressive words and forward movements often mean the enemy is preparing to retreat.

When light chariots are positioned on the flanks, it signals the enemy is getting ready for battle.

Peace offers that come without a sworn agreement usually signal a trap.

If the enemy's soldiers are running about and quickly forming up, the decisive moment is near.

If some soldiers advance while others retreat, it is likely a trick designed to confuse and mislead you.

Soldiers leaning on their spears are likely weak from hunger, and if they drink water immediately after getting it, the army is suffering from thirst.

If the enemy hesitates to act even when given an opportunity, it is a sign their troops are exhausted.

If birds are gathering in a specific area, it means that spot is unoccupied.

Noise at night suggests the enemy is anxious, while disorder in their camp indicates the general has lost control.

If the enemy's banners are being moved around frequently, it could mean there is rebellion in the ranks. Anger among the officers suggests that the soldiers are worn out.

When an army begins feeding its horses with grain, slaughtering cattle for food, and not hanging up its cooking pots, it means they are prepared to fight to the death.

When soldiers whisper in small groups, it indicates unrest in the ranks. Frequent rewards suggest the enemy is running low on resources, while excessive punishments point to severe internal problems.

If a general talks boldly but then hesitates out of fear of the enemy's numbers, it reveals a lack of intelligence. When envoys come with polite words, it usually means the enemy is seeking a truce.

If the enemy's troops stand facing yours for a long time without fighting or retreating, they may be preparing a surprise attack. Stay alert.

If your forces are roughly equal to the enemy's, you should be able to hold your position, but attacking head-on would be risky. Instead, gather your strength, watch the enemy closely, and wait for reinforcements.

A leader who underestimates the enemy and doesn't plan ahead will ultimately be defeated.

Punishing soldiers before they are loyal to you will lead to disobedience. However, if they are not disciplined after they become loyal, they will be ineffective in battle.

That's why it's important to first treat soldiers with kindness, then later enforce strict discipline. This is the path to victory.

If commands are enforced consistently, the army will be disciplined. If not, the soldiers will become disorderly. A general who trusts his men while making sure his orders are followed will strengthen both his leadership and his army.

Chapter 10 - Terrain

Sun Tzŭ said: We can identify six kinds of terrain:

(1) Accessible ground;

(Mei Yao-ch'en explains this as ground that is well-supplied with roads and ways of communication.)

(2) Entangling ground;

(Mei Yao-ch'en describes this as "net-like" terrain, where if you enter, you may become entangled.)

(3) Temporizing ground;

(This is ground where you can delay or hold off.)

(4) Narrow passes; (5) Steep heights; (6) Positions far from the enemy.

(It is hardly necessary to point out the issues with this classification. There is a strange lack of logical reasoning in the unquestioning acceptance of these overlapping categories.)

Ground that both sides can freely move across is called accessible.

On this type of terrain, you should arrive before the enemy, take the higher, sunnier spots, and carefully guard your supply lines.

(The general meaning of this last phrase, as Tu Yu explains, is "not to allow the enemy to cut your communications." In view of Napoleon's statement, "the secret of war lies in the communications," it would have been helpful if Sun Tzŭ had elaborated more on this important subject here and in other sections. Col. Henderson says: "The line of supply is as vital to the life of an army as the heart is to a human being. Just as a duelist who finds his opponent's weapon threatening his life and his own guard out of place must adjust to his opponent's movements, the commander whose communications are suddenly threatened finds himself in a bad position. He may be forced to change all his plans, divide his forces into isolated groups, and fight with fewer troops on unprepared ground. In such a situation, defeat could mean the ruin or surrender of his entire army.")

If you follow these steps, you will be able to fight with an advantage.

Ground which can be abandoned but is hard to re-occupy is called entangling ground.

From a position of this sort, if the enemy is unprepared, you may sally forth and defeat him. But if the enemy is prepared for your coming, and you fail to defeat him, then, return being impossible, disaster will ensue.

When the position is such that neither side will gain by making the first move, it is called temporizing ground.

(Tu Mu says: "Each side finds it inconvenient to move, and the situation remains at a deadlock.")

In a position of this sort, even though the enemy should offer us an attractive bait,

(Tu Yu says, "turning their backs on us and pretending to flee." But this is only one of the lures which might induce us to quit our position.)

it will be advisable not to stir forth, but rather to retreat, thus enticing the enemy in his turn; then, when part of his army has come out, we may deliver our attack with advantage.

With regard to narrow passes, if you can occupy them first, let them be strongly garrisoned and await the advent of the enemy.

(Because then, as Tu Yu observes, "the initiative will lie with us, and by making sudden and unexpected attacks we shall have the enemy at our mercy.")

Should the enemy forestall you in occupying a pass, do not go after him if the pass is fully garrisoned, but only if it is weakly garrisoned.

With regard to precipitous heights, if you are beforehand with your adversary, you should occupy the raised and sunny spots, and there wait for him to come up.

(Ts'ao Kung says: "The particular advantage of securing heights and defiles is that your actions cannot then be dictated by the enemy." [For the enunciation of the grand principle alluded to, see VI. § 2]. Chang Yu tells the following anecdote of P'ei Hsing-chien (A.D. 619-682), who was sent on a punitive expedition against the Turkic tribes. "At night he pitched his camp as usual, and it had already been completely fortified by wall and ditch, when suddenly he gave orders that the army should shift its quarters to a hill nearby. This was highly displeasing to his officers, who protested loudly against the extra fatigue which it would entail on the men. P'ei Hsing-chien, however, paid no heed to their remonstrances and had the camp moved as quickly as possible. The same night, a terrific storm came on, which flooded their former place of encampment to the depth of over twelve feet. The recalcitrant officers were amazed at the sight and owned that they had been in the wrong. 'How did you know what was going to happen?' they asked. P'ei Hsing-chien replied: 'From this time forward be content to obey orders without asking unnecessary questions.' From this it may be seen," Chang Yu continues, "that high and sunny places are advantageous not only for fighting, but also because they are immune from disastrous floods.")

If the enemy has occupied the high ground before you, do not pursue him, but instead retreat and try to lure him away.

(Li Shih-min's turning point in his campaign in 621 A.D. against the rebels Tou Chien-te, King of Hsia, and Wang Shih-ch'ung, Prince of Cheng, was his capture of the heights of Wu-lao. Despite this, Tou Chien-te still tried to help his ally in Lo-yang and was defeated and captured. See Chiu T'ang Shu, ch. 2, fol. 5 verso, and also ch. 54.)

If you are far from the enemy and the strength of both armies is equal, it is not easy to provoke a battle,

(The key is that you shouldn't undertake a long, tiring march, which would leave you exhausted while the enemy remains fresh and alert, as Tu Yu explains.)

and fighting in such conditions will put you at a disadvantage.

These six are the principles related to the terrain.

(Or, "principles relating to the ground." See I. § 8.)

A general in a position of responsibility must carefully study them.

Now, an army can face six different calamities, not due to natural causes, but because of the general's mistakes. These are: (1) Flight; (2) Insubordination; (3) Collapse; (4) Ruin; (5) Disorganization; (6) Rout.

If one force is thrown against another ten times its size, the outcome will be the flight of the smaller force.

When the common soldiers are too strong, and their officers are too weak, the result is insubordination.

(Tu Mu refers to the case of T'ien Pu [Hsin T'ang Shu, ch. 148], who was sent to Wei in 821 A.D. to lead an army against Wang T'ing-ts'ou. While he was in command, his soldiers treated him with disdain, openly disrespecting him by riding donkeys around the camp in large numbers. T'ien Pu couldn't control this behavior, and when he finally tried to engage the enemy, his troops scattered in all directions. Afterward, he tragically committed suicide.)

When the officers are too strong and the common soldiers too weak, the result is collapse.

(Ts'ao Kung says: "The officers are eager to advance, but the soldiers are weak and suddenly collapse.")

When higher-ranking officers act out of anger and fight the enemy on their own initiative, without waiting for the commander-in-chief to assess whether they are ready for battle, the result is ruin.

(Wang Hsi comments: "This refers to a general who becomes angry without reason and fails to recognize the capabilities of his subordinate officers. This leads to intense resentment and ultimately brings disaster upon him.")

When the general is weak and lacks authority, and when his orders are not clear or precise,

(Wei Liao Tzŭ in chapter 4 says: "If the commander gives his orders decisively, the soldiers will not need to hear them twice. If his actions are carried out without hesitation, the soldiers will not have doubts about following them." General Baden-Powell also emphasizes, saying: "The key to getting good results from your trained men lies in clear instructions." Wu Tzŭ, in chapter 3, adds: "The worst flaw in a military leader is indecision; the greatest disasters in an army come from hesitation.")

when officers and men are not given specific duties,

(Tu Mu explains: "Neither the officers nor the soldiers have any set routines.")

and when the troops are assembled in a careless and disorganized manner, the result is complete chaos.

When a general fails to properly assess the enemy's strength and sends a smaller force against a much larger one, or orders a weak unit to engage a stronger force without placing the best soldiers at the front, the outcome will be a disastrous defeat.

(Chang Yu explains this by saying: "Whenever there is fighting, the most determined soldiers should be placed at the front, both to inspire confidence in our own troops and to intimidate the enemy." This concept aligns with Caesar's use of the primi ordines in "De Bello Gallico," V. 28, 44, and elsewhere.)

These are six ways to invite defeat, and they must be carefully observed by any general who holds a position of responsibility.

(See earlier discussion in § 13.)

The natural landscape is the soldier's greatest ally;

(Ch'en Hao notes: "The advantages of weather and timing are not as significant as those related to the terrain.")

but the ability to assess the enemy, control the factors that lead to victory, and accurately judge difficulties, dangers, and distances is what defines a truly great general.

He who knows these principles and in fighting puts his knowledge into practice, will win his battles. He who knows them not, nor practises them, will surely be defeated.

If fighting is sure to result in victory, then you must fight, even though the ruler forbids it; if fighting will not result in victory, then you must not fight even at the ruler's bidding.

(Chang Yu also quotes the saying: "Decrees from the Son of Heaven do not penetrate the walls of a camp." Huang Shih-kung of the Ch'in dynasty, who is said to have been the patron of Chang Liang and to have written the San Lueh, has these words attributed to him: "The responsibility of setting an army in motion must devolve on the general alone; if advance and retreat are controlled from the Palace, brilliant results will hardly be achieved. Hence the god-like ruler and the enlightened monarch are content to play a humble part in furthering their country's cause [literally, kneel down to push the chariot wheel]." This means that "in matters lying outside the zenana, the decision of the military commander must be absolute.")

The general who advances without coveting fame and retreats without fearing disgrace,

(It was Wellington, I think, who said that the hardest thing of all for a soldier is to retreat.)

whose only thought is to protect his country and do good service for his sovereign, is the jewel of the kingdom.

(A noble presentiment, in few words, of the Chinese "happy warrior." Such a man, says Ho Shih, "even if he had to suffer punishment, would not regret his conduct.")

Regard your soldiers as your children, and they will follow you into the deepest valleys; look on them as your own beloved sons, and they will stand by you even unto death.

(Cf. I. § 6. In this connection, Tu Mu draws for us an engaging picture of the famous general Wu Ch'i, from whose treatise on war I have frequently had occasion to quote: "He wore the same clothes and ate the same food as the meanest of his soldiers, refused to have either a horse to ride or a mat to sleep on, carried his own surplus rations wrapped in a parcel, and shared every hardship with his men. One of his soldiers was suffering from an abscess, and Wu Ch'i himself sucked out the virus. The soldier's mother, hearing this, began wailing and lamenting. Somebody asked her, saying: 'Why do you cry? Your son is only a common soldier, and yet the commander-in-chief himself has sucked the poison from his sore.' The woman replied, 'Many years ago, Lord Wu performed a similar service for my husband, who never left him afterwards, and finally met his death at the hands of the enemy. And now that he has done the same for my son, he too will fall fighting I know not where.'")

Li Ch'uan mentions the Viscount of Ch'u, who invaded the small state of Hsiao during the winter. The Duke of Shen said to him: "Many of the soldiers are suffering severely from the cold." So he made a round of the whole army, comforting and encouraging the men; and straightway they felt as if they were clothed in garments lined with floss silk.

If, however, you are lenient but unable to assert your authority; kind-hearted but unable to enforce your commands; and also incapable of maintaining order, then your soldiers will be like spoiled children—they will be useless in any real situation.

[Li Ching once said that if you could make your soldiers fear you, they wouldn't be afraid of the enemy. Tu Mu recounts a strict example of military discipline from 219 A.D., when Lu Meng was holding the town of Chiang-ling. He had ordered his army not to bother the local people or take anything from them by force. However, one officer under his command, who happened to be from the same town, took a bamboo hat from a villager to wear over his helmet in the rain. Despite being a fellow townsman, Lu Meng didn't excuse the breach of discipline. He ordered the officer's execution, though tears fell down his face as he gave the command. This strict action instilled a healthy sense of fear in the army, and from that point on, even items left in the road were not touched.]

If we know our own men are ready to attack but don't know that the enemy is not vulnerable to attack, we've only come halfway to victory.

[As Ts'ao Kung says, "in this case, the outcome is uncertain."]

If we know the enemy is vulnerable but don't realize that our own men aren't ready to attack, we've again only come halfway to victory.

If we know the enemy is vulnerable, and we know our men are ready to attack, but we don't realize that the terrain makes fighting impossible, we're still only halfway to victory.

Hence, the seasoned soldier, once on the move, is never confused; once he breaks camp, he is never lost.

[According to Tu Mu, this is because he has planned everything so thoroughly that victory is ensured before any action is taken. Chang Yu adds, "He doesn't act rashly, so when he does move, he makes no mistakes."]

Thus the saying goes: If you know the enemy and know yourself, you won't have to worry about the outcome of a hundred battles; if you know both Heaven and Earth, your victory will be complete.

[Li Ch'uan concludes: "If you understand three things—the affairs of men, the seasons of Heaven, and the natural advantages of Earth—, you will always win your battles."]

Chapter 11 - The Nine Situations

Sun Tzu said: The art of war recognizes nine types of ground: (1) Dispersive ground; (2) facile ground; (3) contentious ground; (4) open ground; (5) ground of intersecting highways; (6) serious ground; (7) difficult ground; (8) hemmed-in ground; (9) desperate ground.

When a leader is fighting in his own territory, it is called dispersive ground. This is because the soldiers, being near their homes and eager to see their wives and children, are likely to seize the opportunity of a battle to scatter in every direction. As Tu Mu explains, "They will lack the desperation needed to fight with full valor, and when they retreat, they will find places of refuge."

When the army has crossed into enemy territory, but not deeply, it is called facile ground. Li Ch'uan and Ho Shih say this is because retreat is still easy, and other commentators give similar explanations. Tu Mu adds, "When your army has crossed the border, you should burn your boats and bridges to show everyone there is no turning back."

Ground that offers great advantage to either side is called contentious ground. Tu Mu defines this as ground "worth fighting for." Ts'ao Kung says it is ground "on which the few and weak can defeat the many and strong," such as "the neck of a pass," which Li Ch'uan mentions as an example. Thermopylae fits this description because holding it for even a short time delayed an entire invading army, providing invaluable time. As Wu Tzu says in his writings: "When facing odds of one against ten, there is nothing better than a narrow pass."

When Lu Kuang was returning from his successful expedition to Turkestan in 385 A.D., and had reached I-ho with many spoils, Liang Hsi, the administrator of Liang-chou, took advantage of the death of Fu Chien, King of Ch'in, to plot against him. Yang Han, governor of Kao-ch'ang, advised him, saying, "Lu Kuang has just won victories in the west, and his soldiers are strong and confident. If we face him in the desert sands, we will not stand a chance. Instead, let's take control of the defile at the mouth of the Kao-wu pass. By cutting off his water supply, we can wait until his troops are weakened by thirst and then dictate our terms. Or, if that pass is too far, we could confront him at the I-wu pass, which is closer. Even a skilled strategist like Tzŭ-fang could not overcome the strength of these two positions." Liang Hsi, however, refused this advice and was overwhelmed and defeated by the invader.

Ground where both sides can move freely is called open ground.

[There are different interpretations of the word used for this type of ground. Ts'ao Kung says it means "ground covered with roads, like a chessboard." Ho Shih suggests it means "ground where communication is easy."]

Ground that forms the key to three neighboring states is ground of intersecting highways.

[Ts'au Kung defines this as "our country next to the enemy's, with a third country adjoining both." Meng Shih uses the example of Cheng, a small state bordered by Ch'i to the northeast, Chin to the west, and Ch'u to the south.]

Whoever takes control of this area first has a strategic advantage over most of the region.

[The one who holds this important position can force many neighboring states to become allies.]

When an army has moved deep into enemy territory, leaving fortified cities behind, it is on serious ground.

[Wang Hsi says it is called serious ground because "the army's situation becomes serious when it reaches this point."]

Mountain forests, steep terrain, marshes, and fens—all areas that are difficult to pass—are called difficult ground.

Ground that is reached through narrow gorges, where retreat can only happen through winding paths, and where a small enemy force could easily defeat a large army, is called hemmed-in ground.

Ground where the only way to avoid destruction is to fight immediately is called desperate ground.

[The situation, as described by Ts'ao Kung, is much like hemmed-in ground but worse, with no way out: "A tall mountain in front, a large river behind, no way to advance, no way to retreat." Ch'en Hao says being on desperate ground is "like sitting in a sinking boat or standing in a burning house." Tu Mu shares a vivid description from Li Ching of an army caught in this type of trap: "Imagine an army in enemy territory with no local guides. The army stumbles into a deadly trap, at the enemy's mercy. A ravine on the left, a mountain on the right, and a path so dangerous that horses must be tied together and chariots lifted with slings. There's no way forward, and retreat is blocked. The soldiers move in single file, barely forming ranks before an overwhelming enemy force appears. There's no time to rest, no escape. We try to fight, but there's no space; we try to defend ourselves, but there's no respite. Staying put means wasting time, but any move invites enemy attacks from the front and rear. The land is wild, with no food or water. The soldiers are exhausted, the horses worn out, and every effort seems hopeless. The path is so narrow that one person could stop an army of ten thousand. The enemy controls all the advantages, while we have lost all our options. Even with the bravest soldiers and sharpest weapons, how could they possibly be effective?" Students of Greek history may recall the tragic end of the Sicilian expedition and the suffering of the Athenians under Nicias and Demosthenes. [See Thucydides, VII. 78 sqq.]]

Do not fight on ground where you're scattered. Do not stop on easy ground. Do not attack when there's a lot of opposition.

[Instead, focus all your energy on getting the upper hand first. So says Ts'ao Kung. However, Li Ch'uan and others believe this means the enemy has already beaten us to it, so attacking would be foolish. In the Sun Tzŭ Hsu Lu, when the King of Wu asks what to do in this situation, Sun Tzŭ responds: "The rule for contested ground is that whoever holds the ground first has the advantage. If the enemy has secured this type of position, do not attack. Trick them into moving by pretending to flee—show your flags and beat your drums—rush to other spots they can't afford to lose—drag branches and kick up dust—confuse their senses—send your best troops to secretly ambush them. Then your enemy will rush out to save the situation."]

On open ground, don't try to block the enemy's path.

[Because it would be pointless and would put the blocking force in danger. There are two interpretations here. I follow Chang Yu's view. The other is found in Ts'ao Kung's short note: "Come closer together"—which means making sure part of your army isn't cut off.]

On ground with crossing roads, join up with your allies.

[Or perhaps, "make alliances with neighboring states."]

On serious ground, take what you need.

[Li Ch'uan adds an interesting note: "When an army moves deep into enemy territory, it's important not to anger the local people by treating them unfairly. Follow the example of the Han Emperor Kao Tsu, who during his march into Ch'in territory didn't harm women or steal valuables. [Note: this was in 207 B.C., a lesson that could embarrass Christian armies that marched into Peking in 1900 A.D.] This is how he won the hearts of the people. In this passage, I think the right reading is not 'take what you need,' but 'don't take what you don't need.' Sadly, the commentator's emotions may have clouded his judgment. Tu Mu, at least, isn't under any such illusions. He says: 'When camped on serious ground, where there's no reason to advance and no chance to retreat, one should prepare for a long defense by gathering supplies from all around, while keeping a close watch on the enemy.'"]

In tough terrain, keep moving steadily forward.

[Or, in the words of VIII. § 2, "don't stop and make camp."]

When trapped, use a clever strategy.

[Ts'ao Kung says, "Try something unusual or unexpected," and Tu Yu adds, "In such situations, you must come up with a plan that fits the moment. If you can trick the enemy, you might escape the danger." This is exactly what happened when Hannibal was trapped in the mountains on the road to Casilinum, seemingly caught by the dictator Fabius. Hannibal came up with a clever trick, similar to one used by T'ien Tan 62 years earlier. [See IX. § 24, note.] At nightfall, they tied bundles of twigs to the horns of around 2,000 oxen and set them on fire. The terrified animals were driven towards the mountain passes held by the enemy. The sight of these fast-moving lights frightened the Romans, causing them to retreat, and Hannibal's army safely passed through the narrow pass. [See Polybius, III. 93, 94; Livy, XXII. 16, 17.]]

When in desperate situations, fight.

[As Chia Lin notes, "If you fight with everything you've got, you have a chance to survive. But if you just stay in your corner, death is certain."]

In the past, skilled leaders knew how to divide the enemy's front from their rear;

[In more exact terms, "They would make sure the front and rear were no longer in touch with each other."]

They knew how to stop the enemy's big and small divisions from working together, and how to prevent strong troops from saving the weak, and officers from rallying their soldiers.

When the enemy's troops were scattered, they made sure the enemy couldn't regroup. Even when the enemy's forces were united, they still managed to keep them disorganized.

When it was to their advantage, they moved forward; if not, they stayed put.

[Mei Yao-ch'en links this to the previous point: "After successfully disrupting the enemy, they would advance to secure any advantage; if there was no advantage, they would stay where they were."]

If asked how to handle a large, organized enemy force about to launch an attack, I would say: "Start by capturing something your opponent values; this will force him to act according to your will."

[There are different views on what Sun Tzŭ meant here. Ts'ao Kung thinks it refers to "some strategic advantage the enemy relies on." Tu Mu says: "The three things an enemy is eager to do, and on which his success depends, are: (1) to capture our key positions; (2) to destroy our farmlands; and (3) to protect his own supply lines." Our goal should be to disrupt his plans in these three areas, rendering him powerless. [Cf. III. § 3.] By boldly seizing the initiative, you force the enemy into a defensive position.]

Speed is the essence of war.

[Tu Mu explains, "This is a summary of the main principles of warfare," and adds, "These are the deepest truths of military science, and the general's most important duty." The following stories, told by Ho Shih, show how important speed was to two of China's greatest generals. In 227 A.D., Meng Ta, governor of Hsin-ch'eng under the Wei Emperor Wen Ti, was planning to defect to the House of Shu, and had begun communicating with Chu-ko Liang, the Prime Minister of that state. The Wei general Ssu-ma I, who was then the military governor of Wan, heard about Meng Ta's treachery and immediately set out with an army to stop him, after having tricked him with a friendly message. Ssu-ma's officers suggested that they should investigate more thoroughly before making a move. Ssu-ma I replied, "Meng Ta is an unreliable man, and we should go and punish him right away, while he is still uncertain and before he has fully betrayed us." Then, with a series of forced marches, he brought his army to the walls of Hsin-ch'eng in just eight days. Now, Meng Ta had earlier written in a letter to Chu-ko Liang: "Wan is 1,200 li from here. When news of my revolt reaches Ssu-ma I, he will inform the emperor, but it will take a whole month before any action is taken. By that time, my city will be well fortified. Besides, Ssu-ma I is not likely to come himself, and the generals that will be sent are not worth worrying about." But his next letter was full of panic: "Though only eight days have passed since I revolted, an army is already at the gates. What incredible speed!" Two weeks later, Hsin-ch'eng fell, and Meng Ta was executed. [See Chin Shu, ch. 1, f. 3.] In 621 A.D., Li Ching was sent from K'uei-chou in Ssu-ch'uan to defeat the rebel Hsiao Hsien, who had declared himself Emperor in the modern-day Ching-chou Fu in Hupeh. It was autumn, and the Yangtze River was in flood, so Hsiao Hsien did not expect Li Ching to risk coming down through the gorges, and as a result made no preparations. But Li Ching immediately prepared his army and was about to set off when the other generals begged him to delay his departure until the river was less dangerous to navigate. Li Ching replied, "For a soldier, overwhelming speed is of the utmost importance, and he must never miss an opportunity. Now is the time to strike, before Hsiao Hsien even knows we have gathered an army.

If we attack while the river is in flood, we will reach his capital with such unexpected speed, like thunder that is heard before you have time to cover your ears." [See VII. § 19, note.] This is a key principle of war. Even if Hsiao Hsien hears of our approach, he will have to raise his soldiers in such a rush that they will not be fit to fight us. This way, we will secure total victory." Everything happened as predicted, and Hsiao Hsien was forced to surrender, nobly asking that his people be spared and he alone face death.]

Take advantage of the enemy's lack of readiness, move by unexpected routes, and attack where they are not guarded.

Here are the principles for an invading force to follow: The deeper you go into a country, the stronger the unity among your troops will become, and the defenders will struggle to defeat you.

Make raids in fertile lands to provide your army with food.

[Cf. § 13. Li Ch'uan does not provide a note here.]

Pay close attention to the well-being of your soldiers,

[By "well-being," Wang Hsi means, "Take good care of them, indulge them, make sure they have enough food and drink, and generally keep them in good condition."]

and do not overwork them. Focus your energy and save your strength.

[Ch'en recalls the approach used in 224 B.C. by the brilliant general Wang Chien, whose leadership was key to the First Emperor's success. He invaded the Ch'u State, where a mass mobilization had been raised against him. However, uncertain about the mood of his troops, he refused to engage in battle and stayed strictly on the defensive. The Ch'u general tried repeatedly to provoke a fight, but day after day, Wang Chien remained inside his fortifications. Instead of rushing into battle, he focused on winning the trust and loyalty of his soldiers. He ensured they were well-fed, even sharing meals with them, provided opportunities for bathing, and used every possible method to keep them content and united. After some time, he sent people to check on how his soldiers were spending their free time. The report came back that they were competing in activities like weightlifting and long jumping. When Wang Chien heard this, he knew their morale was high, and they were ready for battle. By then, the Ch'u army, frustrated by their unanswered challenges, had marched away to the east. At that moment, Wang Chien broke camp and pursued them. In the battle that followed, the Ch'u forces were crushed, and shortly after, the entire state of Ch'u was conquered by Ch'in, with their king, Fu-ch'u, taken captive.]

Keep your army constantly on the move,

[So the enemy never knows where you are. However, it has occurred to me that the true meaning might be "link your army together."]

and develop plans that are impossible for the enemy to understand.

Put your soldiers in positions where there is no escape, and they will choose death over retreat. If they are ready to face death, there is nothing they cannot accomplish.

[Chang Yu quotes Wei Liao Tzǔ (ch. 3): "If a single man ran wild with a sword in a marketplace, and everyone else fled from him, it wouldn't mean that he alone was brave and the rest were cowards. The truth is, a man with nothing to lose and a man who values his life are not in the same position."]

Both officers and soldiers will give their full strength.

[Chang Yu says: "If they find themselves in a difficult situation together, they will definitely combine their strength to get out of it."]

When soldiers are in desperate situations, they lose all sense of fear. If they have nowhere to run, they will stand firm. If they are deep in enemy territory, they will fight with determination. If there is no other option, they will fight fiercely.

Thus, without needing to be organized, soldiers will always be alert; without needing to be asked, they will follow your orders.

[Literally, "Without asking, you will receive."]

Without strict rules, they will stay loyal; without needing commands, they can be trusted.

Ban the taking of omens, and eliminate superstitious doubts. Then, until the moment of death, no disaster will be feared.

[Superstition and fear can turn men into cowards who "die many times before their deaths." Tu Mu quotes Huang Shih-kung: "Spells and incantations should be strictly forbidden, and no officer should inquire about the fate of the army through divination, as this can unsettle the soldiers' minds." He continues, "If all doubts and superstitions are cast aside, your soldiers will remain resolute until the very end."]

If our soldiers are not burdened with wealth, it is not because they dislike riches; if their lives are not overly long, it is not because they do not want longevity.

[Chang Yu explains this well: "Wealth and long life are natural desires for all men. So, if soldiers burn or throw away valuables and give up their lives, it is not because they hate them, but because they have no choice." Sun Tzŭ hints that since soldiers are only human, it is the general's responsibility to make sure they are not tempted to avoid battle and seek riches instead.]

On the day your soldiers are ordered to battle, they may cry,

[The word used here is "snivel," which suggests deeper sorrow than just tears.]

some of them sitting up and soaking their clothes with tears, while others lying down let the tears roll down their faces.

[This isn't because they are afraid, but because, as Ts'ao Kung says, "they have all made a firm decision to fight to the death." We can also remember that the heroes of the Iliad were similarly open in showing their emotions. Chang Yu references the sad farewell at the I River between Ching K'o and his friends, when Ching K'o was sent to assassinate the King of Ch'in (who would later become the First Emperor) in 227 B.C. As he said goodbye, tears flowed like rain, and he recited these lines: "The wind blows sharp, the river is cold; Your hero goes forth—never to return."]

But when they are cornered, they will show the courage of a Chu or a Kuei.

[Chu was the personal name of Chuan Chu, a native of the Wu State and a contemporary of Sun Tzŭ. He was hired by Kung-tzu Kuang, also known as Ho Lu Wang, to assassinate the king Wang Liao with a dagger hidden inside a fish at a banquet. He succeeded, but was immediately cut down by the king's guards. This happened in 515 B.C. The other hero, Ts'ao Kuei (also known as Ts'ao Mo), became famous 166 years earlier, in 681 B.C. After Lu had been defeated three times by Ch'i, they were about to sign a treaty giving up a large part of their territory. At that moment, Ts'ao Kuei grabbed Huan Kung, the Duke of Ch'i, at the altar and held a dagger to his chest. None of the Duke's men dared move, and Ts'ao Kuei demanded that all of Lu's territory be returned, arguing that Lu was unfairly treated because it was smaller and weaker. Fearing for his life, Huan Kung agreed. Ts'ao Kuei then calmly put away his dagger and sat back down, showing no fear. Although the Duke wanted to break the agreement later, his wise counselor Kuan Chung advised him that it would be unwise to go back on his word. As a result, Lu regained all the land they had lost in the three battles.]

A skilled strategist can be compared to the shuai-jan. The shuai-jan is a snake found in the Ch'ang mountains.

["Shuai-jan" means "suddenly" or "rapidly," and the snake got this name because of how quickly it moves. Over time, the term came to refer to military maneuvers.]

If you strike at its head, its tail will attack you; if you strike at its tail, its head will attack you; if you strike at its middle, both head and tail will attack you together.

If asked whether an army can be made to act like the shuai-jan,

[As Mei Yao-ch'en says, "Is it possible to make the front and rear of an army respond quickly to an attack on the other, just as if they were parts of one living body?"]

I would answer, Yes. The men of Wu and the men of Yüeh are enemies;

[Cf. VI. § 21.]

yet if they are crossing a river in the same boat and a storm strikes, they will help each other, just as the left hand helps the right.

[The meaning is: If two enemies will cooperate when faced with a shared danger, how much more should two parts of the same army, bound together by shared interests and camaraderie, work together? Still, it is well known that many campaigns have been lost because of a lack of cooperation, especially when allied armies are involved.]

Therefore, it is not enough to rely on tethering horses or burying chariot wheels in the ground to keep an army from fleeing.

[These strange methods, meant to stop soldiers from running away, remind us of the Athenian hero Sophanes, who carried an anchor into battle at Plataea and used it to tie himself to one spot. [See Herodotus, IX. 74.] Sun Tzŭ is saying that merely making flight impossible through such mechanical means is not enough. You will only succeed if your men have strong willpower, unity of purpose, and, most importantly, a spirit of cooperation. This is the lesson we can learn from the shuai-jan.]

The way to manage an army is to set one standard of courage that everyone must meet.

[Literally, "make the courage of all equal as if it were that of one." If the ideal army is to act as one cohesive unit, then the determination and spirit of its members must be of the same quality, or at least not below a certain level. Wellington's comment about his army at Waterloo, calling it "the worst he had ever commanded," was likely a reflection of its lack of this essential trait—unity of courage and spirit. If he hadn't anticipated the Belgian defections and kept those troops in the background, he almost certainly would have lost the battle.]

How to make the best use of both strong and weak soldiers is a matter of how you use the terrain.

[Mei Yao-ch'en explains: "The way to erase the differences between strong and weak and make both useful is by using the natural features of the ground." Weaker troops, if placed in strong defensive positions, can hold out as effectively as better troops on more vulnerable ground. A good position can make up for a lack of stamina and courage. Col. Henderson comments: "With all due respect to textbooks and standard tactics, I believe the study of terrain is often neglected, and that too little attention is given to the selection of positions and the great benefits that come from using natural features, whether attacking or defending." [2]]

Thus, the skillful general leads his army as easily as if he were leading a single person by the hand, whether they want to follow or not.

[Tu Mu says: "The comparison refers to how easily this is done."]

A general must stay calm to ensure secrecy and be upright and just to maintain order.

He must be able to confuse his officers and soldiers with false reports and deceptive appearances,

[Literally, "to deceive their eyes and ears."]

so that they remain in complete ignorance of his true plans.

[Ts'ao Kung gives a wise saying: "Troops should not be allowed to know your plans at the beginning; they may only share in your success when it is achieved." One of the key principles of war is "to mystify, mislead, and surprise the enemy." But how about deceiving your own troops? Those who think Sun Tzŭ overstates this would benefit from reading Col. Henderson's comments on Stonewall

Jackson's Valley campaign: "The great care Jackson took to hide his movements, intentions, and thoughts, even from his most trusted staff officers, would have been seen as unnecessary by a less meticulous commander." [3] In 88 A.D., according to ch. 47 of the Hou Han Shu, Pan Ch'ao led 25,000 men from Khotan and other Central Asian states to attack Yarkand. The King of Kutcha sent his commander with 50,000 troops from Wen-su, Ku-mo, and Wei-t'ou to defend it. Pan Ch'ao called a war council with his officers and the King of Khotan and said, 'We are outnumbered and cannot defeat the enemy directly. The best plan is to split up and go in different directions. The King of Khotan will march east, and I will head west. We will leave after the evening drum sounds.' Pan Ch'ao secretly released some prisoners, who informed the King of Kutcha of these plans. Feeling confident, the King of Kutcha took 10,000 horsemen to block Pan Ch'ao's retreat in the west, while the King of Wen-su led 8,000 cavalry east to intercept the King of Khotan. Once Pan Ch'ao knew the enemy leaders had left, he quickly reunited his troops and launched a surprise attack at dawn on Yarkand's camp. The enemy fled in confusion, and Pan Ch'ao pursued them, killing over 5,000 and seizing many horses, cattle, and other valuables. After Yarkand surrendered, Kutcha and the other states withdrew their forces. From then on, Pan Ch'ao's influence dominated the western regions." In this case, the Chinese general not only kept his officers in the dark about his real plans, but also used the bold tactic of splitting his army to deceive the enemy.]

By altering his tactics and changing his plans,

[Wang Hsi believes this means not using the same strategy twice.]

he keeps the enemy unsure and without clear information.

[Chang Yu, in a quote from another work, says: "The idea that war is based on deception doesn't only apply to tricking the enemy. You must also deceive your own soldiers. Make them follow you without letting them know the reasons behind your decisions."]

By shifting his camp and taking indirect routes, he prevents the enemy from predicting his intentions.

At the crucial moment, the leader of an army acts like someone who has climbed a high wall and then kicks away the ladder behind him. He takes his soldiers deep into enemy territory before revealing his true plans.

[Literally, "releases the spring" (see V. § 15), meaning that he takes a decisive action that makes retreat impossible—similar to Hsiang Yu, who sank his ships after crossing a river. Ch'en Hao, followed by Chia Lin, interprets this less clearly as "uses every trick at his disposal."]

He burns his boats and destroys his cooking pots; like a shepherd driving a flock of sheep, he directs his soldiers this way and that, and no one knows where they are headed.

[Tu Mu says: "The army only understands orders to advance or retreat; it doesn't know the true goals of attacking or conquering."]

To gather his forces and lead them into danger—this is the duty of a general.

[Sun Tzŭ means that once the army is mobilized, there should be no delay in striking at the enemy's core. Note how he returns to this idea again and again. In the warring states of ancient China, desertion was likely a much more immediate and serious threat than in today's armies.]

The different strategies suitable for the nine types of ground;

[Chang Yu says: "One should not rigidly apply the rules for the nine types of ground."]

the need for either aggressive or defensive tactics, and the basic laws of human nature: these are things that must absolutely be studied.

When invading hostile territory, the general principle is that penetrating deeply creates unity, while penetrating only a little leads to division.

[Cf. § 20.]

When you leave your homeland and lead your army into neighboring lands, you are on critical ground.

This kind of ground is mentioned earlier, but it is not listed among the Nine Situations or the Six Calamities in another chapter. At first glance, you might think it means "distant ground," but according to commentators, this is not correct. Mei Yao-ch'en explains that it's ground that is neither far enough to be called "easy" nor close enough to be "scattered." It is somewhere in between. Wang Hsi says that it is ground separated from home by a state whose territory we had to cross to reach it, so it is important to finish our task there quickly. He adds that this situation is rare, which is why it is not included among the Nine Situations.

When you have roads in all directions, it is ground of intersecting highways.

When you go deep into enemy territory, it is serious ground. When you advance only a little, it is easy ground.

When the enemy's strongholds are behind you, and narrow paths are in front, it is hemmed-in ground. When there is no place to retreat, it is desperate ground.

Therefore, on scattered ground, I would unite my men under a common goal.

To achieve this, Tu Mu suggests staying on the defensive and avoiding battle.

On easy ground, I would keep all parts of my army closely connected.

Tu Mu explains that this is to prevent two dangers: the possibility of soldiers deserting or a sudden enemy attack. Mei Yao-ch'en adds that during the march, the troops should stay close together, and in camp, the fortifications should be continuous.

On contested ground, I would hurry to bring up my rear forces.

Ts'ao Kung offers this view, and Chang Yu agrees, saying that the head and tail of the army must reach their destination together without straggling. Mei Yao-ch'en suggests another view: If the enemy hasn't yet reached the desired position and we are behind them, we should move quickly to claim it. Ch'en Hao takes another approach, thinking the enemy may have already chosen their ground. He quotes a passage where Sun Tzŭ warns against attacking when exhausted. If a favorable position lies ahead, Ch'en Hao advises sending a strong unit to secure it, and if the enemy tries to fight for it, the main force can strike their rear, leading to victory.

On open ground, I would stay alert and defend carefully. On ground of intersecting highways, I would strengthen my alliances.

On serious ground, I would make sure to maintain a steady flow of supplies.

Commentators believe this refers to gathering forage and plunder, not maintaining a connection with home, as you might expect.

On difficult ground, I would keep moving forward.

On hemmed-in ground, I would block any escape routes.

Meng Shih explains that this would make it seem like I am defending the position, but my real plan is to break through the enemy's lines unexpectedly. Mei Yao-ch'en adds that this would make my soldiers fight with desperation. Wang Hsi suggests that this would prevent my men from being tempted to flee. Tu Mu points out that this is the opposite of a previous situation, where it is the enemy who is surrounded. An example of this is from 532 A.D., when Kao Huan, who later became Emperor, was surrounded by a much larger army led by Erh-chu Chao and others. Despite his smaller force, which included only 2000 horsemen and fewer than 30,000 foot soldiers, Kao Huan blocked all remaining escape routes by driving oxen and donkeys into the gaps. When his officers and men saw there was no escape, they fought with extraordinary bravery and broke through the enemy ranks with fierce determination.

On desperate ground, I would tell my soldiers there is no hope of survival.

Tu Yu suggests making it clear to the soldiers that survival is impossible by burning their baggage, throwing away supplies, blocking wells, and destroying cooking stoves. The only way to live is to fight as if they expect to die. Mei Yao-ch'en adds that their only chance of survival is to abandon all hope of it.

This concludes what Sun Tzŭ says about "grounds" and their corresponding "variations." Reviewing these passages, it is clear that the subject is treated in a somewhat scattered and unstructured manner. Sun Tzŭ begins by listing a few variations before discussing "grounds" but only mentions five variations, which are later expanded. Some types of ground are addressed earlier, while chapter X introduces six new types of ground, each with a variation to match. However, none of these six types are revisited, and one closely resembles a type of ground described later. In chapter XI, we encounter the Nine Grounds, followed by a list of their variations. By sections 43-45, new definitions for several of these grounds are provided, as well as for another type not previously mentioned. Finally, the nine variations are listed again, though many of them differ from earlier versions.

Although we cannot definitively explain the current state of Sun Tzŭ's text, a few interesting observations stand out: (1) Chapter VIII is titled "Nine Variations," but only five are listed. (2) This chapter is unusually short. (3) Chapter XI is called "The Nine Grounds," but some of the grounds are defined more than once, and two separate lists of variations are given. (4) This chapter is much longer than any other, except chapter IX. While no specific conclusions can be drawn from these facts, it seems likely that Sun Tzŭ's work has not reached us exactly as he originally wrote it. Chapter VIII appears incomplete and possibly out of place, while chapter XI contains material that may have been added later or misplaced from another part of the text.

For it is the soldier's nature to offer a determined resistance when surrounded, to fight fiercely when there is no way out, and to follow orders quickly when faced with danger. Chang Yu refers to the actions of Pan Ch'ao's loyal followers in 73 A.D. The story is found in the Hou Han Shu, chapter 47: "When Pan Ch'ao arrived at Shan-shan, the king, Kuang, initially treated him with great politeness and respect; but soon after, his attitude changed abruptly, and he became negligent and indifferent. Pan Ch'ao spoke of this to the officers with him: 'Have you noticed,' he said, 'that Kuang's courtesy is fading? This must mean that envoys from the Northern barbarians have arrived, leaving him uncertain about which side to support. That is surely the reason. The wise man, we are told, can foresee events before they happen; how much more easily can he observe what is already taking place!' Then he called one of the locals assigned to his service and set a trap by asking, 'Where are those envoys from the Hsiung-nu who arrived a few days ago?' The man, startled and afraid, quickly revealed the whole truth. Pan Ch'ao, having secured the man, then summoned a meeting with his officers, thirty-six in all, and began drinking with them. As the wine took effect, he encouraged their spirits further by saying: 'Gentlemen, here we are in a remote region, eager to achieve riches and honor through a great deed. Recently, an ambassador from the Hsiung-nu has arrived, and because of this, the respectful treatment we've received from the king has faded. If this envoy persuades him to capture us and deliver us to the Hsiung-nu, our bones will be left for the wolves of the desert. What are we to do?' The officers, as one, replied, 'With our lives at risk, we will follow you through life and death.' The rest of this story can be found in chapter twelve, section one."

We cannot form alliances with neighboring rulers until we understand their intentions. We are not fit to lead an army on the march unless we know the landscape—its mountains and forests, its traps and cliffs, its marshes and swamps. We cannot make use of the land's advantages unless we employ local guides. These three statements are repeated from chapter seven to stress their importance, according to the commentators. However, I believe they are placed here as a lead-in to the next statements. Regarding local guides, Sun Tzŭ might have added that there is always a risk of error, either due to their betrayal or through misunderstanding. Livy, for instance, recounts a case where Hannibal ordered a guide to take him near Casinum, where an important pass was to be secured; but Hannibal's Carthaginian accent, not well-suited to Latin names, led the guide to mishear Casilinum instead of Casinum. The mistake was not discovered until the army had nearly reached the wrong location.

To be ignorant of any one of the following four or five principles is unworthy of a warlike leader.

When a prince who is ready for war attacks a strong nation, his skill as a leader comes from stopping the enemy from gathering their forces. He intimidates his opponents, and their allies are scared off from uniting against him.

[Mei Tao-ch'en offers one of the logical chains of thought that the Chinese are fond of: "When attacking a strong state, if you can separate its forces, you gain the advantage in strength; if you have the advantage in strength, you can intimidate the enemy; if you intimidate the enemy, neighboring states will become fearful; and if neighboring states are fearful, the enemy's allies will be stopped from joining her." The following interpretation gives an even stronger meaning: "If the powerful state is defeated before they can call on their allies, then the smaller states will hesitate and avoid bringing their forces together." Ch'en Hao and Chang Yu understand this in a very different way. Ch'en Hao says: "Even though a prince may be strong, if he attacks a large state, he won't have enough troops and will have to rely on outside help. If he ignores this and, with too much confidence in his own strength, tries to scare the enemy, he will certainly lose." Chang Yu explains it this way: "If we recklessly attack a large state, our own people will be unhappy and hesitant. And if our military power is clearly weaker than the enemy's, other leaders will be too scared to join us."]

So, he does not try to form alliances with everyone, nor does he help other states become stronger. He carries out his secret plans, keeping his enemies in fear.

[Li Ch'uan explains the thinking like this: Confident that his enemies won't join forces, "he can afford to turn down risky alliances and just focus on his own secret plans, with his reputation allowing him to do without external friendships."]

In this way, he can capture their cities and bring down their kingdoms.

[Even though this paragraph was written long before the state of Ch'in became a serious threat, it sums up well the strategy that the Six Chancellors used to pave the way for Ch'in's final victory under Shih Huang Ti. Chang Yu, expanding on his earlier note, thinks that Sun Tzŭ is criticizing this cold, selfish, and isolated approach.]

Bestow rewards without regard to rules,

[Wu Tzŭ, less wisely, says: "Let advancement be richly rewarded and retreat be heavily punished."]

issue orders

[Literally, "hang" or post them up.]

without regard to previous arrangements;

["In order to prevent treachery," says Wang Hsi. The general meaning is made clear by Ts'ao Kung's quotation from the Ssu-ma Fa: "Give instructions only upon sighting the enemy; give rewards when you see worthy deeds." Ts'ao Kung paraphrases: "The final instructions you give to your army should not match those that were previously posted." Chang Yu simplifies this to "your plans should not be revealed in advance." And Chia Lin adds: "There should be no fixed rules in your arrangements." Not only is there risk in letting your plans be known, but war often requires reversing them at the last moment.]

and you will be able to manage a whole army as though you were dealing with just one man.

[Cf. supra, § 34.]

Confront your soldiers with the action itself; never let them know your plan.

[Literally, "do not tell them words," meaning do not give reasons for any order. Lord Mansfield once told a junior colleague to "give no reasons" for his decisions, and this rule applies even more to a general than to a judge.]

When the situation looks promising, show it to them; but when the outlook is bleak, tell them nothing.

Place your army in deadly peril, and it will survive; throw it into desperate situations, and it will come out safely.

[These words of Sun Tzŭ were once quoted by Han Hsin to explain the tactics he used in one of his most brilliant battles, mentioned earlier. In 204 B.C., Han Hsin was sent against the army of Chao, halting ten miles from the Ching-hsing pass, where the enemy had gathered in full strength. At midnight, he sent out 2000 light cavalry, each equipped with a red flag. Their orders were to pass through narrow defiles and secretly observe the enemy. "When the men of Chao see me retreating in full flight," Han Hsin said, "they will abandon their defenses and chase us. This will be your signal to rush in, pull down the Chao banners, and raise the red flags of Han instead." He then told his other officers: "The enemy holds a strong position and won't attack us until they see the standard and drums of the commander-in-chief, fearing I might retreat through the mountains." With this, he sent out a division of 10,000 men, ordering them to form a line of battle with their backs to the River Ti. Upon seeing this maneuver, the entire Chao army burst into laughter. By morning, Han Hsin raised his general's flag and marched out of the pass with drums beating, quickly engaging the enemy. A fierce battle followed, lasting for some time, until Han Hsin and his colleague,

Chang Ni, left the drums and flag on the battlefield and fled to the division by the river, where another intense fight was underway. The enemy rushed after them to claim the trophies, leaving their defenses exposed, but the two generals managed to join their army, which was fighting desperately. Now it was time for the 2000 horsemen to act. When they saw the men of Chao pursuing the fleeing forces, they galloped behind the abandoned fortifications, tore down the enemy's flags, and replaced them with the banners of Han. When the Chao army looked back during the chase and saw the red flags, they were struck with terror. Convinced that the Hans had overpowered their king, they panicked and scattered, despite their leader's attempts to stop them. Then the Han forces attacked from both sides, completely routing the Chao army, killing many and capturing the rest, including King Ya himself. After the battle, some of Han Hsin's officers approached him and said: "In the Art of War, we are taught to position troops with a hill or mound on the right rear and a river or marsh on the left front. Yet you ordered us to draw up with the river at our backs. How did you manage to win under such conditions?" The general replied: "I'm afraid you haven't studied the Art of War carefully enough. Does it not say, 'Plunge your army into desperate straits, and it will come off in safety; place it in deadly peril, and it will survive'? Had I followed the usual methods, I wouldn't have been able to bring my colleague around. As the Military Classic says, 'Swoop down on the marketplace and drive the men off to fight.' If I hadn't placed my troops where they had no choice but to fight for their lives, and instead allowed them to act freely, they would have scattered, and we couldn't have accomplished anything." The officers acknowledged the wisdom of his argument and said: "These are tactics beyond our own abilities."]

For it is precisely when a force finds itself in danger that it becomes capable of striking a blow for victory.

[Danger has a motivating effect.]

Success in warfare is achieved by carefully adapting to the enemy's intentions.

[Ts'ao Kung says: "Feign ignorance" by appearing to comply with the enemy's wishes. Chang Yu explains: "If the enemy shows a desire to advance, encourage him to do so; if he wishes to retreat, delay deliberately to allow him to carry out his plan." The goal is to make him overconfident and careless before launching our attack.]

By constantly keeping pressure on the enemy's flank,

[I understand this to mean "moving alongside the enemy in the same direction." Ts'ao Kung says: "Unite the troops and advance towards the enemy." But such a rearrangement of words is not defensible.]

we will eventually succeed,

[Literally, "after a thousand li."]

in killing the enemy's commander.

[This was always a significant aim in Chinese warfare.]

This is what it means to achieve something through sheer strategy.

On the day you take command, block the frontier passes, destroy the official tallies,

[These were tablets of bamboo or wood, half of which was used as a permit by an official. When returned within a set period, the gate could be opened for the traveler.]

and stop all communication,

[Whether to or from the enemy's territory.]

Be firm in the council-chamber,

[Show no weakness, and ensure your plans are approved by the ruler.]

so that you can maintain control over the situation.

[Mei Yao-ch'en interprets this to mean: Take the strictest measures to maintain secrecy in your discussions.]

If the enemy leaves an opening, you must charge through it.

Outsmart your opponent by seizing what he values most,

[See earlier, § 18.]

and subtly manipulate the timing of his arrival at the battlefield.

[Ch'en Hao explains: "If I seize a favorable position but the enemy doesn't show up, the advantage gained is meaningless. To control an important position, you must create a kind of 'appointment' with the enemy, tricking him into arriving there as well." Mei Yao-ch'en says this "appointment" can be made by using the enemy's own spies, who will bring back only the information we want them to have. Once we've cunningly revealed our plans, we can make sure, by starting after the enemy, that we arrive before him (VII. § 4). Starting later forces him to move there; arriving first allows us to capture the position without resistance. This supports Mei Yao-ch'en's reading of § 47.]

Walk the path guided by strategy,

[Chia Lin says: "Victory is all that matters, and this cannot be won by strictly following conventional rules." Unfortunately, this interpretation relies on weak authority, though it makes much more sense. As we know, Napoleon, according to the veterans of the old school whom he defeated, won his battles by breaking all the traditional rules of warfare.]

and adapt to the enemy until the moment comes for a decisive battle.

[Tu Mu says: "Follow the enemy's tactics until a favorable moment arises; then engage in a battle that will be conclusive."]

At first, show the reserve of a shy maiden until the enemy gives you an opening; then strike with the speed of a running hare, and it will be too late for the enemy to resist you.

[Though the hare is known for its timidity, Sun Tzŭ was clearly referring to its speed. The words have sometimes been interpreted to mean fleeing from the enemy as fast as a hare, but Tu Mu rightly rejects this idea.]

Chapter 12 - The Attack by Fire

Sun Tzŭ said: There are five ways to attack using fire. The first is to set fire to soldiers in their camp.

[Tu Mu agrees. Li Ch'uan adds: "Set the camp on fire, and kill the soldiers as they try to escape from the flames." Pan Ch'ao, on a diplomatic mission to the King of Shan-shan, found himself in great danger when an envoy from the Hsiung-nu, China's mortal enemies, unexpectedly arrived. During a meeting with his officers, he declared: "Nothing ventured, nothing gained! Our only option now is to attack the barbarians with fire under the cover of night, when they won't be able to see how many we are. Taking advantage of their panic, we can wipe them out, discourage the King, and achieve glory, ensuring the success of our mission." The officers suggested discussing the plan with the Intendant first, but Pan Ch'ao was outraged: "Today is the day our fate will be decided! The Intendant is a mere civilian and will be too scared when he hears our plan, leading to its exposure. Dying ingloriously is not the fate for brave warriors." The officers then agreed to follow his lead. That night, Pan Ch'ao and his small group approached the barbarian camp. A strong wind was blowing. Pan Ch'ao ordered ten men to hide behind the enemy barracks with drums, ready to make a loud noise when they saw the fire. The rest of his men, armed with bows and crossbows, were placed in ambush at the camp's gate. Pan Ch'ao set the camp on fire from the windward side, and immediately, the drums began to beat, and shouts filled the air. The Hsiung-nu ran out in panic. Pan Ch'ao personally killed three of them, while his men beheaded the envoy and thirty others. More than a hundred of the enemy perished in the flames. The next day, Pan Ch'ao, aware of the Intendant's concerns, assured him, "Although you didn't join us last night, I won't take sole credit for the success." This satisfied Kuo Hsun, and Pan Ch'ao presented the head of the barbarian envoy to the King of Shan-shan, causing fear throughout the kingdom. Pan Ch'ao calmed the situation by issuing a public proclamation, took the king's sons as hostages, and then reported his success to Tou Ku." *Hou Han Shu,* ch. 47, ff. 1, 2.]

The second is to burn stores.

[Tu Mu says: "Food, fuel, and fodder." During the Sui dynasty, to subdue the rebellious population of Kiangnan, Kao Keng advised Emperor Wen Ti to make periodic raids and burn their grain stores, a strategy that ultimately succeeded.]

The third is to burn baggage trains.

[An example is Ts'ao Ts'ao's destruction of Yuan Shao's wagons and supplies in 200 A.D.]

The fourth is to burn arsenals and magazines.

[Tu Mu explains that arsenals and magazines contain the same items, listing weapons, bullion, and clothing. See VII. § 11 for comparison.]

The fifth is to hurl fire into the enemy's camp.

[Tu Yu mentions in the *T"ung Tien*: "To drop fire into the enemy camp, dip arrowheads into a brazier to set them alight and then shoot them from powerful crossbows into the enemy's lines."]

In order to carry out an attack, we must have the necessary means available.

[T'sao Kung believes this refers to "traitors in the enemy's camp." However, Ch'en Hao more likely means: "We must have favorable circumstances in general, not just rely on traitors." Chia Lin adds: "We should take advantage of wind and dry weather."]

The material for raising fire should always be kept ready.

[Tu Mu suggests materials for starting a fire like "dry vegetation, reeds, brushwood, straw, grease, oil, etc." This is the material cause. Chang Yu adds: "Containers for hoarding fire and things for lighting fires."]

There is a proper season for making attacks with fire and specific days for starting a blaze.

The proper season is during very dry weather, and the specific days are when the moon is in the constellations of the Sieve, the Wall, the Wing, or the Cross-bar;

[These correspond roughly to the 7th, 14th, 27th, and 28th of the Twenty-eight Stellar Mansions, which are Sagittarius, Pegasus, Crater, and Corvus.]

because these four are all days when the wind rises.

When attacking with fire, you must be prepared for five possible outcomes:

(1) When fire breaks out inside the enemy's camp, immediately launch an attack from outside.

(2) If a fire starts but the enemy's soldiers remain calm, wait and do not attack.

[The main goal of attacking with fire is to create confusion among the enemy. If that doesn't happen, it means the enemy is prepared for you. Therefore, caution is necessary.]

(3) When the flames reach their peak, follow up with an attack if possible; if not, stay where you are.

[Ts'ao Kung advises: "If you see an opportunity, advance; but if the difficulties seem too great, retreat."]

If it is possible to make an assault with fire from the outside, do not wait for it to break out within, but launch your attack at a favorable moment.

[Tu Mu explains that the previous sections referred to fire breaking out inside the enemy's camp, either by accident or through arson. He adds: "But if the enemy is camped in a waste area filled with grass, or if he has set up camp in a location that can easily be burned, we should attack with fire at any good opportunity instead of waiting for a fire to start within. Otherwise, the enemy might burn the surrounding vegetation themselves, rendering our efforts useless." The famous Li Ling once outsmarted a leader of the Hsiung-nu this way. The latter, taking advantage of a favorable wind, attempted to set fire to the Chinese general's camp, but found that all combustible vegetation had already been burned down. On the other hand, Po-ts'ai, a general of the Yellow Turban rebels, was badly defeated in 184 A.D. for neglecting this basic precaution. While leading a large army, he was besieging Ch'ang-she, which was defended by Huang-fu Sung. Although the garrison was small and nervous, Huang-fu Sung called his officers together and said: "In war, there are various indirect ways to attack, and numbers are not everything." [Here the commentator quotes Sun Tzŭ, V. §§ 5, 6, and 10.] "The rebels have set up camp in thick grass that will easily catch fire when the wind blows. If we set fire to it at night, they will panic, and we can attack from all sides, just like T'ien Tan did." [See page 90.] That night, a strong breeze arose, so Huang-fu Sung ordered his soldiers to bind reeds into torches and guard the city walls. Then, he sent out a group of brave men who sneaked through the enemy lines and started the fire with loud shouts and yells. At the same time, a bright light flared up from the city walls, and Huang-fu Sung, sounding the drums, led a swift charge, throwing the rebels into confusion and sending them fleeing." *Hou Han Shu,* ch. 71.]

When you start a fire, make sure you are upwind from it. Do not attack from the downwind side.

[Chang Yu, following Tu Yu, explains: "When you start a fire, the enemy will retreat away from it; if you block their retreat and attack, they will fight desperately, which will not lead to your success." Tu Mu offers a simpler explanation: "If the wind is blowing from the east,

114

begin burning to the east of the enemy and follow up your attack from that direction. If you start the fire on the east side and attack from the west, both you and the enemy will suffer."]

A wind that rises during the day lasts long, but a night breeze dies down quickly.

[Lao Tzŭ says: "A violent wind does not last the space of a morning." (Tao Te Ching, chap. 23.) Mei Yao-ch'en and Wang Hsi explain: "A daytime breeze fades at nightfall, and a night breeze ends at daybreak. This is usually the case." While this observation may be accurate, how this applies in the context is not immediately clear.]

In every army, the five developments related to fire must be understood, the movements of the stars calculated, and attention paid to the proper days.

[Tu Mu says: "We must calculate the paths of the stars and watch for the days when wind will rise before launching a fire attack." Chang Yu seems to interpret the text differently, suggesting: "We must not only know how to attack our opponents with fire but also guard against similar attacks from them."]

Those who use fire as a tool for attacking show intelligence, while those who use water as a tool for attacking gain additional strength.

By means of water, an enemy may be intercepted, but not stripped of all his possessions.

[Ts'ao Kung comments: "We can only obstruct the enemy's path or divide his forces, but we cannot wipe out all his stores." Water can be helpful, but it lacks the overwhelming destructive power of fire. This, Chang Yu concludes, is why water is dismissed in just a few lines, while fire attacks are discussed in detail. Wu Tzŭ (ch. 4) remarks: "If an army is camped on low-lying marshy ground, where water can't drain away, and where rainfall is heavy, it may be flooded. If an army is camped in wild marshlands overgrown with weeds and brambles, and frequently visited by gales, it may be wiped out by fire."]

Unhappy is the fate of one who tries to win his battles and succeed in his attacks without fostering a spirit of initiative; for the result is wasted time and general stagnation.

[This is one of the most puzzling passages in Sun Tzŭ. Ts'ao Kung says: "Rewards for good service should not be delayed even for a single day." Tu Mu adds: "If you don't seize the opportunity to advance and reward those who deserve it, your subordinates will not follow your orders, and disaster will follow." However, I prefer the interpretation suggested by Mei Yao-ch'en, whose words I will quote: "Those who want to ensure success in their battles and attacks must seize favorable opportunities when they arise and not shy away from bold measures. That means they must use such means of attack as fire, water, and the like. What they must avoid, which will lead to failure, is sitting still and merely holding on to the advantages they have already gained."]

Hence the saying: The enlightened ruler plans well in advance; the capable general builds up his resources.

[Tu Mu quotes from the *San Lueh,* ch. 2: "The warlike prince controls his soldiers through his authority, unites them through trust, and makes them serve through rewards. If trust fades, there will be disorder; if rewards are insufficient, orders will not be obeyed."]

Move not unless you see an advantage; use not your troops unless there is something to be gained; fight not unless the position is critical.

[Sun Tzŭ may seem overly cautious at times, but he never goes as far as the passage in the *Tao Te Ching,* ch. 69: "I dare not take the initiative but prefer to act defensively; I dare not advance an inch but prefer to retreat a foot."]

No ruler should send troops into the field merely to satisfy personal anger; no general should fight a battle out of resentment.

If it benefits you, make a forward move; if not, stay where you are.

[This repeats from XI. § 17. It feels like an interpolation here because § 20 clearly follows from § 18.]

Anger may eventually turn into gladness; frustration may be replaced by contentment.

But a kingdom once destroyed can never be restored;

[The Wu State serves as a sad example of this saying.]

nor can the dead ever be brought back to life.

Therefore, the enlightened ruler is cautious, and the wise general is full of care. This is the way to keep a country at peace and an army intact.

["Unless you enter the tiger's lair, you cannot catch its cubs."]

Chapter 13 - The Use of Spies

Sun Tzŭ said: Raising an army of a hundred thousand men and marching them over long distances causes heavy losses to the people and drains the State's resources. The daily cost will amount to a thousand ounces of silver.

[Cf. II. §§ 1, 13, 14.]

There will be unrest both at home and abroad, and men will collapse from exhaustion along the highways.

[Cf. *Tao Te Ching,* ch. 30: "Where troops have been stationed, thorns and brambles spring up." Chang Yu notes: "We are reminded of the saying: 'On serious ground, gather in plunder.' So why does transport cause such exhaustion on the highways?—The answer lies in the fact that it is not just food but all sorts of munitions that must be transported to the army. Additionally, the command to 'forage on the enemy' means that, when deeply engaged in enemy territory, food shortages must be anticipated. Therefore, while not entirely dependent on the enemy for supplies, we must forage to ensure a continuous flow. Moreover, in places like salt deserts, where provisions are unavailable, supplies from home become indispensable."]

As many as seven hundred thousand families will be hindered in their work.

[Mei Yao-ch'en comments: "There will be a shortage of men to work the fields." The reference is to the system of dividing land into nine parts, with the central plot farmed for the State by the tenants of the other eight plots. It was here, as Tu Mu notes, that the families built their cottages and shared a common well. [See II. § 12, note.] During wartime, one family had to serve in the army, while the other seven provided support. Therefore, when 100,000 men were conscripted (with one able-bodied soldier per family), the agricultural work of 700,000 families would be affected.]

Hostile armies may face each other for years, striving for a victory that is decided in a single day. Given this, to remain ignorant of the enemy's condition simply because one begrudges the cost of a hundred ounces of silver for rewards and payments

["For spies" is implied here, though it is not explicitly mentioned to maintain the effect of this elaborate introduction.] is the height of inhumanity.

[Sun Tzŭ's argument is quite clever. He starts by acknowledging the immense misery and staggering cost in lives and resources that war brings. If you remain uninformed about the enemy's situation and fail to strike at the right moment, a war can drag on for years. The only way to get this information is by employing spies, and reliable spies cannot be found unless they are well paid. It is false economy to begrudge such a small amount when each additional day of war costs vastly more. This burden falls hardest on the poor, so neglecting the use of spies is, in Sun Tzŭ's view, nothing less than a crime against humanity.]

One who acts in this way is no leader of men, no true support to his sovereign, and no master of victory.

[This notion, that the ultimate goal of war is peace, has deep roots in the Chinese national temperament. Even as far back as 597 B.C.,

Prince Chuang of the Ch'u State said: "The [Chinese] character for 'prowess' is formed by the characters for 'to stay' and 'a spear' (the cessation of hostilities). Military prowess is seen in the suppression of cruelty, the laying down of weapons, upholding the mandate of Heaven, establishing merit, bringing happiness to the people, promoting harmony among the princes, and spreading wealth."]

Thus, what enables the wise sovereign and the good general to strike and conquer, achieving things beyond the reach of ordinary men, is foreknowledge.

[That is, understanding the enemy's plans and intentions.]

Now, this foreknowledge cannot be gained from spirits; it cannot be derived from experience,

[Tu Mu explains: "[Knowledge of the enemy] cannot be obtained by reasoning from similar cases."]

nor can it be deduced through calculation.

[Li Ch'uan notes: "Quantities like length, breadth, distance, and magnitude can be determined mathematically, but human actions cannot be calculated in the same way."]

Knowledge of the enemy's plans can only be obtained from other men.

[Mei Yao-ch'en adds an interesting point: "Divination can provide knowledge of the spirit-world; inductive reasoning can reveal truths in natural science; and mathematical calculation can verify the laws of the universe. But the enemy's plans can only be learned through spies, and spies alone."]

Hence the use of spies, of whom there are five types: (1) Local spies; (2) inward spies; (3) converted spies; (4) doomed spies; (5) surviving spies.

When all five types of spies are working together, no one can unravel the secret system. This is called "divine manipulation of the threads." It is the sovereign's most valuable skill.

[Cromwell, one of the greatest and most practical cavalry leaders, had officers called 'scout masters,' whose task was to gather all possible intelligence regarding the enemy through scouts and spies. Much of his success in warfare was due to the prior knowledge of the enemy's movements gained in this way.]

Having local spies means using the inhabitants of a region.

[Tu Mu advises: "In the enemy's country, win people over through kind treatment and use them as spies."]

Having inward spies means using officials of the enemy.

[Tu Mu lists several groups likely to be useful in this regard: "Worthy men who have been disgraced, criminals who have been punished, favorite concubines greedy for gold, men frustrated with being in subordinate positions or passed over for promotions, others hoping for their side's defeat so they can showcase their talents, and turncoats who always try to keep a foot in both camps. Officials of these types should be secretly approached and won over with rich gifts. In this way, you can discover the state of affairs in the enemy's country, learn their plans, and also cause discord between the ruler and his ministers." However, dealing with inward spies requires extreme caution, as illustrated by an incident related by Ho Shih: "Lo Shang, Governor of I-Chou, sent his general Wei Po to attack the rebel Li Hsiung of Shu in his stronghold at P'i. After several victories and defeats on both sides, Li Hsiung employed the services of a certain P'o-t'ai, a native of Wu-tu. He had P'o-t'ai whipped until blood flowed, then sent him to deceive Lo Shang by pretending to cooperate from inside the city and promising to light a fire signal for a coordinated assault. Lo Shang trusted these promises, sent out his best troops, and ordered Wei Po and others to attack when P'o-t'ai signaled. Meanwhile, Li Hsiung's general, Li Hsiang, prepared an ambush along their path. P'o-t'ai then raised long scaling ladders against the city walls and lit the signal fire. Wei Po's men rushed in upon seeing the signal, climbed the ladders, and were pulled up by ropes. More than a hundred of Lo Shang's soldiers entered the city, where they were immediately beheaded. Li Hsiung then charged with his full forces, both inside and outside the city, and completely routed the enemy." This occurred in 303 A.D. Though Ho Shih does not provide his source, it is not mentioned in the biographies of Li Hsiung or his father, Li T'e, in *Chin Shu,* ch. 120, 121.]

Having converted spies means capturing the enemy's spies and using them for our own purposes.

[This involves offering them large bribes and making generous promises to turn them against their original side, so they will send false information back to the enemy and spy on their own people. Another approach, mentioned by Hsiao Shih-hsien, is to pretend that we haven't caught on to the spy, allowing him to leave with a false understanding of what is happening. Some commentators accept this as an alternative interpretation, but it's not what Sun Tzŭ intended, as shown by his later comments on treating the converted spy well. Ho Shih gives three examples of successful use of converted spies: (1) T'ien Tan in his defense of Chi-mo, (2) Chao She on his march to O-yu, and (3) Fan Chu in 260 B.C., when Lien P'o was conducting a defensive campaign against Ch'in. The King of Chao, unhappy with Lien P'o's slow and cautious methods, listened to reports from spies who had secretly switched sides and were already being paid by Fan Chu. The spies said, "The only concern Ch'in has is if Chao Kua becomes general. They see Lien P'o as an easy target who will be defeated eventually." Chao Kua, the son of the famous general Chao She, had been obsessed with war and strategy since childhood, believing no one could defeat him. His father, worried about his arrogance, warned that if Kua ever became a general, he would ruin the army of Chao. Despite warnings from his mother and the statesman Lin Hsiang-ju, Chao Kua was appointed to replace Lien P'o. He proved no match for the skilled general Po Ch'i and the mighty Ch'in army. His army was split, his supply lines were cut, and after a 46-day resistance, during which his starving soldiers resorted to cannibalism, he was killed by an arrow, and his entire force, reportedly 400,000 men, was slaughtered.]

Having doomed spies means openly doing certain things to deceive the enemy and letting our own spies know about it so they can report back.

[Tu Yu explains it best: "We deliberately do things to fool our own spies into thinking they've uncovered real secrets. When they are caught by the enemy, they will give false reports, causing the enemy to prepare for something that won't happen." Once the enemy realizes the deception, the spies will be executed. Ho Shih gives the example of prisoners released by Pan Ch'ao during his campaign against Yarkand. He also mentions T'ang Chien, who was sent by T'ai Tsung in 630 A.D. to lull the Turkish Kahn Chieh-li into a false sense of security until Li Ching could launch a surprise attack. Some say the Turks killed T'ang Chien in revenge, but both the old and new T'ang histories record that he escaped and lived until 656. Li I-chi played a similar role in 203 B.C., when sent by the King of Han to negotiate with Ch'i. Li I-chi may be a more fitting example of a doomed spy, as the King of Ch'i, feeling betrayed after an unexpected attack by Han Hsin, had Li I-chi boiled alive.]

Surviving spies are those who return with information from the enemy's camp.

[These are the typical spies, forming a regular part of the army. Tu Mu says: "A surviving spy must be intelligent but appear foolish; he should look shabby on the outside but possess a strong will. He must be active, tough, physically strong, and brave; accustomed to doing dirty work, able to endure hunger and cold, and capable of handling shame and humiliation." Ho Shih tells a story about Ta'hsi Wu of the Sui dynasty: "When he was governor of Eastern Ch'in, Shen-wu of Ch'i launched an attack on Sha-yuan. Emperor T'ai Tsu sent Ta'hsi Wu to spy on the enemy, accompanied by two others. They rode on horseback, wearing the enemy's uniform. After nightfall, they dismounted a few hundred feet from the enemy's camp and sneaked closer to listen. They managed to overhear the army's passwords. Then they got back on their horses and, pretending to be night watchmen, boldly rode through the camp. Several times, they even punished soldiers who were breaking the rules, beating them as if they were enforcing discipline! This way, they gathered detailed information about the enemy's position and returned to report. The Emperor was so impressed by their intelligence that he used it to achieve a major victory over the enemy."]

Hence, none in the entire army should be more closely connected with than spies.

[Tu Mu and Mei Yao-ch'en note that spies have the privilege of entering even the general's private tent.]

No one should be rewarded more generously, and no other work should be kept more secret.

[Tu Mu adds that all communication with spies should be done "mouth-to-ear," in utmost secrecy. The following advice on spies can be quoted from Turenne, who used them more than any previous commander: "Spies work for those who pay them the most. A commander who pays poorly will never be well-served. They should remain unknown to others, and they should not know one another. When they propose something important, secure their loyalty by holding them or their families as hostages for their faithfulness. Only share with them what is absolutely necessary for them to know."]

Spies cannot be effectively used without a certain intuitive sagacity.

[Mei Yao-ch'en says: "To use them well, you must be able to distinguish truth from lies and recognize honesty from deceit." Wang Hsi interprets this more as "intuitive perception" and "practical intelligence." Tu Mu, however, strangely attributes these qualities to the spies themselves: "Before employing spies, we must confirm their integrity and assess their experience and skills." But he adds: "A bold face and a cunning mind are more dangerous than mountains or rivers; it takes a genius to see through them." This leaves some uncertainty as to his true view of the passage.]

They cannot be properly managed without benevolence and straightforwardness.

[Chang Yu says: "After attracting spies with good offers, you must treat them with complete sincerity, so they will serve you with full dedication."]

Without subtle ingenuity, one cannot be sure of the accuracy of their reports.

[Mei Yao-ch'en warns: "Beware of the possibility that spies might defect to the enemy."]

Be subtle! Be subtle! And use your spies for all kinds of tasks.

If a spy leaks a secret before the time is right, he must be executed along with the person who received the information.

[The literal translation is: "If spy matters are heard before [our plans] are carried out," etc. Sun Tzŭ's point is that the spy is executed as punishment for revealing the secret, while the other person is killed, as Ch'en Hao explains, "to keep his mouth shut" and prevent further leaks. If the information has already been shared with others, this would be ineffective. Sun Tzŭ's advice may seem harsh, though Tu Mu defends it, saying the recipient deserves punishment because he must have pressured the spy into revealing the secret.]

Whether the goal is to defeat an army, storm a city, or assassinate a leader, it is crucial to start by learning the names of the attendants, aides-de-camp,

[Literally "visitors," referring to those who supply the general with information, requiring regular meetings with him.]

the doorkeepers, and sentries of the general in command. Our spies must be assigned to find out these details.

[This would be the first step toward determining whether any of these key figures can be bribed.]

The enemy's spies who come to spy on us must be identified, tempted with bribes, and then won over and treated well. This way, they become converted spies and can work for us.

It is through the information provided by the converted spy that we can recruit and use local and inward spies.

[Tu Yu explains: "By converting the enemy's spies, we learn the true state of the enemy." Chang Yu adds: "We must entice the converted spy into our service because he knows which local inhabitants are greedy for profit and which officials are open to corruption."]

It is also through the converted spy's information that we can use doomed spies to send false reports to the enemy.

[Chang Yu says, "The converted spy knows the best ways to deceive the enemy."]

Finally, the converted spy's information allows us to use the surviving spy on special occasions.

The ultimate purpose of all five types of spies is to gain knowledge of the enemy; and this knowledge primarily comes from the converted spy.

[As outlined in §§ 22-24. The converted spy not only provides direct information but also makes it possible to effectively employ the other types of spies.]

Therefore, it is crucial to treat the converted spy with the greatest generosity.

Of old, the rise of the Yin dynasty

[Sun Tzŭ is referring to the Shang dynasty, founded in 1766 B.C., which was later renamed Yin by P'an Keng in 1401.]

was due to I Chih

[Also known as I Yin, the famous general and statesman who played a key role in Ch'eng T'ang's campaign against Chieh Kuei.]

who had served under the Hsia. Likewise, the rise of the Chou dynasty was due to Lü Ya

[Lü Shang, who rose to prominence under the tyrant Chou Hsin, later helped to overthrow him. He is widely known as T'ai Kung, a title given to him by Wen Wang, and is said to have authored a treatise on war, though it has been wrongly identified with the *Liu T'ao.*]

who had served under the Yin.

[The Chinese wording here is less precise than this translation, and the commentaries are not clear. However, in the context, it seems likely that Sun Tzŭ is presenting I Chih and Lü Ya as examples of converted spies or something similar. His point is that the Hsia and Yin dynasties fell because these former ministers had intimate knowledge of their weaknesses, which they shared with the opposing side. Mei Yao-ch'en objects to this interpretation, saying: "I Yin and Lü Ya were not traitors. The Hsia dynasty failed to employ I Yin, so the Yin did. The Yin dynasty failed to employ Lü Ya, so the Chou did. Their great deeds were for the benefit of the people." Ho Shih is also offended: "How could divinely inspired men like I and Lü have been mere spies? Sun Tzŭ is not suggesting that they were spies, but rather that using spies requires the highest level of intelligence, which people like I and Lü possessed. That is why they are mentioned here." Ho Shih believes they are referenced for their wisdom in using spies, but this interpretation is weak.]

Hence, only the enlightened ruler and the wise general will use the highest intelligence in the army for spying, and by doing so, they achieve great results.

[Tu Mu concludes with a note of caution: "Just as water, which can carry a boat across a river, can also sink it, so relying on spies can bring great success but also lead to disaster."]

Spies are a crucial part of warfare because the movement of the army depends on them.

Meditations

Marcus Aurelius

Introduction

I. Biography of Marcus Aurelius

Marcus Aurelius, one of history's most revered philosopher-emperors, was born on April 26, 121 AD, in Rome. His birth name was Marcus Annius Verus, reflecting his noble lineage. The Annii Verus family was well-established and influential within the Roman aristocracy, known for their wealth and connections to the imperial court. Marcus's father, Annius Verus, held the esteemed position of a praetor, a senior official in the Roman Republic, but he passed away when Marcus was only three years old. Raised primarily by his grandfather, Marcus Annius Verus, a revered figure in Roman society, young Marcus was imbued with a sense of duty and moral fortitude from an early age.

His upbringing was characterized by the highest standards of Roman education, emphasizing rhetoric and philosophy, the cornerstones of intellectual development in the ancient world. This background laid the foundation for his later philosophical pursuits and writings. Marcus was betrothed at a young age to the daughter of Lucius Aelius Caesar, the first adopted heir of Emperor Hadrian, aligning him closely with the line of succession.

Rise to Power and Role as Roman Emperor

Marcus Aurelius's path to power was paved by the foresight of Emperor Hadrian, who saw potential in the young nobleman. After the death of Aelius Caesar, Hadrian adopted Antoninus Pius as his successor, with the condition that Antoninus would, in turn, adopt Marcus and Lucius Verus, the son of Aelius Caesar. This arrangement placed Marcus directly in line for the imperial throne.

In 138 AD, upon Hadrian's death, Antoninus Pius ascended to the throne and took on the role of a mentor and father figure to Marcus. Marcus's political and philosophical education continued under Antoninus's guidance, preparing him for future leadership. During this period, he became deeply engaged with Stoic philosophy, profoundly influencing his thinking and governance approach.

Marcus's reign as emperor began in 161 AD, following Antoninus Pius's death. Uniquely, he shared this role with his adoptive brother, Lucius Verus, marking the first instance of co-emperors in Roman history. However, Marcus was recognized as the senior partner, entrusted with greater authority and responsibilities. His reign was marked by a series of military conflicts, most notably the Marcomannic Wars against Germanic tribes along the Danube frontier and the Parthian War in the East. Despite these challenges, Marcus remained committed to the principles of Stoicism, which emphasized rationality, self-control, and the importance of duty.

As emperor, Marcus Aurelius strove to balance his philosophical ideals with the demands of leadership. His writings, now known as the Meditations, reflect his internal struggles and dedication to self-improvement amidst the pressures of ruling a vast empire. The text offers timeless wisdom on resilience, virtue, and the human condition, making it as relevant today as it was in antiquity.

Marcus Aurelius passed away in 180 AD, leaving a legacy as both a philosopher and a ruler who sought to harmonize the complexities of power with the pursuit of ethical living. His life and works continue to inspire those who seek to navigate the challenges of modern life with wisdom and integrity.

Historical Context

The Roman Empire during the reign of Marcus Aurelius was a vast and complex entity, stretching from the Atlantic Ocean in the west to the Euphrates River in the east. At its height, the empire included regions that are now parts of over 40 modern countries, encompassing diverse cultures, languages, and economies. Governed from Rome, this massive realm was held together by a sophisticated network of roads, a shared legal system, and the might of the Roman legions.

Marcus Aurelius ascended to the throne in 161 AD, a time when the Roman Empire was the preeminent power in the Western world. The city of Rome, with its monumental architecture, bustling markets, and teeming population, served as the heart of this empire. Roman society was highly stratified, with a rigid class system, yet it was also a melting pot of peoples and ideas, influenced by centuries of conquest and trade.

Despite its grandeur, the empire faced numerous challenges. The economy relied heavily on agriculture, supplemented by trade with far-flung regions. The social fabric was underpinned by slavery, which fueled the empire's economy and infrastructure but also posed moral and practical dilemmas. Culturally, the empire was a mosaic of traditions, as Roman religion and customs intertwined with those of conquered peoples.

During Marcus's reign, the empire maintained its prosperity but was also stretched to its limits. The sheer size of the empire made it difficult to govern effectively, with distant provinces often acting semi-autonomously. This complexity required a delicate balance of power and diplomacy, alongside military might, to keep the empire stable.

The reign of Marcus Aurelius was marked by significant events and challenges that tested the resilience of the Roman Empire and its leader.

The Marcomannic Wars

One of the primary challenges Marcus faced was the Marcomannic Wars, a series of battles against Germanic tribes and other barbarian groups along the Danube frontier. These wars spanned much of his reign, from 166 to 180 AD, and required constant vigilance and military engagement. The conflicts were driven by pressures from migrating tribes displaced by other groups farther north and the empire's attempts to secure its borders.

The Marcomannic Wars were not just a test of military strategy but also of Marcus's leadership. As a Stoic philosopher, he struggled to reconcile his duties as a warrior emperor with his philosophical ideals of peace and rationality. The wars strained the empire's resources and highlighted the fragility of its frontiers, forcing Marcus to adopt new military tactics and fortify the empire's defenses.

The Parthian War

Another significant challenge during Marcus Aurelius's reign was the Parthian War, which began shortly after he ascended to the throne in 161 AD. The conflict arose when the Parthian Empire, Rome's rival in the East, invaded the Roman client state of Armenia, a strategic buffer region between the two empires. The Parthian King Vologases IV sought to expand his influence, prompting a Roman military response.

The Parthian War demanded significant resources and military attention. Marcus appointed his co-emperor Lucius Verus to oversee the campaign, which involved a series of complex military operations across the eastern provinces. Despite initial setbacks, the Roman forces ultimately succeeded in repelling the Parthian advance, capturing the Parthian capital, Ctesiphon, and re-establishing Roman authority in the region.

The war was a testament to the strategic acumen of Roman military leaders and the resilience of the Roman army. However, it also revealed the strains on the empire's resources, as the cost of sustaining such distant military campaigns was immense. Marcus's ability to manage these military operations while addressing other challenges underscores his effectiveness as a leader who balanced military necessity with philosophical reflection.

The Antonine Plague

In addition to military conflicts, Marcus Aurelius's reign was plagued—quite literally—by a devastating pandemic known as the Antonine Plague. This epidemic, believed to have been smallpox or measles, struck the empire in 165 AD and continued for over a decade, causing widespread mortality and economic disruption.

The plague significantly impacted the Roman military, reducing the number of available soldiers and weakening the empire's defensive capabilities. It also affected civilian populations, leading to labor shortages and a decline in agricultural productivity. The social and economic ramifications of the plague were profound, contributing to a sense of instability and uncertainty within the empire.

Marcus Aurelius's response to these challenges demonstrated his commitment to duty and resilience. He worked tirelessly to support the empire's recovery, overseeing relief efforts and implementing measures to stabilize the economy. Despite personal losses, including the death of his co-emperor Lucius Verus, Marcus maintained a stoic resolve, viewing the trials as opportunities for personal and philosophical growth.

Political and Economic Struggles

Throughout his reign, Marcus Aurelius also contended with internal political and economic challenges. The Roman economy was heavily reliant on agriculture and trade, both of which were disrupted by the ongoing military conflicts and the Antonine Plague. To address financial shortfalls, Marcus took measures such as debasing the currency, which temporarily alleviated fiscal pressures but also contributed to long-term economic difficulties.

Politically, Marcus faced challenges in maintaining the loyalty and cooperation of the Roman Senate and provincial governors. His reign saw occasional uprisings and conspiracies, which he addressed through a combination of clemency and strategic governance. Marcus's leadership style was characterized by his emphasis on justice, reason, and the importance of leading by example.

Domestic Reforms and Legal Contributions

During his reign, Marcus Aurelius undertook several domestic reforms aimed at improving governance and addressing social issues within the empire. His legal reforms reflected his commitment to justice and equity, as he sought to ensure that Roman law was fair and accessible to all citizens.

Marcus introduced measures to protect the rights of slaves and orphans, reflecting his Stoic belief in the inherent worth of all individuals. He also worked to improve the administration of justice, emphasizing the importance of legal integrity and reducing corruption among provincial governors.

These reforms were consistent with his philosophical ideals, as Marcus believed that a just and equitable society was essential for the well-being of its citizens. His legal contributions helped shape Roman law, leaving a legacy that influenced legal systems in later Western civilizations.

The Rise of Christianity

The rise of Christianity posed another challenge during Marcus Aurelius's reign. As a new religious movement, Christianity was often viewed with suspicion by Roman authorities, who perceived it as a threat to traditional Roman religious practices and social order.

While Marcus Aurelius is not known to have actively persecuted Christians, his reign saw instances of local persecutions, as Christian communities were often scapegoated for societal problems. The tension between traditional Roman values and the growing Christian faith reflected broader cultural and religious shifts within the empire.

Marcus's philosophical writings, while not directly addressing Christianity, emphasize tolerance and understanding, values that resonate with contemporary discussions on religious freedom and coexistence. His emphasis on rationality and virtue provided a framework for navigating the complex religious landscape of his time.

The Succession and Legacy

One of the enduring challenges for Roman emperors was ensuring a stable succession. Marcus Aurelius faced the difficult task of securing the future of the empire beyond his reign. Unlike his predecessors,

Marcus chose to appoint his son Commodus as his successor, a decision that proved contentious.

Commodus's rule, marked by autocracy and instability, contrasted sharply with his father's philosophical and principled leadership. The transition highlighted the inherent risks in dynastic succession and the challenges of maintaining imperial stability. Despite the difficulties of his son's reign, Marcus Aurelius's legacy as a philosopher-emperor endured, with his writings continuing to inspire future generations.

II. The Duality of Marcus Aurelius

Philosopher and Emperor

Marcus Aurelius is celebrated as both a philosopher and an emperor, two roles that may seem fundamentally at odds with one another. His life presents a fascinating duality, as he was tasked with wielding immense political power while simultaneously pursuing the introspective path of a philosopher. This intersection of roles makes Marcus a compelling figure in history and philosophy.

As a philosopher, Marcus Aurelius was deeply influenced by Stoicism, a school of thought that emphasized reason, self-discipline, and the pursuit of virtue as the highest good. Stoicism taught that the key to a fulfilling life was living in harmony with nature and accepting the things beyond one's control. Marcus's philosophical journey was driven by a relentless pursuit of self-improvement and wisdom, as he sought to align his actions with the Stoic ideals of rationality and virtue.

Conversely, as emperor of Rome, Marcus faced the practical demands of governance, leading a vast empire fraught with challenges such as military conflicts, political intrigue, and economic pressures. His role required decisive action and strategic thinking to maintain the stability and prosperity of the Roman Empire. Balancing these demands with his philosophical aspirations created a profound tension in his life.

Exploration of the Tension Between His Philosophical Pursuits and Imperial Duties

As a Stoic, Marcus believed in the importance of rational thought and virtuous living. However, as an emperor, he was often required to engage in warfare and make difficult decisions that could seem at odds with Stoic principles.

This tension is evident in his personal writings, where Marcus frequently reflects on the challenges of maintaining his philosophical integrity while fulfilling his imperial responsibilities. The Meditations reveal his internal struggles with anger, fear, and the burdens of leadership. He grappled with the idea of duty versus desire, questioning how to remain true to his philosophical beliefs while effectively governing an empire.

One of the key challenges Marcus faced was reconciling the Stoic ideal of peace with the necessity of war. The Marcomannic Wars required him to take on the role of a military leader, directing campaigns against invading tribes to protect the empire's borders. Despite his personal distaste for conflict, Marcus viewed these actions as necessary to fulfill his duty to Rome. He approached these decisions with a sense of Stoic detachment, striving to act in accordance with reason and the greater good.

Contrast Between His Public Role and Private Philosophical Reflections

The contrast between Marcus Aurelius's public and private lives is striking. As emperor, he was the most powerful man in the world, responsible for the welfare of millions of people. Yet, his Meditations reveal a private individual who was introspective, self-critical, and often doubtful of his own abilities.

In public, Marcus was expected to project confidence and authority, maintaining the image of a strong and capable ruler. He was seen as a wise and just leader, dedicated to the well-being of his subjects. However, his personal writings reveal a different side—a man who continually questioned his own motives and actions, seeking to improve himself in the face of life's challenges.

His writings are a testament to Marcus's commitment to self-reflection and personal growth. They offer insight into his efforts to reconcile his public responsibilities with his private philosophical aspirations. Through his writings, Marcus sought to hold himself accountable, using Stoic philosophy as a guide to navigate the complexities of his dual role.

In this way, Marcus Aurelius serves as a timeless example of the struggle to balance personal ideals with external demands. His life and writings demonstrate the enduring relevance of philosophy in providing guidance and perspective in the face of life's challenges. For contemporary readers, Marcus's duality offers valuable lessons on how to integrate philosophical principles into everyday life, even amidst the pressures of modern society.

III. Philosophical Background

Stoicism is a philosophical school that emerged in Athens during the early 3rd century BC. Founded by Zeno of Citium, it gained prominence in the Hellenistic world and later found a home in Rome, where it deeply influenced thinkers like Seneca, Epictetus, and Marcus Aurelius. Stoicism offers a practical guide for living a virtuous life, emphasizing the development of personal wisdom and self-control as pathways to true happiness.

At its core, Stoicism teaches that the universe is governed by a rational and divine order, often referred to as "Logos." This belief in a rational cosmos shaped the Stoics' understanding of human nature and their emphasis on living in harmony with this natural order. For the Stoics, philosophy was not merely a theoretical pursuit but a way of life that required continuous practice and reflection.

Marcus Aurelius, as a Stoic philosopher, was deeply influenced by these teachings. His writings reflect his efforts to apply Stoic principles to his daily life and challenges, offering timeless insights into the human condition.

Core Principles of Stoicism

The philosophy of Stoicism is built upon several core principles that guide individuals toward a life of virtue and tranquility. Understanding these principles provides a foundation for exploring Marcus Aurelius's Meditations and their relevance to modern life.

1. The Dichotomy of Control

One of the fundamental tenets of Stoicism is the distinction between what is within our control and what is not. The Stoics taught that we should focus on our thoughts, intentions, and actions, as these are within our control. External events, the opinions of others, and the outcomes of our efforts are beyond our control and should be accepted with equanimity. This principle encourages individuals to cultivate inner peace by letting go of concerns about things they cannot change.

2. Living in Accordance with Nature

Stoicism emphasizes living in harmony with nature, which means aligning our actions with the rational order of the universe. This principle involves understanding and accepting our place in the world, recognizing that we are all part of a larger whole. Living in accordance with nature also means acknowledging our human nature, which is characterized by reason and social interconnectedness.

3. The Pursuit of Virtue

For the Stoics, virtue is the highest good and the only true source of happiness. Virtue encompasses qualities such as wisdom, courage, justice, and temperance. By cultivating these virtues, individuals can achieve a state of moral excellence and live a fulfilling life. The Stoics believed that external goods, such as wealth and fame, are indifferent and do not contribute to genuine happiness.

4. The Practice of Mindfulness and Reflection

Stoicism encourages regular self-examination and mindfulness as tools for personal growth. By reflecting on one's thoughts and actions, individuals can identify areas for improvement and reinforce their commitment to living virtuously. This practice of self-awareness helps cultivate resilience and adaptability in the face of life's challenges.

5. The Acceptance of Fate

The Stoics taught the importance of accepting the unfolding of events with grace and composure. This principle, often referred to as "amor fati" or love of fate, involves embracing life's circumstances, both good and bad, as part of the natural order. By accepting fate, individuals can maintain their inner tranquility and focus on what truly matters: their response to life's challenges.

6. Universal Brotherhood

Stoicism emphasizes the interconnectedness of all human beings. The Stoics believed that we are all part of a universal community and have a responsibility to care for one another. This principle encourages empathy, compassion, and cooperation, promoting a sense of shared humanity that transcends individual differences.

These core principles form the foundation of Stoic philosophy and offer a practical framework for navigating the complexities of life. Marcus reflects on his engagement with these ideas, providing a timeless guide for those seeking wisdom and resilience in a rapidly changing world. By embracing Stoic principles, contemporary readers can find guidance and inspiration to lead more meaningful and virtuous lives.

Influence of Stoic Philosophy on Marcus Aurelius

Stoicism offered Marcus a framework for understanding the world and his place within it. It provided him with the tools to navigate the complexities of leadership and personal development.

1. Stoicism as a Guide to Leadership

For Marcus Aurelius, Stoicism was more than an abstract philosophy; it was a practical guide to governance and leadership. The Stoic emphasis on virtue and ethical conduct informed his approach to these responsibilities, guiding him to prioritize justice, fairness, and the common good.

Marcus's adherence to Stoic principles helped him maintain a sense of balance and perspective amidst the challenges of his reign. The Stoic idea of focusing on what is within one's control and accepting what is not enabled him to remain composed and effective in the face of external pressures, such as wars, political intrigue, and natural disasters.

2. Personal Resilience and Inner Strength

Stoicism taught Marcus the importance of cultivating inner strength and resilience, qualities that were crucial for his personal development and effectiveness as a ruler. The philosophy's focus on self-discipline and emotional regulation helped Marcus manage his reactions to the inevitable difficulties and frustrations of life.

Marcus reflects on his efforts to practice Stoic exercises, such as self-examination and mindfulness. These practices allowed him to maintain a sense of inner peace and clarity, even when confronted with adversity. By striving to align his thoughts and actions with Stoic principles, Marcus was able to build a foundation of personal integrity and resilience.

3. The Pursuit of Virtue

Central to Marcus's philosophical journey was the pursuit of virtue, which the Stoics regarded as the highest good. Stoicism taught him that true happiness and fulfillment come from living a life in accordance with virtue, rather than seeking external rewards such as wealth or fame.

Marcus's commitment to this ideal is evident throughout the book He continually emphasizes the importance of wisdom, courage, justice, and temperance as guiding principles for his conduct. These virtues served as a moral compass, helping him navigate the complexities of imperial rule and personal challenges.

4. Acceptance and Tranquility

The Stoic concept of "amor fati," or love of fate, profoundly influenced Marcus Aurelius's outlook on life. Stoicism encourages acceptance of the natural order and the unfolding of events, teaching that peace of mind comes from embracing life as it is, rather than how one wishes it to be.

Marcus applied this principle to his role as emperor, striving to accept the burdens and responsibilities that came with his position. By practicing acceptance, he was able to maintain a sense of tranquility and purpose, even when faced with the uncertainties of leadership and the transience of life.

5. A Legacy of Stoic Thought

The influence of Stoicism on Marcus Aurelius is perhaps most clearly reflected in the legacy of his writings. They serve as a timeless testament to the practical wisdom of Stoic philosophy, offering insights that continue to resonate with readers today.

Through his engagement with Stoic principles, Marcus Aurelius exemplified the possibility of integrating philosophy into everyday life. His reflections encourage contemporary readers to consider how Stoic teachings can inform their own pursuit of a virtuous and meaningful existence.

IV. The Meditations

Purpose and Nature of the Text

The Meditations is a remarkable work of philosophical reflection and personal introspection. Unlike typical philosophical treatises of the time, it was not intended for public consumption or scholarly debate. Instead, it serves as a private journal where Marcus recorded his thoughts, struggles, and insights as he endeavored to live according to Stoic principles.

Personal Reflections

Written during the last decade of his life, the text was crafted during military campaigns on the frontiers of the Roman Empire. This setting highlights the personal and practical nature of the work, as Marcus wrote in stolen moments of solitude, often in the midst of hardship and uncertainty. The text is composed of twelve books, each a collection of thoughts and reflections that offer a glimpse into Marcus's inner life and philosophical journey.

The primary purpose of this text was self-improvement. Marcus Aurelius used his writings as a tool for self-examination, aiming to reinforce his commitment to Stoic ideals and cultivate personal virtue. By reflecting on his experiences and challenges, he sought to better understand himself and align his actions with his philosophical beliefs. In this sense, the text serves as a manual for personal development, guiding the reader—both Marcus and modern readers—toward a life of wisdom and integrity.

Not a Public Philosophical Treatise

Unlike the works of other philosophers such as Plato or Aristotle, Meditations was not intended as a systematic exposition of philosophical doctrines. It lacks the formal structure and argumentative rigor typical of philosophical texts. Instead, the work is characterized by its fragmented and spontaneous nature, reflecting the fact that it was written for Marcus's eyes alone.

Marcus's writings are deeply personal and candid, revealing his vulnerabilities, doubts, and aspirations. The text does not seek to instruct or persuade others; rather, it is a record of Marcus's ongoing dialogue with himself as he grapples with the challenges of being both a philosopher and an emperor. This introspective quality makes it unique among ancient texts, offering a rare insight into the personal application of Stoic philosophy.

A Timeless Guide for Self-Reflection

While Meditations was written as a private journal, its insights and reflections have transcended time, offering timeless guidance to those seeking to lead a life of virtue and purpose. The text's appeal lies in its universality; Marcus's reflections on the human condition, the nature of happiness, and the pursuit of wisdom resonate with readers across cultures and eras.

For contemporary readers, this book serves as a powerful reminder of the value of self-reflection and the importance of living in accordance with one's principles. The text encourages individuals to examine their own lives, confront their weaknesses, and strive for personal growth. In an age where external distractions and pressures abound, the book invites readers to turn inward, fostering a deeper understanding of themselves and their place in the world.

Relevance for Today

The enduring relevance of Meditations is a testament to the universal nature of its themes. In a fast-paced and often chaotic world, Marcus's reflections on inner peace, resilience, and the pursuit of virtue offer a source of inspiration and guidance. His writings remind us that true fulfillment comes not from external achievements but from living a life aligned with our deepest values.

Contemporary readers can explore the transformative power of Stoic philosophy, gaining insights into how to navigate life's challenges with grace and wisdom. Marcus Aurelius's personal reflections continue to illuminate the path to self-improvement, encouraging us to cultivate the qualities that define a meaningful and virtuous life.

Structure and Style

Overview of the Organization of the Text

Meditations is organized into twelve books, each containing a series of reflections, aphorisms, and philosophical musings.

Each book varies in length and content, reflecting the episodic nature of Marcus's reflections. The entries are not organized thematically but are rather a spontaneous outpouring of his inner dialogue. This structure highlights the deeply personal nature of the work, as Marcus uses writing as a tool for self-examination and personal growth.

Despite the lack of formal organization, certain themes and topics recur throughout the text, such as the pursuit of virtue, the transience of life, and the importance of rationality and self-discipline. These themes provide a unifying thread, connecting Marcus's reflections across different contexts and periods.

Literary Style and Use of Language

Meditations is written in a direct and unadorned style, reflecting Marcus Aurelius's commitment to clarity and sincerity. The language is often concise and pointed, capturing the essence of his philosophical reflections with minimal embellishment. This straightforward style aligns with Stoic values, emphasizing the importance of truth and simplicity.

The text is rich in metaphor and imagery, using vivid language to illustrate philosophical concepts. Marcus often employs analogies drawn from nature, daily life, and the military to convey his insights. For example, he likens the soul to a citadel, emphasizing the importance of inner strength and resilience against external challenges.

The use of the second person is a distinctive feature of the text, as Marcus frequently addresses himself directly. This creates an intimate and introspective tone, inviting readers to engage with his reflections as a form of personal dialogue. By writing in this manner, Marcus underscores the self-directed nature of his philosophical practice, encouraging readers to apply similar introspection in their own lives.

The text also incorporates elements of rhetorical questioning and paradox, challenging readers to think critically about their assumptions and beliefs. Marcus's style reflects his philosophical rigor and his desire to provoke thoughtful reflection.

A Living Document

The literary style is marked by its variability, ranging from meticulously crafted passages to fragmented and cryptic notes. This variability reflects the conditions under which the text was written—often during military campaigns and moments of solitude—and the dynamic nature of Marcus's thought process.

The text is best understood as a living document, capturing the evolution of Marcus's philosophical understanding over time. This fluidity allows readers to witness his struggles and growth, making it a powerful testament to the ongoing journey of self-improvement.

V. Themes and Content of Meditations

Key Themes

Meditations explores a rich tapestry of themes that delve into the nature of the human experience and the quest for a virtuous life. Written as a series of personal reflections, these themes reflect Marcus's struggle to reconcile his philosophical beliefs with the demands of his role as Roman Emperor. Despite the centuries that separate us from his time, the insights Marcus offers remain profoundly relevant, providing guidance on how to navigate the complexities of modern life.

The Pursuit of Virtue and Self-Improvement

Central is the Stoic ideal of virtue as the highest good. Marcus Aurelius constantly emphasizes the importance of living in accordance with virtue, which encompasses wisdom, courage, justice, and temperance. For Marcus, the pursuit of virtue is not just an abstract goal but a practical guide for everyday conduct.

His reflections encourage readers to cultivate self-discipline and strive for personal improvement. He believed that by consistently practicing virtue, individuals could achieve a state of inner harmony and fulfillment. This pursuit requires continuous self-examination and the willingness to confront one's weaknesses, making virtue a dynamic and lifelong journey.

Marcus's dedication to self-improvement is evident in his commitment to Stoic exercises and practices. These exercises, which include mindfulness, reflection, and the repetition of core principles, serve as tools to strengthen his resolve and maintain focus on what truly matters. By sharing these practices, Marcus provides a roadmap for readers to follow in their quest for personal growth and ethical living.

The Nature of Death and Impermanence

Another significant theme is the contemplation of death and the transient nature of life. Marcus Aurelius often reflects on the inevitability of death, viewing it as a natural part of the human experience. For the Stoics, acceptance of mortality is crucial for living a meaningful life, as it encourages individuals to focus on the present moment and prioritize their values.

Marcus's writings offer a sober yet empowering perspective on death. By accepting the impermanence of life, he argues, we can free ourselves from the fear of death and the anxieties that come with it. This acceptance allows us to appreciate the fleeting nature of existence and inspires us to live each day with intention and purpose.

For contemporary readers, Marcus's reflections on death serve as a reminder to cherish life's fleeting moments and to align our actions with our core values. His insights encourage us to let go of trivial concerns and focus on what is truly important, fostering a sense of gratitude and mindfulness in our daily lives.

The Insignificance of Fame and External Validation

Marcus frequently contemplates the futility of seeking fame and external validation. As emperor, he was acutely aware of the transient nature of power and the superficiality of public acclaim. He urges readers to recognize that true fulfillment comes from within, rather than from the fleeting approval of others.

Marcus's reflections challenge us to question the societal emphasis on status, wealth, and recognition. He encourages us to pursue intrinsic values, such as integrity and authenticity, rather than relying on external measures of success. By shifting our focus away from external validation, we can cultivate a deeper sense of self-worth and contentment.

In today's world, where social media and external pressures often dictate our self-image, Marcus's insights are particularly relevant. His writings invite us to reevaluate our priorities and seek fulfillment through personal growth and self-acceptance, rather than through the opinions of others.

Dealing with Anger and Maintaining Composure

A recurring theme is the challenge of managing anger and maintaining composure in the face of adversity. Marcus Aurelius candidly acknowledges his struggles with anger and frustration, particularly in his role as a leader. He draws upon Stoic principles to navigate these emotions, emphasizing the importance of reason and self-control.

Marcus encourages readers to adopt a detached perspective, viewing challenges and setbacks as opportunities for growth rather than sources of distress. By practicing patience and understanding, we can cultivate resilience and respond to difficult situations with grace and equanimity.

His reflections remind us that anger is a natural human emotion but one that must be managed to maintain inner peace. By practicing mindfulness and cultivating a rational mindset, we can transform anger into a catalyst for personal development and positive change.

Stoic Practices and Exercises

Marcus Aurelius not only reflects on Stoic philosophy but also demonstrates how to integrate its principles into daily life through practical exercises. These Stoic practices are designed to cultivate self-awareness, resilience, and personal growth, offering valuable tools for navigating the complexities of modern life. By engaging in these exercises, Marcus sought to strengthen his character and live in harmony with his philosophical ideals.

1. Daily Reflection and Journaling

One of the most prominent practices in Meditations is the use of daily reflection and journaling as a means of self-examination. Marcus Aurelius utilized writing as a tool for introspection, recording his thoughts, challenges, and aspirations. This exercise allowed him to evaluate his actions, assess his adherence to Stoic principles, and identify areas for improvement.

For contemporary readers, daily reflection and journaling can serve as powerful tools for personal development. By setting aside time each day to write about our thoughts and experiences, we can gain clarity, foster self-awareness, and reinforce our commitment to living in accordance with our values.

2. The Dichotomy of Control

A fundamental Stoic exercise practiced by Marcus is the dichotomy of control, which involves distinguishing between what is within our control and what is not. By focusing on our thoughts, intentions, and actions—elements within our control—we can cultivate inner peace and resilience. Marcus frequently reminded himself to accept external events and outcomes, understanding that they are beyond his control.

This exercise encourages modern readers to let go of anxiety and frustration over things they cannot change, allowing them to concentrate on their responses and attitudes. By embracing the dichotomy of control, we can develop a sense of empowerment and tranquility in the face of life's uncertainties.

3. Mindfulness and Presence

Mindfulness, or the practice of being present in the moment, is another key Stoic exercise. Marcus emphasized the importance of living in the present, avoiding distractions from the past and future. He believed that by fully engaging with the present moment, individuals could act with intention and purpose.

For today's readers, mindfulness can be a transformative practice, helping to reduce stress and enhance focus. By cultivating presence and awareness, we can make more deliberate choices and appreciate the richness of our experiences.

4. Negative Visualization

Negative visualization, or premeditatio malorum, is a Stoic exercise that involves contemplating potential challenges and setbacks in advance. Marcus used this practice to prepare himself mentally for difficulties, reducing their impact when they occurred. By envisioning possible obstacles, he was able to develop strategies for coping and maintaining a sense of equanimity.

This exercise can be valuable for contemporary readers as a means of building resilience and adaptability. By anticipating potential challenges, we can reduce fear and anxiety, allowing us to respond to adversity with greater confidence and composure.

5. Practicing Virtue

Central to Marcus's practice was the active pursuit of virtue, which the Stoics considered the highest good. Marcus continually sought to embody qualities such as wisdom, courage, justice, and temperance in his daily life. He believed that by practicing virtue, individuals could achieve true fulfillment and happiness.

For modern readers, focusing on the cultivation of virtue can provide a meaningful framework for personal growth. By striving to embody these qualities, we can develop a strong moral character and live a life aligned with our deepest values.

6. Reflection on Mortality

Marcus frequently reflected on the impermanence of life and the inevitability of death, using this awareness to inspire a sense of urgency and purpose. This exercise encouraged him to prioritize meaningful actions and relationships, reminding him of the preciousness of each moment.

Contemplating mortality can help contemporary readers clarify their priorities and make choices that align with their core values. By embracing the finite nature of life, we can focus on what truly matters and cultivate gratitude for the present.

VI. The Legacy of Marcus Aurelius

Meditations has resonated with readers for centuries, influencing a wide range of philosophers, writers, and leaders. Its appeal lies in its practical wisdom and deeply personal reflections, which provide a window into the mind of a ruler grappling with the challenges of leadership and life.

Throughout history, it has inspired prominent figures in philosophy, literature, and politics. During the Renaissance, the revival of classical learning brought renewed interest in Stoic philosophy, with Meditations serving as a key text for thinkers seeking to integrate Stoic ideals into their own work. Renaissance humanists, such as Erasmus and Montaigne, drew upon Marcus's reflections to explore themes of virtue, reason, and self-governance.

In the modern era, the text has continued to influence philosophers like Friedrich Nietzsche, who admired Marcus's ability to maintain philosophical ideals while fulfilling his duties as emperor. The existentialists, including Jean-Paul Sartre and Albert Camus, also found resonance in Marcus's reflections on meaning, choice, and the human struggle for authenticity.

Beyond philosophy, Meditations has inspired leaders seeking to apply Stoic principles to the complexities of governance and decision-making. Figures such as Thomas Jefferson and Theodore Roosevelt found guidance in Marcus's writings, using his insights to navigate the challenges of leadership with integrity and wisdom.

A Timeless Guide to Leadership and Ethics

For those in positions of leadership, Meditations provides a timeless guide to ethical decision-making and the cultivation of moral character. Marcus's reflections on justice, courage, and empathy offer valuable insights for leaders seeking to navigate the complexities of modern governance with integrity and compassion.

In a world where ethical leadership is increasingly important, Marcus's example serves as a reminder of the power of philosophy to shape not only personal conduct but also the governance of society. His writings encourage leaders to prioritize the common good, act with wisdom and fairness, and remain true to their principles in the face of adversity.

Inspiration for Personal and Collective Resilience

Finally, Meditations inspires both personal and collective resilience, offering guidance on how to confront life's challenges with courage and grace. Marcus's reflections on the impermanence of life and the importance of accepting fate resonate with readers seeking to find meaning and purpose in an uncertain world.

By embracing the Stoic ideals, individuals and communities can cultivate a deeper sense of connection, purpose, and resilience. Marcus Aurelius's legacy continues to inspire and guide those who seek to lead lives of virtue and meaning, demonstrating the enduring power of philosophy to transform both individuals and society.

VII. Personal Reflections

This book offers an extraordinary glimpse into the mind of a philosopher-king, providing insights into his lifelong quest for wisdom and virtue. As you embark on this journey through Meditations, I invite you to explore the text as a source of guidance and inspiration for your own personal development. Marcus Aurelius's reflections offer a wealth of wisdom that can help you navigate the complexities of modern life with grace and resilience. His teachings remind us of the importance of cultivating self-discipline, embracing challenges as opportunities for growth, and living in accordance with our values.

In a world that often emphasizes external achievements and validation, the text encourages us to turn inward, fostering a deeper understanding of ourselves and our place in the world. By engaging with Marcus's reflections, you can develop a greater sense of self-awareness and clarity, empowering you to make more deliberate choices and lead a more fulfilling life.

Consider using the book as a tool for daily reflection, drawing upon its insights to guide your actions and decisions. Allow the Stoic exercises and principles outlined in the text to inspire your own journey of self-improvement, helping you cultivate a mindset of mindfulness and resilience.

Ultimately, the wisdom of Marcus Aurelius offers a timeless reminder that true fulfillment comes not from external success but from living a life of virtue and authenticity. Let the journey be an invitation to explore the richness of Stoic philosophy and its potential to illuminate the path toward a life well-lived. As you read and reflect on Marcus Aurelius's words, may you find inspiration to cultivate the qualities that define a virtuous and meaningful existence.

Book 1

From my grandfather Verus, I learned to be a good person and control my temper.

From my father's reputation and memory, I learned how to be humble and act like a man.

From my mother, I learned to be religious, generous, and to avoid not only bad actions but even bad thoughts. I also learned to live simply, far from the habits of the rich.

From my great-grandfather, I learned not to attend public schools and to have good teachers at home, knowing that it's worth spending money on education.

From Diognetus, I learned not to care about trivial things and not to believe in magic or people who claim to banish demons. I learned not to get obsessed with things like raising quails for fighting. I learned to accept free speech and became interested in philosophy, attending lectures first of Bacchius, then Tandasis and Marcianus, and to write dialogues when I was young. I also learned to desire a simple bed and lifestyle, following Greek customs.

From Rusticus, I learned that my character needed improvement and discipline. He taught me not to get caught up in the love of fancy arguments, not to write about things just to show off, not to give little moral speeches, or to pretend I was someone who practiced a lot of self-discipline or did good deeds just to look impressive. I also learned to stay away from using fancy words, writing poems, or trying to sound too sophisticated. He showed me not to walk around the house in formal clothes or do anything similar. I learned to write letters in a simple and straightforward way, like the letter Rusticus wrote to my mother from Sinuessa. He also taught me to be quick to make peace with those who have wronged me as soon as they show they want to make up. From him, I learned to read carefully and not be satisfied with just a shallow understanding of a book, and not to agree too quickly with people who talk a lot. I owe it to him that I got to know the discourses of Epictetus, which he shared with me from his own collection.

From Apollonius, I learned to have freedom of will and unwavering steadiness of purpose. He taught me to focus on nothing else, not even for a moment, except reason. He showed me how to stay the same person, whether in sharp pain, during the loss of a child, or in long illness. He was a clear example of how the same man can be both determined and flexible, and he was never irritable when teaching. He considered his experience and skill in explaining philosophical ideas as the least of his talents. From him, I also learned how to accept favors from friends without feeling humbled by them or letting them go unnoticed.

From Sextus, I learned to have a kind disposition and the example of a family led by a fatherly figure. He taught me the idea of living according to nature and to have dignity without being pretentious. He showed me how to carefully look after the interests of friends and to tolerate ignorant people and those who form opinions without thinking. He was able to adapt easily to everyone, making interactions with him more pleasant than any flattery. At the same time, he was highly respected by those who knew him. He had the ability to discover and organize the important principles of life intelligently and methodically. He never showed anger or any other strong emotion, remaining completely free from passion, yet he was very affectionate. He could express approval without making a big show and had a lot of knowledge without being boastful.

From Alexander the grammarian, I learned not to find fault with others, and not to scold those who used incorrect or strange expressions in a harsh way. Instead, he would skillfully introduce the correct expression that should have been used, either by answering, confirming, or engaging in a discussion about the thing itself, rather than focusing on the word, or by some other fitting suggestion.

From Fronto, I learned to understand what envy, deceit, and hypocrisy are in a tyrant, and that generally, those among us who are called Patricians often lack paternal affection.

From Alexander the Platonic, I learned not to frequently or unnecessarily say to anyone, or write in a letter, that "I am toobusy". He also taught me not to constantly excuse neglecting the duties required by our relationships with others by claiming urgent business.

From Catulus, I learned not to be indifferent when a friend criticizes me, even if the criticism seems unreasonable, but to try to restore the friend to their usual good feelings. He also taught me to be ready to speak well of my teachers, as is said of Domitius and Athenodotus, and to truly love my children.

From my brother Severus, I learned to love my family, to love truth, and to love justice. Through him, I came to know Thrasea, Helvidius, Cato, Dion, and Brutus. From him, I received the idea of a government in which there is the same law for everyone, a government that respects equal rights and freedom of speech. I also learned from him the idea of a monarchy that values the freedom of its people above all. He taught me consistency and unwavering steadiness in my commitment to philosophy. He showed me how to be generous, to give to others readily, to hold on to good hopes, and to believe that I am loved by my friends. I noticed in him that he never hid his opinions about those he disapproved of, and his friends never had to guess what he wanted or did not want—it was always clear.

From Maximus, I learned self-control and not to be easily led astray by anything. He showed me how to be cheerful in all circumstances, even in illness. His character was a perfect blend of gentleness and dignity. He did whatever was required of him without complaining. I observed that everyone believed he thought as he spoke, and that in everything he did, he never had any bad intentions. He never showed amazement or surprise, was never in a hurry, and never put off doing something. He was never confused or dejected, nor did he ever laugh to hide his irritation, and he was never passionate or suspicious. He was used to doing kind acts, was always ready to forgive, and was free from all falsehood. He appeared to be someone who couldn't be turned away from doing the right thing, rather than someone who had to be improved. I also observed that no one ever thought they were looked down upon by Maximus or dared to think they were better than him. He had a pleasant sense of humor in an agreeable way.

In my (adoptive) father, I observed a mild temper and unchangeable determination in the things he decided after careful thought. He had no vanity in those things that men call honors. He had a love for hard work and perseverance, and he was always ready to listen to those who had something to suggest for the common good. He was unwavering in giving everyone what they deserved. He had knowledge from experience about when to take vigorous action and when to be lenient. I noticed that he had overcome any desire for young boys and saw himself as no better than any other citizen. He released his friends from any obligation to dine with him or to accompany him when he went abroad. Those who couldn't join him because of urgent circumstances always found him the same. I also observed his habit of careful inquiry in all matters of decision-making, and his persistence. He never stopped investigating a matter just because he was satisfied with the first impression. He was loyal to his friends and was not quick to tire of them, nor was he extravagant in his affection. He was satisfied in all situations and cheerful. He could foresee things far ahead and took care of the smallest details without making a show of it. He immediately checked popular applause and all flattery. He was always watchful over the things necessary for running the empire, and he was a good manager of expenses. He patiently endured the criticism he received for such conduct. He was not superstitious with respect to the gods, nor did he try to win over men by giving them gifts, by trying to please them, or by flattering the public. He showed sobriety in all things and firmness, never having any mean thoughts or actions, nor a love of novelty. The things that contributed to the comfort of life, which fortune gave him in abundance, he used without arrogance and without excuses. When he had them, he enjoyed them without showing off, and when he didn't have them, he didn't miss them. No one could ever say that he was either a sophist or a flippant servant or a pedant. Everyone recognized him as a man mature, perfect, beyond flattery, capable of managing his own and other people's affairs. He also honored those who were true philosophers and did not criticize those who pretended to be philosophers, nor was he easily swayed by them. He was easy in conversation, and he made himself pleasant without any offensive affectation. He took reasonable care of his health, not because he was attached to life, nor out of concern for his appearance, nor in a careless way, but so that through his own attention, he very seldom needed a doctor or medicine or external treatments. He was most ready to give without envy to those who had any special skill, such as eloquence or knowledge of the law or morals or anything else, and he gave them his help so that each might enjoy the reputation they deserved. He always acted according to the traditions of his country without pretending to do so. He was not fond of change nor was he unsteady. He liked to stay in the same places and to focus on the same things. After his headaches, he would return immediately fresh and vigorous to his usual activities. His secrets were very few and rare, and only about public matters. He showed prudence and economy in arranging public spectacles and in constructing public buildings, in his donations to the people, and in other such things. He was a man who looked at what needed to be done, not at the reputation that might come from doing it. He didn't take baths at odd hours. He wasn't interested in building houses, or curious about what he ate, or about the texture and color of his clothes, or about the beauty of his slaves. His clothes came from Lorium, his villa on the coast, and from Lanuvium generally. We know how he behaved toward the toll-collector at Tusculum who asked his pardon. All his behavior was like this. There was nothing harsh, implacable, or violent in him. You could say that he never broke a sweat. He examined everything one by one as if he had all the time in the world, without confusion, in an orderly way, energetically and consistently. The saying about Socrates could be applied to him: that he was able both to abstain from and to enjoy those things which many are too weak to abstain from and cannot enjoy without excess. But to be strong enough both to bear one and to be moderate in the other is the mark of a man who has a perfect and invincible soul, as he showed in the illness of Maximus.

I owe to the gods that I had good grandfathers, good parents, a good sister, good teachers, good relatives, and friends—almost everything good. I also owe it to the gods that I was not pushed into any offense against any of them, though I had a nature which, if the opportunity had come, might have led me to do something wrong. But through their favor, there was never such a combination of circumstances as put me to the test. I am also thankful to the gods that I was not raised for a long time with my grandfather's concubine, that I kept the flower of my youth, and that I did not prove my manhood before the proper time, but even delayed it. I was subjected to a ruler and a father who was able to take away all pride from me and to bring me to the realization that it is possible for a man to live in a palace without wanting guards, fancy dresses, torches, statues, and other such showy things. A man in such a position can bring himself very close to living like an ordinary person, without being any lower in thought or more careless in action with respect to the things that must be done for the public good in a way that fits a ruler. I thank the gods for giving me such a brother who was able, by his moral character, to make me watchful over myself, and who at the same time pleased me with his respect and affection. I am thankful that my children have not been stupid or deformed in body. I am grateful that I didn't make more progress in rhetoric, poetry, and other studies, in which I might have been completely absorbed if I had seen that I was improving in them. I am glad that I quickly placed those who brought me up in the position of honor that they seemed to desire, without making them wait with the hope that I would do it later because they were still young. I am thankful that I knew Apollonius, Rusticus, and Maximus, and that I received clear and frequent impressions about living according to nature and what kind of life that is. So far as it depended on the gods, their gifts, help, and inspirations, nothing stopped me from living according to nature, though I still fall short of it because of my own fault and because I don't pay attention to the warnings of the gods, and, I may almost say, their direct instructions. I am grateful that my body has held out so long in such a life. I am thankful that I never touched either Benedicta or Theodotus, and that, after falling into romantic passions, I was cured. Even though I was often upset with Rusticus, I never did anything that I had reason to regret. I am thankful that, even though it was my mother's fate to die young, she spent the last years of her life with me. Whenever I wanted to help someone in need, or on any other occasion, I was never told that I didn't have the means to do it. I am also grateful that I never had to receive anything from another. I am thankful that I have such an obedient, affectionate, and simple wife. I am thankful that I had many good teachers for my children. I am also grateful that remedies have been shown to me by dreams, both for other things and for spitting blood and dizziness. I am thankful that when I wanted to study philosophy, I didn't fall into the hands of any sophist, and that I didn't waste my time on writers of histories, or in resolving complex arguments, or in studying appearances in the heavens. All these things required the help of the gods and fortune.

These reflections were written while I was among the Quadi, near the Granua River.

Book 2

Begin each morning by reminding yourself: today, I will meet people who are nosy, ungrateful, arrogant, deceitful, jealous, and unfriendly. They behave this way because they don't understand what is truly good or bad. But I know that the nature of good is what is right, and the nature of bad is what is wrong. I understand that those who do wrong are related to me, not just by blood, but because we share the same intelligence and divine spark. Therefore, they cannot truly harm me, nor can I be angry or hate them, for we are meant to work together, like feet, hands, eyelids, or the rows of upper and lower teeth. To fight against each other is against our nature, just as it is to be annoyed or to turn away from one another.

Remember that you are made up of a little flesh, some breath, and a guiding mind. Let go of distractions, like books, and focus on your true self. You don't have time to waste as if you were on the edge of death. Disregard the flesh—it is just blood and bones, a network of nerves, veins, and arteries. Consider your breath, too—it is just air, which is constantly expelled and drawn in. The most important part is the guiding mind: remember that you are aging and should not allow it to be controlled by unsocial impulses or be dissatisfied with life or fearful of the future.

Everything from the gods is full of purpose. What comes from fortune is connected with nature and is part of the divine plan. Everything flows from this source, including necessity and what benefits the entire universe, of which you are a part. What is good for every part of nature is what maintains and supports it. The universe is preserved by the changing elements and the transformation of things made from these elements. Let these principles be your foundation, and hold them as unshakeable truths. Set aside your desire for books so that you may die content and grateful to the gods.

Remember how long you've been delaying, how often the gods have given you opportunities, yet you've not taken them. It is time to understand which universe you are part of and recognize the divine source from which you come. There is limited time for you to clear your mind of confusion, and if you don't use it, it will be gone and will not return.

In every moment, act as a Roman and a human being by doing your tasks with dignity, kindness, freedom, and justice. Let go of all other thoughts by acting as if each task were your last. Let go of carelessness, resistance to reason, hypocrisy, selfishness, and dissatisfaction with your life. Notice how few things are needed to live a life that flows with peace and resembles the existence of the gods. The gods require nothing more from someone who follows these principles.

My soul, don't harm yourself any longer; you may not have another chance to honor yourself. Every person's life is complete, yet yours is nearly over, and you have not yet respected your own soul, instead seeking happiness in others' opinions.

Do external distractions bother you? Give yourself time to learn new and good things and stop being whirled around. But avoid being led astray by trivial activities that leave you without a purpose or clear thoughts.

People rarely become unhappy by not knowing what's in another person's mind, but those who don't understand their own minds will inevitably be unhappy.

Always keep in mind the nature of the whole universe and your nature and how they relate. No one can stop you from doing and saying things that align with your true nature.

The philosopher Theophrastus said that offenses driven by desire are worse than those caused by anger. When someone is angry, they may act against reason with pain and impulse, but someone driven by desire is controlled by pleasure and acts without self-control. He rightly said that actions driven by pleasure are more blameworthy than those driven by pain. Someone who acts out of anger may feel wronged, but someone who acts out of desire is driven to do wrong by their impulses.

Since you could leave this life at any moment, act and think as if this were true. Leaving this world shouldn't frighten you if the gods exist, for they wouldn't harm you. And if they don't exist, or don't care for human affairs, then why should it matter to live in a world without gods or purpose? But the gods do exist, and they do care for humans, and they've given us the means to avoid true evils. If there were real evils, they would ensure that we wouldn't fall into them. What doesn't make a person worse can't make their life worse. The universe hasn't overlooked this, nor made mistakes by letting good and bad happen randomly. Death, life, honor, dishonor, pain, and pleasure all happen to both good and bad people, and they don't make us better or worse, so they are neither good nor bad.

All things quickly fade: bodies disappear, and even their memories vanish. The nature of all things that bring pleasure or cause fear or are celebrated by fame are worthless and fleeting. It is up to our mind to observe this. We should also notice who gives us a reputation and understand death. When analyzed, death is just a natural process, and to fear it is childish. It is not only a natural process but also serves nature's purposes. Consider how humans are close to the divine, and what part of us connects with it when we are aligned with nature.

There is nothing more miserable than a person who is constantly running around in circles, trying to figure out everything. Like the poet said, they dig deep into the earth, searching for signs to guess what others are thinking. They don't realize that it's enough to focus on the divine spirit within themselves and serve it sincerely. This service means keeping it free from passion, trivial thoughts, and dissatisfaction with what happens, whether it comes from gods or men. What comes from the gods should be respected for its goodness, and what comes from men should be accepted because of our kinship. Sometimes, we may even feel pity for people due to their ignorance of what is good and bad, which is as serious a flaw as not being able to tell the difference between light and dark.

Even if you were going to live for three thousand years or even ten times that, remember that no one loses any life other than the one they are living now, nor lives any life other than the one they are losing. So, the longest and the shortest lives end up the same. The present moment is the same for everyone, though what is passing is different. Therefore, what is lost seems like just a brief moment. No one can lose either the past or the future, because how could someone take away what you don't have?

Remember these two things: First, everything has been the same from eternity and will keep coming back in a cycle, so it doesn't matter if a person sees the same things for a hundred years, two hundred, or forever. Second, both the longest-lived and the one who dies soonest lose the same thing—the present moment. This is the only thing we can be deprived of because it's the only thing we truly have, and we cannot lose what we don't have.

Remember that everything is just as we think it is. The Cynic philosopher Monimus pointed this out, and it's clear that his saying is useful if we take what is true from it.

The soul harms itself first when it becomes like a sore or tumor on the universe, as much as it can. To be upset by anything that happens is to separate ourselves from nature, of which we are all a part. Second, the soul harms itself when it turns away from another person or moves toward them with the intention of harming them, as with those who are angry. Third, the soul harms itself when it is overpowered by pleasure or pain. Fourth, when it acts insincerely, saying or doing anything false. Fifth, when it allows any action of its own to be without a purpose, acting thoughtlessly without considering what it's doing. Even the smallest things should be done with a goal in mind. The goal for rational beings is to follow reason and the law of the oldest and most respected state—the Universe.

In human life, time is just a moment, everything is in flux, our perception is dull, our bodies are rotting, our minds are spinning, fortune is hard to predict, and fame is lacking in judgment. To sum it up, everything related to the body flows away like a river, everything related to the soul is like a dream and vapor, life is a battle and a temporary stay in a strange land, and after fame comes oblivion. What, then, can guide us? One thing, and one thing only—philosophy. This means keeping the divine spirit within us free from harm and violence, superior to pleasure and pain, acting with purpose, truthfully and without hypocrisy, and not needing others to act or refrain from acting. It also means accepting everything that happens and everything that is allotted to us as coming from the same place from which we ourselves came. Finally, it means waiting for death with a cheerful mind, knowing that death is nothing more than the dissolution of the elements of which every living being is made. If the elements themselves are not harmed by constantly changing into each other, why should we fear the change and dissolution of all the elements? This is according to nature, and nothing that follows nature is evil.

This was written during my time in Carnuntum.

Book 3

Written in Carnuntum.

We should think about how our life is getting shorter every day, and how we have less and less time left. But there's something else to consider too: even if we live longer, we can't be sure that our mind will stay sharp enough to understand things the way we do now, and to keep thinking about both the divine and human things. If our mind starts to weaken, things like breathing, eating, imagining, and desiring will still work, but our ability to use our mind properly, to understand what we need to do, to separate truth from lies, and to decide if it's time to leave this life, all of these important abilities will be gone. So, we must act quickly, not just because we're getting closer to death every day, but also because our understanding and clarity of thought will fade away before our life does.

We should also notice that even the little things that happen in nature have their own kind of beauty. For example, when bread is baking, it sometimes cracks open on the top. These cracks might seem like a mistake, but they actually look nice and make us want to eat the bread. When figs are fully ripe, they split open, and even though this might look like they're about to rot, it still makes them look beautiful. The same goes for ripe olives and many other things in nature. If you look at these things by themselves, they might not seem beautiful, but because they happen naturally, they add beauty to the whole. So, if someone understands how nature works, they will find beauty in almost everything, even in things that might not look nice at first. Such a person can even enjoy the sight of wild animals, not just the paintings or sculptures of them. They can see beauty in an old woman or man, and even in young people, they will see beauty in a pure and respectful way. But this kind of appreciation is not for everyone, only for those who truly understand and love nature and its works.

Hippocrates, a famous doctor who cured many diseases, eventually got sick and died himself. The Chaldeans, who were known for predicting the future, couldn't avoid their own fates. Great leaders like Alexander, Pompey, and Julius Caesar, who destroyed entire cities and killed many soldiers, eventually died too. Heraclitus, who spent his life thinking about the universe, died from an illness that filled him with water. Democritus was killed by lice, and Socrates was also killed by vermin. What does all this mean? It means that life is like a journey on a ship—you board, you sail, and then you reach the shore. When you get there, it's time to leave. If there's another life after this one, the gods will be there too. But if there's nothing after, you'll stop feeling pain and pleasure, and you'll no longer be a slave to your body, which is just made of earth and blood, while your mind is something divine.

Do not waste the rest of your life by thinking about what others are doing unless it is relevant to some common good. When you spend time thinking about what someone else is doing, why they are doing it, what they are saying, what they are thinking, or what they are planning, you lose the chance to focus on your own mind. We should stop any thoughts that have no purpose and are useless, especially those that are overly curious or harmful. A person should train themselves to think only about things that, if someone suddenly asked, "What are you thinking about now?" you could answer immediately and honestly, "This or that." Your answer should show that everything in your mind is simple, kind, and fitting for a social being. Your thoughts should not be about pleasure or indulgence, rivalry, envy, suspicion, or anything else that would make you ashamed to admit what you are thinking.

A person like this, who no longer delays becoming one of the best, is like a priest and servant of the gods, using the divine spirit within them. This makes the person pure, unaffected by pleasure, unharmed by pain, untouched by insults, and free from feeling wronged. Such a person fights the noblest fight, one where no passion can overpower them. They are deeply just, accepting with all their soul everything that happens and is given to them as their share. They rarely, and only when absolutely necessary for the common good, think about what others are saying, doing, or thinking. They focus only on their own actions and the part of life that has been assigned to them. They make sure their own actions are good and believe that their own portion of life is good. Each person's destiny is part of them, and they move forward together with it.

They also remember that every rational being is a relative, and that caring for others is part of human nature. However, they do not hold on to the opinions of everyone, only of those who clearly live according to nature. As for those who do not live this way, they always remember what kind of people they are, both in private and in public, both day and night, and the kind of company they keep. Therefore, they do not value the praise of such people because those people are not even satisfied with themselves.

Do not work unwillingly, selfishly, or without careful thought, or while being distracted. Do not try to make your thoughts sound fancy, and do not be a person who talks too much or tries to do too many things. Additionally, let the divine spirit within you be the protector of a person who is mature, manly, involved in public affairs, Roman, and a leader. Be someone who is ready to leave life when the signal comes, without needing oaths or other people's approval. Be cheerful, and do not seek help from outside or rely on the peace that others can give. A person must stand upright, not be held up by others.

If you find anything in human life better than justice, truth, temperance, fortitude, and, in short, anything better than your own mind's satisfaction in doing what is right according to reason, and in accepting the life given to you without your own choice, then turn to that with all your soul and enjoy what you have found to be the best. But if nothing seems better than the divine spirit within you, which controls all your desires, carefully examines all your thoughts, and, as Socrates said, separates itself from the influence of the senses and submits to the gods while caring for mankind, then do not give any space to anything else. If you let anything else take its place, you will not be able to focus without distraction on the good that is truly yours.

It is not right that anything else, like praise from others, power, or enjoyment of pleasure, should compete with what is rational and truly good. These other things may seem to fit with what is better in a small way, but they quickly take control and lead us away. So, I say, simply and freely choose the better and stick to it.

What is useful is the better. If it is useful to you as a rational being, then keep to it; but if it is only useful to you as an animal, say so and stick to your judgment without arrogance. Just be sure that you make this decision carefully.

Never consider anything good for yourself that would force you to break a promise, lose your self-respect, hate anyone, be suspicious, curse, act dishonestly, or desire anything that requires secrecy. The person who puts their intelligence, spirit, and worship of what is excellent above everything else does not act tragically, does not groan, and does not need either solitude or large crowds. Most importantly, they live without either chasing after or running away from death. Whether they live with the soul inside their body for a long time or a short time, they do not care at all. Even if they must leave immediately, they will do so as readily as they would perform any other action that can be done with decency and order. Throughout life, they only make sure that their thoughts do not stray from what belongs to an intelligent animal and a member of a community.

In the mind of someone who is disciplined and pure, you will find no corruption, no festering wounds, and no sores that are just covered up. Their life does not feel incomplete when fate comes for them, just as an actor does not leave the stage before finishing the play. There is nothing servile, fake, overly attached, or detached in them, nothing that deserves blame, and nothing that seeks to hide.

Respect the ability that forms your opinions. Everything depends on whether your opinions agree with the nature and constitution of a rational being. This ability promises freedom from rash judgments, friendship towards others, and obedience to the gods.

Therefore, hold on to these few things and let go of everything else. Remember that every person lives only in the present moment, which is a small, indivisible point in time, and that the rest of their life is either in the past or uncertain. The time each person lives is short, the part of the earth where they live is small, and even the longest-lasting fame is short and will be passed on by people who will soon die and who do not even know themselves, much less someone who died long ago.

To the aids that have been mentioned, add this one: Make for yourself a clear description of whatever comes to your mind so that you can see clearly what kind of thing it is in its true form, completely and entirely, and tell yourself its proper name, the names of its parts, and what it will become. Nothing is more effective in elevating the mind than being able to examine each thing you encounter in life methodically and truthfully. Always look at things in a way that allows you to see what kind of universe this is, what role everything plays in it, what value everything has for the whole, and what value it has for a person, who is a citizen of the highest city, of which all other cities are like families. Consider what each thing is, what it is made of, how long it will last, and what virtue you need to face it, such as gentleness, courage, truthfulness, loyalty, simplicity, or contentment. On every occasion, a person should say, "This comes from God," or "This is according to the plan of destiny," or "This is from someone who is like me, a relative, but who does not know what is truly natural." But I know, and for this reason, I behave towards them with kindness and justice, following the natural law of fellowship. At the same time, in things that are indifferent, I try to determine their true value.

If you work on what is in front of you, following right reason seriously, vigorously, calmly, and without letting anything distract you, while keeping your divine part pure as if you had to give it back immediately, if you hold on to this, expecting nothing, fearing nothing, and being satisfied with your present actions according to nature, and if you speak the truth in every word and action, you will live happily. And no one can prevent this.

Just as doctors always have their instruments and knives ready for emergencies, you should always have principles ready for understanding both divine and human things and for doing everything, even the smallest task, with an awareness of the bond that unites the divine and human. You will not do anything well that belongs to humans without also referring to the divine, and the same is true in reverse.

No longer wander aimlessly; you will not read your own memoirs, nor the acts of the ancient Romans and Greeks, nor the selections from books that you were saving for old age. Hurry then to the goal before you, and, abandoning idle hopes, help yourself if you care for yourself while it is still possible.

They do not know how many things are signified by the words stealing, sowing, buying, staying quiet, or seeing what needs to be done, for this is not done by the eyes, but by a different kind of vision.

Body, soul, and mind: the body perceives through the senses, the soul has desires, and the mind has principles. Receiving sensory impressions is something even animals do; being driven by desires is common to both wild beasts and men who have become weak, and to tyrants like Phalaris and Nero. Having the mind to guide what seems appropriate is also found in those who do not believe in the gods, betray their country, and commit immoral acts in secret. If everything else I mentioned is shared by many, then what remains unique to a good person is being pleased and content with what happens, and with the fate assigned to them, not polluting the divine spirit within, and not disturbing it with a flood of images. Instead, they keep it calm, following it obediently as a god, never saying anything untrue or doing anything unjust. If everyone doubts that this person lives a simple, modest, and content life, he is not angry with them, nor does he stray from the path that leads to the end of life, which he should reach pure, calm, ready to leave, and in complete acceptance of his fate.

Book 4

The ruling part within us, when aligned with nature, adapts easily to whatever happens and is presented to it. It doesn't need specific materials but works toward its purpose under certain conditions. It creates its own path from obstacles, just as fire consumes what falls into it, making it grow stronger and higher.

Let every action have a purpose and align with the perfect principles of the art of life. People seek retreats for themselves—houses in the country, by the sea, or in the mountains—and you might desire such things too. But this is common thinking, for you can retreat into yourself anytime you choose. Nowhere can a person find more quiet or freedom from trouble than within his own soul, especially when he has thoughts that bring immediate tranquility. I affirm that tranquility is nothing more than the proper ordering of the mind. Constantly give yourself this retreat and renew yourself. Let your guiding principles be brief and fundamental, so they can cleanse your soul and free you from discontent with the world.

What are you upset about? Is it because of the bad behavior of others? Remember this: rational creatures are made to help each other, and being patient with others is part of being just. People don't do wrong on purpose. Think about how many people have fought, hated, and hurt each other, only to end up dead and turned to ashes. So calm yourself. Or maybe you're unhappy with what life has given you. Then remember this choice: either there is a higher plan guiding everything, or everything happens by chance. Or think about the arguments that prove the world is like a big community, and find peace in that.

But maybe physical things still bother you. In that case, remember that your mind is separate from the body, whether the body is calm or troubled. Once your mind realizes its own power, it doesn't need to be affected by the body. Also, think about everything you've learned about dealing with pain and pleasure, and find peace.

Or maybe you're worried about fame. Think about how quickly people forget everything and how endless time stretches out before and after us. Fame is empty, and the opinions of those who praise you are often unreliable. The space in which people praise you is so small, and the people who do it are so few and insignificant.

So, retreat into your own mind and be free. Don't let yourself be distracted or stressed. Look at things as a human being, as a citizen, and as someone who is mortal. Keep two ideas in mind: first, that things outside of you don't really touch your soul; they remain outside and can't move you unless you let them. Second, that all the things you see are constantly changing and will soon be gone. Remember how many changes you've already seen. The universe is always changing, and life is shaped by our opinions.

If our minds are shared, then so is the reason that makes us rational beings. If that's true, then the reason that tells us what to do and what not to do is also shared. If that's true, then we share a common law. If that's true, then we are fellow citizens. If that's true, then we are part of a community. And if that's true, then the world is like a single city. What other community could all humans be members of? And from this shared community comes our very mind, our reason, and our sense of law. Where else could they come from? Just as my body comes from the earth, and the water in me comes from some source, and the heat in me from another, so too my mind must come from some source.

Death is just like birth—a mystery of nature. It's the same elements being combined and then separated. It's nothing to be ashamed of because it's not unnatural for a rational being, and it's not against the reason we are made with.

It's natural for certain people to act a certain way, and it's unavoidable. If you wish it were different, it's like wanting figs to stop producing juice. But remember that in a short time, both you and the person who bothers you will be dead, and soon after, not even your names will be remembered.

If you take away your opinion that you've been hurt, then the hurt itself disappears. And if you take away the feeling that you've been harmed, then there is no harm.

Whatever doesn't make a person worse in themselves doesn't make their life worse either. It can't hurt them from the outside or the inside.

The nature of what is beneficial had to act this way.

Think about it: everything that happens, happens justly. If you look closely, you'll see this is true, not just in how events follow each other, but in the sense that everything happens as it should, as if someone were assigning each thing its place. So keep observing, and in whatever you do, aim to be good and to act as a good person should in every situation.

When someone wrongs you, don't see things the way they do or the way they want you to see them. Instead, see things as they truly are.

Always keep these two principles ready: first, to do only what reason and fairness suggest is good for people. Second, to be willing to change your opinion if someone convinces you that you're wrong. But this change should only come from a clear understanding of what is just or beneficial, not just because it feels good or brings approval.

Do you have reason? Yes, you do. So why not use it? If reason is doing its job, what else could you want?

You have existed as part of the Whole. You will disappear into what made you, but really, you will be taken back into the source that created everything.

Many grains of incense are placed on the same altar. One burns away first, another later, but it doesn't matter.

In just a few days, you could seem like a god to the people who now see you as an animal or a fool—if you return to your principles and the worship of reason.

Don't act as if you're going to live for ten thousand years. Death hangs over you. While you live, while it's in your power, be good.

Think about how much peace you gain when you don't worry about what your neighbor says, does, or thinks, but focus only on making sure your own actions are just and pure. Or as Agathon said, don't look around at the bad behavior of others, but keep your path straight.

If you're obsessed with posthumous fame, consider this: everyone who remembers you will soon be dead too. Then those who come after them will also die, until all memory of you is extinguished. Even if people remember you forever, what does that matter to you? I don't mean just to the dead, but to the living—what's the point of praise, except if it has some practical benefit? By focusing on fame, you are rejecting the gift of nature and clinging to something else.

Everything that is beautiful is beautiful in itself and is complete in itself. Praise is not part of what makes it beautiful. Whether or not it's praised, it's neither better nor worse. This is true even of things commonly considered beautiful, like material objects or works of art. Something that is truly beautiful doesn't need anything else, not more than law, not more than truth, not more than kindness or modesty. Which of these things becomes beautiful because it is praised or is ruined by being blamed? Is an emerald less valuable if no one praises it? What about gold, ivory, purple, a lyre, a knife, a flower, or a bush?

If souls continue to exist, how does the air hold all of them from the beginning of time? But how does the earth hold all the bodies that have been buried since time began? Just as the earth eventually breaks down these bodies to make room for others, so too the air transforms souls, making room for new ones. This could be one explanation if we believe that souls live on. But we should also think about the number of animals eaten every day by us and other creatures—an enormous number, yet the earth still has room for them because they transform into blood and other elements.

How do we seek the truth in this matter? By separating what is material from what is the cause of form.

Don't let yourself be swept away. In every action, keep justice in mind, and in every thought, stick to what is certain.

Everything that happens is in harmony with you, O Universe. Nothing is too early or too late if it happens at the right time for you. Everything that comes to me is like fruit from your seasons, O Nature. From you come all things, in you are all things, and to you, all things return. The poet says, "Dear city of Cecrops," and should you not say, "Dear city of Zeus"?

Keep yourself occupied with few things, says the philosopher, if you want to be calm. But consider if it wouldn't be better to do only what is necessary, what reason and the social nature of humans demand, and to do it in the way that reason requires. This brings both the peace that comes from doing good and the peace that comes from doing few things. Most of what we say and do is unnecessary. If you can remove unnecessary things, you will have more time and less stress. So on every occasion, ask yourself, "Is this one of the unnecessary things?" And don't just remove unnecessary actions, but unnecessary thoughts too, so that unnecessary actions won't follow.

Try living the life of a good person—someone who is satisfied with their place in the world and with their own just actions and kind disposition.

Have you seen these things? Then look at them again. Don't upset yourself. Be simple. Does someone do wrong? They do wrong to themselves. Has something happened to you? Well, everything that happens has been arranged by the universe from the beginning and has been given to you as part of your destiny. In short, life is short. Use the present moment wisely with reason and justice. Be calm and relaxed.

Either the universe is well-organized, or it's a chaotic mix of elements, but still a universe. But can there be order within you if there is disorder in the whole? Especially when all things are connected and influence each other.

A black character, a weak character, a stubborn character, a beastly character, a childish character, a foolish character, a false character, a cruel character, a deceitful character, a tyrannical character.

If someone doesn't understand what's in the universe, they are a stranger in it. If they don't understand what's happening in it, they are also a stranger. They are like someone running away if they reject social reason. They are blind if they close their mind's eye. They are poor if they depend on others and don't have everything they need within themselves. They are a tumor on the universe if they separate themselves from the common nature through dissatisfaction with what happens because the same nature produces everything, including them. They are torn away from the community if they separate their soul from the soul of all rational beings, which is one.

One philosopher has no shirt, another has no book. Here is someone else who is half-naked: "I have no bread," he says, "but I stick to reason." But I have all the food of learning, and yet I am not faithful.

Love the art you have learned, and take comfort in it. Go through the rest of your life with sincere commitment to the gods, never making yourself a tyrant or a slave to anyone.

Consider, for example, the time of Vespasian. You will see the same things happening: people marrying, having children, getting sick, dying, fighting, feasting, trading, farming, flattering, being arrogant, suspecting others, plotting, wishing for others to die, complaining about their lot, falling in love, gathering wealth, wanting political power. And now, that life is gone. Look at the time of Trajan. Again, the same things happened, and that life too is gone. Similarly, look at the histories of other times and nations, and see how many lives, after much effort, quickly fell apart and returned to the elements. But most importantly, remember those you have known yourself, who distracted themselves with empty things and neglected to live according to their true nature, to hold on to it firmly and find contentment in it. And remember that the attention you give to each action should be in proportion to its importance. This way, you won't be dissatisfied if you only devote as much time as necessary to less important matters.

Words that were common long ago are now outdated, and so too are the names of people who were once famous—like Camillus, Caeso, Volesus, Dentatus, and later Scipio and Cato, then Augustus, and then Hadrian and Antoninus. All things quickly fade and turn into mere stories, and complete oblivion soon buries them. And I'm talking about those who shone with great brilliance. For the rest, as soon as they breathe their last, they are gone, and no one talks about them. And in the end, what is even an eternal memory? It's nothing. So what should we focus on? Only this: just thoughts, social actions, honest words, and a disposition that gladly accepts everything that happens as necessary, understandable, and coming from a reasonable source.

Willingly submit yourself to Clotho, one of the Fates, allowing her to spin your thread into whatever she chooses.

Everything is fleeting—both the memory of things and the things themselves.

Constantly observe how everything changes and get used to the idea that the universe loves nothing more than to change old things into new ones. Everything that exists is like a seed of what will come next. But you might be thinking only of seeds that are planted in the earth or a womb. That's a very simple way of thinking.

You will soon die, and you are not yet calm, free from disturbances, unafraid of external harm, kind to all people, or convinced that acting justly is the only wisdom.

Look into the minds of others, even those who are wise, and see what they avoid and what they pursue.

What is evil to you does not exist in the mind of another, nor in any change of your body. Where is it, then? It is in your own mind, in the part that forms opinions about what is evil. Let this part not form such opinions, and all will be well. Even if your body is hurt, burned, or decays, let the part of you that judges these things remain calm. It should understand that nothing is truly bad or good that can happen equally to both bad and good people. For what happens equally to those who live according to nature and those who live against nature is neither in line with nature nor against it.

Always think of the universe as one living being, made of one substance and one soul. Notice how everything is connected to one understanding, how everything works together, and how all things are part of everything else. Observe the continuous weaving of the threads and the interconnection of the web.

You are a small soul carrying a dead body, as Epictetus used to say.

It's not bad for things to change, and it's not good for things to stay the same because of change.

Time is like a river of events, a powerful stream. As soon as one thing appears, it's swept away, and another takes its place, and this too will be carried away.

Everything that happens is as natural and expected as roses in spring and fruit in summer—like disease, death, slander, and betrayal, and all the things that either delight or trouble foolish people.

In the chain of events, those that come after always fit with those that came before. This chain is not just a list of disconnected things but a rational connection. Just as everything that exists is harmoniously arranged, so too do the things that happen show a wonderful relationship.

Always remember Heraclitus's saying that the death of earth is to become water, the death of water is to become air, and the death of air is to become fire, and vice versa. Remember also that people forget where the path leads and that they quarrel with the reason that governs the universe, even though they interact with it constantly. They find everyday things surprising, but we should not act and speak as if we were asleep, even though in sleep we seem to act and speak. We should not simply accept what we are taught like children with their parents.

If a god told you that you would die tomorrow or the day after tomorrow, you wouldn't care much whether it was the third day or the next day, unless you were extremely fearful because the difference is so small. So think it's no big deal to die after however many years you can name rather than tomorrow.

Think constantly about how many doctors have died after worrying about their patients, how many astrologers have died after predicting the deaths of others, how many philosophers have died after debating endlessly about death or immortality, how many heroes have died after killing thousands, how many tyrants have died after using their power over life and death with cruelty, as if they were immortal. And think about how many cities are now completely gone, like Helice, Pompeii, Herculaneum, and countless others. Consider all the people you've known, one after the other: one man buries another, and then he is buried, and all this happens in a short time. The conclusion is that you should always see human life as brief and of little value. Yesterday, you were just a drop of semen; tomorrow, you'll be a mummy or ashes. So live according to nature, and when your time comes, leave life content, like an olive that falls when it is ripe, blessing the earth that bore it and thanking the tree on which it grew.

Be like the rocky headland against which the waves constantly break. It stands firm and calms the fury of the water around it.

You might think, "It's my bad luck that this happened to me." But you should say, "It's my good luck that although this happened to me, I can endure it without pain, without being crushed by the present or afraid of the future." Because something like this could happen to anyone, but not everyone could bear it without pain. So why consider the event more of a misfortune than your ability to endure it a good fortune? And would you call anything a misfortune for a person that isn't a deviation from human nature? And does something seem to you to be a deviation from human nature if it doesn't go against what human nature intends? Well, you know what the purpose of nature is. So will this thing that has happened stop you from being just, courageous, self-controlled, wise, careful in your decisions, truthful, honorable, and free? Or from having all the other qualities that, when combined, fulfill human nature? So, in any situation that might make you sad, remember this principle: "This is not a misfortune, but to bear it well is good fortune."

It's a simple but effective way to lessen your fear of death by thinking about those who clung to life for a long time. What did they gain compared to those who died young? In the end, they all lie in their graves—like Caedicianus, Fabius, Julianus, Lepidus, and all the others who attended many funerals and then had their own. The time we have to live is short, and we drag it out with such effort, in poor company, in weak bodies. So don't consider life a great thing. Look at the endless time behind you and the infinity ahead of you. In this vastness, what is the difference between someone who lives for three days and someone who lives for three generations?

Always take the shortest path, and the shortest path is the natural one. Do and say everything according to the soundest reason. For such a purpose frees a person from trouble, from conflict, and from all artifice and display.

Book 5

When you wake up in the morning and don't feel like getting up, remind yourself: "I'm getting up to do the work of a human being." So why am I unhappy if I'm about to do what I was made for, the purpose for which I was brought into the world? Or was I made just to stay in bed and keep warm? But staying in bed feels so nice. Were you made to enjoy comfort, or were you made for action and effort? Don't you see how little plants, birds, ants, spiders, and bees all work together to make the world what it is? And yet you're unwilling to do the work of a human being and hurry to do what's natural to you? But we need rest too. Yes, rest is necessary, but nature has set limits to this, just like with eating and drinking, and yet you often go beyond these limits, beyond what's enough; but in your actions, you stop short of what you could do. This means you don't really love yourself, because if you did, you would love your nature and its purpose. Other people who love their work push themselves to the point of neglecting washing and eating. But you value your own nature less than a craftsman values his craft, or a dancer values dancing, or a lover of money values his wealth, or a person who loves fame values his reputation. Such people, when they are passionate about something, will skip meals and sleep rather than stop perfecting what they care about. But do you see the acts that benefit society as less important and less deserving of your effort?

It's easy to push away or erase any troubling or inappropriate thoughts and immediately find calm.

Consider any word or action that aligns with nature to be appropriate for you; don't let criticism or the opinions of others make you doubt yourself. If something is good to do or say, don't consider it beneath you. Others have their own principles and follow their own paths; don't be distracted by them. Stay on your path, which is aligned with both your nature and the universal nature—they are one and the same.

I continue through life according to nature until I fall and rest, breathing my last breath into the air from which I draw it daily, and returning to the earth that gave my father his seed, my mother her blood, and my nurse her milk; the earth that has fed and watered me for so many years; the earth that bears my footsteps and endures all the ways I use and abuse it.

People may not admire you for your intellect. So be it. But there are many other qualities you can't say you lack by nature. So show those virtues that are entirely within your power—honesty, dignity, hard work, self-discipline, contentment with what you have, kindness, openness, simplicity, moderation, and magnanimity. Don't you see how many qualities you can display without needing any special talent?

And yet you still choose to fall short. Or do you think your lack of natural talent forces you to complain, to be stingy, to flatter, to criticize your own body, to try to please others, to boast, or to let your mind be so restless? No, by the gods, it does not! You could have freed yourself from these things long ago. If you are slow to understand, work on it—don't ignore it or take pleasure in your dullness.

Some people, when they do a favor for someone else, expect to be thanked. Others don't expect thanks but still think of the other person as owing them something, and they remember what they've done. A third kind doesn't even think about what they've done, just like a vine that produces grapes and expects nothing more after it's borne its fruit. Just like a horse that runs, a dog that hunts, or a bee that makes honey, a person who does a good deed doesn't call for others to notice, but moves on to the next good deed, just as a vine moves on to bear grapes again in its season. So you should aim to be like those who are almost unaware of the good they do. But you might say, "Shouldn't I be aware of my actions? Isn't it part of being a social creature to know when I'm acting in a social way and to want others to recognize it too?" That's true, but you're misunderstanding my point. If you focus on understanding this, you won't fall into the trap I mentioned before. Even those who misunderstand what I'm saying do so because of a seemingly logical reason. But if you want to understand, don't worry that this will make you neglect your social duties.

The Athenians prayed:
"Rain, rain, O dear Zeus,
on the plowed fields
and plains of the Athenians."
We should pray in this simple and honest way, or not pray at all.

Just as people say that Asclepius prescribed horse-riding, or cold baths, or going barefoot to someone, we should think of nature as prescribing disease, injury, loss, or anything else of the kind. In the first case, "prescribed" means that it was ordered for the person's health. In the second, it means that what happens to each person is arranged as part of their destiny. We talk about things "fitting" just as masons say that stones fit together in walls or pyramids when they join in a certain way. In the whole of the universe, there is one harmony, and just as all bodies combine to make one harmonious whole, so all causes combine to make one harmonious destiny. Even those who don't know much can sense what I mean. They say, "It was fate that brought this on him." So if "brought," then also "prescribed." So let's accept these things as we accept Asclepius's prescriptions, even if some of them are harsh, because we trust they will lead to health.

You should take the same view of what happens to you as you do of your own health, and welcome everything that happens, even if it seems harsh, because it contributes to the health of the universe and the prosperity of Zeus. He wouldn't bring anything upon anyone unless it also benefited the Whole, just as no natural principle brings anything unsuitable to what it governs.

So there are two reasons you should be content with what happens to you. One, because it was meant for you and is related to you, like a thread of destiny spun for you from the very beginning. The other, because what happens to each individual contributes to the welfare, perfection, and even the very continuity of what governs the universe. For the integrity of the Whole is compromised if you cut off even the smallest part of its connection and continuity, whether of its parts or its causes. And you do cut something off when you fret about your lot; in a sense, this is an act of destruction.

Don't be disheartened or impatient if you don't succeed in doing everything according to the right principles. If you stumble, get back up, and be glad if most of your actions align with human nature. And love what you return to. Don't return to philosophy like a schoolboy returning to his teacher, but like a person with sore eyes returning to his sponge and ointment, or someone else returning to their bandage or compress. In this way, you'll show that following reason isn't a burden but a relief. Remember, philosophy requires only what your nature requires, but you wanted something unnatural. And what could be more pleasant than following your nature? This is how pleasure deceives us, but think whether there isn't something more pleasant in magnanimity, generosity, simplicity, consideration, or piety. And what could be more pleasant than wisdom itself, when you think of the security and peace it brings through understanding and knowledge?

Things are so wrapped up that several philosophers have thought them completely beyond understanding, and even the Stoics find them difficult. Every agreement we give to our perceptions is open to error. No one is infallible. So look at the objects of our experience—how short-lived they are, how poor in quality: even a criminal, a prostitute, or a thief could own them. Look also at the character of the people around you; it's hard to put up with even the best of them, let alone endure yourself. In all this darkness and filth, with everything constantly changing and passing away, what could possibly be worth valuing or pursuing? Instead, we should comfort ourselves with the thought of natural release, not being impatient for it, but holding on to two principles: one, that nothing will happen to me that isn't in line with the nature of the Whole, and two, that it's within my power not to act against my god and daemon, because no one can force me to do that.

What am I using my soul for right now? I must ask myself this on every occasion. I must examine myself and ask, "What kind of soul do I have right now?" Is it like that of a child, a young man, a woman, a tyrant, a domestic animal, or a wild beast?

We can understand what most people consider to be "good" by looking at their behavior. If someone truly valued qualities like wisdom, self-control, justice, and courage, they wouldn't be interested in anything that didn't align with those values. But if someone values what most people think is good, they'll readily agree with the comic writer who said that some people have so many goods they have no room to relieve themselves. This difference is obvious to most people. Otherwise, the saying wouldn't be offensive or rejected when applied to real goods, but we accept it when it's about wealth, luxury, and fame.

I'm made up of form and matter, and neither will disappear into nothingness, just as neither came into existence out of nothing. So every part of me will change and become some other part of the universe, and that part will change again into another part of the universe, and so on forever. The same process that brought me into existence also brought my parents into existence, and so on infinitely backward. Nothing prevents us from saying this, even if the universe follows definite cycles.

Reason and philosophy are powers that are sufficient for themselves and their own actions. They move from their own first principles to the end they aim for, which is why these actions are called "right" actions—they proceed along the right path.

You should ignore anything that isn't a part of your role as a human being. These things aren't required of you; they don't fulfill your nature or help you achieve your purpose. Therefore, they aren't good. Moreover, if any of these things were truly a part of you, it wouldn't be right for you to disdain them or resist them. We wouldn't praise someone for not needing them. If these things were truly good, then a person who deprives themselves of them or tolerates being deprived of them wouldn't be a good person. But in fact, the more a person deprives themselves of such things or tolerates their loss, the better they are.

Your mind will take on the character of your most frequent thoughts, for the soul is dyed by your thoughts. So dye your soul with a continuous series of thoughts like these: "Wherever a person can live, they can live well." But you must live in a palace. Well, then, you can live well in a palace. And again: "Each thing is made for a purpose, and it moves toward that purpose; its end lies in that toward which it moves; and where its end is, there also is its advantage and good." The good for a rational creature is community. It has been shown above that we are born for community. Is it not clear that the inferior exists for the sake of the superior? But things that have life are superior to those without life, and those with reason are superior to those without.

To seek what is impossible is madness, and it is impossible for bad people not to act according to their nature.

Nothing happens to any person that they are not naturally equipped to endure. The same things happen to others, and either because they don't realize it or because they show great spirit, they remain calm and unharmed. Isn't it strange that ignorance and arrogance can be stronger than wisdom?

Things themselves don't touch the soul at all; they have no entry to the soul and can't move it. The soul alone moves itself and makes whatever judgments it sees fit about the things presented to it.

In one respect, other people are the closest things to me because I must do good to them and tolerate them. But when some people obstruct my proper work, they become indifferent to me, no different than the sun, the wind, or a wild animal. These may impede some actions, but they don't impede my will or my disposition, which have the power to adapt and change. The mind converts and changes every hindrance to its activity into a help, so that what was an obstacle becomes a furtherance to the work.

Revere what is best in the universe: the power that uses all things and directs all things. Similarly, revere what is best in yourself: the power that uses everything else in you and governs your life.

What doesn't harm the community doesn't harm the citizen. Apply this rule in every situation where you think you've been harmed: if the community isn't harmed, neither am I. But if the community is harmed, you shouldn't be angry with the person who caused the harm—show them where they went wrong.

Think often of how quickly things pass by and disappear, both the things that are and the things that are produced. Existence is like a river in constant flow, with its actions always changing and its causes working in endless ways. Hardly anything stands still. And think of the vastness of the past and future, in which all things vanish. How foolish is it, then, to be puffed up with ambition, to struggle and worry over things, or to be upset about them as if they were permanent or could trouble you for long?

Think of the whole of existence, of which you are a tiny part; think of the whole of time, of which you have been assigned a brief and fleeting moment; think of destiny—what a small fraction of it are you?

Another person wrongs me. What's that to me? Let them deal with their own actions and disposition. I now have what the universal nature has given me, and I do what my own nature requires me to do.

Let the part of your soul that leads and governs stay undisturbed by the movements in the flesh, whether they are of pleasure or pain. Don't let it unite with them, but let it stay within its own bounds and limit those effects to their proper parts. But when these effects reach the mind through the natural connection that exists in a unified body, you shouldn't resist the sensation, for it is natural. But don't let the ruling part of yourself add the judgment that the sensation is either good or bad.

Live with the gods. And you live with the gods if you constantly show them that your soul is content with what is assigned to you and that it does everything your daemon wishes, which Zeus has given to every person as a guardian and guide—a part of himself. This is every person's understanding and reason.

Are you angry with someone whose armpits smell? Are you angry with someone whose breath is foul? What good will your anger do you? That's just the way his armpits or mouth are, and it's necessary that they produce such smells. But you might say, "He has reason, and if he tries, he can realize where he's offending." Good for you if he does! And you have reason too, so use your rational faculty to stir his rational faculty. Show him his mistake; correct him. If he listens, you'll cure him, and there's no need for anger.

You can live your life here on earth just as you intend to live when you've left it. But if people don't allow you to live as you wish, then leave life, but don't see it as a misfortune. "The house is smoky, so I'm leaving it." Why think this is such a big deal? But as long as nothing like that drives me out, I stay, I am free, and no one can stop me from doing what I choose to do. And I choose to do what is in line with the nature of a rational and social being.

The intelligence of the universe is social. It has made the lower things for the sake of the higher, and it has harmonized the higher with each other. You can see how it has arranged everything to fit together and work together, bringing the best things into unity.

How have you behaved so far toward the gods, your parents, siblings, wife, children, teachers, tutors, friends, relatives, and servants? Have you followed the principle of "do no harm" with all of them? Remind yourself of all you've been through and how much you've endured. Your life story is complete, your service is done. Think of how often you've seen beauty, disregarded pleasure and pain, rejected glory, and been kind to those who were unkind to you.

Why do unskilled and ignorant minds confuse those who have skill and knowledge? What kind of mind has true skill and knowledge? It's the mind that knows the beginning and the end and understands the reason that governs all existence, guiding the Whole through its appointed cycles for all eternity.

Soon, very soon, you'll be ashes or a skeleton, just a name or not even that. If you do have a name, it will be just a sound and an echo. The things people value in life are empty, rotten, and trivial—like little dogs biting each other or children quarreling, laughing, and then crying. But fidelity, modesty, justice, and truth have fled up to Olympus from the wide-spread earth.

So what's left to keep you here if the objects of sense are constantly changing and never stable, if our senses are dull and easily misled, and if the soul itself is just an exhalation of blood? To have a good reputation in such a world is meaningless. Why not wait calmly for your end, whether it's extinction or transition to another state? And until that time comes, what's enough? Only to worship and praise the gods, to do good to others, to practice tolerance and self-restraint.

And as for everything beyond the limits of your body and breath, remember that it's neither yours nor in your control.

You can always keep your life on the right path if you follow reason in your judgments and actions. Two things are common to the souls of all rational beings, both gods and humans: they are free from any external hindrance, and their good lies in a just disposition and just actions, with these being the limit of their desire.

If something isn't caused by my own wrongdoing, or if it isn't the result of any wrong done to me, and if it doesn't harm the community, then why should it trouble me? And what harm could it do to the community?

Don't let other people's grief carry you away indiscriminately. Help them as best you can and as the situation deserves, even if their grief is for the loss of something insignificant. But don't imagine their loss as any real harm—that's the wrong way to think. Instead, be like the old man in the play who reclaimed his foster child's favorite toy at the end, never forgetting that it was only a toy. So when you feel pity for others, remind yourself of what things are really worth. "Yes, but these things are important to them." Is that any reason for you to join in their foolishness?

"There was a time when everything seemed to go my way." But good fortune is what you make for yourself: and good fortune is having good inclinations, good impulses, and good actions.

Book 6

The universe is made up of a substance that can be shaped and directed, and the reason behind it has no intention to do harm. There is no malice in it, and nothing it creates is done wrongly or with ill intent. Everything that exists is made according to this reason.

If you are doing what you should be doing, it shouldn't matter whether you are cold or warm, sleepy or well-rested, praised or criticized, or even if you're close to death or busy with something else.

Dying is just another part of life, and in this, as in everything else, it's enough to do your best.

Look inside yourself. Don't overlook the unique quality or value of anything.

Everything that exists changes quickly. Things either turn into vapor if all substance is one, or they disperse into smaller parts.

The reason that governs everything knows its own nature, what it creates, and the material it uses to create.

The best way to get back at someone who has wronged you is not to become like them.

Take joy and find peace in moving from one good action to another, keeping your thoughts on the divine.

The mind is what wakes itself up, shapes itself, and decides how it wants to see everything that happens to it.

Everything in the universe happens according to its nature. It couldn't happen according to anything else—whether something outside controls it or it controls something within it.

The universe is either a random mix of things, where everything is jumbled together and eventually falls apart, or it is a unified whole with order and purpose. If it's the first, why do I care about anything? Why do I worry about anything other than the fact that I'll return to the earth someday? And if it's the second, I should respect it, stay firm, and trust in the one who governs it all.

When something upsets you, quickly return to your calm state. Don't stay out of harmony longer than necessary. You'll master this more by constantly returning to it.

If you had a stepmother and a mother at the same time, you'd pay attention to your stepmother, but you'd always go back to your mother. The court and philosophy should be like that to you: the court is your stepmother, and philosophy is your mother. Return to philosophy often and rest in her. She will help you see the court's demands as bearable, and make you bearable in the court.

When we have meat before us and other types of food, we should recognize that what we are seeing is the dead body of a fish, or the dead body of a bird, or the dead body of a pig. Similarly, when we look at Falernian wine, we should remember that it is nothing more than a little grape juice, and when we see a purple robe, we should realize that it is just some sheep's wool dyed with the blood of a shellfish. These are the real impressions of what these things truly are, and when we see them in this way, we penetrate their real nature and understand them for what they truly are. In the same way, throughout our lives, we should act by revealing the true nature of things that seem most worthy of our approval, laying them bare, and examining their lack of value. We should strip away all the words that make them seem grander than they are. Outward appearances can be a powerful deceiver of reason, and when you are most convinced that you are dealing with things that are worth your effort, it is then that they deceive you the most. So, consider what Crates said about Xenocrates himself.

Most of the things that the masses admire are basic objects, those that are held together by cohesion or natural structure, such as stones, wood, fig trees, vines, or olives. But the things that are admired by people who are slightly more reasonable are connected to things that are held together by a living principle, like flocks or herds of animals. The things admired by people who are even more educated are those that are connected to a rational soul, but not a universal soul, only rational to the extent that it is skilled in some art, or expert in some other way, or simply rational to the extent that it possesses a number of slaves. But the person who values a rational soul, a soul that is universal and fit for social life, cares for nothing else except this. Above all things, they keep their soul in a state and activity that conforms to reason and social life, and they work together with others who share the same kind of values.

Some things are rushing into existence, while others are rushing out. Even as something is born, part of it is already dying. The world is constantly being renewed by motions and changes, just as time keeps flowing endlessly. In this river of life, where nothing stays still, what is really worth valuing among all the things that rush by? It's like falling in love with a sparrow that flies by, but it's already gone out of sight. Life is just like that—transient, like a breath you take in and let out.

Breathing and taking in impressions are not things to be valued, just like how plants transpire and animals breathe. Nor is it valuable to be driven by desires like a puppet on strings or to gather in groups. Even eating is just about getting rid of the waste later. So, what should be valued? Applause? No. Nor should we value the clapping of tongues, which is just empty praise from the crowd. If you've given up on trivial fame, what's left to value? To me, it's this: to act or refrain from acting according to your own nature, as skills and crafts teach. Every craft aims to make its product fit for its purpose, just as a gardener, a horse-trainer, or a dog-trainer does. The same goes for educating and teaching young people. That's where the real value lies, and if you hold onto this, you won't need anything else. Will you not stop valuing so many other things too? Otherwise, you'll never be free, never be self-sufficient, and never be without passion. You'll be envious, jealous, and suspicious of those who can take away what you value, and you'll plot against those who have what you want. If you desire any of these things, you'll be in a state of turmoil, and you'll often find yourself blaming the gods. But if you honor and respect your own mind, you'll be content with yourself, in harmony with society, and in agreement with the gods, praising all that they give and have arranged.

Everything around you—the earth, the sky, the elements—is constantly in motion. But the movement of virtue doesn't follow these; it's something more divine and moves forward along a path that's hard to understand.

People act in strange ways! They won't praise those who are alive at the same time and living alongside them, but they place great value on being praised by future generations, by people they have never seen and never will see. This is very much like being upset because those who lived before you didn't praise you.

If something is difficult for you to accomplish, don't think that it is impossible for any person. But if something is possible for a human and in line with their nature, then you should believe that you can achieve it as well.

In gymnastic exercises, suppose someone scratches you with their nails or hits your head and causes a wound. We don't show signs of anger, nor are we offended, nor do we suspect them afterward as being treacherous. Yet, we remain cautious around them, not as an enemy, nor with suspicion, but simply by quietly staying out of their way. Let your behavior be like this in all parts of life. Let us overlook many things in people who are like opponents in the gymnasium. It is within our power, as I said, to avoid them without suspicion or hatred.

If anyone can convince me and show me that I am not thinking or acting correctly, I will gladly change, for I seek the truth, by which no one was ever harmed. But the person who stays in their error and ignorance is the one who is injured.

I do my duty; other things do not trouble me because they are either things without life, or things without reason, or things that have lost their way and do not know the right path.

As for animals that have no reason, and generally for all things and objects, since you have reason and they do not, make use of them with a generous and liberal spirit. But towards human beings, who do have reason, behave with a social spirit. And on all occasions, call on the gods, and do not trouble yourself about how long you shall do this; for even three hours spent this way are sufficient.

Alexander the Macedonian and his groom were brought to the same state by death; they were either received into the same primary elements of the universe, or they were equally dispersed among the atoms.

Consider how many things happen at the same moment within each of us—things that concern the body and things that concern the soul. So do not be surprised if many more things, or rather all things that exist in the one whole, which we call the Cosmos, exist at the same time.

If someone should ask you how the name Antoninus is written, would you loudly and impatiently shout out each letter? What if they become angry—will you become angry too? Wouldn't you rather calmly spell out each letter in order? In the same way, in this life, remember that every duty is made up of certain parts. It is your duty to observe these parts, and without being disturbed or showing anger towards those who are angry with you, continue on your way and complete what is set before you.

How cruel it is not to allow people to strive after the things that seem suitable to their nature and beneficial! Yet in some way, you do not allow them to do this when you are vexed because they do wrong. For they are certainly moved towards things because they believe them to be suitable to their nature and beneficial to them. But if it is not so, then teach them, and show them without being angry.

Death is the end of impressions through the senses, the end of the pulling strings that move our desires, the end of the wandering thoughts, and the end of serving the flesh.

It is a shame for the soul to be the first to give up in this life when your body does not give up.

Take care that you do not become like a Caesar, that you are not stained with that dye; for such things happen. Keep yourself simple, good, pure, serious, free from affectation, a friend of justice, a worshipper of the gods, kind, affectionate, and diligent in all proper acts. Strive to remain the kind of person that philosophy intended to make you. Reverence the gods, and help people. Life is short. There is only one true fruit of this earthly life—a pious disposition and social acts. Do everything as a disciple of Antoninus. Remember his consistency in every act that was in line with reason, his even temper in all things, his piety, the calmness of his expression, his gentleness, his disregard for empty fame, and his efforts to understand things; and how he never let anything pass without first carefully examining it and clearly understanding it; and how he bore with those who blamed him unjustly without blaming them in return; how he did nothing in a hurry; how he ignored slander; how exact he was in examining manners and actions; how he did not reproach people, nor was he timid, suspicious, or a sophist; and how little he was satisfied with—such as his lodging, bed, clothes, food, and servants; and how hardworking and patient he was; and how, because of his frugal diet, he could last until evening without needing to relieve himself except at the usual hour; and his steadiness and consistency in his friendships; and how he tolerated free speech from those who opposed his opinions; and the pleasure he took when someone showed him a better way; and how religious he was without being superstitious. Imitate all of this so that you may have as clear a conscience when your last hour comes as he had.

Return to your sober senses and call yourself back. When you have awakened from sleep and realized that it was only dreams that troubled you, now in your waking hours look at the things around you as you did at those dreams.

I am made of a small body and a soul. Now to this small body, all things are indifferent because it cannot perceive differences. But to the mind, those things are indifferent only if they are not the works of its own activity. Whatever things are the works of its own activity, all these are within its power. However, of these, only those which are done with reference to the present matter; for as to the future and past activities of the mind, even these are indifferent at the present moment.

Neither the labor that the hand does nor that of the foot is against nature, as long as the foot does the foot's work and the hand does the hand's. So then, neither is a person's labor against nature, as long as they do the things of a person. But if the labor is not against their nature, neither is it harmful to them.

How many pleasures have been enjoyed by robbers, parricides, and tyrants.

Do you not see how craftsmen adapt themselves, up to a certain point, to those who are not skilled in their craft—yet they hold firmly to the reason and principles of their art, and do not allow themselves to depart from it? Is it not strange if the architect and the physician show more respect for the reason and principles of their own arts than a person does for their own reason, which is shared with the gods?

Asia and Europe are small corners of the universe; all the sea is just a drop in the universe; Athos is just a small clod of earth in the universe; all of the present time is just a point in eternity. All things are small, changeable, and perishable. All things come from there, from that universal ruling power, either directly or as part of a sequence. Accordingly, the lion's gaping jaws, that which is poisonous, and every harmful thing, like thorns or mud, are byproducts of the grand and beautiful. Do not then imagine that they are different from what you venerate, but form a just opinion of the source of all.

He who has seen the present has seen all—both everything that has taken place from all eternity and everything that will happen for time without end. For all things are of one kind and one form.

Frequently consider the connection of all things in the universe and their relation to one another. For in a way, all things are intertwined with one another, and all are friendly to one another. One thing comes in order after another, and this is by virtue of the active movement and mutual cooperation and the unity of the substance.

Adapt yourself to the things with which your lot has been cast, and love the people among whom you have received your portion, but do it sincerely.

Every instrument, tool, or vessel is good if it does what it was made to do, even though the one who made it is not there. But in the things held together by nature, there is within them, and there remains in them, the power that made them; therefore, it is more fitting to revere this power, and to think that if you live and act according to its will, everything in you is in harmony with intelligence. And thus also in the universe, the things that belong to it are in harmony with intelligence.

Whatever things are not within your power that you suppose to be good or evil, it must necessarily follow that if such a bad thing befalls you, or if you lose such a good thing, you will blame the gods and hate people—those who are the cause of the misfortune or the loss, or those who are suspected of being likely to be the cause. Indeed, we do much injustice because we make a difference between these things, because we do not regard these things as indifferent. But if we judge only those things which are within our power as good or bad, there remains no reason to either find fault with God or to stand in a hostile attitude towards people.

We are all working together towards one end, some with knowledge and intention, and others without knowing what they do; as with people who are asleep, as Heraclitus, I think, said that they too are laborers and cooperators in the things that take place in the universe. But people cooperate in different ways: even those who find fault with what happens and those who try to oppose it and hinder it also cooperate; for the universe had a need for such people too. So it remains for you to understand what kind of worker you place yourself among; for he who rules all things will certainly make good use of you, and he will place you among some part of the cooperators and those whose labor contributes to one end. But do not be such a part as the mean and ridiculous verse in the play, which Chrysippus speaks of.

Does the sun try to do the work of the rain, or Aesculapius the work of the earth, which bears fruit? And how is it with each of the stars? They are different, yet they all work together towards the same end.

If the gods have determined about me and the things that must happen to me, they have determined well, for it is not easy even to imagine a god without forethought. As for doing me harm, why should they have any desire for that? What advantage would result to them from this or to the whole, which is the special object of their providence? But if they have not determined about me individually, they have certainly determined about the whole, and the things that happen as part of this arrangement should be accepted with pleasure, and I should be content with them. But if they decide about nothing— which is wicked to believe—then we should neither sacrifice nor pray nor swear by them or do anything else as if the gods were present and living with us. But if the gods don't decide about anything that concerns us, I can still decide for myself, and I can seek what is useful, and what is useful to everyone is what aligns with their nature. My nature is rational and social, and my city and country, as far as I am Antoninus, is Rome, but as far as I am a human, it is the world. So, the things that are useful to these cities are also useful to me.

Whatever happens to each person is for the good of the whole. That should be enough. But if you look closer, you will also see that whatever benefits one person also benefits others. However, let the word "benefit" be understood here in its common sense, referring to things that are neither good nor bad.

Just as you find the continuous sight of the same things in the amphitheater and similar places tiresome and boring, so it is with life as a whole. Everything above and below is the same and comes from the same source. How much longer will this continue?

Think often about how many different types of people, with different professions and from different nations, have died, and let your thoughts go down to even Philistion, Phoebus, and Origanion. Now think about other types of people. We too must eventually move to that place where there are so many great orators, noble philosophers like Heraclitus, Pythagoras, and Socrates, so many heroes of old, and so many generals and kings who came after them.

Add Eudoxus, Hipparchus, Archimedes, and other men of great intellect, vision, and dedication, as well as rogues, bigots, and even satirists like Menippus who mocked this short and fleeting human life. Think about how all of them have long been in the dust. What harm has come to them? And what about those whose names are completely forgotten? There is only one thing of value in this life: to live in truth and justice and be tolerant of those who are neither true nor just.

Whenever you want to cheer yourself up, think about the good qualities of the people around you—for example, one person's energy, another's decency, a third's generosity, and another's talent. Nothing cheers you up more than seeing virtues in the character of those you live with, especially when they are abundant. So keep these examples in your mind.

You don't resent your weight, do you—that you weigh only a certain amount and not three hundred pounds? So don't resent that your life span is only so many years and not more. Just as you are content with the amount of matter given to you, so be content with the amount of time you have.

Try to persuade people, but act even if they don't agree when the principles of justice demand it. But if someone uses force to stop you, accept it peacefully, and use the obstacle as an opportunity to practice another virtue. And remember that you started on this path with a condition—you didn't aim for the impossible. So, what were you aiming for? A certain effort, which you have accomplished if the things you were driven to do are not completed.

A person who loves fame thinks another person's actions are his own good; a person who loves pleasure thinks his own sensations are his good, but a person with understanding considers his own actions as his good.

It's within our power to have no opinion about something and not be disturbed in our soul because things themselves have no natural power to form our judgments.

Get used to listening carefully to what others say and try as much as possible to understand what is in the speaker's mind.

What isn't good for the hive isn't good for the bee either.

If sailors spoke badly of their captain or patients of their doctor, would they listen to anyone else? If not, how could the captain ensure the safety of the passengers or the doctor the health of those in his care?

How many people who were born around the same time as me are already gone?

Appearances: to someone with jaundice, honey tastes bitter; to someone bitten by a mad dog, water is terrifying; to little children, a ball is a wonderful thing. So why am I angry? Do you think a false opinion has less power than the bile in someone with jaundice or the poison in someone bitten by a mad dog?

No one will stop you from living according to the reason of your own nature. Nothing will happen to you that goes against the reason of universal nature.

Think about the kind of people others want to please, the things they aim for, and the actions they take. How quickly time will cover everything—and how much it has already covered.

Book 7

What is badness? It is what you have often seen. Remember this when anything happens: it is what you have seen before. Everywhere you look, you will find the same things, as in ancient histories, medieval times, and in our day; cities and houses are filled with them now. There is nothing new: all things are both familiar and short-lived.

How can our principles die unless the thoughts corresponding to them are extinguished? But you have the power to keep these thoughts alive. I can hold the opinion about anything that I should hold. If I can, why am I disturbed? External things have no relation to my mind.

Let this be your state, and you will stand tall. You have the power to reclaim your life. Look at things as you once did, for this is how to reclaim your life.

The idle business of show, stage plays, flocks of sheep, herds, spear exercises, bones cast to little dogs, bits of bread in fishponds, laboring ants, scurrying mice, and puppets on strings—all alike. Your duty is to show good humor amid such things, not pride; to understand that every man is worth as much as the things he busies himself with.

In conversation, focus on what is said; in every movement, observe what is happening. In conversation, see what end it refers to; in movement, carefully watch what is signified.

Is my understanding sufficient for this or not? If it is, I use it as an instrument given by universal nature. If not, I either step aside for someone more capable unless there's a reason I shouldn't, or I do my best, aided by someone who, with my guidance, can do what is fit and useful for the general good. Whatever I do, alone or with another, should be directed to what is useful and suited to society.

Many celebrated by fame are forgotten; many who celebrated others' fame are long dead.

Do not be ashamed to be helped; it is your duty to do your part like a soldier in a town assault. What if you are lame and cannot climb the battlements alone, but can with help?

Let not future things disturb you, for you will face them, if necessary, with the same reason you use for present things.

All things are interconnected, and the bond is sacred; hardly anything is unconnected with any other thing. Things are coordinated and form the same universe (order). There is one universe of all things, one God who pervades all, one substance, one law, one common reason in all intelligent animals, and one truth; if there is one perfection for all animals of the same stock and reason.

Everything material soon disappears into the whole's substance; everything formal (causal) is taken back into universal reason; and the memory of everything is soon overwhelmed in time.

To the rational animal, the same act is natural and reasonable.

Stand tall, or be made tall.

Just as members in one body are united, rational beings, though separate, are constituted for one cooperation. This is more apparent if you often say to yourself that you are a member of rational beings. But if you say you are a part, you do not yet love people from your heart; beneficence does not delight you for its own sake; you do it as propriety, not as good for yourself.

Let external things fall as they may on parts that feel them. Those parts may complain if they choose. But I am not harmed unless I think it is evil, and I have the power not to think so.

Whatever anyone does or says, I must be good, as gold, emerald, or purple says, "Whatever anyone does or says, I must keep my color."

The ruling faculty does not disturb itself; it does not frighten or cause pain to itself. If someone else can frighten or pain it, let them. The faculty itself will not turn into such ways by its own opinion. Let the body take care not to suffer, and let it speak if it suffers. But the soul, subject to fear and pain, has the power of opinion about these things, and it will suffer nothing, for it will not deviate into such a judgment. The leading principle wants nothing unless it creates a want for itself; it is free from disturbance and unimpeded if it does not disturb and impede itself.

Eudaemonia (happiness) is a good daemon, or a good thing. What are you doing here, imagination? Go away, I beg you by the gods, as you came, for I do not want you. But you have come as you always do. I am not angry with you: only go away.

Is anyone afraid of change? Why, what happens without change? What is more pleasing or suitable to universal nature? Can you take a bath unless the wood changes? Can you be nourished unless the food changes? Can anything useful be accomplished without change? Do you not see that you, too, must change, just like everything in the universe?

Through the universal substance, as through a torrent, all bodies are carried, united with and cooperating with the whole, like body parts with one another. How many Chrysippus, Socrates, and Epictetus has time swallowed? Let this thought occur to you with reference to everyone and everything.

One thing only troubles me: lest I do something against human nature, or in a way it does not allow, or at the wrong time.

Near is forgetfulness of all things; near is forgetfulness of you by all.

It is unique to man to love even wrongdoers. This happens when you remember they are kin, do wrong through ignorance and unintentionally, and both will soon die. Above all, the wrongdoer has not harmed you, for he has not worsened your ruling faculty.

Universal nature, like wax, molds a horse, then a tree, then a man, then something else, each for a short time. It is no hardship for the vessel to be broken, just as there was none in its making.

A scowling look is unnatural; when often assumed, it extinguishes comeliness. From this, conclude it is contrary to reason. If even the perception of doing wrong departs, why live longer?

Nature, which governs the whole, will soon change all things you see and make new things from them, to keep the world new.

When someone wrongs you, consider with what opinion of good or evil they did it. When you see this, you will pity them, not wonder or be angry. For you either think the same thing is good or another similar thing. Your duty is to pardon them. If you do not think such things are good or evil, you will more readily be kind to the errant.

Think not of what you lack but of what you have. Select the best of what you have and reflect on how eagerly you would have sought it if you lacked it. However, do not overvalue them so as to be disturbed if you lose them.

Retire into yourself. The rational ruling principle is content when it does what is just, securing tranquility.

Wipe out imagination. Stop the pulling of strings. Confine yourself to the present. Understand well what happens to you or others. Divide and distribute every object into the causal (formal) and material. Think of your last hour. Let the wrong done by someone stay where it was done.

Focus on what is said. Let your understanding enter into the things being done and those doing them.

Adorn yourself with simplicity, modesty, and indifference to things between virtue and vice. Love mankind. Follow God. The poet says Law rules all. It is enough to remember Law rules all.

About death: Whether it is dispersion, resolution into atoms, or annihilation, it is either extinction or change.

About pain: Intolerable pain carries us off; long-lasting pain is tolerable. The mind maintains tranquility by retreating into itself, and the ruling faculty is not worsened. Let harmed parts, if they can, express their opinion.

About fame: Observe the minds of those seeking fame, what they are, what they avoid, and what they pursue. As piles of sand hide former sands, life's events soon cover past ones.

From Plato: Can a man with an elevated mind and view of all time and substance think human life is great? It is not possible. Such a man thinks death is not evil. Certainly not.

From Antisthenes: It is royal to do good and be abused. It is base for the countenance to obey and compose itself as the mind commands, but the mind not to be self-regulated and composed.

Do not vex yourself over things, for they care not about it.

To the immortal gods and us, give joy.

Life must be reaped like ripe corn: One is born, another dies.

If gods do not care for me and my children, there is a reason.

For the good and the just are with me.

No joining in others' wailing, no violent emotion.

From Plato: A sufficient answer is: You say wrong if you think a good man should consider the hazard of life or death, rather than whether he does just or unjust works of a good or bad man.

For men of Athens, truly: wherever a man places himself, thinking it best, or is placed by a commander, he should stay and abide hazard, considering nothing, death or anything else, above deserting his post.

Reflect if the noble and good differ from saving and being saved. A real man should dismiss such thoughts. A man must entrust these matters to the deity, believing women say no man can escape destiny. The next inquiry is how best to live the time given.

Look at the courses of stars as if traveling with them; consider the elements changing into one another; such thoughts purge the filth of earthly life.

Plato says: He who talks about men should view earthly things from above, in assemblies, armies, agriculture, marriages, treaties, births, deaths, courts, deserted places, barbarians, feasts, lamentations, markets, a mix of all things and orderly combination of contraries.

Consider the past's political changes. Foresee future things; they will be similar, not deviating from the present order: contemplating life for forty years is like contemplating ten thousand. What more will you see?

That which has grown from earth returns to earth;

That which springs from heavenly seed returns to heavenly realms.

This is dissolution of atoms' involution or dispersion of unsentient elements.

With food, drinks, and cunning magic arts,

Turning the channel to escape death,

The breeze heaven sent

We must endure and toil without complaint.

Another may cast his opponent better; but he is not more social, modest, or better disciplined to meet what happens, nor more considerate of neighbors' faults.

Where work can be done conformably to gods' and men's reason, fear nothing: where activity proceeds according to our constitution, no harm is suspected.

Everywhere and always, you can piously accept your condition, behave justly to those around you, and focus on present thoughts, examining them well.

Do not look around for others' principles; look to what nature leads you, the universal nature through events and your own nature through your actions. Every being should act according to its constitution; all else is for rational beings, like inferior things for superior ones, but rational for one another.

The primary principle in man's constitution is social. The second is not yielding to the body's persuasions, as rational and intelligent motion circumscribes itself, never overpowered by senses or appetites, both animal; intelligent motion claims superiority, not allowing itself to be overpowered. With good reason, for it is formed to use all. The third thing in rational constitution is freedom from error and deception. Let the ruling principle hold these things and go straight on, with what is its own.

Consider yourself dead and have completed life up to now; live according to nature the remainder allowed.

Love only what happens to you and is spun with destiny's thread. What is more suitable?

In everything that happens, consider those who experienced the same, how they were vexed and treated them as strange. Where are they now? Nowhere. Why act the same? Why not leave these agitations, foreign to nature, to those causing and moved by them? Why not focus on the right use of things happening to you? Use them well; they will be material for you. Only attend to yourself and resolve to be good in every act.

Look within. Within is the fountain of good, ever bubbling if you dig.

The body should be compact, showing no irregularity in motion or attitude. The mind's intelligence and propriety should show in the face and the whole body without affectation.

Life's art is more like wrestling than dancing: stand ready and firm for sudden, unexpected onsets.

Observe those whose approval you want and their principles. You will not blame involuntary offenders or want their approval if you know their opinions and appetites' sources.

Every soul is involuntarily deprived of truth; it is deprived of justice, temperance, benevolence, and everything of the kind. Bear this in mind, and you will be gentler towards all.

In every pain, remember it is not dishonorable nor worsens the governing intelligence; it does not harm intelligence rationally or socially. Epicurus said most pains are neither intolerable nor everlasting if you remember they have limits and add nothing in imagination: remember many disagreeable things are like pain, such as drowsiness, heat, lack of appetite. When discontented with these, say you yield to pain.

Do not feel toward the inhuman as they feel toward men.

How do we know if Telauges wasn't a better person than Socrates? It's not enough that Socrates died in a more honorable way, argued better with the sophists, endured a cold night more strongly, or that when he was told to arrest Leon of Salamis, he thought it was more honorable to refuse, or that he walked confidently in the streets—though we might doubt if this last part is true. Instead, we should ask what kind of soul Socrates had. Was he able to be satisfied with being fair to people and respectful to the gods? Did he avoid being upset by people's wrongdoings, or becoming a slave to anyone's ignorance? Did he accept everything that happened to him as part of life without thinking it was too much to bear? Did he keep his mind from being affected by the troubles of the body?

Nature hasn't mixed your mind with your body in a way that stops you from controlling yourself and mastering what is truly yours. It's entirely possible to be a great person without anyone noticing. Always remember this: very little is needed to live a happy life. And even if you've given up on becoming a great thinker or scientist, don't lose hope of being free, modest, social, and obedient to God. You have the power to live free from pressure with a peaceful mind, even if the whole world shouts at you, and even if wild animals tear apart this body that surrounds you. What stops the mind, in all this, from staying calm, judging everything around it fairly, and using what it has wisely? So that the mind can say to what it sees: "This is what you really are, even if people think you're something else." And the mind can say to what it uses: "You're exactly what I was looking for." For me, whatever happens is always an opportunity for virtue, whether it's rational or social, and in short, for the practice of the art that belongs to humans or gods.

Everything that happens is connected to either God or humans and is neither new nor hard to deal with. It's familiar and useful material to work with. The perfection of moral character is to live each day as if it were your last, without getting overly excited, sluggish, or pretending to be someone you're not. The gods, who never die, aren't upset that they have to put up with humans for so long, even though many of them are bad. In fact, they still care for them in every way. But you, who will die so soon, are you tired of putting up with the bad, even though you're one of them yourself?

It's ridiculous for a person not to escape their own badness, which is possible, but to try and escape other people's badness, which is impossible. Whatever the rational and social part of us finds to be neither intelligent nor social, it rightly judges to be below itself. When you've done something good and someone else has benefited from it, why do you still look for something else, like fools do? Whether it's to gain a reputation for doing good or to get something in return? No one gets tired of receiving what's useful. But it's useful to act according to nature. So don't get tired of receiving what's useful by doing good for others.

The nature of everything decided to create the universe. Now, either everything that happens is a result of that, or the main things that the universe's ruling power moves towards are governed by no rational principle. If you remember this, it will help you stay calm in many situations.

Book 8

This thought can help you stop caring about empty fame: you no longer have the chance to live your whole life, or even just your adult life, as a philosopher. It's clear to many, including yourself, that you are far from being a philosopher. Your life has become disordered, making it hard to gain the reputation of a philosopher, and your way of living goes against it too. If you truly understand this, stop worrying about how you appear to others. Instead, be happy if you can live the rest of your life the way your nature wants. Focus on what your nature desires and let nothing else distract you. You've already wandered through many paths without finding happiness anywhere—not in logical arguments, not in wealth, not in fame, not in pleasure, not in anything. So where can happiness be found? It's found in doing what human nature requires. And how do you do this? By having principles that guide your feelings and actions. What principles? Those that relate to what is good and bad: understanding that nothing is good unless it makes you just, self-controlled, brave, and free; and nothing is bad unless it does the opposite.

Before every action, ask yourself: "How does this affect me? Will I regret it?" In a short time, I will be dead, and all will be gone. What more do I need if what I am doing now is the work of an intelligent, social being who follows the same laws as God?

Alexander, Julius Caesar, and Pompey—how do they compare to Diogenes, Heraclitus, and Socrates? The latter understood things, their causes, and their essence, and their guiding principles were in harmony with their pursuits. But as for the others, how many things did they have to worry about, and how many things were they slaves to?

Remember that people will keep doing the same things, even if you burst with frustration.

The most important thing is not to be disturbed, for everything happens according to the nature of the universe, and soon you will be nobody and nowhere, just like Hadrian and Augustus. Then, focus steadily on your task, look at it, and remember that your duty is to be a good person and to do what human nature demands. Do this without straying, and speak as you think is most just, but do so kindly, modestly, and sincerely.

The nature of the universe constantly works to change things, to move them from one place to another. Everything is changing, but there's no need to fear anything new. Everything is familiar; what happens is neither new nor hard to deal with but is a usual part of the whole.

Every living thing is satisfied when it follows its nature. A rational being follows its nature when it agrees with truth, directs its actions towards social good, limits its desires to what is within its power, and accepts everything that happens as part of the universal order. This universal nature includes every individual nature, just as a leaf is part of the plant's nature. However, the nature of a leaf is part of a plant that cannot perceive or reason and can be stopped in its growth, while human nature is part of a larger nature that is not impeded and is intelligent and just, giving everything its fair share of time, substance, cause, action, and experience. But don't expect everything to be exactly equal in all respects; instead, look at the whole picture and how one thing compares to the sum of another.

You may not have time to study, but you do have time to control your arrogance. You have time to rise above pleasure and pain, to let go of the love of fame, and not to be upset by foolish or ungrateful people, but to care for them instead.

Don't let anyone hear you complaining about your life or the life in the court.

Regret is a form of self-blame for missing out on something useful. But if something is truly good, it must be useful, and a truly good person should pursue it. No good person would ever regret not indulging in a sensual pleasure, so pleasure is neither good nor useful.

Ask yourself, "What is this thing, really? What is it made of? What is its purpose in the world? How long will it last?"

When you wake up and feel reluctant to get out of bed, remember that it is in your nature, as a human being, to perform social duties. Sleeping is something you share with animals, but acting according to your nature is something that belongs uniquely to you and is more fitting and pleasant.

Constantly examine your impressions—every single one if possible—look at its cause, identify the feeling it brings, and analyze it logically.

Whenever you meet someone, immediately ask yourself: "What opinions does this person hold about what is good and bad?" If he believes certain things about pleasure, pain, fame, dishonor, life, and death, it won't be surprising if he acts in a certain way, and you'll understand that he's compelled to do so.

It's as silly to be surprised at a fig tree producing figs as it is to be surprised when the world produces things that are natural to it. Similarly, it would be foolish for a doctor to be surprised by a patient having a fever or a sailor by an unfavorable wind.

Remember that changing your mind and following someone who corrects your mistake is just as much a part of your freedom as sticking to your original opinion. This change comes from your own choice, your own judgment, and your own understanding.

If something is within your control, why aren't you doing it? But if it's under someone else's control, why do you blame atoms or gods? Both are senseless. You should blame no one. If you can, fix the cause; if you can't, at least fix the effect. But if even that's not possible, what good does it do to complain? Everything should have a purpose.

What dies does not leave the universe. If it remains here, it changes here and dissolves into its basic parts, which are elements of the universe and of yourself. These elements also change, and they don't complain about it.

Everything has a purpose—like a horse or a vine. Why are you surprised? Even the sun would say, "I exist for a purpose," and the other gods would say the same. So what is your purpose—to enjoy pleasure? See if that makes sense.

Nature's purpose includes everything, from the beginning to the end. Just like someone tossing a ball, how is it good for the ball to go up and bad for it to come down or even to hit the ground? The same could be said of a bubble when it forms and when it bursts. Or a candle, when it is lit and when it goes out.

Turn it (the body) inside out and see what kind of thing it is, what it becomes when it grows old, and when it is sick. Both the praiser and the praised, the rememberer and the remembered, are short-lived, and all this happens in a tiny corner of the world. Not even here do people agree, not even with themselves. And the whole earth is just a point in space.

Focus on the matter at hand, whether it's an opinion, an action, or a word. You deserve what you're going through because you choose to become good tomorrow instead of today.

Am I doing something? I do it with the good of humanity in mind. Is something happening to me? I accept it as coming from the gods and the source of all things, from which everything is connected.

Just like bathing seems—oil, sweat, dirt, filthy water, all things disgusting—so is every part of life and everything in it.

Lucilla saw Verus die, and then Lucilla died. Secunda saw Maximus die, and then Secunda died. Epitynchanus saw Diotimus die, and then Epitynchanus died. Antoninus saw Faustina die, and then Antoninus died. And so it goes for everyone. Celer saw Hadrian die, and then Celer died. Where are those sharp-witted men now, those prophets or proud individuals? Charax, Demetrius the Platonist, and Eudaemon— where are they? All of them were just temporary, and now they're dead. Some haven't been remembered at all, some became legends, and others have even disappeared from legends. So remember that this little body of yours will either be scattered, your breath will be extinguished, or you will be moved to another place.

A man finds satisfaction in doing the right work for a man. And the right work for a man is to be kind to others, to rise above the distractions of the senses, to judge things fairly, and to understand the nature of the universe and everything that happens in it.

There are three relationships: one to the body that surrounds you, the second to the divine source from which everything comes, and the third to the people you live with.

Pain is either an evil to the body—let the body say what it thinks of it—or to the soul. But the soul has the power to keep itself calm and not to think that pain is an evil. Every judgment, movement, desire, and aversion is within, and no evil can rise above it.

Erase your harmful thoughts by often reminding yourself: "Now it's in my power to keep this soul free from any badness, from any desire, from any disturbance at all. By looking at things as they are, I can use each one according to its value." Remember this power that nature has given you.

Speak plainly, whether in the senate or to any person, without being pretentious. Use straightforward language.

The court of Augustus—wife, daughter, descendants, ancestors, sister, Agrippa, relatives, friends; Areius, Maecenas, doctors, and priests—all are dead. Then think of others, not just one person's death but the end of a whole family, like the Pompeii. And consider the words written on the tombs: "The last of his race." Then think of all the effort those before them put in to leave behind an heir, and that eventually, one must be the last. Again, think about the end of an entire family.

You must organize your life action by action, and be content if each action achieves its purpose as well as it can. No one can prevent you from achieving this. "But there will be some external obstacle." No obstacle can stop you from acting justly, with self-control, and with reason. "But maybe some other action will be blocked." Accept the block gladly and make a wise change to meet the situation. Another opportunity for action will immediately take its place and fit into the plan for your life.

Receive wealth or prosperity without arrogance, and be ready to let it go.

If you've ever seen a hand, foot, or head cut off and lying apart from the body, that's what you do to yourself when you refuse to accept your lot or do something unsocial. Imagine you've cut yourself off from the natural whole—you were born to be part of it, but now you've separated yourself. But here's the amazing thing: it's within your power to reunite with the whole. God has allowed this to no other part, once it's been cut off, to come together again. But think of the kindness by which he has distinguished humans, giving them the ability not to be separated at all, or to return and reunite if they are.

Just as the nature of the whole has given every rational being all other powers, so we have received this power too. Just as the universal nature turns everything that stands in its way into a part of itself and uses it, so the rational animal can turn every obstacle into material for its own purpose and use it to achieve its goal.

Don't let the thought of your whole life overwhelm you, and don't dwell on all the troubles that may have happened in the past or may happen in the future. Just ask yourself, "What is there in this situation that I can't bear or handle?" You'll be ashamed to admit it. Then remember that it's neither the future nor the past that burdens you, but only the present. This present burden is very small if you isolate it and challenge your mind if it can't handle even this.

Does Panthea or Pergamus still sit by the tomb of Verus? Does Chabrias or Diotimus sit by the tomb of Hadrian? That would be ridiculous. Even if they did, would the dead be aware of it? And if they were aware, would they be pleased? And if they were pleased, would that make their mourners immortal? Was it not their fate also to grow old—old women and men like everyone else—and then to die? And with them dead, what would those they mourned do then? It's all just foul-smelling decay in a bag of bones.

If you have sharp sight, use it, but also add wise judgment.

In the structure of a rational being, I see no virtue that opposes justice, but I do see a virtue that opposes pleasure, and that is self-control.

If you take away your judgment about something that seems painful, you yourself remain unharmed by it. "Who is this self?" The reason. "But I'm not just reason." True, so let your reason not trouble itself. But if another part of you suffers, let it have its own judgment about itself.

An obstacle to sense perception is harmful to animal nature. An obstacle to desires is also harmful to animal nature. And something else is equally an obstacle and a harm to the nature of plants. So, anything that blocks the mind is harmful to intelligent nature. Apply this to yourself. Is pain or pleasure affecting you? That's for the senses to deal with. Have you met an obstacle in your efforts? If this effort was unconditional, then yes, the obstacle is harmful to your rational nature. But if you consider the usual course of things, you haven't yet been harmed or even impeded. Nothing can impede the proper functions of the mind. The mind can't be touched by fire, steel, tyranny, or slander in any way. When it's made perfect, it remains complete.

I shouldn't harm myself, as I've never intentionally harmed anyone else.

Different things bring different people joy, but my joy comes from keeping my mind clear, not turning away from anyone or anything that happens, but looking at and accepting everything with kind eyes and using each thing according to its value.

See that you make the most of this present moment. Those who chase after fame after death don't realize that the people of the next generation will be just like those they dislike now. Both groups will die. And what does it matter to you if those future people say this or that about you?

Take me and put me wherever you will; wherever I am, I'll keep my inner self calm and satisfied if it can act according to its nature. Is this situation any good reason for my soul to be unhappy and worse than it was? Expanded, shrinking, scared? And what would be a good reason for that?

Nothing can happen to any human being that isn't natural to humans, just as nothing happens to an ox that isn't natural to oxen, or to a vine that isn't natural to vines, or to a stone that isn't natural to a stone. So if everything happens as is usual and natural for it, why should you complain? The universal nature brings nothing that you can't handle.

If something outside you is causing distress, it's not the thing itself that's bothering you, but your judgment of it—and you can erase that judgment right now. But if it's something in your own attitude that's bothering you, who's stopping you from changing it? If you're upset because you're not doing something that seems right, why not do it instead of complaining? "But there's an obstacle in the way that I can't overcome." Then don't be upset, because the reason it's not being done isn't your fault. "But life isn't worth living if I can't do this." Then leave life as graciously as someone who has achieved their goal, and in peace with those who stood in your way.

Remember that your inner self is invincible when it withdraws into its own self-sufficiency, doing nothing that it doesn't choose to do, even if that choice is stubborn. How much stronger will it be when it acts according to reason and deliberation? That's why a mind free from passions is a fortress—people have no stronger place of retreat, and someone who takes refuge here is invincible. Anyone who hasn't realized this is ignorant, and anyone who knows it but doesn't take refuge is unlucky.

Say nothing more to yourself than what your first impressions report. Suppose you're told that someone speaks ill of you. That's all you've been told, nothing more. I see that my child is sick. I do see that, but I don't see that he's in danger. So always stick to your first impressions and don't add anything from your own thoughts. Then nothing more will happen to you. Or better yet, add something like a person who understands everything that happens in the world.

A cucumber is bitter—throw it away. There are thorns in the road—go around them. That's all you need to do. Don't ask, "Why are these things in the world?" because you'll be laughed at by someone who understands nature, just as a carpenter or shoemaker would laugh at you if you complained about seeing shavings or scraps in their workshop. And yet they have places to throw those scraps, while the universal nature has no external space. But her amazing skill is that even though she's confined herself, she changes everything within her that seems to decay, grow old, or become useless into something new, so she doesn't need any material from outside or a place to throw away what decays. She's content with her own space, her own material, and her own skill.

Don't be sluggish in your actions, unclear in your speech, or wandering in your thoughts. Don't let your mind become troubled or overjoyed. Allow some leisure in your life.

Suppose people kill you, cut you into pieces, or curse you. What can these things do to stop your mind from staying pure, wise, sober, and just? For example, if someone were to stand by a clear, sweet spring and curse it, the spring would still keep sending out good water to drink. If someone threw mud or filth into it, the spring would quickly disperse it, wash it away, and not be polluted at all. How can you make your mind like an everlasting spring and not just a well? By training yourself every hour to be free, kind, simple, and decent.

Someone who doesn't know what the world is doesn't know where he is. Someone who doesn't know the purpose of the world doesn't know who he is or what the world is. And if someone fails in any of these things, he couldn't even say what his own purpose is. What do you think of someone who seeks or avoids the praise of people who don't even know where they are or who they are?

Do you want to be praised by someone who curses himself three times an hour? Do you want to please someone who doesn't even please himself? Can someone who regrets almost everything he does be pleased with himself?

Don't just breathe the surrounding air—breathe in the thoughts of the mind that embraces all things. The power of the mind spreads everywhere and penetrates everything, just like the air for those who can breathe it.

Wickedness does no harm to the universe as a whole, and one person's wickedness doesn't harm another person. It only harms the one who commits it, and he can get rid of it as soon as he decides to.

My neighbor's will is as indifferent to me as his breath and his body. We're born to help each other, but the ruling mind of each of us is sovereign. Otherwise, my neighbor's wickedness would harm me, which God didn't intend, so that my misfortune wouldn't depend on another person.

The sun seems to pour its light everywhere, and it does spread out in all directions, but it doesn't run out. This spreading is an extension, and that's why its rays are called "extensions." You can see what a ray is if you look at sunlight entering a dark room through a narrow opening. It extends in a straight line and stops when it hits a solid object. The light stays there and doesn't slide or fall off. This is how the mind should spread and shine, not pouring out or colliding violently with obstacles, but staying fixed and illuminating whatever receives it. Anything that doesn't reflect the light will only deprive itself of it.

He who fears death fears either losing all sensation or gaining a different kind of sensation. But if you have no sensation, you won't feel any harm, and if you gain a different kind of sensation, you'll be a different kind of living being and won't stop living.

People exist to help each other. So either teach them or put up with them.

An arrow moves one way, and the mind moves another. But even when the mind is cautious or curious, it still moves directly towards its goal.

Enter into the mind of everyone you meet, and let them enter yours.

Book 9

When someone acts unjustly, they are acting against the will of the universe. The universe has created rational beings to help each other, not to harm one another. So, when someone goes against this, they are disrespecting the highest power. Similarly, lying is also disrespectful to this power because the universe is based on truth. Everything that exists is connected, and truth is the foundation of it all. A person who lies on purpose is guilty because they are being unjust by deceiving others. Even someone who lies without meaning to is still guilty because they are going against the nature of the universe. They disturb the order by opposing truth, using the abilities nature has given them incorrectly.

A person who chases after pleasure won't avoid doing wrong, and this is clearly against the will of the universe. Now, when it comes to things like pain and pleasure, or life and death, or honor and dishonor, the universe treats them all the same. It wouldn't have created these opposites unless it viewed them equally. So, those who want to live according to nature should also see them the same way. If someone doesn't, they are clearly going against nature. When I say the universe treats these things equally, I mean that they happen to everyone as a result of cause and effect. Everything that exists comes from a plan that the universe set in motion from the beginning, creating everything and allowing changes and cycles to happen.

It would be best for a person to leave this world without having ever lied, pretended, indulged in excess, or been proud. But if someone has experienced these things, the next best thing for that person is to become tired of them before he or she dies.If you choose to stay with such behaviors, has your experience not yet shown you that you should avoid them? The corruption of the mind is much worse than any disease of the body. The latter only affects animals, but the former destroys what makes us human.

Do not fear death, but be content with it, since it is also something that nature wants. Just like being young, growing old, maturing, getting teeth, a beard, and gray hair, having children, and giving birth, all the other natural events that happen throughout life, so is dying. This, then, is fitting for a thoughtful person—to be neither careless nor impatient nor scornful about death, but to wait for it as just another natural process. Just as you now wait for the time when your wife will give birth, so be ready for the time when your soul will leave this body.

But if you also need a more vulgar kind of comfort that can touch your heart, you will find it easier to accept death by thinking about the things you will leave behind, and the kind of people you won't have to deal with anymore. It's not right to be angry with others, but you should care for them and treat them kindly. Still, remember that when you die, you will be leaving behind people who don't share your values. If there is anything that could make us want to stay alive, it's the chance to live with people who think like us. But now, you see how difficult it is to live with people who don't agree with you, so you might say, "Come quickly, death, before I too forget who I am."

When someone does something wrong, they are really hurting themselves. When someone acts unfairly, they are making themselves worse.

Sometimes, doing nothing can be just as wrong as doing something bad.

It is enough for you to have clear thoughts, act in a way that helps others, and accept whatever happens with a calm mind.

Erase your imaginations, stop your impulses, control your desires, and keep your mind in charge.

Animals that don't have reason share one life, but animals with reason share one intelligent mind. Just like how all things of the earth share one earth, and we all see by the same light and breathe the same air.

All things that share something in common naturally move towards others like them. Everything that is earthy goes back to the earth, everything watery flows together, and everything airy does the same, unless something separates them. Fire moves upward because it is drawn to other fire, and it is so ready to join with any fire that even dry things easily catch fire because they don't have much to stop them from burning.

In the same way, everything that shares the same intelligent nature moves towards others like itself, even more strongly than the elements. The higher something is, the more it wants to mix with things like it. That's why among animals without reason, we see bees forming hives, cattle forming herds, birds caring for their young, and a kind of love. Even in animals, there is a kind of soul that brings them together, stronger than what we see in plants or stones or trees. But in animals with reason, there are communities, friendships, families, and gatherings of people; even in wars, there are treaties and truces. But in things that are even higher, like the stars, there is a kind of unity even when they are far apart. So, as we go higher, we find more sympathy and connection, even in things that are separated. But look at what happens now: only intelligent creatures, like us, have forgotten this desire to be united. Only among us do we see no coming together. Even though we try to avoid it, we are still drawn together, because our nature is too strong. If you look closely, you'll see what I mean. It's easier to find something earthy that doesn't return to the earth than to find a person who is completely separated from others.

Both people, gods, and the universe produce results in their own time. Even though we usually talk about this when we discuss vines and similar things, it doesn't matter. Reason also produces results for everyone and itself, and it creates other things that are like reason itself.

If you can, teach those who do wrong; if you can't, remember that you have the ability to be kind. The gods are also kind to such people, and they even help them achieve things like health, wealth, and reputation. You can do the same. So, who is stopping you?

Work, but not like someone who is miserable or looking for pity or admiration. Focus on just one thing: doing what you need to do or holding yourself back, as reason requires.

Today I escaped all my troubles, or rather, I got rid of them, because they were not outside of me, but inside, in my own thoughts.

Everything is the same: familiar in experience, short-lived in time, and worthless in substance. Everything now is just like it was in the time of those who have died.

Things stand outside of us, by themselves, without knowing anything or judging themselves. What judges them, then? Our minds.

Good or bad for a rational being comes not from feeling but from action, just as our virtue or vice comes not from what we feel, but from what we do.

A stone thrown into the air isn't harmed by falling down, and it isn't helped by being thrown up.

Look into the minds of those you fear and see what kind of people they are. You'll realize that there is no reason to be afraid of their judgment, and you'll see how poorly they judge themselves.

Everything is changing: and you yourself are constantly changing and, in a way, being destroyed. The whole universe is, too.

You should leave another person's wrong act where it is.

The end of an action, the stopping of a movement or thought, is like a death, but it's not something to fear. Think about the different stages of your life: your childhood, your youth, your adulthood, your old age. In each of these, every change was like a death. Is there anything to fear in that? Now think about your life with your grandfather, then with your mother, then with your father. Just as you find many differences and changes and endings, ask yourself, is there anything to fear? In the same way, the end and change of your whole life is nothing to be afraid of.

Quickly examine your own mind, the mind of the universe, and the mind of your neighbor: your own mind, so you can make it just; the universe's mind, so you can remember what you are a part of; and your neighbor's mind, so you can know whether they are acting out of ignorance or understanding, and remember that their mind is like yours.

As you are a part of a social system, let every act of yours be a part of social life. Any act that doesn't contribute to a social goal tears apart your life and makes it incomplete, like when someone in a meeting stands apart from the group.

Children's arguments and games, and poor souls carrying around dead bodies—such is everything. What we see in depictions of the underworld seems clearer.

Look closely at the form of an object, separate it from its material part, and then think about how long it is naturally made to last.

You have gone through so many troubles by not being satisfied with your mind when it does what it was naturally meant to do. But that's enough of this.

When someone blames or hates you, or says something hurtful about you, look into their soul, see what kind of person they are. You'll realize that there's no reason to be troubled by their opinions of you. But still, be kind to them because, by nature, they are your friends. And the gods help them in many ways, through dreams, signs, and other means, to achieve the things they care about.

The cycles of the universe are always the same, up and down, from age to age. Either the universal mind moves everything for a reason, and if so, be content with the result, or it started everything in motion once, and everything else follows naturally. Or everything is made up of atoms. In any case, if there is a god, all is well, and if it's just chance, don't let yourself be controlled by it. Soon, the earth will cover us all, and then the earth will change, and the things that come from change will keep changing forever. When a person thinks about the changes that come one after another, like waves, and how quickly they happen, they will lose respect for everything that is temporary.

The universal cause is like a winter flood: it carries everything along with it. But how worthless are those people who are busy with political matters, thinking they are being philosophers! They are just wasting their time. So, what should you do? Do what nature requires right now. If you can, act, and don't worry about whether anyone notices. Don't wait for some perfect situation like Plato's Republic. Be content if even the smallest thing goes well, and consider that to be no small achievement. Because who can change people's opinions? And without a change in opinions, what is left but the slavery of people who pretend to obey but are really suffering? Now, tell me about Alexander, Philippus, and Demetrius of Phalerum. They can judge for themselves whether they understood what nature required and trained themselves accordingly. But if they acted like tragic heroes, no one has forced me to imitate them. Philosophy is simple and modest. Don't lead me to arrogance and pride.

Look down from above on the countless groups of people and their countless activities, all the different journeys in storms and calm weather, the differences among those who are born, live together, and die. And think about the life of people who lived long ago, the life of those who will live after you, and the life being lived now in other parts of the world. How many people don't even know your name, how many will soon forget it, and how many who might praise you now will soon criticize you. Realize that neither a lasting name, nor reputation, nor anything else is really important.

Accept calmly whatever comes from an external cause, and act justly in everything that comes from your own actions. In other words, let your thoughts and actions be fulfilled in social conduct, as that is an expression of your own nature.

You can remove many unnecessary troubles that only exist in your own opinion. And by doing so, you will make a lot of room for yourself by understanding the whole universe, contemplating the eternity of time, and noticing how quickly each thing changes—how short the time is from birth to death, and the limitless time before birth and after death.

All that you see will soon disappear, and those who witness this disappearance will soon disappear too. Whether you die in extreme old age or before your time, it will all be the same.

What are the leading thoughts of these people? What are they focused on, and what do they care about? Train yourself to look at their minds, without any disguise. When they think their criticism will hurt you or their praise will help you, what a silly thought that is!

Loss is nothing more than change. The universal nature loves change, and everything that comes from nature happens for a reason. Similar things have happened forever, and will continue to happen forever. So why would you say that everything has always been bad and always will be, and that the gods have never had the power to fix these things, leaving the world condemned to constant misery?

The decay of everything that is the foundation of everything: water, dust, bones, filth. Or, marble rocks, the hard parts of the earth; and gold and silver, just sediments; and clothes, only bits of hair; and purple dye, just blood; and everything else is the same. And what we call the soul is also just something that changes from one thing to another.

Enough of this miserable life, complaining and acting like a fool. Why are you upset? What is new here? What is bothering you? Is it the way something looks? Look at it. Or is it the material? Look at that. But besides these, there is nothing else. Now, finally, become simpler and better in your thoughts toward the gods. It's the same whether we examine these things for a hundred years or three.

If someone has done wrong, the harm is theirs. But maybe they haven't done wrong.

Either everything comes from one intelligent source and works together like one body, and the part shouldn't complain about what is done for the good of the whole, or there are only atoms, and nothing else but a mix and scattering. So, why are you upset? Say to your mind, "Are you dead, are you corrupted, are you pretending, are you just going along with the crowd?"

Either the gods have power or they don't. If they have no power, why do you pray to them? But if they do have power, why not pray for them to give you the strength not to fear the things you fear, or to stop desiring the things you desire, or to not be upset by anything, instead of praying for those things to not happen or to happen? Because if they can help people, they can help with these things too. But maybe you'll say that the gods have left these things in your control. Well then, isn't it better to use what is in your power like a free person than to desire in a weak and helpless way what isn't in your control? And who told you that the gods don't help us with the things that are in our power? Start praying for these things, and you'll see. One person prays, "How can I get to be with that woman?" You pray, "How can I stop wanting to be with her?" Another prays, "How can I get rid of that person?" You pray, "How can I stop wanting to get rid of them?" Another says, "How can I keep my little child safe?" You say, "How can I learn not to be afraid of losing them?" In short, turn your prayers this way, and see what happens.

Epicurus says, "In my sickness, I didn't talk about the pains of my poor body, and I didn't go on about it to those who visited me. Instead, I kept discussing the main points of philosophy, focusing especially on how the mind, even when affected by what happens to the body, can still stay calm and keep its own good. I didn't give the doctors a chance to act like they were doing something great, but my life went on fine and happy." Do the same as he did, whether you are sick or in any other situation. Never abandon philosophy, no matter what happens, and don't engage in silly talk with people who don't know any better. Focus only on what you are doing right now and the tool you are using to do it.

When you are offended by someone's bad behavior, immediately ask yourself, "Is it possible for the world to not have people like this?" It's not possible. So don't ask for the impossible. This person is just one of the many bad people who must exist in the world. Think the same way when you deal with dishonest people, unfaithful people, or anyone who does wrong in any way. When you remind yourself that it's impossible for the world to be without people like this, you'll find yourself being kinder to each person individually. It's also helpful to remember what virtue nature has given you to deal with each wrong action. Nature gave us gentleness to deal with unkind people, and other qualities to deal with other kinds of wrongs. In every case, you can teach the person who has gone astray because every person who does wrong is missing the mark and has gone off course. Also, how have you been harmed? You'll find that none of the people you're angry with has done anything that could make your mind worse; the only thing that can harm you is in your own mind. And what harm is there, or what is so strange, if someone who hasn't been taught does the things an untaught person would do? Think about whether you should blame yourself instead, because you didn't expect this person to make that mistake. Your reason should have helped you see that it was likely they would make this mistake, and yet you are surprised that they did. But most of all, when you blame someone for being untrustworthy or ungrateful, look at yourself. The fault is clearly yours if you trusted that a person with that character would keep their promise, or if you did something kind without doing it completely and without expecting anything in return. What more do you want when you've done someone a favor? Isn't it enough that you've done something that fits your nature? Why do you seek to be paid back for it? It's like if the eye demanded something in return for seeing, or the feet for walking. Just as these parts of the body are made for a certain purpose, and by doing what they were made to do, they get what they need; in the same way, when a person does something kind or helpful for others, they have done what they were made for, and they get what they need from it.

Book 10

My soul, will you ever be good, simple, and clear, without any confusion, brighter than the body that surrounds you? Will you ever enjoy being kind and content? Will you ever be full and satisfied, without wanting anything, not desiring anything, either living or non-living, just for the sake of pleasure? Will you ever stop wishing for more time to enjoy things, or a better place, or a nicer climate, or the company of people who agree with you? Instead, will you be happy with your present condition, pleased with everything around you, and convinced that you have everything you need, that it all comes from the gods, that everything is good for you, and will continue to be good, no matter what the gods decide to give you? Will you finally become someone who can live peacefully with gods and men, without finding fault with them or being judged by them?

Observe what your nature requires as long as you are just a living being: then do it and accept it, as long as your nature as a living being is not harmed by it. Next, observe what your nature requires as a rational being. Follow all these things, as long as your rational nature is not harmed by them. And remember, a rational being is also a social being. Use these rules, and don't worry about anything else.

Everything that happens either happens in a way that you are naturally able to bear it, or it happens in a way that you are not naturally able to bear it. If it happens in a way that you are naturally able to bear it, don't complain, but bear it as you were made to do. But if it happens in a way that you are not naturally able to bear, don't complain, because it will end after it has affected you. Remember that you are made to bear everything, as long as you believe it is either in your interest or your duty to do so.

If someone is mistaken, kindly teach them and show them their error. But if you can't do that, blame yourself, or perhaps don't even blame yourself.

Whatever happens to you was prepared for you from all time; and the causes have been working since forever, creating your being and everything that happens to it.

Whether the universe is made of atoms or is a natural system, the first thing to understand is that you are part of the whole that is governed by nature; second, that you are closely related to other parts that are like you. With this in mind, since you are a part, you will not be upset by anything that happens to you, because nothing that benefits the whole can harm the part. And the whole contains nothing that is not good for it. All living things have this in common, but the universe also has this additional feature: no external cause can force it to create anything harmful to itself. Remembering that you are part of such a whole will make you content with everything that happens. And since you are closely related to other parts like you, you will act in a social manner, focusing on what is good for everyone and avoiding the opposite. If you live this way, life will go smoothly, just as the life of a citizen who acts in ways that benefit others and accepts what the state gives them is happy.

The parts of the whole—all the things that naturally exist in the universe—must perish; but understand this as a change. If this change is naturally both harmful and necessary for the parts, the whole could not stay in good condition if its parts are always changing and are made to perish in various ways. Did nature design itself to harm its own parts and make them fall into harm by necessity, or did it just not notice? Both ideas seem impossible. But even if someone drops the idea of nature as a force and just says things happen as they do, it's still ridiculous to be surprised or upset that things naturally change, especially when everything dissolves back into its basic elements. Things either break down into the elements they are made of, or they change from solid to earth and from air to air, returning to the universe's reason, whether it is consumed by fire or renewed through eternal cycles. And don't think that the solid and airy parts belong to you from birth. They only recently came from the food you ate and the air you breathed. What changes is what you've added, not what your mother gave you. Even if what your mother gave you is deeply connected to this added part that changes, this doesn't change what's been said.

When you've taken on names like good, modest, truthful, rational, calm, and noble, make sure you don't lose them. And if you do lose them, return to them quickly. Remember that being rational means paying close attention to everything and not being careless; that calmness is accepting what nature gives you willingly; and that nobility is raising your mind above the pleasures or pains of the body, above fame, death, and all such things. If you can keep these names without needing others to call you by them, you will become a different person and start a new life. Continuing to live as you have been, while being torn apart and corrupted, is the sign of a foolish person who is too attached to life, like those gladiators who, though covered in wounds and blood from wild animals, still beg to live another day, only to face the same claws and bites again. So, hold onto these few names, and if you can stay true to them, do so as if you were living in the islands of the blessed. But if you find yourself falling away from them and losing control, retreat to a quiet place where you can regain them, or leave life altogether—not in anger, but simply, freely, and with dignity, having at least achieved this one good thing in your life: leaving it in this way. To help you remember these names, it will be very useful to remember the gods and that they do not want flattery, but want all rational beings to become like them. And remember that what makes a fig tree a fig tree is doing the work of a fig tree, what makes a dog a dog is doing the work of a dog, what makes a bee a bee is doing the work of a bee, and what makes a man a man is doing the work of a man.

Every day, farce, war, surprise, dullness, and slavery will wipe out those principles of yours if you don't constantly study nature. It's your duty to think and act in a way that perfects your ability to deal with circumstances while also exercising your understanding, maintaining confidence in what you know without showing off, but also without hiding it. Because when will you finally enjoy simplicity, dignity, and the knowledge of each thing—what it really is, its place in the world, how long it lasts, what it's made of, who owns it, and who can give or take it away?

A spider feels proud when it catches a fly, and a man feels proud when he catches a hare, a fish in a net, a wild boar, a bear, or captures Sarmatians. But if you look closely at their motivations, aren't they all just robbers?

Adopt the habit of seeing how all things change into one another, and constantly practice this part of philosophy. Nothing helps you develop a great mind more than this. A person trained this way has detached themselves from the body and, knowing that they will soon leave this world and everything in it, focuses entirely on being just in their actions and accepting whatever happens as part of nature. They don't worry about what others say, think, or do against them, but are content with two things: acting justly in the present moment and accepting what is assigned to them now. They set aside all distractions and desires, wanting nothing more than to follow the straight path of law, and by following this path, they follow God.

What need is there for fear when you can always ask yourself what should be done? And if you see the way clearly, follow it contentedly, without hesitation. But if you don't see clearly, stop and ask the best advisers. If other things block you, proceed with caution, but always do what seems just. Justice is the best goal, and if you fail, let it be because you aimed for justice. A person who follows reason in everything is both calm and active, cheerful and collected.

As soon as you wake up, ask yourself: "Will it matter to me if someone else does what is just and right?" It won't matter. You haven't forgotten, I hope, that those who act arrogantly when praising or blaming others are the same as they are when they eat and sleep, and you haven't forgotten what they do, what they avoid, what they pursue, how they steal, and how they rob—not with their hands and feet, but with their most valuable part, the part that can produce trust, modesty, truth, law, and happiness.

To nature, who gives and takes back all things, the educated and humble person says, "Give what you want; take back what you want." And they say this not with pride, but with obedience and satisfaction.

The little time you have left to live is short. Live as if you were on a mountain. It doesn't matter whether you live there or here, as long as you live everywhere in the world as part of a community. Let people see and know a real person who lives according to nature. If they can't handle it, let them end your life. That's better than living as they do.

No more talk about what a good person should be. Just be one!

Always keep in mind the whole of time and existence, and consider that each thing, in terms of substance, is like a grain of a fig, and in terms of time, like the turn of a drill.

Look at everything around you and realize that it is already breaking down, changing, and decaying, or that everything is made to die.

Think about what people are when they are eating, sleeping, having sex, going to the bathroom, and so on. Then think about what they are like when they have power over others—arrogant, quick to anger, and harsh in their punishment. And yet, just a little while ago, they were slaves to all those needs, and soon they will be slaves again.

What nature brings to each thing is good for it. And it is good for it at the time when nature brings it.

"Earth loves the rain, and the sky loves to give it." The whole world loves to create the future. I say to the world, "I share your love." Isn't that what it means when we say, "This loves to happen"?

Either you live on here, getting used to it; or you leave by your own decision; or you die, having done your duty. There's no other choice. So be cheerful.

Always keep in mind that "the grass is not greener" anywhere else, and that everything is the same here as it is on top of a mountain, by the sea, or anywhere else you choose to be. You'll find Plato's words fitting: "living within the walls of a city as if in a fold on a mountain."

What is my mind to me right now? What am I turning it into? What am I using it for? Is it lacking understanding? Has it become disconnected from social life? Has it become so mixed with the body that it just follows along with it?

A slave who runs away from their master is a fugitive. Law is our master, so breaking the law makes you a fugitive. In the same way, feeling pain, anger, or fear means you are rejecting something that has happened, is happening, or will happen—something that has been determined by the one who governs all things, who is law and assigns to everyone what is right. So, feeling fear, pain, or anger makes you a fugitive.

A man deposits his seed in a womb and leaves. Then another force takes over and makes a child. What an amazing result from such a simple beginning! Then the child takes in food, and another force creates sensation, movement, life, strength, and all sorts of other things. Look closely at these mysterious processes and see the power at work, just as we see gravity pulling things down or up—not with our eyes, but just as clearly.

Constantly remember that all the things happening now have happened before and will happen again in the future. Keep in mind the full stories from history or your own experience, like the court of Hadrian, the court of Antoninus, the court of Philip, Alexander, or Croesus. All the same as now, just with different actors.

Picture everyone who complains about anything as being like a pig that's being sacrificed, kicking and squealing. And think of the person who silently resents things as being like this pig too. Consider how we are all bound together and how only rational creatures can choose to willingly accept what happens; everything else must submit.

For everything you do, ask yourself if losing it through death makes death something to fear.

When you're offended by someone's wrongdoing, immediately think about how you might be doing something similar—like valuing money, pleasure, or reputation too much, and so on. This will help you quickly forget your anger, especially if you also remember that the person may be acting out of compulsion—what else could they do? Or, if you can, remove the cause of their compulsion.

When you see Satyrion, Eutyches, or Hymen, think of Socrates' circle; when you see Eutychion or Silvanus, think of Euphrates; when you see Tropaeophorus, think of Alciphron; when you see Severus, think of Crito or Xenophon; and when you look at yourself, think of one of the Caesars. In each case, think of someone similar from the past. Then, let this thought strike you: Where are those people now? Nowhere, or wherever. In this way, you will always see human life as nothing but smoke and dust, especially if you remind yourself that what has changed once will never exist again for the rest of time. So why stress? Why not be content with moving through this short life in an orderly way? What situation or role are you trying to avoid? What is all of this other than an exercise for your reason, which has carefully studied and understood life? Stay until you have taken in everything, just as a strong stomach digests all food, or a bright fire turns everything you throw into it into flame and light.

Don't let anyone truthfully say that you are not sincere or good; make sure that anyone who thinks this is lying. This is entirely within your power—who can stop you from being sincere and good? Just decide that you will not live any longer if you can't have these qualities. And reason will abandon anyone who won't have them.

In any situation, what can be done or said that is most reasonable? Whatever that is, it's within your power to do or say it—don't pretend there are obstacles. You will never stop complaining until you find the same joy in responding appropriately to each situation as a hedonist finds in their indulgences. Because you should consider it enjoyable to do what fits your nature, and you can do that anywhere.

A roller doesn't have the power to roll wherever it wants, nor do water or fire, or anything else controlled by nature or an irrational soul—many things can block them. But mind and reason have the power to move through everything that opposes them, by their nature and choice. Keep in mind this ability of reason to move through everything, like fire rising, a stone falling, or a roller going down a slope, and don't look for anything more. Any remaining obstacles either affect only the body, which is dead, or, without the judgment and consent of your own reason, they cannot hurt or harm you in any way; if they could, then the person affected would immediately become worse. But in the case of all other things that have a certain constitution, whatever harm happens to them makes them worse; however, a person becomes better and more praiseworthy by making good use of whatever happens to them. Finally, remember that nothing harms a citizen of nature unless it harms the city, and nothing harms the city unless it harms the law. None of the things we call misfortunes harms the law. So, what doesn't harm the law doesn't harm the city or the citizen either.

For someone who truly understands the principles of life, even the shortest and simplest reminder is enough to remove all pain and fear—for example:

"The wind blows last year's leaves to the ground ... and in the same way, the generations of men come and go."

Your children are like leaves, and so are those who praise you or curse you, or secretly blame or mock you. And those who will carry on your reputation in the future are like leaves too. All these things are like "leaves that grow in spring," as the poet says; then the wind blows them down, and the forest produces more leaves in their place. Everything is short-lived—that's their common fate—but you chase after things as if they would last forever. Soon, you will close your eyes, and soon someone else will mourn the person who buries you.

A healthy eye should see all there is to see and not say, "I only want to see green things"; that's a sign of disease. A healthy ear and nose should be ready to perceive all sounds and smells. A healthy stomach should be ready to accept all food, just as a mill grinds whatever it is made to grind. And in the same way, a healthy mind should be ready for all situations. A mind that says, "My children must live" or "Everyone must praise everything I do" is like an eye that only wants to see green or teeth that only want to chew soft things.

No one is so fortunate that there aren't people who will be pleased when they die. Even if they were a good and wise person, someone might still think, "At last, we can breathe freely, now that we're rid of this teacher. He was never harsh to any of us, but I could feel his silent judgment of us all." That's what they might say about a good person. But in your case, how many more reasons are there for people to want to get rid of you? Think about this when you're dying, and you'll leave more peacefully, thinking, "I'm leaving a life where even those I've worked, prayed, and cared for want me gone, hoping to get some small benefit from it." So why should anyone cling to a longer life here? But don't leave with less kindness towards them because of this. Instead, keep true to your own character—friendly, kind, generous—and leave life as easily as a soul leaving the body in a peaceful death. Nature connected you to them and made them your companions, but now she's releasing you. My release is like parting from family, but I do not resist or need to be forced. This, too, is part of following nature.

As much as you can, get into the habit of asking yourself, whenever someone else does something, "What is their purpose?" But start with yourself: examine yourself first.

Remember that what controls your actions is the part of you that's hidden inside: that's where the power to act comes from, that's the principle of life, and that's what you could call the real you. So, don't give as much thought to the body or the tools attached to it. These are just instruments like an axe, differing only in being attached to the body. There's no more use in these parts without the mind that moves and controls them than in a shuttle without the weaver, a pen without the writer, or a whip without the coachman.

Book 11

The rational mind has certain abilities: it can understand itself, shape itself, and make itself into whatever it chooses to be. It benefits from the results of its own actions—unlike plants and animals, whose fruits are used by others. The rational mind achieves its purpose no matter when life ends. It's not like a play or a dance where the whole performance is ruined if interrupted. Instead, at any moment, the rational mind is complete and fulfilled, and it can confidently say, "I have what is mine." It also explores the entire universe and the empty space around it, thinking about its shape. It stretches its understanding into infinite time, embracing the idea that everything renews in cycles. It understands that those who come after us won't see anything new, just as those before us didn't see anything different. Since things are so similar, a person who is 40 years old, if they understand anything, has in a way seen everything—both past and future.

Another quality of the rational mind is its love for others, its honesty, and its integrity. It values nothing more than itself, just like the law, which values justice above all. Therefore, true wisdom is no different from justice.

You'll think less of music, dancing, or wrestling if you break down a song into its separate notes and ask yourself about each one: "Is this something that controls me?" You'll be too embarrassed to admit that it does. Do the same with dance, analyzing each movement and pose, and with wrestling, too. For everything, except for virtue and virtuous actions, break it down into its parts, and you'll come to value it less. Apply this rule to your whole life as well.

What a noble soul it is, ready to leave the body at any moment, prepared for whatever happens next—whether that's disappearing, scattering, or continuing to exist. But this readiness should come from a thoughtful decision, not out of stubbornness like the Christians, but with dignity and in a way that others can respect, without being overly dramatic.

Have I done something good for others? Then I've also benefited. Keep this thought always in your mind, and never stop doing good.

What is your job? To be a good person. And how do you do this well, except by understanding the nature of the universe and the proper way for humans to live?

Tragedies were first performed to remind us of what can happen in life, showing that these events are natural. If you are moved by a play, you should not be upset by the larger stage of life because things must happen the way they do. Even those who cry out "Oh, Cithaeron!" in pain must bear it.

There are some wise sayings in tragedies, like,

"If my children and I are no longer cared for by the gods, this too has a reason,"

and,

"We should not get angry at mere things,"

and,

"Just as ripe corn is harvested, so are lives."

And there are many others like this.

After tragedies came the old comedies, which had value in their straightforward and honest humor, warning us against arrogance. Diogenes used this type of humor for the same purpose. Then came middle comedy and new comedy, which became more about imitation than teaching. Although these later works had some useful sayings, it's important to ask what the overall goal of this type of art was.

It's clear that there is no better way of life for practicing philosophy than the one you are currently living.

If a branch is cut from a tree, it is separated from the whole tree. In the same way, when a person separates from another person, they are cut off from the entire community. The branch is cut by someone else, but a person separates themselves by rejecting or hating their neighbor, not realizing they are cutting themselves off from society. But Zeus, who created human society, gave us the ability to reconnect with our neighbors and become part of the whole again. However, frequent separation makes it harder to reunite and return to the original state. In short, a branch that grows with the tree from the beginning is different from one that is cut off and then reattached, no matter what gardeners might say.

Share in their substance, but not in their beliefs.

Just as those who try to stop you from following reason won't succeed in diverting you from doing the right thing, don't let them push you away from your goodwill toward them. Keep an even balance, maintaining steady judgment and action while also being gentle with those who try to hinder you or who are against you. Being angry with them is just as much a weakness as abandoning your course out of fear. Both are failures to fulfill your duty—whether by running away in fear or by turning against your natural friends and fellow humans.

No nature is lower than art because art imitates nature. If this is true, then the most perfect and comprehensive nature could never be surpassed by any artistic invention. All arts create lower things for the sake of higher ones, and this is also how universal nature works. Justice originates from this, and all other virtues come from justice because justice cannot be maintained if we focus on indifferent things or are easily misled or changeable.

The things outside of you that you chase or avoid don't force themselves on you, but you go after them. If you keep your judgment of them calm, they will remain still, and you won't be seen as either chasing after or avoiding them.

The soul is like a sphere that keeps its shape if it does not stretch out toward anything or contract inward, flare up, or sink down. It should stay constant in its light, seeing the truth of all things and the truth within itself.

If someone looks down on me, that is their concern. But I will make sure that I don't say or do anything that deserves contempt. If someone hates me, that is their concern. But I will be kind and good to everyone, and I will be ready to show that person their mistake, not with criticism or showing off my tolerance, but with genuine goodwill, like the famous Phocion (if he wasn't being sarcastic). This should be the quality of our inner thoughts, which are open to the gods' eyes: they should see a person not complaining or feeling sorry for themselves. And what harm can come to you if you are acting in line with your own nature and accepting what suits the purpose of the universe as a human being at your post, working for the common good?

People may despise each other and flatter each other at the same time. They may want to surpass each other and yet bow down to each other.

How fake it is for someone to say, "I prefer to be honest with you!"—What are you talking about? There's no need to announce it. Your actions will show it soon enough. It should be obvious in your voice and the look in your eyes, just as a lover can read everything in their beloved's eyes. In short, a good and honest person should be like someone with a strong smell—anyone nearby will notice it, whether they want to or not. But pretending to be simple is like being a crooked stick. Nothing is more disgraceful than fake friendship. Avoid it most of all. The good, honest, and kind person shows these qualities clearly in their eyes, unmistakably.

Living well is within the power of the soul if it is indifferent to things that don't matter. It will be indifferent if it looks at each of these things separately and together, remembering that none of them forces an opinion about itself on us or comes to us on its own. These things remain still, and we create judgments about them, writing them into our minds. But we don't have to write them, and if any judgments slip into our minds, we can erase them. Remember, our attention to these things is brief, then life ends. So what trouble is there in doing this? If these things are natural, embrace them, and they will be easy; but if they are against nature, look for what fits your nature and go after that, even without recognition. Everyone is allowed to seek their own good.

Think about where each thing comes from, what it consists of, what it changes into, and what it will become when it changes. It will not be harmed.

If someone offends you, first consider: What is my relationship to others? We are made for each other. In another sense, I was made to lead them, like a ram leading its flock or a bull leading its herd. But start from the beginning: If everything is not just atoms, then nature governs everything. If this is true, then lower things exist for the sake of higher ones, and the higher ones for each other.

Next, consider what kind of people they are in private, and under what pressures they act as they do. Regarding their actions, consider how proud they are of their deeds.

Third, if what they do is right, you should not be upset; but if it's wrong, they are acting out of ignorance and not on purpose. Just as no soul likes to be robbed of truth, no soul wants to treat others worse than they deserve. People are upset when accused of being unjust, ungrateful, or selfish—wronging their neighbors.

Fourth, you also have many faults, and you are no different from them. Even if you avoid some wrongs, you still have the tendency to commit them, though you may abstain because of fear, concern about your reputation, or some other low motive.

Fifth, you may not even understand whether they are wrong, as many actions are done with regard to circumstances. A person must know a lot to judge another's actions correctly.

Sixth, when you are angry or upset, remember that human life is brief, and soon we will all be dead.

Seventh, it is not their actions that upset us, because these lie in their own minds, but our judgments of them. Remove these judgments, decide to dismiss your belief that an act is harmful, and your anger will disappear. How do you remove these judgments? By reflecting that no wrongful act of another harms you unless you also do many wrongs, becoming a thief and worse.

Eighth, more pain comes from our anger and frustration about these acts than from the acts themselves.

Ninth, a kind disposition is unbeatable if it is sincere, not fake or forced. What can the most aggressive person do to you if you remain kind? If, when they try to hurt you, you gently correct them and show them what they're doing wrong, saying, "Not so, my friend; we were meant for something better. You can't hurt me, but you are hurting yourself." Show them kindly how things are, without being ironic or critical. Your advice should be friendly, without bitterness or a desire to impress, whether alone or in the presence of others.

Remember these nine rules as gifts from the Muses, and start to be a good person while you are still alive. Avoid flattering others and being angry in your interactions, as both are harmful to society. When you feel anger rising, remind yourself that there is nothing strong about being angry; calmness and gentleness are more human and, therefore, more manly. Those who are gentle have strength, resilience, and courage, unlike those who are angry and upset. The more a person controls their emotions, the closer they are to real power. Anger and pain show weakness, as both have been wounded and have surrendered.

Finally, remember this tenth lesson from the leader of the Muses: It is madness to expect bad people not to do wrong, as this is impossible. But it is cruel to allow them to act this way toward others while demanding they do no wrong to you.

There are four main errors of the rational mind you should watch out for and remove when you notice them, saying to yourself: "This thought is unnecessary," "This thought harms social unity," "This is not an honest thought," and "This is a failure of the higher, rational part to the lower, bodily part, giving in to physical pleasures."

The air and fire elements in you naturally tend to rise, but they obey the order of the whole and stay within the body. The earth and water elements naturally tend to sink, but they are also raised up and stay in place. So even the elements obey the universe, staying in their assigned places until the universe signals their release.

So isn't it strange that only your intelligent part rebels and complains about its place? And yet nothing is forced on it—only what fits its own nature. But still, it refuses to comply and goes in the opposite direction. Any movement toward injustice, excess, anger, pain, or fear is a rejection of nature. When the rational mind feels resentment about anything, it is deserting its proper role. It was created not only for justice toward others but also for reverence and service to the gods, which is another form of fellowship, perhaps even more important than justice.

A person who does not have one consistent goal in life cannot remain the same throughout their life. We need to decide what that goal should be. People have different ideas about what is good, but only one thing is universally recognized as good, and that is the well-being of the community. Therefore, we should aim to benefit others, and a person who directs all their efforts toward this goal will be consistent in all their actions, remaining the same throughout their life.

Think of the country mouse and the town mouse and how the town mouse was frightened and anxious.

Socrates called the common beliefs of many people "bogeymen," things to scare children.

At public events, the Spartans set up shaded seats for visitors but sat wherever they could find a spot.

Socrates once declined an invitation to visit Perdiccas of Macedon, saying, "I don't want to die the worst death," meaning accepting a favor and then not being able to return it.

The writings of Epicurus tell us to constantly think of those who followed the path of virtue before us.

The Pythagoreans advised looking at the sky at dawn to remind ourselves of the constancy of the stars, their unchanging duty, order, purity, and openness. No star is covered by a veil.

Think of Socrates, who wore just a skin when Xanthippe took his cloak, and how he spoke to his friends who were embarrassed when they saw him dressed like that.

In writing and reading, you must learn before you can teach. This is even truer in life.

You were born a slave: you have no voice.

And my heart laughed within.

And virtue they curse, speaking harsh words.

It is foolish to look for figs in winter, just as it is to hope for a child when it is no longer possible.

When you kiss your child, Epictetus said, you should remind yourself, "Tomorrow, they may die." But some people think these are bad words. Epictetus replied, "Nothing is bad if it reflects nature's process. Otherwise, it would be bad to talk about corn being harvested."

The unripe grape, ripe bunch, and dried grape all change, not into nothing, but into something else that is not yet.

No one can take away our free will. Epictetus also said, "We must develop a skill in agreeing with things, and in all our actions, we should ensure they are appropriate to the situation, have a social purpose, and match the value of the goal. We must avoid personal motivation and not reject anything outside our control."

The dispute, Epictetus said, is not about a small matter, but about whether we are sane or mad.

Socrates used to ask, "What do you want? The souls of rational or irrational people?" "Rational souls." "What kind of rational souls? Healthy or unhealthy?" "Healthy." "Then why don't you seek them?" "Because we already have them." "Then why are you fighting and quarreling?"

Book 12

Everything you want to achieve through a long and difficult path, you can have right now if you allow it. This means if you stop worrying about the past, trust that the future will take care of itself, and focus on doing the right thing in the present. Be satisfied with what life has given you because nature chose it for you, and you were made for it. Always be truthful and fair, saying what is right and doing what matches the worth of every person. Don't let someone else's bad actions, opinions, or words, or even the feelings in your body, stop you. Let your mind take care of that. If, when you are close to death, you focus only on your mind and the spirit within you, and if you fear not that life will end, but that you might not have lived it according to nature, then you will be a person worthy of the universe that made you. You will no longer feel like a stranger in the world, surprised by what happens as if it were unexpected or dependent on this or that.

God sees our minds without the covering of the body and all its impurities. His connection is only between His intelligence and the intelligence He gave us. If you learn to do the same, you will free yourself from many distractions. It is unlikely that someone who ignores the body would waste time worrying about clothes, houses, reputation, or other superficial things.

You are made up of three things: a little body, a little breath, and intelligence. The first two are yours to care for, but the third—your intelligence—is truly yours. If you separate your mind from what others do or say, from what you have done or said, from worries about the future, from what your body experiences or what the breath (life) within you feels, and from all the chaos around you, then your mind will be free to act justly, accept what happens, and speak the truth. If you can do this, you will be able to live the rest of your life peacefully and in harmony with the spirit inside you.

I often wonder why people love themselves more than anyone else but value other people's opinions more than their own. If a god or a wise teacher told you to only think and plan things you would openly share as soon as you think of them, you wouldn't be able to do it for even one day. This shows that we respect what others think of us more than what we think of ourselves.

How could the gods, who arranged everything so well for us, overlook one thing—that good people, who have the most connection with the divine through their actions, would completely cease to exist when they die? But if this is true, trust that if it should have been different, the gods would have made it so. If it were fair, it would be possible; if it were natural, nature would have made it so. Since it isn't different, be sure it should not be different—for in questioning this, you are arguing with the divine. And we should not argue with the gods unless we believe they are just and good—if so, they would not let anything in the universe be neglected unfairly or without reason.

Even if you don't think you can achieve something, practice it anyway. Just like how your left hand might be weaker, but with practice, it can hold the reins stronger than your right.

Think about what kind of person you should be when death comes for you. Consider how short life is, how vast the past and future are, and how weak all material things are.

Look at things without their coverings; think about the reasons behind actions; consider what pain, pleasure, death, and fame really are, and how no one can truly harm you unless you let them.

In applying your beliefs, be like a boxer, not a gladiator. The gladiator can drop his sword and be killed, but the boxer always has his hands ready to defend himself.

See things as they truly are by breaking them down into their basic parts—material, cause, and purpose.

Remember that humans have the power to do what is right and accept what happens according to nature. We should not blame the gods, for they do no wrong, nor blame humans, as they only do wrong without meaning to. So, we should blame no one.

How silly it is to be surprised by anything that happens in life.

There is either an unchangeable destiny, kind Providence, or complete chaos without a plan. If it is destiny, why fight it? If Providence, make yourself worthy of divine help. If chaos, be happy that you have a mind to guide you. Even if chaos takes your body, breath, and everything else, it cannot take away your mind.

A lamp's light keeps shining until it goes out; will the truth, justice, and self-control within you stop before you die?

When you think someone has done wrong, ask yourself, "How do I know this is really wrong?" And even if it is, how do I know they haven't already punished themselves for it? Wanting a bad person not to do wrong is like wanting a fig tree not to produce figs, babies not to cry, or horses not to neigh—these things must happen. What should you do if someone has a bad character? If you get angry, work on fixing that in yourself.

If it's not right, don't do it; if it's not true, don't say it.

Whenever something makes an impression on you, break it down into its basic parts—what causes it, what it's made of, what its purpose is, and how long it will last.

Understand that inside you is something stronger and more divine than the emotions that make you act like a puppet on strings. Ask yourself, "What's in my mind right now? Fear, suspicion, desire, or something else?"

First, do nothing without purpose. Second, make sure everything you do is for the common good.

Remember that soon you will be nobody and nowhere, and the same is true for everything and everyone you see now. Everything is made to change, die, and transform so that new things can come into being.

Remember that everything is just how you think about it, and you have control over your thoughts. So, whenever you want, you can change your thoughts, and like a sailor who has safely sailed past a dangerous cape, you'll find calm waters and a peaceful bay.

When any activity ends at the right time, it doesn't suffer because it has ended. And the person who did this activity doesn't suffer either just because it stopped. In the same way, when all the activities that make up a person's life come to an end at the right time, it doesn't suffer because of that. The person who finishes their life at the right time hasn't been treated unfairly either. Nature decides the right time and end, sometimes because of old age, and always because of the universal nature, which keeps the whole world fresh and young by constantly changing its parts.

Everything that helps the whole universe is always good and happens at the right time. So, the end of life for every person isn't bad because it's not shameful. It isn't something we can control, and it doesn't harm the common good. In fact, it's good because it happens at the right time and helps the universe. When we follow this natural process, we're moving in the same direction as the divine will.

There are three important principles to remember: First, in everything you do, act thoughtfully and justly, just as justice itself would. Second, when things happen to you from outside, understand that they happen either by chance or by divine guidance, and don't blame chance or accuse divine providence. Third, think about what each living being is, from the moment it's conceived to when it first receives a soul, and from that moment until it gives the soul back. Think about what each being is made of and what it will become after it dies. If you were suddenly lifted high above the earth and could look down at all human activities, you'd see how small and short-lived they are. You'd realize that every time you looked down, you'd see the same things—things that aren't worth being proud of.

If you get rid of your judgment, you save yourself. Who is stopping you from letting go of it?

When you worry about something, you've forgotten that everything happens according to the universal nature. You've forgotten that someone else's wrong act doesn't harm you. You've also forgotten that everything that happens has always happened this way and will continue to happen everywhere. Lastly, you've forgotten how closely connected you are to the whole human race—not just by blood, but by shared intelligence. You've forgotten that each person's intelligence is divine, that nothing truly belongs to you, not even your child, your body, or your soul, because they all come from the divine. You've forgotten that everything is just opinion and that every person only lives in the present moment, losing only that moment.

Think often about those who have complained a lot or who have been famous, unfortunate, or successful in any way. Then ask yourself, where are they now? They're nothing but smoke and ashes, just a story or maybe not even a story anymore. Remember people like Fabius Catellinus in the countryside, Lucius Lupus in his gardens, Stertinius at Briae, Tiberius at Capri, and Velius Rufus. Think about how they chased after things with pride, but how worthless those things are now. It's much wiser to use the opportunities you have to be just, self-controlled, and obedient to the gods, and to do this simply and without pride. The worst kind of pride is the kind that's proud of not being proud.

To those who ask, "Where have you seen the gods, or how do you know they exist and worship them?" I would answer first that the gods can be seen with our eyes. Secondly, even though I haven't seen my own soul, I still honor it. In the same way, from all the experiences I've had of the gods' power, I'm sure they exist, and I respect them.

The safety of life lies in examining everything completely—what it is, what it's made of, and why it exists. With all your heart, do what is right and tell the truth. What else is there but to enjoy life by doing good things one after another, without leaving any gaps between them?

There is one light from the sun, even though it is blocked by walls, mountains, and many other things. There is one common substance, even though it is spread out among many different bodies with their own qualities. There is one soul, even though it is shared among many different living beings. There is one intelligent soul, even though it seems divided among many individuals. All these parts—like air and matter—don't have feelings and don't naturally connect with each other. But even these parts are held together by an intelligent force that pulls them towards each other. The mind, in a special way, reaches out to others like itself and connects with them, so the sense of fellowship isn't broken.

What do you want—to keep living? Do you want to keep feeling, moving, growing, and then stop growing, speaking, and thinking? Which of these things seems worth desiring to you? If you can easily set aside all these things, focus on what remains—following reason and God. But if you value these other things and worry about losing them because of death, you're going against reason and God.

How small a part of endless and unknowable time is given to each of us, and how quickly it disappears into eternity! How small a part of all the matter in the universe! How small is the tiny piece of earth you crawl on! When you think about all this, don't think anything is important except acting according to your nature and accepting whatever happens according to universal nature.

How does your ruling mind use itself? Everything depends on this. Everything else, whether you can control it or not, is just lifeless ashes and smoke.

A powerful reminder to think little of death is that even those who think pleasure is good and pain is bad have not feared death.

For someone whose only good is what happens at the right time, who is equally satisfied with more or fewer opportunities to act according to reason, and who doesn't care whether they view the world for a long or short time, death has no fear.

Mortal human, you have been a citizen in this great world; what difference does it make if it's for five years or fifty? For what follows the laws is fair for everyone. So where is the difficulty, if it's not a tyrant or an unjust judge sending you away from the world, but nature itself, which brought you into it? It's like a director who hired an actor dismissing him from the stage. "But I haven't finished my five acts, only three," you might say. You're right, but in life, three acts can be the whole play. What makes a complete drama is decided by the one who caused its beginning and now its end; you are not the cause of either. So leave satisfied, for the god who releases you is also satisfied.

The Tao Te Ching

Laozi

Shang Pian

Chapter 1

The Dao that can be spoken is not the eternal Dao;
The name that can be named is not the eternal name.
The nameless is the source of heaven and earth;
The named is the mother of all things.
Therefore,
Without desire, you see the mystery's beginning;
With desire, you see its manifestations.
Though they come from the same source, they are different in
    name;
Both are called the Mystery.
Mystery within Mystery, the gateway to all wonders.

Chapter 2

Everyone understands what beauty is;
That is because there is ugliness.
Everyone knows what goodness is;
That is because there is evil.
Therefore,
Being and nothingness give birth to one another,
Hard and easy create each other,
Long and short define each other,
High and low complete each other,
Music and sound harmonize with each other,
Front and back follow one another.
Thus,
The sage focuses on non-action in his works,
Practices silence in his words.
The myriad things arise but are left alone,
The sage creates but does not possess,
Acts but does not claim,

Achieves but does not take credit.
Because he does not seek credit, it never leaves him.

Chapter 3

Not seeking virtue
keeps the people from competing.
Not valuing rare treasures
keeps the people from becoming thieves.
Not displaying what is desirable
keeps the people's hearts undisturbed.
Therefore, in the sage's peaceful and quiet world,
People's minds are calm,
Their bellies are full,
Their ambitions are reduced,
Their bodies are strong.
People are kept unknowing and without desire,
And even those who know do not dare to act.
Acting without action,
Nothing is left undone.

Chapter 4

The Dao is empty,
Not seeking virtue
keeps the people from competing.
Not valuing rare treasures
keeps the people from becoming thieves.
Not displaying what is desirable
keeps the people's hearts undisturbed.
Therefore, in the sage's peaceful and quiet world,
People's minds are calm,
Their bellies are full,
Their ambitions are reduced,
Their bodies are strong.
People are kept unknowing and without desire,

And even those who know do not dare to act.
Acting without action,
Nothing is left undone.

Chapter 5

The sky and the earth do not show kindness,
They treat the myriad things like straw dogs.
The sage does not show kindness,
He treats people like straw dogs.
The space between heaven and earth, how like a great bellows!
Empty, yet never exhausted,
Move it, and wind comes forth.
Too many words lead to nothing.
It is better to stay balanced between extremes.

Chapter 6

The valley-spirit never dies; it is called the primal mother.
The gate of the primal mother is the root of the world.
Her supply is endless,
Using her will never deplete her.

Chapter 7

Heaven and earth are eternal.
The reason heaven and earth endure
Is because they do not live for themselves,
Therefore, they last forever.
Because of this, the sage places himself behind others,
Yet finds himself ahead.
He is unconcerned with discomfort and danger,
Yet he survives.
Is it not because he is selfless
That he ultimately achieves fulfillment?

Chapter 8

The best character is like water.
Water's virtue is that it benefits all things without competing,
And it flows to places that others avoid,
Thus, it is close to the Dao.
It is good to live on solid ground,
To deepen the heart,
To love people when among them,
To keep one's word when speaking,
To be at peace when governing,
To do what one is capable of,
To act at the right moment.
Because it does not compete,
It is without blame.

Chapter 9

Rather than filling a cup until it overflows, it is better to stop in
   time.
Hammering and sharpening will soon wear it down.
Filling a hall with riches, one cannot protect it.
The man who is arrogant from great wealth invites disaster.
Stepping back after success aligns with the way of the universe.

Chapter 10

If the soul keeps being controlled by the body,
How can the body and soul not separate?
Forcing oneself to appear delicate,
How can one remain like a baby?
Clean the mirror of the true source,
How can it not reveal its flaws?
To love people and govern a country,
How can one not appoint the wise?
The gate of heaven opens and closes constantly,
How can one act like a passive observer?

Having understood causes and effects,
How can one stick to unfinished tasks?
Nurture and nourish them,
Create without possessing,
Act without claiming,
Lead without controlling.
This is called profound virtue.

Chapter 11

Join thirty spokes to a single hub,
It is the empty space at the center that makes the wheel useful.
Shape clay into a vessel,
It is the empty space inside that makes the vessel useful.
Cut doors and windows for a room,
It is the empty space within that makes the room useful.
Thus, what is made provides only the form,
But what we use is the original empty space.

Chapter 12

Beautiful colors blind people's eyes,
Appealing music deafens people's ears,
Delicious flavors dull people's taste,
Indulging in hunting drives people's hearts wild,
Pursuing rare treasures leads to improper behavior.
Thus, the sage focuses on the inner world, not the outer.
He discards the outer and embraces the inner.

Chapter 13

Honor and disgrace are equally alarming,
And great troubles arise because of the body.
What does it mean by "Honor and disgrace are equally alarming"?
Honor is fleeting,
It is frightening to receive it, and frightening to lose it.

This is what is meant by "Honor and disgrace are equally
    alarming."
What does it mean by "Great trouble is like the body"?
The reason I have great trouble is because I have a body;
If I had no body, what trouble could I have?
Therefore, if you view your body as the world,
you can be trusted to govern the world;
If you cherish your body as the world,
you are worthy of caring for the world.

Chapter 14

That which can be seen but not observed is called invisible;
That which can be heard but not perceived is called soundless;
That which can be touched but not grasped is called intangible.
These three cannot be fully understood, and so they merge into
    one.
Above, it is not bright; below, it is not dark.
A continuous thread without a name returns to the formless.
It is called the form of the formless, the image of the imageless.
This is called the indistinct and mysterious.
Approach it, and you cannot see its front; follow it, and you cannot
    see its back.
By holding onto the Dao of the present, you can master the
    present moment and understand the origins of the past.
This is called the thread of the Dao.

Chapter 15

Once upon a time, those who knew the Way were mysterious and
    subtle people,
Fleeting yet deep, tranquil yet utterly unfathomable.
Since they are difficult to describe, I can only speak of what they
    seemed like:
Cautious, as if crossing a winter river,
Wary, as if fearful of their neighbors.

Solemn, like courteous house guests.

Elusive, like melting ice.

Pure and natural, like uncut gems.

Vast and open, like a deep valley.

Yet mysterious, oh yes, like troubled waters.

Who can stay calm amidst the turbulence, allowing clarity to emerge from within?

Who can remain at peace eternally, allowing movement to give birth to nature?

For those who follow the Way, fulfillment was never their goal.

Only because they are never fully satisfied, they can continuously find renewal.

Chapter 16

Immersed in the heart of the void, hold on to the essence of tranquility.

The myriad things arise together,

And through this, I see their returning.

Now things bloom, and in blooming, each one returns to its source.

Returning to the source is called tranquility,

This is the return to destiny,

The return to destiny is eternal,

To know the eternal is wisdom.

Not knowing wisdom leads to disaster!

Knowing the eternal brings vast understanding,

Vast understanding leads to open-mindedness,

Open-mindedness leads to being regal,

Being regal leads to being heavenly,

Being heavenly leads to the Dao,

The Dao leads to everlasting.

Thus, one can face the perishing of the body without fear.

Chapter 17

Great rulers are barely known by their subjects,
Next come those the people draw near and praise,
Then those the people fear,
And finally, those the people despise.
If a ruler lacks trust, trust will not be given.
Act without arrogance;
Achieve without boasting;
When deeds are done, the people will say it happened naturally.

Chapter 18

When the Dao is lost, benevolence and righteousness arise.
When prudence and wisdom emerge, hypocrisy grows.
When family relationships are in disorder, filial piety and parental
    affection appear.
When the state is in chaos, loyalty and faithfulness are proclaimed.

Chapter 19

Abandon holiness, relinquish wisdom; the people will thrive a
    hundredfold.
Abandon benevolence, relinquish righteousness; the people will
    return to filial piety and affection.
Abandon cleverness, relinquish profit; and thieves and robbers
    will disappear.
As I know these three are not just empty words,
Hold fast to what is trustworthy.
Embrace simplicity, cherish purity,
Lessen the self, and diminish desires.

Chapter 20

Discard conventional doctrines, and be free from anxieties.
Flattery or reprimand, what difference does it make?
Good or evil, what does it matter?
Just because people are in awe, must you remain indifferent?

Ridiculous! Baseless!
When everyone is celebrating with joy,
As if they've achieved a spiritual victory,
As if they're enjoying a great feast,
I alone am empty, contemplating the endless future,
Dazed like a newborn,
Living in the moment, pondering the unknown.
When everyone feels full,
I alone feel hollow.
I am a fool! Confused!
When everyone seems enlightened, I alone am in doubt;
When everyone is alert, I alone am lost.
Mysterious! Like the dim twilight,
Vast! Like the infinite universe.
When everyone is focused, I alone am stubborn and lowly.
I alone am different from the ordinary,
I find refuge in the embrace of this profound Dao.

Chapter 21

Where the greatest Virtue resides,
Only the Dao can reveal it.
Things that embody the Dao
Shine with freedom and ease.
Eased! Liberated from form, yet perfectly shaped;
Freed! At ease with its place, yet steady.
Mesmerizing! Mysterious!
A light shines from within;
Its radiance so pure, it reveals the truth.
Through all time,
Its name remains undiminished,
Gathering all the marvels of human understanding.
How do I know the essence of all these wonders?
By observing things that embody the Dao.

Chapter 22

Fractured, one seeks unity,
Crooked, one strives for straightness,
Depressed, one appears fulfilled,
Exhausted, one shows freshness,
Ignorant, one expresses wisdom,
Excessive, one becomes misguided.
Thus, the master upholds integrity,
And sets an example for the people.
Without professing, enlightenment is revealed,
Without contending, brilliance shines,
Without proclaiming, praises are won,
Without demanding dignity, respect is earned.
The master does not compete,
Therefore remains uncontested.
"Fractured, one seeks unity"—
Such timeless wisdom!
With true integrity, one rediscovers oneself.

Chapter 23

Speak less, and words will naturally express themselves.
Thus, gusts cannot chill a vibrant day,
Showers cannot turn daylight into dusk.
Why is this so?
Even heaven and earth cannot resist their own force,
How can people do so?
Therefore, those who follow the Dao find joy in knowing that:
The Dao is the teaching,
Virtue is the Virtue,
And perplexity is simply perplexity.
Aligned with the Dao, the Dao welcomes them;
Aligned with Virtue, Virtue appreciates them;
Aligned with perplexity, even perplexity satisfies them.
A lack of faith

Explains why disbelief persists in this seeming futility.

Chapter 24

Those who tip-toe cannot stand firm,
Those who stride cannot walk steadily,
Those who show off do not shine,
Those who are self-righteous lack true justification.
Those who assert themselves achieve nothing,
Those who esteem themselves do not endure.
According to the Dao,
These are called excess and arrogance,
Which the people despise.
Therefore, those who embrace the Dao do not dwell in such ways.

Chapter 25

Before existence,
Before the birth of heaven and earth,
It was tranquil, desolate!
Independent and unmoved,
Cyclic and unbroken,
The mother of all nature.
Its true name is unknown,
I call it the Art of the Dao,
And describe it as great.
Being great, it is far-reaching,
Being far-reaching, it is distant,
Being distant, it returns.
Thus, the Dao is great,
Heaven is great,
Earth is great,
And the master is also great.
These are the four noble greatnesses,
And the master is one of them.
Humanity follows the earth,

The earth follows heaven,
Heaven follows the Dao,
The Dao follows nature.

Chapter 26

Heaviness is the root of lightness,
Temperance is the master of temperament.
Therefore, the master stays close to essential resources in their
    endeavors;
Even when there are sights and distractions,
They remain calm and composed.
Why then would a leader of many followers,
Risk their own body in pursuit of the world?
Being light, they lose their root;
Being tempestuous, they forfeit mastery.

Chapter 27

Good traveling leaves no tracks;
Good speech leaves no room for reproach;
Good strategies require no scheming;
Good fastening needs no hinges, yet no door can be opened;
The good knot is tied without a rope, and it cannot be undone.
Thus, the Sage never fails to save people,
Therefore, no one is rejected;
The Sage never fails to save things,
Therefore, nothing is abandoned.
This is true illumination.
Thus, the good are teachers to the bad,
And the bad are resources for the good.
One who fails to respect their teacher,
And does not cherish their resources,
No matter how intelligent, is deeply confused.
This is the essential mystery!

Chapter 28

Gain knowledge of the external, but
Acquaint yourself with the internal, and
Become the wellspring of the earth.
Be the earth's fountain, be Virtuous and unwavering,
And be renewed.
Recognize the brilliance of the spotlight, but
Stay in the shadows, and
Become an example for the people.
Be the people's example, be Virtuous without excess,
And find peace.
Know the glory, but
Show humility, and
Become the world's refuge.
Be the world's refuge, be Virtuous and content,
And return to your roots.
When uprooted, wood can be shaped into tools;
The master uses it to become a respected leader.
Thus, a great tailor seldom trims.

Chapter 29

It is futile to try to possess the universe,
Or to shape it according to one's ambitions.
The workings of the universe cannot be controlled,
One cannot act upon them.
Act upon them, and you will fail;
Grasp them, and they will slip away.
For everything, there is a time to advance and a time to retreat,
A time to blow and a time to breathe,
A time for strength and a time for weakness,
A time to carry and a time to ride.
Thus, the master avoids extremes,
Avoids extravagance, and avoids grandeur.

Chapter 30

Those who offer advice on the Art of governance
Do not recommend using force to dominate the world,
Understanding it invites retaliation.
Where troops march, thorns grow.
After great armies, years of resentment follow.
Thus, the master aims only to achieve the goal,
Daring not to seek dominance.
Accomplish, but avoid glorification,
Accomplish, but restrain aggression,
Accomplish, but reject pride,
Accomplish only because it is necessary,
Accomplish, but refuse domination.
Things that mature grow old,
This is not the Way of the Dao.
Without following the Dao, one perishes prematurely.

Chapter 31

Where everyone is heavily armed, the state is in vain,
Such actions are resented,
Therefore, the master does not dwell there.
Thus, the master finds refuge in what remains,
And acts based on righteousness.
Weapons are tools of destruction,
They are not the instruments of a master.
Used only when absolutely necessary,
Peace and reconciliation are paramount,
Victory is achieved without glorification.
Those who glorify victory take pleasure in bloodshed,
And those who take pleasure in bloodshed
Cannot win the hearts of the people.
Therefore, in times of prosperity, remain humble,
In adversity, act with righteousness.
Thus, the general stands on the left,

The admiral stands on the right,
In solemn remembrance.
Casualties are mourned with consolation,
And victories are remembered with solemnity.

Chapter 32

The Dao remains eternally unknowable.
Its unexploited nature may seem insignificant,
Yet no one under heaven can control it.
When kings and nobles abide by it,
The myriad things naturally follow.
Heaven and earth work together,
To bring about the morning dew,
Without human intervention, the droplets spread evenly.
In society, establishments come with titles;
Once titles are given, one must learn restraint.
With self-restraint, disaster can be avoided.
In this way, the Dao manifests in the world,
Like rivers merging into the vast oceans.

Chapter 33

Knowing others is intelligence,
Knowing oneself is enlightenment.
Conquering others is strength,
Conquering oneself is true invincibility.
Those who are content are truly wealthy,
Those who are driven by ambition are enslaved by it.
Those who hold to their principles will endure,
Those who pass but are not forgotten live on.

Chapter 34

The implications of the Tao are vast and far-reaching. Ubiquitous!
It can influence and sway everything, to the left or right.
The myriad things depend on it, yet it never turns away,

Fulfilling all without seeking recognition.
It supports the myriad things without claiming ownership,
Always without desire,
Thus, it is called modest.
It is immersed in all things without taking possession,
Thus, it is called great.
Therefore, the master avoids seeking greatness,
And is thereby able to accomplish great deeds.

Chapter 35

Herald a great symbol,
And the people will come.
Come toward teachings that do no harm,
And the people will find safety,
Peace, and prosperity.
Music and temptations make the visitor linger.
The words of the Dao
Are tasteless and without sensation.
Look, and it cannot be seen,
Listen, and it cannot be heard,
Use it, and it cannot be exhausted.

Chapter 36

If one wishes to shrink something, one must first expand it greatly;
If one wishes to weaken something, one must first strengthen it greatly;
If one wishes to discard something, one must first allow it to flourish greatly;
If one wishes to obtain something, one must first give it abundantly.
This is the Knowledge of Subtlety.
Gentleness overcomes hardness,
Vulnerability overcomes dominance.
Fish cannot leave the depths,

Deadly weapons should not be shown to the people.

Chapter 37

The Dao remains in non-action, yet nothing is left undone.
When leaders follow this way,
The myriad things transform naturally.
When transformed, desires arise,
I would quiet them with the unexploited and unknowable.
Without knowledge or exploitation, one is led to no desire.
Without desire and in tranquility,
The world corrects itself.

Xia Pian

Chapter 38

Those with great Virtue are not confined by virtues,
Thus, they remain with Virtue.
Those without Virtue cannot free themselves from the rules of
    virtue,
Thus, they remain without Virtue.
Those with great Virtue act without seeking credit,
Those without Virtue act and demand recognition.
The humane act charitably without seeking reputation.
The righteous act in the name of justice and seek glory.
The moral act, but when there is no response,
They force the issue, alas, to no avail.
Thus, when the Dao is lost, there is Virtue;
When Virtue is lost, there is humanity;
When humanity is lost, there is righteousness;
When righteousness is lost, there is morality.
When the rituals of morality become customary,
Devotion and faith grow shallow, and turmoil begins to stir.
When scholars are given priority,
The Dao becomes glorified and used to deceive the masses.

Therefore, the master is concerned with depth,
Not with appearances;
Focuses on integrity, not on glory.
Thus, let go of the exterior and embrace the interior.

Chapter 39

When aligned with the Dao:
When heaven is at one, it is clear,
When earth is at one, it is fertile,
When the spirit is at one, it is calm,
When shelter is at one, it is secure,
When the myriad things are at one, there is life,
When leaders are at one, the people are respectful,
And all things become united.
If heaven loses its clarity, there is fear of collapse;
If earth becomes barren, there is dread of disaster;
If the spirit is disturbed, there is anxiety over death;
If shelter is deprived, there is panic over decline;
If the myriad things are lifeless, there is fear of extinction;
If leaders become disrespectful,
Obsessed with admiration for their own power,
The people grow terrified under authority.
Thus, true admiration stems from humility,
Supremacy finds its foundation in lowliness.
When leaders remain uninvolved, detached, and undeserving,
Is it not rooted in humility?
Therefore, prepare your chariots and set them aside.
Desire not crowns and jewels,
But remain composed in the grit and gravel.

Chapter 40

Resilience reflects the Dao in action,
Vulnerability shows the Dao in expression.
The myriad things in the universe are born from existence,

And existence is born from non-existence.

Chapter 41

The learned discover the Dao and follow it naturally;
The seeker discovers the Dao and questions its power;
The unlearned discover the Dao and burst into laughter,
Without their laughter, it wouldn't be the Dao.
Thus, the words of wisdom say:
Those enlightened by the Dao appear confused,
Those moving toward the Dao seem to fall behind,
Those who discredit the Dao seem honorable,
The Virtuous seem empty and desolate,
The honest seem humiliated,
Those with noble Virtue seem to lack,
Those who build on Virtue seem deceitful,
Those with principled character seem uncertain.
Great squareness has no sharp corners,
Great tools take time to craft,
Great vocalists rarely raise their voices,
Great symbols are formless.
The Dao is the master of providing and empowering.

Chapter 42

The Dao gives birth to unity,
Unity gives birth to duality,
Duality gives birth to trinity,
Trinity gives birth to the myriad things.
The myriad things carry shadows and embrace radiance,
Infused with the breath of life to achieve the harmony of darkness,
    light, and soul.
(People dislike being uninvolved, irrelevant, and undeserving,
Yet true leaders align themselves with these qualities.)
Thus, things may be gained by losing,
And may be lost by gaining.

What others proclaim, I will also declare:
"Forcing principles will not make them sustainable."
Let this be the heart and soul of the message.

Chapter 43

The softest in the world
Overcomes the hardest in the world.
What has no substance enters where there is no space.
Thus, we come to appreciate the benefits of non-action.
The teachings of unspoken words,
The power of inaction,
Few things in this world can compare.

Chapter 44

Fame and honor, which is more relatable?
Health and wealth, which is more essential?
Success and failure, which is more damaging?
Thus, great admiration comes with a heavy cost,
Accumulating treasures leads to the loss of modesty.
Embrace humility to avoid humiliation,
Know your limits to become limitless and enduring.

Chapter 45

Great support appears insufficient,
Yet when used, it does not fail.
Great buoyancy seems hollow,
Yet when utilized, it never runs out.
Great honesty appears flawed,
Great skill seems inept,
Great speech seems inarticulate.
Movement overcomes cold,
Stillness overcomes heat,
Through tranquility, the world finds its righteousness.

Chapter 46

When the world follows the Dao,
Carriages are used to transport manure.
When the world strays from the Dao,
Armed chariots line the city gates.
There is no greater sin than temptation,
No greater fault than discontent,
No greater guilt than constant desire.
Therefore, know contentment, and you will always have enough.

Chapter 47

Without leaving home,
You can understand the universe.
Without looking through windows of knowledge,
You can grasp the Dao.
The farther you travel, the less you may know.
Thus, the master does not travel, yet is wise,
Does not see, yet is insightful,
Does not act, yet is accomplished.

Chapter 48

In pursuing scholarship, each day brings something to gain.
In practicing the Dao, each day brings something to lose.
When you have lost all that can be lost,
You arrive at a state of non-action.
Act without acting, and nothing will be left undone!
Thus, those who can master the universe
Often remain unoccupied;
Those who are preoccupied
Cannot master the universe.

Chapter 49

The masters never close their minds,
But align their minds with the minds of the people.

To those who are kind, be kind;
To those who are unkind, be kind as well.
Kindness is the way of Virtue.
To those who are faithful, have faith in them;
To those who are unfaithful, have faith in them as well.
Faithfulness is the way of Virtue.
The master remains ever watchful over the world,
And is concerned for the people.
The people pay attention to the master's words and actions,
And the master nurtures them all in innocence.

Chapter 50

Emerging from birth and disappearing into death:
Three out of ten are followers of life,
Three out of ten are followers of death,
And three out of ten pursue life,
But end up in the place of death.
Why is this so?
Because they overindulge in their pursuit of life.
Those who truly understand the essence of living
Can walk through the forest without being attacked by tigers,
Enter battlefields without being harmed by weapons.
Brutality finds no way to strike,
Tigers find no place to lay their claws,
Enemies find no opening to lodge their swords.
Why is this so?
Because they never enter a realm of death.

Chapter 51

The Dao conceives,
Virtue nurtures,
Things take form,
Movement gives them power.
Thus, among the myriad things,

None fail to respect the Dao and honor Virtue.
Respect for the Dao,
Honor for Virtue,
Are not commanded, yet arise naturally.
Therefore, the Dao conceives, and Virtue nurtures,
Guides and educates,
Empowers and matures,
Raises and redeems.
Conceiving without possessing,
Acting without dwelling,
Leading without dictating—
These are the subtleties of Virtue.

Chapter 52

The origin of existence began with the mother of all nature.
Understand the mother,
And you will know the being of the child;
Understand the being of the child,
And you will reconnect with the mother.
One can face the perishing of the body without fear.
Close the exchanges,
Shut the doors,
And you will live without burdens.
Open the exchanges,
Engage in business,
And you will live without peace.
Seeing small details is to have insight,
Holding to gentleness is to have strength.
Use the radiance,
But return to your insight.
Remember, striving to leave nothing behind will leave yourself
    empty.
This is the practice of timeless truth.

Chapter 53

What makes one principled is having knowledge,
Walking the path of the Dao,
The only fear is becoming too instructive.
The way of the Dao is unmarked,
Yet people prefer having a clear path.
When many are appointed to offices, while fields grow wild,
And storages remain empty,
When fashion is overly adorned,
And people carry weapons,
When they indulge in feasts,
And revel in extravagance,
This is behaving like thieves!
It is not the way of the Dao.

Chapter 54

Proficient builders do not destroy,
Noble embracers do not abandon.
They remain honored through generations.
Cultivate the Dao within yourself,
And the Virtue lies in understanding the truth.
Cultivate the Dao within your family,
And the Virtue lies in finding fortune.
Cultivate the Dao within your community,
And the Virtue lies in earning respect.
Cultivate the Dao within your nation,
And the Virtue lies in reaping prosperity.
Cultivate the Dao within the universe,
And the Virtue is universally enjoyed.
Therefore, observe yourself to know yourself,
Observe your family to know your family,
Observe your community to know your community,
Observe your nation to know your nationality,
Observe the universe to know the universe.

How do I know the essence of the universe?
By observing all of this.

Chapter 55

The profoundness of being embraced by Virtue
Is like being a newborn.
Wild wasps, poisonous scorpions, and venomous snakes find no
    sting,
Fierce beasts find no grip,
Predatory birds find no claws.
The bones are weak, the muscles tender, yet the grasp is strong.
Without knowing the union of male and female,
Yet wholly united with integrity, embodying true purity.
Crying all day, yet the voice is not strained,
The very sound of harmony.
Understanding harmony leads to eternity,
Understanding eternity brings enlightenment.
Nurturing life is an act of grace,
Channeling energy inward is true strength.
Things that mature grow old,
Because they go against the Dao.
To go against the Dao
Is to meet an early end.

Chapter 56

Those who know do not speak,
Those who speak do not know.
Block its exchanges,
Constrain its ideas,
Temper its cleverness,
Unravel its complexity,
Soften its intensity,
And merge into its boundless nature.
This is the subtlety of the all-encompassing.

It cannot be possessed for love,
Cannot be possessed for hate,
Cannot be possessed for gain,
Cannot be possessed for harm,
Cannot be possessed for respect,
Cannot be possessed for contempt.
Thus, it is honored by the universe.

Chapter 57

Be just in governance,
Be unpredictable in battle,
Be unoccupied to master the universe.
How do I understand the essence of leadership?
With this:
When the world is full of taboos and prohibitions,
The people are steeped in poverty.
When the people are armed with weapons,
The nation is riddled with corruption.
When the people are consumed by professions,
Strange obsessions arise.
When laws and regulations multiply,
Thievery becomes common.
Therefore, the master maintains:
"I act not, and the people naturally flourish.
I believe in peace, and the people naturally become righteous.
I remain unoccupied, and the people naturally prosper.
I desire nothing, and the people naturally become serene."

Chapter 58

When governance is idle,
The people are calm and mellow;
When governance is strict,
The people become mischievous.
Adversity! Where fortune may lean,

Fortune! Where adversity hides.
How can the ultimate be known?
It has no fixed pattern!
As righteousness regresses into confusion,
Goodwill regresses into deception,
And the days become long and difficult.
Thus, the master remains square without being sharp,
Upright without being severe,
Straightforward without being thoughtless,
Radiant without seeking glory.

Chapter 59

In governance and management, nothing compares to being
    conservative.
Only by being conservative,
Can withdrawal lead to advancement.
Advancing through withdrawal means focusing on cultivating
    Virtue.
Focusing on Virtue,
Nothing becomes insurmountable.
When nothing is insurmountable, limitations become unknown.
When one's limitations are unknown,
One can inspire a nation.
A nation inspired is a nation that thrives.
This is being deeply rooted
In the viability and vision of the Dao.

Chapter 60

Governing a nation is like frying small fish—handle with care.
Approach the world with the Dao,
And evil will find no place to dwell.
It's not that evil spirits don't exist,
But they will cause no harm.
Not only will the spirits cause no harm,

The master will also cause no harm.

When the master and the people do not harm each other,

Virtue can be restored and shared among all.

Chapter 61

Superior nations are positioned downstream,

Where heaven and earth converge,

There the feminine remains.

Femininity often overcomes masculinity with calmness,

Maintaining composure is maintaining a low profile.

Thus, when a great nation humbles itself beneath a smaller nation,

It can surpass the smaller nation.

When a small nation humbles itself beneath a great nation,

It can surpass the greater nation.

Therefore, by staying low, one can conquer,

Or by staying low, one can be conquered.

The greatest mistake for a powerful nation is obsession with
domination,

The critical mistake for a small nation is obsession with asserting
dominance.

True greatness is achieved only when both desires are met,

Thus, the superior always stay humble.

Chapter 62

The Dao holds the key to all things,

It is the treasure of goodness,

It is the redeemer of evil.

Eloquent words can influence economies,

Respectable actions can win the hearts of the people.

How can one distance themselves from temptation?

Thus, when a leader is chosen,

And officers are appointed,

Though treasures of honor and chariots of pride may be offered,

Nothing compares to offering a vision rooted in the Dao.

Why is the value of the Dao cherished eternally?
Because it provides without being asked,
And forgives even the gravest sins.
That is why it is cherished by the world.

Chapter 63

Act without acting,
Work without working,
Taste without tasting.
Enlarge the small, increase the diminished,
Reward condemnation with Virtue.
Complexity arises from simplicity,
Greatness is found in the trivial.
Difficult problems must be solved through simplicity,
Great achievements are built on small steps.
Thus, the master remains unconcerned with grand deeds,
And is therefore capable of achieving greatness.
Light promises draw few believers,
The more you simplify, the more complexity arises.
Thus, the master addresses complexity,
And continually avoids complications.

Chapter 64

What is settled is easily maintained,
What is without form is easily planned,
What is fragile is easily broken,
What is small is easily scattered.
Act on it before it materializes,
Manage it before it becomes chaotic.
A towering tree grows from a tiny sprout;
A sky-reaching tower is built from a modest mound,
A long journey begins with a single step.
Those who act upon things will fail,
Those who cling to things will lose.

The master acts not, thus never fails;
Holds onto nothing, thus never loses.
Amateurs often fail at the brink of success.
Stay focused at the end as in the beginning,
And there will be no failure.
Thus, the master desires without attachment,
Values no precious possessions.
Learn to unlearn,
Free the people from their past.
Assist all things in returning to their essence,
And dare not to intervene.

Chapter 65

The timeless masters of the Dao
Do not seek to enlighten the people with it,
But rather to humble them with it.
The people are complex,
Govern them by tempering their intelligence.
To rule a nation with intelligence is to invite betrayal,
To rule without relying on intelligence is to bring blessings to a
    nation.
Understand these two, and set them as guiding principles.
Being wise in setting these standards
Is to possess intricate Virtue.
This intricate Virtue is profound and far-reaching,
Contrary to what it governs, yet leading to peacefulness and
    harmony.

Chapter 66

Lakes and oceans can be the masters of all streams
Because they are good at staying low,
Thus they can be masters of all streams.
So, one who desires to be honored
Must speak humbly of oneself;

One who desires to lead must keep themselves behind.
Thus, the master is above, yet the people do not feel burdened,
Is in front, yet the people do not feel pushed aside.
Therefore, the world gladly pushes the master forward
Without feeling displaced.
Because the master does not contend,
They remain uncontested.
The world says the Dao is great, but it seems useless.
I say that it is great precisely because it seems useless.
If it appeared to be useful,
Its greatness would have diminished over time.

Chapter 67

I have three precious things that I hold dear and cherish.
The first is called mercy,
The second is called prudence,
The third is not daring to be above the world.
With mercy, one can be truly courageous;
With prudence, one can be truly generous;
Not daring to be on top of the world,
One can become a true leader, both influential and respected.
Without mercy, yet seeking courage,
Without prudence, yet seeking generosity,
Without reservation, yet pushing ahead—this is futile!
With mercy, battles are won,
Defense is secured,
The heavens will come to your aid,
And grant protection in its mercy.

Chapter 68

Great gladiators are not violent,
Great warriors are not driven by rage,
Great champions remain uncontested,
Great leaders act with humility.

This is the Virtue of not contesting,
This is the strength of true leadership,
This is the ultimate unity with timelessness.

Chapter 69

There is a saying on the battlefield:
"Dare not be the host, and thus be the guest,
Dare not advance an inch, and thus retreat a foot."
This means to move without moving,
Be armed without weapons,
Cast out without casting,
And be forceful without force.
There is no greater fault than underestimating one's opponent,
To underestimate an opponent is to lose one's caution.
Therefore, when forces clash,
Those who remain reserved are victorious!

Chapter 70

These words are easy to understand and easy to follow,
Yet for worldly people, none can understand, none can follow.
Words create legends,
Deeds create heroes.
Because there is nothing to be known in this, it remains unknown.
Those who know are rare, and those who live by it are worthy of
    respect.
Thus, the master wears humility outwardly and keeps treasures in
    the heart.

Chapter 71

Knowing that you do not know is true wisdom;
Not knowing that you lack this knowledge is a flaw.
Only by recognizing and correcting flaws
Can one be free from defectiveness.
The master is free from defectiveness,

Because they acknowledge and correct their flaws,
Thus, they remain without defectiveness.

Chapter 72

When the people are not threatened by imposing authority,
Authority is imposed without intruding on their lives,
Without belittling their creations.
Because there is no belittling,
There is no resentment.
Thus, the master is introspective and does not proclaim;
Self-loving, but not self-righteous.
Therefore, they are free and at peace.

Chapter 73

Courage in daring brings death,
Courage in not daring brings life.
These two can be favorable or harmful, depending on the moment.
What the heavens detest,
Who can truly know?
Thus, the master approaches the complexity with care.
The heavenly Dao:
Contend not and master victory,
Speak not and master oration,
Summon not and things come naturally,
Be honest and master cunning.
The heavenly net is vast and wide,
Its mesh may seem loose, but nothing escapes its reach.

Chapter 74

When people are not afraid of death,
Why threaten them with it?
If someone causes the people to live in constant fear of death,
And bewilders them with confusion, they must be seized and
    executed—

But who would dare?
There are natural executioners who carry out this task,
But those who take the executioner's role upon themselves,
Are like taking the carpenter's job to carve wood.
Those who take the carpenter's job to carve wood,
Seldom avoid cutting their own hands.

Chapter 75

The people's poverty
Is caused by the parasitic exploitation of their superiors,
Thus, there is poverty.
The people's complexity
Is caused by the ambitions of their superiors,
Thus, there is complexity.
The people's willingness to sacrifice
Is due to the weight placed on life,
Thus, there are sacrifices.
Only those who are not ambitious for worldly achievements
Are truly capable of appreciating life.

Chapter 76

People are born gentle and fragile,
They die stiff and tough.
The myriad things, plants and trees, are born tender and fresh,
They die dried and withered.
Thus, those who are stiff and tough are followers of death,
Those who are gentle and fragile are followers of life.
When the armed forces are strong, the nation does not succeed,
When resources are forceful, the arms grow naturally powerful.
True strength comes from staying humble,
Superiority is achieved through gentleness and fragility.

Chapter 77

The heavenly Dao

Is like an arching bow!
What is high is brought low,
What is low is lifted high.
The excessive is diminished,
The lacking is replenished.
The way of the Dao is heavenly,
It supplements the deprived at the expense of the excessive.
The way of the people is different,
They give to the excessive and take from the deprived.
How, then, can there be any excess to offer to the world?
There is none but the Dao.
Thus, the master acts without presumption,
Accomplishes without dwelling on achievements,
And is free from the desire to display their abilities!

Chapter 78

Of all gentleness and submissiveness in the world,
Nothing compares to water.
In tackling stiffness and toughness, nothing is better,
And nothing can easily replace it.
By being submissive, one overcomes dominance,
By being gentle, one overcomes toughness.
Everyone in the world knows this,
Yet few are able to follow it.
Therefore, the master says:
"Accepting the nation's shame is being truly noble;
Accepting the nation's hardships is being truly majestic."
Righteous words often seem contradictory.

Chapter 79

When hateful hostility is resolved,
There will still be lingering resentment.
How can this be cured?
Thus, the master holds onto agreements,

Without blaming anyone.
Those with Virtue focus on working out agreements,
Those without Virtue focus on scrutinizing disagreements.
The Dao is impartial,
It always brings healing to the people.

Chapter 80

A small nation with a small population,
Even without advanced tools or technologies,
The people would rather stay than migrate elsewhere.
Though there are vessels and vehicles for travel,
No one feels the need to use them.
Though there are national guards,
They do not line up for inspection.
People return to simple ways, measuring with straps and knots.
They fulfill their desires and aspirations,
Adorn their clothing,
Secure their homes and quarters,
And find comfort in their beliefs and customs.
Even if the neighboring nation is within sight,
And the sounds of roosters and dogs can be heard,
The people live out their lives without any desire to serve or
    engage with the other nation.

Chapter 81

Truthful words are not always pleasant,
And pleasant words are not always trustworthy.
Those who are good do not argue,
And those who are argumentative are not good.
Those who truly know are not necessarily learned,
And those who are learned may not truly know.
The Sage does not hoard possessions;
The more he does for others, the more he has.
The more he gives, the more he gains.

The Way of Heaven
Is to benefit without causing harm.
The Way of the Sage
Is to act without contention.

The Book of Five Rings

Miyamoto Musashi

Introduction

I have spent many years studying the Way of Strategy, known as Ni Ten Ichi Ryu, and now I think it's time to explain it in writing for the first time. It's now early October in the twentieth year of Kanei (1645). I have climbed Mount Iwato in Higo, Kyushu, to pay my respects to heaven, pray to Kwannon, and bow before Buddha. I am a warrior from Harima province, known as Shinmen Musashi No Kami Fujiwara No Genshin, and I am sixty years old. Since I was young, I've been drawn to the Way of Strategy. My first duel was when I was thirteen, where I defeated Arima Kihei, a strategist from the Shinto school. When I was sixteen, I defeated another strategist, Tadashima Akiyama. At twenty-one, I traveled to the capital, facing many strategists, and never lost a single contest. After that, I traveled from province to province, dueling strategists from different schools, and I never lost, even though I had up to sixty matches. This was between the ages of thirteen and twenty-eight or twenty-nine.

When I turned thirty, I reflected on my past victories. They weren't because I had mastered strategy. Maybe it was natural talent, or the will of heaven, or that the other schools' strategies were not as good. After that, I studied day and night, searching for the deeper meaning, and I came to understand the Way of Strategy when I was fifty. Since then, I've lived without following any particular path. Through the virtue of strategy, I have practiced many skills and arts, learning them all without a teacher. When writing this book, I did not rely on the teachings of Buddha, Confucius, or any old war stories or books on martial arts. I pick up my brush to explain the true spirit of this Ichi school, as it reflects the Way of heaven and Kwannon. The time is the night of the tenth day of the tenth month, during the hour of the tiger (3-5 a.m.).

Chapter 1 - The Ground Book

Strategy is the skill of the warrior. Commanders must put this skill into practice, and soldiers should understand this Way. Today, there is no warrior who truly understands the Way of Strategy. There are many Ways to follow. For example, there is the Way of salvation through the teachings of Buddha, the Way of Confucius guiding learning, the Way of healing for doctors, the Way of poets through Waka, and the arts of tea, archery, and many other skills. Each person follows the Way they feel drawn to. It is said that a warrior's Way is the balance between the pen and the sword, and he should have an appreciation for both. Even if someone doesn't have natural talent, they can still be a warrior by dedicating themselves to both sides of the Way.

In general, the Way of the warrior is about accepting death with resolve. Although many people—whether priests, women, peasants, or others—have been known to face death for duty or out of shame, the warrior's focus is different. The study of strategy is about overcoming others. By gaining victory, whether in a duel or in battle, we achieve power and honor for ourselves or our lord. This is the essence of strategy.

In China and Japan, those who follow this Way have been called "masters of strategy." Warriors must learn this Way. Recently, some people have gained fame as strategists, but they are often just sword-fighters. In the past, the attendants of the Kashima and Kantori shrines in Hitachi province received teachings from the gods and established schools that traveled across the land, teaching men. This is the more recent meaning of strategy. In earlier times, strategy was considered one of the Ten Abilities and Seven Arts, recognized as a valuable practice. Although swordsmanship is certainly an art, strategy as a practice was never limited to just the use of the sword.

The true value of swordsmanship goes beyond mere technique. If we look around us, we see that many arts are turned into commodities. People use their skills to promote themselves. It's as if the nut, the essential part, has become less important than the flower. In this kind of strategy, both teachers and students focus too much on showing off their skills, trying to rush the flower into bloom. They speak of "This Dojo" and "That Dojo," all seeking profit. Someone once said, "Immature strategy causes grief," and that is certainly true.

There are four main paths in life: the paths of the gentleman, the farmer, the artisan, and the merchant. The Way of the farmer is through the use of agricultural tools, observing the changes of the seasons from spring to autumn. The second Way is that of the merchant. A wine maker gathers ingredients and uses them to make his living. The merchant's Way is always to live by seeking profit. This is the Way of the merchant. Third is the gentleman warrior, carrying the tools of his trade. The Way of the warrior is to master the virtue of his weapons. If a gentleman does not care for strategy, he will not see the value in weapons. Shouldn't he at least have a little appreciation for this? Fourth is the Way of the artisan. The Way of the carpenter is to master the use of his tools, first laying out plans with precision, and then following them carefully in his work. This is how he lives his life. These are the four Ways: the gentleman, the farmer, the artisan, and the merchant.

Now, let's compare the Way of the carpenter to strategy. The connection is found in the building of houses. Noble houses, warrior houses, the Four Houses, houses that rise and fall, the style of the house, the traditions of the house, and the reputation of the house all come into play. The carpenter uses a master plan to build, and strategy is similar because there is a plan for a campaign. If you want to learn the art of war, study this book carefully. The teacher is like a needle, and the student is like the thread. You must practice constantly.

Like a chief carpenter, the commander must understand the natural laws, the rules of the land, and the traditions of the people. This is the Way of the chief. The chief carpenter must know the architecture of towers and temples, the plans for palaces, and must direct workers to raise buildings. The Way of the chief carpenter is the same as the commander of a warrior household.

When building, the choice of wood is important. Straight, unblemished timber is used for visible pillars, while straight wood with small flaws is used for interior pillars. Wood that looks good, even if a bit weak, is used for thresholds, lintels, doors, and sliding panels. Strong wood, even if it is knotted or twisted, can still be used discreetly in construction. Timber that is weak throughout is used for scaffolding or later for firewood.

The chief carpenter assigns tasks based on the workers' skills. Some lay floors, others make doors or thresholds, ceilings, and so on. Those with less skill work on floor supports or carve wedges and do smaller tasks. If the chief knows his workers well and uses them wisely, the result will be good. The chief must understand his workers' strengths and weaknesses, keeping morale high and encouraging them when needed. This is the same principle found in strategy.

Like a warrior, a carpenter sharpens his own tools. He carries his equipment in a toolbox and works under the direction of the foreman. He uses an axe to make columns and girders, a plane to shape floorboards and shelves, and cuts fine details as accurately as his skill allows. This is the craft of carpentry. When a carpenter becomes skilled and understands measurements, he can become a foreman. His accomplishments range from making small shrines and writing shelves to tables, lanterns, chopping boards, and pot lids. These are the specialties of a skilled carpenter.

Things are similar for the soldier. You should think deeply about this. The carpenter's skill is in making sure that his work doesn't warp, that the joints fit properly, and that everything is perfectly planed so it all fits together well, not just in parts. This is essential. If you want to learn this Way, carefully study the things written in this book, one at a time. You must research thoroughly.

This Book of Strategy is divided into five sections, each focusing on different aspects: Ground, Water, Fire, Wind (tradition), and Void (the illusory nature of worldly things). The foundation of the Way of Strategy, from the perspective of my Ichi school, is explained in the Ground book. It's difficult to fully understand the true Way by focusing only on sword-fighting. You must understand both the smallest and the largest things, the most shallow and the deepest things. As if the Way were a straight road mapped on the ground, the first section is called the Ground book.

The second section is the Water book. With water as the theme, the spirit should become like water. Water takes the shape of whatever it is in; sometimes it flows gently, other times it crashes like the sea. Water has a clear, blue color. Through clarity, the teachings of the Ichi school are revealed in this book. If you master the principles of sword-fighting, when you can defeat one man, you can defeat any man in the world. The spirit of defeating one person is the same as defeating many. A strategist can make small things into big things, like building a great Buddha from a small model. I cannot explain in full detail how this is done, but the principle of strategy is to know one thing in order to know ten thousand things. The principles of the Ichi school are explained in the Water book.

The third section is the Fire book. This book is about combat. The spirit of fire is fierce, whether it is a small flame or a large one; the same goes for battles. The way of fighting is the same whether it's a one-on-one duel or a battle with ten thousand soldiers. You must understand that a spirit can be large or small. What is large is easy to see; what is small is harder to notice. For large groups of people, it's hard to change positions, so their movements can be predicted. But an individual can change his mind easily, making his actions harder to foresee. You must grasp this. The key to this section is that you must train day and night to make quick decisions. In strategy, training should become part of daily life, and your spirit should remain steady. This section on combat is explained in the Fire book.

The fourth section is the Wind book. This part does not focus on my Ichi school, but on other schools of strategy. By Wind, I mean old traditions, present-day traditions, and family traditions in strategy. I explain the strategies of the world clearly here. This is tradition. It is hard to know yourself if you don't understand others. Every Way has side paths. If you study a Way every day and your spirit strays, you might think you're following the right path, but in reality, it is not the true Way. If you follow the true Way but stray just a little, over time, this small deviation will turn into a large one. You must recognize this. Other strategies have come to focus too much on sword-fighting, and it's understandable that this happened. However, my strategy's true value lies in a different principle, though it includes sword-fighting. I explain what strategy means in other schools in the Wind book.

The fifth section is the Void book. By Void, I mean that which has no beginning and no end. To grasp this principle means not grasping it at all. The Way of Strategy is the Way of nature. When you understand the power of nature and the rhythm of every situation, you will naturally know how to strike the enemy. This is the Way of the Void. I aim to show how to follow the true Way, according to nature, in the Void book.

The name "Ichi Ryu Ni To" means "One school, two swords." Warriors, both commanders and soldiers, carry two swords at their belts. In earlier times, these were called the long sword and the short sword. Today, they are known as the sword and the companion sword.Let it be enough to say that, in our country, for whatever reason, a warrior carries two swords at his belt. This is the Way of the warrior. "Nito Ichi Ryu" shows the advantages of using both swords. The spear and halberd are weapons used outdoors. Students of the Ichi school Way of Strategy should start training with a sword in one hand and a long sword in the other. This is a truth: when you are ready to sacrifice your life, you must make the fullest use of your weapons. It is wrong not to do so and to die without even drawing a weapon.

If you hold a sword with both hands, it's harder to swing it freely to the left and right. That's why my method is to carry the sword in one hand. This doesn't apply to large weapons like spears or halberds, but swords and companion swords can be used with one hand. Holding a sword with both hands can be a burden when you're on horseback, running over rough roads, swampy ground, muddy rice fields, stony paths, or in a crowd of people. Using both hands to hold the long sword isn't the true Way because if you're carrying a bow, spear, or other weapons in your left hand, you'll only have one hand free for the long sword. However, when it's too hard to strike an enemy down with one hand, you should use both hands.

It isn't hard to wield a sword with one hand; the Way to learn this is by training with two long swords, one in each hand. It will seem difficult at first, but everything is difficult in the beginning. Bows are hard to draw, halberds are hard to use, but as you practice with the bow, your pull becomes stronger. As you get used to handling the long sword, you will gain power and skill with it. As I will explain in the Water Book, there is no quick method to mastering the long sword. The long sword should be used in broad strokes, and the companion sword should be used in close combat. This is the first thing to understand.

According to the Ichi school, you can win with a long weapon, but you can also win with a short one. In short, the Way of the Ichi school is the spirit of victory, no matter what weapon you use or its size. It's better to use two swords rather than one when fighting a crowd, especially if you want to take a prisoner. These things are hard to explain in detail. From one thing, you can learn ten thousand things. When you truly understand the Way of Strategy, nothing will be hidden from you. You must study hard.

The Meaning of the Two Characters for "Strategy"

Masters of the long sword are called strategists. In other military arts, those who master the bow are called archers, those who master the spear are spearmen, those who master the gun are marksmen, and those who master the halberd are halberdiers. But we don't call masters of the long sword "longswordsmen" or "companion swordsmen." Since bows, guns, spears, and halberds are part of a warrior's equipment, they are certainly part of strategy. To master the long sword is to govern oneself and the world. The principle is "strategy by means of the long sword." If someone masters the long sword, one man can defeat ten. And just as one man can defeat ten, one hundred can defeat one thousand, and one thousand can defeat ten thousand. In my strategy, one man is equal to ten thousand, making this strategy the complete skill of the warrior.

The Way of the warrior does not include other Ways like Confucianism, Buddhism, certain traditions, artistic accomplishments, or dancing. But even though these are not part of the Way, if you understand the Way broadly, you will see it reflected in everything. Men must polish their own Way.

The Benefit of Weapons in Strategy

There is a time and place for using different weapons. The best use of the companion sword is in tight spaces or when you are engaged closely with an opponent. The long sword is effective in almost any situation. The halberd, however, is not as good as the spear on the battlefield. The spear gives you the advantage to attack first, while the halberd is more defensive. Between two men of equal skill, the spear offers a slight edge. Both the spear and the halberd have their uses, but neither works well in confined spaces, nor are they good for capturing prisoners. They are mainly for open battlefields.

If you focus too much on "indoor" techniques, you will think too narrowly and forget the true Way, making real-life encounters more difficult. The bow is useful at the start of a battle, especially in open areas like moors, where you can shoot quickly among the spearmen. But the bow is less useful during sieges or when the enemy is farther than forty yards away. For this reason, there are fewer traditional schools of archery today, as this skill is less needed now.

Within fortifications, the gun is unmatched. It is the best weapon before the lines of battle meet, but once swords are drawn, the gun becomes useless. One advantage of the bow is that you can see the arrows in flight and correct your aim, whereas with gunfire, the shots cannot be seen. You must understand the importance of this.

Just as a horse needs endurance and should be free from defects, so too must weapons be strong and reliable. Horses should walk with strength, and swords and companion swords should cut with strength. Spears and halberds must be able to endure heavy use, and bows and guns must be sturdy. Weapons should be tough, not just decorative. You should not favor any particular weapon. Becoming overly attached to one weapon is just as bad as not knowing it well enough. You should not simply imitate others, but use weapons that you can handle well. It's not good for commanders or soldiers to have preferences or aversions when it comes to weapons. These are things you must learn deeply.

Timing in Strategy

There is timing in everything. Mastering timing in strategy requires a great deal of practice. Timing is important in dancing and playing musical instruments like the flute or the lute because rhythm only works if the timing is correct. The same applies to military arts, shooting bows or guns, and riding horses. Every skill and ability involves timing. There is even timing in the Void. Timing governs the entire life of a warrior, from his rise and fall, his harmony and discord. Similarly, timing plays a role in the merchant's life, with the rise and fall of capital. Everything follows a rhythm of rising and falling, and you must learn to recognize this.

In strategy, there are many types of timing. From the beginning, you must know the difference between applicable timing and inapplicable timing. You must also understand the timing of large and small things, as well as fast and slow actions, finding the right timing by first recognizing distance and the background timing. This is the key to strategy. Knowing the background timing is especially important; without it, your strategy will become unstable. You win battles by mastering the timing of the Void, which comes from knowing your enemy's timing and using a rhythm they do not expect.

All five books focus primarily on timing. You must train diligently to truly understand this.

If you practice day and night with the Ichi school's strategy, your spirit will naturally grow. In this way, large-scale strategy and hand-to-hand combat strategy will spread throughout the world. This has been written down for the first time in the five books of Ground, Water, Fire, Wind (Tradition), and Void.

This is the way for those who want to learn my strategy:

1. Do not think dishonestly.

2. The Way is in training.

3. Become familiar with every art.

4. Know the Ways of all professions.

5. Understand the difference between gain and loss in worldly matters.

6. Develop intuitive judgment and understanding for all things.

7. Perceive the things that cannot be seen.

8. Pay attention to even the smallest details.

9. Do nothing that is useless.

It is important to start by placing these broad principles in your heart and train in the Way of Strategy. If you don't look at things from a wide perspective, it will be difficult to master strategy. If you learn and master this strategy, you will never lose, even when facing twenty or thirty opponents.

Most importantly, you must set your heart on strategy and follow the Way with great dedication. Once you do this, you will be able to defeat men in real combat and win with just a glance. With enough training, you will be able to control your body freely, conquer men with your physical presence, and eventually, with enough spirit, defeat ten men at once. When you reach this level, wouldn't that make you invincible?

Furthermore, in large-scale strategy, a superior man will manage many subordinates skillfully, carry himself with proper conduct, govern a country, and care for the people, thus maintaining the ruler's discipline. If there is a Way that involves never being defeated, helping oneself, and gaining honor, it is the Way of Strategy.

Chapter 2 - The Water Book

The spirit of the Ni Ten Ichi school of strategy is based on water, and this Water Book explains methods of victory using the long sword of the Ichi school. Language alone cannot fully describe the Way in detail, but it can be grasped intuitively. Study this book carefully; read a word, then reflect deeply on its meaning. If you interpret the teachings too loosely, you will misunderstand the Way. The principles of strategy written here are expressed in terms of one-on-one combat, but you must think broadly enough to apply them to battles involving ten thousand men. Strategy is different from other practices in that if you stray even slightly from the Way, you will become confused and follow the wrong path.

Simply reading this book will not lead you to the Way of Strategy. You must absorb the ideas within these pages. Do not just read, memorize, or copy; rather, study with dedication so that you come to understand the principles from deep within your own heart and incorporate them into your body.

Spiritual Bearing in Strategy

In strategy, your spiritual bearing should not differ from your normal state. Both in combat and in daily life, you should be calm yet determined. Face situations without tension, but also without carelessness, maintaining a settled spirit that is free from bias. Even when your spirit is calm, do not let your body relax, and when your body is relaxed, keep your spirit alert. Do not let your spirit be controlled by your body, or let your body be controlled by your spirit. Avoid being either too passive or overly intense. A spirit that is too high is weak, and a spirit that is too low is also weak. Do not allow the enemy to sense your spirit.

Smaller individuals must understand the spirit of larger people, and larger individuals must be familiar with the spirit of smaller people. Regardless of your size, do not be misled by your own body's reactions. Keep your spirit open and unrestricted, and view things from a higher perspective. You must cultivate your wisdom and spirit. Sharpen your wisdom by learning public justice, distinguishing between good and evil, and studying various arts one by one. When you reach the point where you cannot be deceived by others, you will have realized the wisdom of strategy. The wisdom of strategy is unique. Even in the heat of battle, when you are under great pressure, you must continuously research the principles of strategy to develop a steady, unwavering spirit.

Stance in Strategy

Take a stance with your head held upright—not drooping, not tilted upward, and not twisted. Your forehead and the space between your eyes should remain relaxed, with no wrinkles. Do not roll your eyes or allow them to blink too often, but keep them slightly narrowed. Maintain a composed expression, keeping your nose aligned straight, and feel a slight flare in your nostrils. Keep the back of your neck straight, infusing energy into your hairline, and let this vigor extend down through your whole body from your shoulders.

Lower your shoulders without sticking out your buttocks. Focus your strength in your legs, from your knees down to your toes. Keep your abdomen braced so that you don't bend at the hips. Wedge your companion sword firmly against your abdomen, ensuring that your belt is not loose—this is known as "wedging in." In all aspects of strategy, it is important to maintain your combat stance in everyday life and make your everyday stance your combat stance. Research this deeply.

The Gaze in Strategy

Your gaze should be large and expansive. This is the twofold gaze, "Perception and Sight." Perception is strong, while sight is weak. In strategy, it is crucial to see distant things as if they were near and to view close things from a distanced perspective. In strategy, it's important to focus on the enemy's sword and not get distracted by small, unimportant movements. You must study this carefully. The gaze used in single combat is the same as in large-scale strategy. In strategy, you must learn to look to both sides without moving your eyes. You cannot master this skill quickly. Learn what is written here, and use this gaze in everyday life without changing it, no matter what happens.

Holding the Long Sword

Hold the long sword with a relaxed grip, using a light touch with your thumb and forefinger, while keeping the middle finger neither too tight nor too loose, and the last two fingers tightly. It's bad to have too much play in your hands. When you take up the sword, your mindset should be focused on cutting the enemy. As you strike, don't change your grip, and don't let your hands tremble. When you deflect the enemy's sword, or block or press it down, slightly adjust the pressure in your thumb and forefinger. Above all, maintain the intent to cut the enemy through the way you grip the sword. The grip for combat and for testing swords is the same. There is no separate "man-cutting grip." Generally, I dislike stiffness in both swords and hands. Stiffness means a dead hand, while flexibility means a living hand. Keep this in mind.

Footwork

Walk with the tips of your toes lightly touching the ground, while stepping firmly with your heels. Whether you move quickly or slowly, with large or small steps, your feet should move naturally, as if walking normally. I dislike the three footwork methods known as "jumping foot," "floating foot," and "fixed steps." The so-called "Yin-Yang foot" is important in this Way. It means not moving only one foot. It involves moving your feet left-right and right-left when cutting, stepping back, or deflecting a strike. You shouldn't favor one foot over the other.

The Five Attitudes

The five attitudes are: Upper, Middle, Lower, Right Side, and Left Side. These are the five. Although there are five different positions, the purpose of all of them is to cut the enemy. These are the only five attitudes. No matter what position you're in, don't focus on forming the attitude; just think about cutting. Your stance should be large or small depending on the situation. The Upper, Lower, and Middle attitudes are decisive, while the Left and Right Side attitudes are flexible. Use Left or Right attitudes when there's something in the way overhead or to the side. The decision to use Left or Right depends on the situation.

The key to understanding attitude lies in mastering the middle attitude. The middle attitude is the core of all the attitudes. If we think of strategy on a larger scale, the Middle attitude is like the leader, and the other four attitudes follow the leader. You must grasp this concept.

The Way of the Long Sword

Knowing the Way of the long sword means being able to wield the sword you usually carry with just two fingers. If you understand the path of the sword, you'll be able to handle it easily. If you try to wield the long sword too quickly, you'll lose sight of the Way. To use the long sword properly, you must handle it calmly. If you try to use it like a fan or a short sword, you'll make the mistake of "short sword chopping." You cannot strike down an enemy with a long sword this way.

After you swing the long sword downward, lift it back up straight. When you swing it sideways, return it along the same path. Always return the sword in a controlled manner, keeping your elbows stretched broadly. Wield the sword with strength. This is the Way of the long sword. If you learn to use the five approaches in my strategy, you will handle the sword well. You must train constantly.

The Five Approaches

The first approach is the Middle attitude. Face the enemy with the tip of your sword aimed at his face. When he attacks, deflect his sword to the right and "ride" it. Alternatively, when the enemy attacks, hit the tip of his sword downward, hold your long sword in place, and when he attacks again, cut his arms from below. This is the first method. The five approaches are like this. You must train repeatedly with the long sword to learn them. When you master my Way of the long sword, you'll be able to control any attack the enemy makes. I guarantee there are no other attitudes beyond the five attitudes of the Ni To long sword.

In the second approach with the long sword, from the Upper attitude, cut the enemy just as he attacks. If the enemy dodges your cut, keep your sword in place and, as he comes in again, cut him from below. You can repeat the cut from this position. In this approach, there are different variations of timing and spirit. You will understand this through training in the Ichi school. You will always win with the five long sword methods. You must train repeatedly.

In the third method, take the Lower stance, preparing to scoop upward. When the enemy attacks, strike his hands from below. He may try to knock your sword down, and if he does, cut his upper arm(s) horizontally, as if "crossing" his attack. This technique involves hitting the enemy at the moment he attacks from the lower stance. You will encounter this often, both as a beginner and later in strategy. You must train with the long sword.

In the fourth method, take the Left Side stance. When the enemy attacks, strike his hands from below. If he tries to knock your sword down, parry his attack and cut across from above your shoulder. This is the Way of the long sword. You win by deflecting the enemy's attack. You must study this technique.

In the fifth method, use the Right Side stance. As the enemy attacks, move your long sword from below to the Upper stance, then cut straight down. This technique is crucial for mastering the long sword. Once you understand this method, you will be able to handle a heavy long sword with ease.

I cannot describe every detail of these five methods. You must become familiar with the "in harmony with the long sword" technique, learn the large-scale timing, understand the enemy's long sword, and practice the five methods from the start. You will always win using these techniques, considering timing and the enemy's intentions. Think carefully about all this.

The "Attitude No-Attitude" Teaching

"Attitude No-Attitude" means there is no need for set long sword stances. However, attitudes do exist as the five ways of holding the long sword. No matter how you hold the sword, it should be in a way that makes it easy to cut the enemy, based on the situation, the place, and your relation to the enemy. From the Upper stance, if your spirit lowers, you can move to the Middle stance. From the Middle stance, you can lift the sword slightly and return to the Upper stance. From the Lower stance, you can raise the sword to adopt the Middle stance as needed.

Depending on the situation, if you move the sword from either the Left or Right Side stance toward the center, you can shift to the Middle or Lower stance. This principle is called "Existing Attitude - Nonexisting Attitude." The most important thing when holding a sword is your intention to cut the enemy, no matter what. Whenever you parry, strike, leap, or touch the enemy's sword, your movement must carry through to cutting the enemy. This is essential. If you only think about hitting, leaping, or striking, you won't be able to cut him. Above all, you must focus on completing the movement by cutting the enemy. You must research this thoroughly.

In large-scale strategy, attitude is referred to as "Battle Array." These stances are all for winning battles. Fixed formations are ineffective. Study this deeply.

To Hit the Enemy "In One Timing"

"In One Timing" means, when you have closed the distance with the enemy, strike him as quickly and directly as possible, without adjusting your body or spirit, while you see that he is still uncertain. The timing of striking before the enemy decides to retreat, block, or strike is the "In One Timing." You must train to achieve this instant timing.

The "Abdomen Timing of Two"

When you attack and the enemy retreats quickly, as you notice him tense up, feint a strike. Then, when he relaxes, follow through and hit him. This is called the "Abdomen Timing of Two." It is hard to fully grasp this through reading alone, but with a little instruction, you will soon understand.

No Design, No Conception

In this method, when the enemy attacks and you also decide to attack, strike with your body, spirit, and sword, moving quickly and strongly from the Void. This is the "No Design, No Conception" strike. It is the most important method of striking and is often used. You must train diligently to understand it.

The Flowing Water Cut

The "Flowing Water Cut" is used when you are locked blade to blade with the enemy. When the enemy pulls back and tries to spring at you with his long sword, expand your body and spirit, and cut him slowly with your long sword, like water flowing steadily. If you master this, you can cut with certainty. You must understand the enemy's level of skill.

Continuous Cut

When you attack and the enemy also strikes, and your swords clash together, in one motion, cut his head, hands, and legs. Cutting multiple parts in one sweep of the long sword is the "Continuous Cut." You must practice this cut often; it is frequently used. With detailed training, you will understand it.

The Fire and Stones Cut

The "Fire and Stones Cut" means that when your long sword clashes with the enemy's, you cut as forcefully as possible without raising the sword at all. This involves cutting quickly with the hands, body, and legs—all three working together with strength. With enough practice, you will strike powerfully.

The Red Leaves Cut

The "Red Leaves Cut" refers to knocking down the enemy's long sword. Your spirit should aim to control his sword. When the enemy is in a long sword stance and intends to cut, hit, or parry, you strike his sword hard using the "Fire and Stones Cut," perhaps with the same spirit as the "No Design, No Conception" Cut. If you beat down his sword with a sticky feeling, he will drop his sword. With enough practice, this cut will allow you to disarm the enemy.

The Body in Place of the Long Sword

Also known as "the long sword in place of the body." Normally, we move our bodies and swords together to strike the enemy. However, depending on the enemy's cutting technique, you can strike him first with your body and then follow with the sword. If the enemy's body is immobile, you can cut first with the long sword, but usually, you strike with your body first and then cut with the long sword. You must study this carefully and practice your strikes.

Cut and Slash

Cutting and slashing are two different things. Cutting is decisive, and it must be done with a determined spirit. Slashing is just making contact with the enemy. Even if you slash powerfully, and the enemy dies immediately, it's still just a slash. When you cut, your spirit must be fully committed. You must understand this. If you first slash the enemy's hands or legs, you must follow up with a strong cut. Slashing, in spirit, is the same as touching. Once you realize this, they will feel similar. Learn this lesson well.

Chinese Monkey's Body

The Chinese Monkey's Body refers to the spirit of not extending your arms. The idea is to close in on the enemy quickly, without fully stretching out your arms, before the enemy has a chance to cut. By keeping your arms from stretching out, you effectively create more distance. The spirit is to advance with your entire body. When you're within arm's reach, it becomes easier to move your body in. Study this well.

Glue and Lacquer Emulsion Body

The "Glue and Lacquer Emulsion Body" is about sticking to the enemy and not separating from him. When you approach, you should connect firmly with your head, body, and legs. Many people advance with their head and legs quickly but let their body lag behind. You should stick firmly so that there is no gap between your body and the enemy's. Think about this carefully.

To Strive for Height

"To strive for height" means that when you close in on the enemy, you should aim to gain the upper position without shrinking back. Stretch your legs, hips, and neck to face the enemy. When you feel that you have gained the upper position, push forward strongly. Learn this method.

To Apply Stickiness

When the enemy attacks and you respond with your long sword, approach with a sticky feeling, holding your long sword against his as you receive his cut. Stickiness doesn't mean hitting hard, but rather making sure the swords don't separate easily. It's best to approach calmly when using this technique. Stickiness is firm, while entanglement is weak. Learn the difference.

The Body Strike

The Body Strike is when you advance through a gap in the enemy's defense and strike him with your body. Turn your face slightly to the side and strike the enemy's chest with your left shoulder pushed forward. Approach with the spirit of bouncing the enemy away, timing your strike with your breath. If you master this method, you will be able to push the enemy back several feet. It's possible to strike with enough force to kill. Train well.

Three Ways to Parry His Attack

There are three ways to parry a cut: First, when the enemy attacks, push his long sword to your right, as if aiming for his eyes. Or, parry by pushing his sword toward his right eye with the feeling of slicing his neck. Lastly, if your long sword is short, close in on him quickly without worrying about parrying, and thrust at his face with your left hand. You should also remember that you can clench your left hand into a fist and strike at his face. Train hard to master these methods.

To Stab at the Face

To stab at the face means that when you are confronting the enemy, your intent should be on stabbing at his face, following the line of your blades with the tip of your long sword. When you aim for the face, the enemy's body will become more vulnerable. When the enemy's body becomes open, there are many chances to win. Keep your focus on this technique. When the enemy becomes exposed, you can win quickly, so don't forget to stab at the face. Train to understand this fully.

To Stab at the Heart

To stab at the heart means that when there are obstacles above or to the sides, and it's hard to cut, thrust directly at the enemy's chest. You must stab him without letting the tip of your long sword waver, showing the ridge of the blade to the enemy while pushing forward with the spirit of deflecting his sword. This method is helpful when you're tired or when your sword is not cutting properly. Understand this technique well.

To Scold "Tut-TUT!"

"Scold" means that when the enemy tries to counterattack as you strike, you cut again from below, as if thrusting, to pin him down. With quick timing, you cut while scolding the enemy. Thrust up with a "Tut!" and cut with a "TUT!" This timing happens often in the exchange of blows. To "scold Tut-TUT" is to time the cut with raising your long sword, as if to thrust. You must practice this frequently to learn it.

The Smacking Parry

The "smacking parry" is when you clash swords with the enemy, meeting his attack with a rhythm of "tee-dum, tee-dum," smacking his sword and cutting him. The point of the smacking parry is not to parry or hit strongly but to match the enemy's attack and quickly cut him. If you understand the timing of smacking, no matter how hard your swords clash, your sword's point will not be knocked back. Train to master this timing.

There are Many Enemies

"There are many enemies" refers to fighting against multiple opponents. Draw both your sword and companion sword and take a wide stance, with your swords covering both sides. The strategy is to chase the enemies around, even if they come from all directions. Watch their order of attack and respond first to those who attack first. Sweep your eyes around, assess their positions, and cut to the left and right with your swords. Don't wait too long. Always return to your stance quickly and cut the enemies down as they approach, crushing them from whichever direction they attack. Keep driving the enemies together, like lining up a row of fish, and when they bunch up, cut them down strongly without giving them a chance to move.

The Advantage when Coming to Blows

You can learn how to win with the long sword through strategy, but it can't be fully explained in writing. You must practice hard to understand how to win.

Oral tradition: "The true Way of Strategy is revealed in the long sword."

One Cut

You can win with certainty through the spirit of "one cut." It's difficult to achieve this without mastering strategy. But if you train well in this Way, strategy will come from within you, and you will be able to win at will. You must train diligently.

Direct Communication

The spirit of "Direct Communication" is how the true Way of the Ni To Ichi school is passed down.

Oral tradition: "Teach your body strategy.

This book outlines the sword-fighting of the Ichi school. To win using the long sword in strategy, first learn the five approaches and the five attitudes. Let the Way of the long sword become natural to your body. Understand spirit and timing, handle the long sword naturally, and move your body and legs in harmony with your spirit. Whether you are fighting one person or two, you will learn the values of strategy. Study the contents of this book, one concept at a time, and by fighting against enemies, you will gradually understand the principles of the Way.

Be patient and deliberate, absorbing the virtue of all this. When you face an enemy, maintain this spirit. Step by step, walk the thousand-mile road. Study strategy over many years and achieve the spirit of the warrior. Today, you must defeat the version of yourself from yesterday; tomorrow, you will defeat lesser men.

To defeat more skilled opponents, train according to this book, and do not let your heart stray from the path. Even if you kill an enemy, if it's not based on what you've learned, it's not the true Way. If you master this Way of victory, you will be able to defeat dozens of men. What remains is to refine your sword-fighting ability, which you will gain through battles and duels.

Chapter 3 - The Fire Book

In this book of the Ni To Ichi school of strategy, I describe fighting like fire. First, people tend to think too narrowly about strategy. They use only the tips of their fingers and understand just a small part of what their whole wrist can do. They let a fight be decided, like using a folding fan, with only the span of their forearms. They focus on small things like hand and leg movements, practicing with a bamboo sword.

In my strategy, learning to defeat enemies comes through many battles, fighting to survive, discovering the meaning of life and death, learning the way of the sword, judging the power of attacks, and understanding the "edge and ridge" of the sword. You can't rely on small tricks, especially when wearing full armor. My way of strategy is the sure way to win when fighting for your life, whether you're facing one person or five or ten. There's nothing wrong with the idea that "one man can defeat ten, and so a thousand can beat ten thousand." You need to study this. Of course, you can't gather a thousand or ten thousand men for daily training. But by training alone with a sword, you can master strategy, understand the enemy's tactics, their strength, and resources, and learn how to defeat ten thousand enemies.

Anyone who wants to master my strategy must study hard, practicing every morning and evening. This is how you refine your skill, let go of your ego, and achieve extraordinary ability. Eventually, you will gain incredible power. This is the practical outcome of strategy.

Depending on the Place

Pay attention to your surroundings. Stand in the sunlight; this means positioning yourself with the sun at your back. If that's not possible, keep the sun on your right side. Indoors, stand with the entrance behind you or to your right. Make sure your back is clear, and that there is open space to your left, with your right side occupied by your stance. At night, if the enemy is visible, keep any light source behind you, with the entrance to your right, and otherwise follow the same rules as before. You should be positioned slightly higher than your enemy. For instance, the Kamiza in a house is considered a high place. In battle, always try to force the enemy to your left. Push them into difficult spots and keep them in awkward positions with their back to those places. Once the enemy is in a bad spot, don't let them look around, but keep pressing them and pin them down. Inside buildings, force them into thresholds, lintels, doors, verandas, or pillars, again preventing them from understanding their situation. Always move the enemy into bad footing or obstacles and use the advantages of the location to gain a better fighting position. You need to study and practice this thoroughly.

The Three Methods to Forestall the Enemy

The first method is to attack first. This is called Ken No Sen (taking the initiative). Another method is to strike as the enemy attacks. This is called Tai No Sen (waiting for the right moment). The last method is to attack at the same time as the enemy. This is called Tai Tai No Sen (matching the enemy's attack and countering). These are the only three ways to take the lead in a fight. Winning quickly by taking the lead is one of the most important aspects of strategy. There are several factors in taking the lead. You need to make the most of the situation, understand the enemy's intentions, and defeat them. This is something that cannot be fully explained in writing.

Ken No Sen

When you choose to attack, stay calm and rush in quickly, taking the initiative before the enemy can react. Alternatively, you can approach with strength but keep your mind focused, taking the lead while remaining composed. Or, you can advance with as much power as possible and, when you reach the enemy, move a little faster than usual with your feet, disrupting and overpowering them sharply. Another option is to attack with a calm spirit, but with the feeling that you're crushing the enemy completely, from start to finish. The spirit is to win deep within the enemy. These are all examples of Ken No Sen.

Tai No Sen

When the enemy attacks, stay composed but pretend to be weak. As the enemy comes near, move away as if you're going to step aside, then quickly rush in and attack strongly when you see the enemy let their guard down. Another way is to attack even harder when the enemy strikes, using the confusion in their timing to win. This is the principle of Tai No Sen.

Tai Tai No Sen

When the enemy attacks quickly, you must attack strongly and calmly, aiming for their weak point as they approach, and defeat them forcefully. Or, if the enemy attacks more cautiously, watch their movements closely and, with your body somewhat light, mirror their movements as they approach. Then move swiftly and cut them down forcefully. This is Tai Tai No Sen. These ideas are hard to explain fully with words. You must study what is written here.

In these three methods of forestalling, you must assess the situation carefully. This doesn't mean you always need to attack first, but if the enemy does attack first, you can still take control. In strategy, once you can anticipate the enemy's moves, you've already gained the upper hand, so you must train well to reach this point.

To Hold Down a Pillow

"To Hold Down a Pillow" means keeping the enemy from rising up. In strategy, it's a mistake to be led around by the enemy. You should always aim to be the one leading the enemy. Of course, the enemy will also try to lead you, but they can't do that if you prevent them from making their move. In strategy, you must block the enemy's attempts to strike, push back against their thrusts, and counter when they try to grapple. That's what "to hold down a pillow" means. Once you understand this concept, you'll be able to see what the enemy is planning before they can act, and stop them. The key is to cut off their attack at the very start: stop them right when they think about attacking. The most important thing in strategy is to block the enemy's useful actions but allow their useless ones. However, if you only block, that's defensive. You must also act according to the Way, stopping the enemy's techniques, ruining their plans, and then taking full control. When you can do this, you'll be a master of strategy. You must train hard and study "holding down a pillow."

Crossing at a Ford

"Crossing at a ford" is like crossing the sea at a narrow point, or sailing across a broad stretch of ocean at a crossing place. I believe we often face "crossing at a ford" moments in life. It means setting out even when your friends stay behind, knowing the way, trusting your ship, and recognizing that the day is in your favor. When everything lines up—maybe with a favorable wind—then you set sail. But if the wind changes just before you reach your goal, you'll have to row the rest of the way. This mindset applies to daily life as well. You should always think about crossing at a ford. In strategy, it's also important to "cross at a ford." Assess the enemy's strengths and weaknesses, understand your own, and attack at the best point, like a skilled captain choosing the right sea route. If you cross at the most favorable point, you can relax afterward. Crossing at a ford means striking at the enemy's weak spot and putting yourself in an advantageous position. This is how to win in large-scale strategy. The spirit of crossing at a ford is important in both large and small strategies. You must study this carefully.

To Know the Times

"To know the times" means understanding the enemy's condition during battle. Is their energy rising or falling? By watching the mood of the enemy's troops and securing the best position, you can figure out their condition and move your forces accordingly. This principle of strategy lets you fight from a position of advantage. In a duel, you must anticipate the enemy and strike after learning their school of strategy, recognizing their strengths and weaknesses, and finding the right moment. Attack when they least expect it, knowing their timing and rhythm. Knowing the times means that if you're skilled enough, you can see through things clearly. If you're experienced in strategy, you'll recognize the enemy's plans and find many opportunities to win. You must study this thoroughly.

To Tread Down the Sword

"To tread down the sword" is a concept often used in strategy. First, in large-scale strategy, when the enemy starts by firing arrows or guns and then charges, it's hard to attack back if you're still busy reloading your own weapons. The idea is to attack swiftly while the enemy is still shooting. The spirit is to win by pressing forward while receiving the enemy's attack. In single combat, you can't secure a victory by following the enemy's sword swings with your own, going back and forth. You must beat them right at the start of their attack, stepping in forcefully so they can't continue. "Treading" doesn't just mean stepping on with your feet. It's about using your whole body, your spirit, and of course, your sword to step in and attack. You need to develop the mindset of not letting the enemy attack a second time. This is the spirit of taking control in every sense. Once you're in position, don't just aim to strike but follow through with your attack. You must study this deeply.

To Know Collapse

Everything can collapse—houses, bodies, and enemies—when their rhythm is thrown off. In large-scale strategy, when the enemy starts to collapse, you must chase them down and not let the chance slip away. If you don't take advantage of their collapse, they might recover. In single combat, the enemy might lose their timing and falter. If you don't act on this, they might regain their balance and become more cautious afterward. Focus on the enemy's collapse, pursue them, and attack without giving them a chance to recover. You must do this.

Your pursuit should be forceful. You need to completely overpower the enemy so they can't regain their position. You must understand how to utterly defeat the enemy.

To Become the Enemy

"To become the enemy" means putting yourself in the enemy's position. People often see a robber trapped in a house as if they're a fortified enemy. But if you think of "becoming the enemy," you'll feel like the whole world is against you with no way out. The one trapped is the prey, while the one coming to capture is the predator. You must recognize this. In large-scale strategy, people often assume the enemy is stronger than they are, making them overly cautious. But if you have strong soldiers, know the principles of strategy, and understand how to defeat the enemy, there's nothing to fear. In single combat, you must also put yourself in the enemy's position. If you think, "Here is a master of the Way, someone who knows strategy," then you'll surely lose. You must consider this deeply.

To Release Four Hands

"To release four hands" is a technique used when both you and the enemy are fighting with equal determination, and neither side is winning. In this case, you need to let go of that mindset and win by using a different tactic. In large-scale strategy, when you find yourself in a "four hands" situation, don't give up—it's part of life. Instead, immediately change your approach and win by doing something the enemy doesn't expect. In single combat, if you feel stuck in a "four hands" situation, defeat the enemy by changing your mindset and using a technique that fits the situation. You must be able to judge when to do this.

To Move the Shade

"To move the shade" is used when you can't see the enemy's intentions. In large-scale strategy, when the enemy's position is unclear, act like you are about to launch a strong attack to force them to reveal their resources. Once you see what they have, it becomes easier to defeat them using another method. In single combat, if the enemy takes a defensive stance with their long sword, hiding their intentions, make a fake attack to draw them out. The enemy will show their sword, thinking they've seen your strategy, and then you can take advantage of what they reveal to secure a victory. Be careful not to miss the right moment. Study this thoroughly.

To Hold Down a Shadow

"Holding down a shadow" is used when you can sense the enemy's intent to attack. In large-scale strategy, when the enemy starts their attack, if you pretend to strongly suppress their technique, they might change their plan. At this point, change your own approach and defeat them by anticipating their next move with an empty, flexible mind. In single combat, when the enemy shows strong intent, you must block it with precise timing, and defeat them by catching them off guard with your timing. You must study this thoroughly.

To Pass On

Many things can be passed on, like sleepiness or yawning. Time itself can be passed on, too. In large-scale strategy, when the enemy becomes agitated and seems ready to rush, remain completely calm. This calmness will affect the enemy, causing them to relax. Once you see that this mood has spread to them, you can defeat them by launching a strong attack with an empty, flexible mind. In single combat, you can win by relaxing your body and spirit, and then, at the moment the enemy relaxes, attacking swiftly and forcefully, taking them by surprise. This is similar to the idea of "getting someone drunk." You can also infect the enemy with boredom, carelessness, or weakness. Study this well.

To Cause Loss of Balance

There are many ways to cause a loss of balance. Danger, hardship, or surprise can all lead to imbalance. You must study this closely. In large-scale strategy, it's important to unbalance the enemy. Attack suddenly where they don't expect it, and while their spirit is unsettled, keep pressing your advantage to defeat them. In single combat, start by moving slowly, then suddenly attack with full force. Don't give them any time to recover; keep the pressure on and seize the opportunity to win. Learn how to do this.

To Frighten

Fear often comes from the unexpected. In large-scale strategy, you can frighten the enemy not just by what they see, but by shouting, making a small force seem larger, or by surprising them with an unexpected attack from the side. All these things can create fear. You can win by taking advantage of the enemy's fearful state. In single combat, you should also take advantage of the enemy's surprise, using your body, sword, or voice to startle and defeat them. Study this well.

To Soak In

When you and the enemy are locked together, and you realize you can't make progress, "soak in" and become one with the enemy. You can win by using the right technique while you are intertwined. In both large and small battles, you can often achieve a decisive victory by learning how to "soak" into the enemy, while drawing apart might cause you to lose your chance to win. Study this carefully.

To Injure the Corners

It's hard to move strong things by pushing them directly, so you should "injure the corners." In large-scale strategy, it's helpful to strike at the edges of the enemy's forces. When the corners fall, the spirit of the entire group will fall apart. To defeat the enemy, you must follow up the attack once the corners have collapsed. In single combat, it becomes easy to win once the enemy's defenses break down. This happens when you injure the corners of his body, weakening him. It's important to know how to do this, so you must study it deeply.

To Throw into Confusion

This means making the enemy lose focus. In large-scale strategy, we can use our troops to throw the enemy into disarray on the battlefield. By observing the enemy's mood, we can make them think,

"Here? There? Like this? Like that? Slow? Fast?" Victory is certain when the enemy gets caught up in a confusing rhythm that distracts their spirit. In single combat, we can confuse the enemy by using a variety of techniques when the moment is right. Fake a thrust or cut, or make the enemy think you're about to engage directly. Once the enemy is confused, it's easy to win. This is the core of fighting, and you must study it carefully.

The Three Shouts

The three shouts happen at different moments: before, during, and after. Shout based on the situation. The voice is a sign of life. We shout at fires, against the wind, and over waves. The voice shows energy. In large-scale strategy, we shout as loudly as possible at the beginning of battle. During the fight, the shout is low and fierce as we strike. After victory, we shout again to proclaim success. These are the three shouts. In single combat, we make a cut and shout "Ei!" at the same time to disturb the enemy, and after the shout, we strike with the long sword. We shout again after cutting down the enemy to announce victory. This is called "sen go no koe" (before and after voice). We do not shout at the same time we swing the sword. Instead, the shout helps establish rhythm. You must study this well.

To Mingle

In battle, when the armies face off, attack the enemy's strong points and, once you've pushed them back, quickly separate and strike another strong point on the edges of their forces. The spirit of this is like a winding mountain path. This is an important tactic when fighting one man against many. Defeat the enemies in one area or drive them back, then time your attack on other strong points to the right and left, moving like a winding path through the mountains, evaluating the enemy's strength. Once you understand the enemy's situation, attack fiercely without any hesitation. "Mingling" means advancing and engaging the enemy without stepping back. You must grasp this concept.

To Crush

This means crushing the enemy, viewing them as weak. In large-scale strategy, if the enemy has few men or even if they have many but their spirit is weak and confused, you must "knock the hat over their eyes," crushing them completely. If you only half-crush them, they might recover. You must learn the spirit of crushing as if with a firm grip. In single combat, if the enemy is less skilled, their rhythm is off, or they're retreating or evading, you should crush them immediately. Do this without giving them space to recover. The key is to crush them all at once. The main goal is to make sure they don't regain their position even a little. Study this deeply.

The Mountain-Sea Change

The "mountain-sea" spirit means that it's a mistake to repeat the same tactic multiple times when fighting the enemy. You may have to do something twice, but don't try it a third time. If you've attacked once and failed, there's little chance you'll succeed using the same approach again. If you try a technique again after it's failed twice, you must change your strategy. If the enemy expects you to act like the mountains, attack like the sea; if they expect you to act like the sea, attack like the mountains. You must study this deeply.

To Penetrate the Depths

When fighting the enemy, even if you can see you're winning on the surface by following the Way, the enemy's spirit might still be strong. They could be beaten on the outside but undefeated inside. With the principle of "penetrating the depths," you can crush the enemy's spirit by quickly shifting your own spirit. This happens often. "Penetrating the depths" means using the long sword, your body, and your spirit to break through. This can't be explained in simple terms. Once you've crushed the enemy in the depths, you don't need to stay aggressive. But if the enemy's spirit remains strong, it's hard to defeat them. You must practice penetrating the depths in both large-scale strategy and single combat.

To Renew

"To renew" applies when you're fighting and the situation feels stuck, with no clear way forward. Abandon your current mindset, think of the situation with a fresh perspective, and win using a new rhythm. To renew, when you're deadlocked with the enemy, means that without changing your surroundings, you change your spirit and win using a different technique. You must also consider how "to renew" applies in large-scale strategy. Study this diligently.

Rat's Head, Ox's Neck

"Rat's head and ox's neck" means that when you and the enemy are both caught up in small, entangled details, you must always remember to think of the Way of Strategy as both small like a rat's head and large like an ox's neck. Whenever you get bogged down in small matters, switch to a large, open spirit, balancing the small with the large. This is one of the key ideas in strategy. A warrior must always think this way in everyday life. You should not stray from this idea in large-scale strategy or single combat.

The Commander Knows the Troops

"The commander knows the troops" applies everywhere in the Way of strategy. Using the wisdom of strategy, treat the enemy like they're your own troops. When you think this way, you can move them as you please and easily chase them around. You become the general, and the enemy becomes your soldiers. You must master this.

To Let Go the Hilt

There are many ways to "let go the hilt." One involves winning without even using a sword. Another is holding the long sword but not winning. These different methods can't be explained fully in writing. You must train well.

The Body of a Rock

When you've mastered the Way of Strategy, you can make your body like a rock, and nothing can touch you. This is the body of a rock. You will be unmoved. (Oral tradition)

Everything written above is what I have always thought about in Ichi school sword fighting, written down as it came to me. This is the first time I've written about my technique, so the order may seem a bit unclear. It's difficult to express it exactly. This book is a spiritual guide for anyone who wants to learn the Way. From my youth, my heart has been set on the Way of Strategy. I have trained my hand, strengthened my body, and developed many spiritual attitudes related to sword fighting.

If we look at men of other schools, they often focus on discussing theories and mastering hand techniques, and though they may seem skilled, they lack true spirit. Of course, men who train like this believe they are strengthening their body and spirit, but this is actually a barrier to the true Way, and its negative influence lingers forever. Because of this, the true Way of Strategy is declining and fading away. The true Way of sword fighting is the craft of defeating the enemy in battle, and nothing more. If you achieve and stick to the wisdom of my strategy, you will never doubt your victory.

Chapter 4 - The Wind Book

In strategy, you must understand the Ways of other schools, so I've written about different traditions of strategy in this Wind Book. Without knowing the Ways of other schools, it's hard to grasp the essence of my Ichi school. When we look at other schools, we find some that focus on using strength with extra-long swords. Some schools study the Way of the short sword, known as the kodachi. Others teach many sword techniques, describing sword positions as the "surface" and the Way as the "interior." I make it clear in this book that none of these are the true Way—along with all their faults, strengths, and rights and wrongs. My Ichi school is different. Other schools use their accomplishments as a way to make a living, like growing flowers and painting decorations to sell. But this is not the Way of Strategy. Some of the world's strategists only focus on sword-fighting and limit their training to handling the long sword and moving their bodies. But is skill alone enough to win? This isn't the essence of the Way. I have written down what's lacking in other schools, one by one, in this book. You must study these points closely to understand the value of my Ni To Ichi school.

Some other schools favor using extra-long swords. From the perspective of my strategy, these schools are weak. This is because they don't understand the idea of cutting the enemy by any means. They rely on the length of the extra-long sword, thinking they can defeat the enemy from a distance. In this world, it's said, "One inch gives the hand an advantage," but this is just idle talk from someone who doesn't know strategy. It shows a weak spirit to depend on the length of a sword, fighting from a distance without the benefit of true strategy. Perhaps this school likes extra-long swords as part of their teachings, but if we compare it to real life, it doesn't make sense. Should we necessarily lose if we have only a short sword and no long sword? It's hard for these people to cut the enemy up close because the long sword is too big and becomes a burden. It puts them at a disadvantage compared to someone with a short sword. As the saying goes: "Great and small go together." So, don't automatically dislike extra-long swords. What I dislike is the tendency to favor the long sword. In large-scale strategy, we can think of large forces as long swords and small forces as short swords. Can't a small group fight a large group? There are many examples of small forces defeating larger ones. Your strategy doesn't matter if you're called to fight in a small space but still wish for a long sword, or if you're in a house and only have your short sword. Besides, some people are not as strong as others. In my teaching, I dislike narrow-minded thinking. You must study this well.

You shouldn't talk about long swords being strong or weak. If you swing a long sword with only strength in mind, your cut will be rough, and it'll be harder to win. If you focus too much on the sword's strength, you'll try to cut too hard and end up not cutting well at all. It's also bad to test your sword by trying to cut too forcefully. Whenever you cross swords with an enemy, you shouldn't think about cutting them either too strongly or too weakly—just focus on cutting and killing them. Be focused entirely on killing the enemy. Don't try to cut too forcefully, and don't worry about cutting too softly either. Just focus on killing. If you rely on strength, when you hit the enemy's sword, you'll hit too hard, and your own sword will get carried away by the impact. That's why the saying "The strongest hand wins" doesn't hold true. In large-scale strategy, if you have a strong army and depend on strength to win, but the enemy also has a strong army, the fight will be fierce on both sides. Without the right principles, the battle can't be won. The spirit of my school is to win with the wisdom of strategy, ignoring unnecessary details. Study this well.

Using a shorter long sword is not the true Way to victory. In ancient times, tachi and katana referred to long and short swords. Men who are strong can handle even a long sword easily, so there's no reason for them to prefer the short sword. They also use long weapons like spears and halberds. Some people use a shorter long sword, thinking they can quickly stab the enemy when his guard is down as he swings his sword. But this way of thinking is wrong. Trying to take advantage of the enemy's unguarded moments is purely defensive and not a good strategy for close combat. Plus, if you face many enemies, you can't use the tactic of jumping in with a short sword. Some believe that if they face a group of enemies with a shorter long sword, they can move freely, cutting wide arcs, but in reality, they'll have to constantly defend themselves and eventually get caught up with the enemy. This approach doesn't align with the true Way of Strategy. The sure way to win is to confuse the enemy by making him move aside, all while keeping your body firm and upright. The same principle applies in large-scale strategy. The essence of strategy is to fall upon the enemy in large numbers and quickly defeat them. People who study strategy tend to get used to countering, dodging, and retreating as normal tactics. They become stuck in this habit and can easily be led around by the enemy. The Way of Strategy is straightforward and direct. You must chase the enemy, making him follow your will.

Other Schools with Many Methods of Using the Long Sword

Placing too much importance on the positions of the long sword is a flawed way of thinking. What is called "attitude" in the world refers to when there is no enemy. This has been the tradition since ancient times, and there should be no idea of "this is the modern way" in dueling. You must put the enemy in uncomfortable positions. Attitude is for times when you must hold your ground, like defending castles, setting up battle formations, and showing that you won't be moved, even by a strong attack. In the Way of dueling, however, you should always focus on taking the lead and attacking. Attitude is about waiting for an attack. You must understand this. In duels of strategy, you should shift the enemy's attitude. Attack where his spirit is weak, confuse him, make him anxious, and frighten him. Use the enemy's unsettled rhythm to your advantage, and you will win. I do not like the defensive spirit known as "attitude." Therefore, in my Way, there is something called "Attitude-No Attitude."

In large-scale strategy, we position our troops for battle by considering our own strength, observing the enemy's numbers, and noting the battlefield's details. This is at the start of the battle. The spirit of attacking first is entirely different from the spirit of being attacked. Withstanding an attack with a strong attitude and defending well is like building a wall of spears and halberds. When you attack the enemy, your spirit must be as strong as pulling the stakes out of the wall and using them as spears and halberds. You must study this closely.

Fixing the Eyes in Other Schools

Some schools teach that you should fix your eyes on the enemy's long sword. Others say you should watch their hands, their face, or their feet, and so on. But if you focus on these spots, your spirit can get confused, and your strategy will fall apart. Let me explain this in detail. Soccer players don't fix their eyes on the ball, but by playing well on the field, they perform skillfully. When you are used to something, your eyes don't limit you. People like master musicians have the music right in front of them, or swordsmen move their blades in different ways when they have mastered the Way. But this doesn't mean they stare directly at these things or make useless movements. It means they can see naturally.

In the Way of Strategy, after you have fought many battles, you will naturally assess the speed and position of the enemy's sword. Once you've mastered the Way, you will also see the strength of their spirit. In strategy, "fixing the eyes" means gazing at the enemy's heart. In large-scale strategy, you should focus on the enemy's strength. "Perception" and "sight" are the two ways of seeing. Perception involves focusing intensely on the enemy's spirit, watching the condition of the battlefield, keeping your gaze steady, noticing the flow of the battle, and observing the changes in advantage. This is the way to win. In single combat, don't focus on small details. As I've said, if you focus on details and ignore what really matters, your spirit will get confused, and victory will slip away. Study this principle carefully and train hard.

Use of the Feet in Other Schools

There are different ways of using the feet: floating foot, jumping foot, springing foot, treading foot, crow's foot, and other nimble walking methods. From the viewpoint of my strategy, all of these are unsatisfactory. I dislike floating foot because the feet tend to float during a fight. The Way must be grounded. I also don't like jumping foot because it leads to a habit of jumping and a restless spirit. No matter how much you jump, it doesn't have a real purpose, so jumping is bad. Springing foot causes a springy, uncertain spirit. Treading foot is a "waiting" method, and I especially dislike it. Besides these, there are various fast walking methods, like crow's foot, and others.

Sometimes, however, you may face the enemy on difficult terrain like marshland, swampy ground, river valleys, rocky areas, or narrow roads. In these situations, you can't jump or move your feet quickly. In my strategy, the footwork remains the same. I walk as I normally do on the street. You should never lose control of your feet. Based on the enemy's rhythm, move either fast or slow, adjusting your body just enough—not too much or too little. Moving your feet properly is also crucial in large-scale strategy. If you attack quickly and carelessly without understanding the enemy's spirit, your rhythm will be thrown off, and you won't be able to win. On the other hand, if you advance too slowly, you won't be able to take advantage of the enemy's disorder, and the chance to win will pass. The battle will drag on, and you won't finish it quickly. You must win by seizing on the enemy's confusion and not giving them even the slightest chance to recover. Practice this thoroughly.

Speed in Other Schools

Speed is not part of the true Way of Strategy. Speed can make things seem fast or slow depending on whether or not they follow the right rhythm. In any Way, a true master of strategy doesn't seem fast. Some people can walk a hundred or even a hundred and twenty miles in a day, but this doesn't mean they run all day long. Untrained runners might seem like they've been running the entire time, but their performance is poor. In dance, skilled performers can sing while dancing, but beginners slow down and become overwhelmed. Similarly, the "old pine tree" melody played on a drum is calm, but beginners make it sound rushed and busy. Very skilled people can handle a fast rhythm, but rushing is bad. If you try to go too fast, you'll fall out of time. Of course, going too slow is also bad. Truly skilled people never lose their timing, and they are always deliberate without seeming busy. This principle can be understood from these examples.

What is known as "speed" is especially harmful in the Way of Strategy. The reason is that in different places—like marshes or swamps—you may not be able to move your body and legs quickly together. And it's even harder to cut quickly with a long sword in these situations. If you try to cut fast, as if you're using a fan or a short sword, you won't make an effective cut at all. You must understand this.

In large-scale strategy, a fast, frantic spirit is also undesirable. Your spirit should be calm, like holding down a pillow, so you won't be even a little late. When your opponent is rushing recklessly, you must act the opposite way—stay calm and steady. Don't let yourself be affected by the opponent's pace. Train diligently to master this spirit.

"Interior" and "Surface" in Other Schools

There is no "interior" or "surface" in strategy. In the arts, people often claim to have hidden meanings, secret traditions, and talk about "interior" and "gate," but in combat, there is no such thing as fighting on the surface or cutting with the interior. When I teach my Way, I start by showing techniques that are easy for students to understand, a straightforward teaching. Gradually, I explain deeper principles, things that are hard to grasp, depending on the student's progress. In any case, because true understanding comes through experience, I don't talk about "interior" or "gate."

In life, if you go deep into the mountains, even deeper, you will eventually reach the gate. Whatever the Way, it has an interior, and sometimes it's useful to point out the gate. In strategy, however, we cannot clearly say what is hidden and what is revealed. That's why I don't like passing on my Way through written pledges or rules. By observing my students' abilities, I teach the direct Way, removing the bad influence of other schools, and gradually introduce them to the true Way of the warrior. The way I teach strategy is through a trustworthy spirit. You must train diligently.

I've tried to outline the strategy of other schools in the nine sections above. I could now go into detail about these schools one by one, from the "gate" to the "interior," but I've intentionally not named the schools or their key points. The reason is that different branches of schools interpret the teachings in various ways. As opinions differ, so must interpretations of the same idea. Therefore, no single person's understanding applies to any school. I've shown the general tendencies of other schools across nine points. If we look at them honestly, we see that people tend to favor either long swords or short swords and focus too much on strength in both large and small matters. This explains why I don't deal with the "gates" of other schools.

In my Ichi school of the long sword, there is no gate or interior. There is no hidden meaning in sword positions. You simply need to keep your spirit true to fully realize the virtue of strategy.

Chapter 5 - The Book Of The Void

The Ni To Ichi Way of Strategy is written down in this Book of the Void. The spirit of the void is what we call a place where nothing exists. It's something beyond human knowledge. The void is, of course, nothingness. By understanding things that exist, you can also understand what does not exist—that is the void. People in this world often misunderstand and believe that whatever they don't understand must be the void. But this isn't the true void; it's confusion. In the Way of Strategy, some warriors believe that anything they don't comprehend in their craft must be the void. This, too, is not the true void.

To truly master the Way of Strategy as a warrior, you must fully study all martial arts and never stray from the Way of the warrior. With a calm spirit, practice every day and every hour. Strengthen both your spirit and mind, and refine both your perception and your sight. When your spirit is completely clear, without even a hint of confusion, that is when you reach the true void. Until you find the true Way—whether in Buddhism or in everyday life—you might think everything is correct and orderly. But when we look at things objectively, through the laws of the world, we see many ideas that have strayed from the true Way.

Understand this well, and let straightforwardness be your foundation, with the true spirit as your Way. Practice strategy broadly, correctly, and openly. Then, you will begin to see things from a wider perspective, and by taking the void as your Way, you will see the Way as the void. In the void, there is virtue and no evil. Wisdom exists, principles exist, the Way exists, but the spirit is nothingness.

Twelfth day of the fifth month,

Second year of Shoho (1645).

Teruro Magonojo

SHINMEN MUSASHI

Translated by Tim Zengerink

As A Man Thinketh

James Allen

Introduction

"Mind is the Master power that moulds and makes,
And Man is Mind, and evermore he takes
The tool of Thought, and, shaping what he wills,
Brings forth a thousand joys, a thousand ills:—
He thinks in secret, and it comes to pass:
Environment is but his looking-glass."

~ James Allen

This little book, which is the result of meditation and experience, is not meant to be a complete work on the often-discussed topic of the power of thought. Instead, it aims to inspire rather than explain, with the goal of encouraging men and women to discover and understand the truth that—

"They themselves are makers of themselves."

This is because of the thoughts they choose and nurture. The mind is the master-weaver, shaping both the inner garment of character and the outer garment of circumstance. Although people may have woven their lives in ignorance and pain before, they can now weave in enlightenment and happiness.

James Allen
Broad Park Avenue,
Ilfracombe,

Chapter 1
Thought and Character

The saying "As a man thinks in his heart, so is he" describes not only a person's entire being but also covers every aspect of their life. A person is truly what they think, as their character is the sum total of all their thoughts.

Just as a plant grows from a seed and cannot exist without it, every action of a person comes from hidden seeds of thought and could not happen without them. This applies to actions that seem "spontaneous" and "unpremeditated" as much as it does to those that are planned.

Action is the blossom of thought, and joy and suffering are its fruits. Thus, a person harvests the sweet and bitter outcomes of their own cultivation.

"Thought in the mind has made us what we are. By thought was wrought and built. If a man's mind has evil thoughts, pain comes to him just as the wheel follows the ox. If one endures in purity of thought, joy follows him like his own shadow—sure."

A person grows by law, not by artificial means, and cause and effect are as absolute and unchanging in the hidden realm of thought as they are in the world of visible and material things. A noble and godlike character is not a gift or a result of chance but is the natural result of consistent right thinking and the effect of dwelling on godlike thoughts for a long time. In the same way, an ignoble and beastly character results from continually harboring lowly thoughts.

A person is made or unmade by themselves. In the workshop of thought, they create the weapons that can destroy themselves or the tools with which they build heavenly mansions of joy, strength, and peace. By choosing the right thoughts and applying them correctly, a person rises to divine perfection; by misusing and wrongly applying thoughts, they fall below the level of a beast. Between these two extremes are all the levels of character, and a person is their creator and master.

Of all the beautiful truths about the soul that have been discovered and brought to light in this age, none is more uplifting or full of divine promise and confidence than this: that a person is the master of their thoughts, the shaper of their character, and the creator of their conditions, environment, and destiny.

As a being of power, intelligence, and love, and the ruler of their own thoughts, a person holds the key to every situation and possesses within themselves the transformative and regenerative ability to become what they desire.

A person is always the master, even in their weakest and most abandoned state. However, in their weakness and degradation, they are a foolish master who mismanages their "household." When they begin to reflect on their condition and diligently search for the Law upon which their being is founded, they become the wise master, directing their energies with intelligence and shaping their thoughts to achieve positive outcomes. This is the conscious master, and a person can only become this by discovering within themselves the laws of thought. This discovery is entirely a matter of application, self-analysis, and experience.

Gold and diamonds are obtained only through much searching and mining, and a person can find every truth related to their being if they dig deep into the mine of their soul. They can prove that they are the maker of their character, the shaper of their life, and the builder of their destiny if they watch, control, and change their thoughts, observing their effects on themselves, on others, and on their life and circumstances. By linking cause and effect through patient practice and investigation, and using every experience, even the most trivial, everyday occurrences, as a means of gaining self-knowledge, they gain understanding, wisdom, and power. In this pursuit, like no other, the law is absolute that "He that seeks, finds; and to him that knocks, it shall be opened;" for only through patience, practice, and constant persistence can a person enter the Door of the Temple of Knowledge.

Chapter 2

Effect of Thought on Circumstances

A man's mind can be compared to a garden, which can be carefully tended or allowed to grow wild. But whether you take care of it or not, it will produce something. If you don't plant good seeds, weeds will grow in abundance.

Just as a gardener takes care of his garden, keeping it free from weeds and growing the flowers and fruits he wants, a person can tend the garden of their mind by removing wrong, useless, and impure thoughts and nurturing right, useful, and pure ones. By doing this, a person eventually realizes that they are the master gardener of their soul and the director of their life. They also discover the laws of thought within themselves and understand more clearly how thoughts shape their character, circumstances, and destiny.

Thought and character are connected, and since character shows itself through environment and circumstances, a person's outer conditions will always be related to their inner state. This doesn't mean that a person's circumstances at any moment fully reveal their entire character, but that these circumstances are deeply linked to some essential thought within them and are necessary for their growth at that time.

Every person is where they are because of the law of their being. The thoughts they have built into their character have brought them there, and nothing in their life happens by chance. Everything is the result of a law that cannot make mistakes. This is true for both those who feel out of harmony with their surroundings and those who are content.

As a growing and evolving being, a person is where they are to learn and grow. As they learn the spiritual lesson in any circumstance, it passes away and makes room for new ones.

People are affected by circumstances as long as they believe they are controlled by outside conditions. But when they realize they are a creative force and can control the inner seeds and soil from which circumstances grow, they become the true master of themselves.

Anyone who has practiced self-control and self-purification knows that circumstances arise from thought. They notice that changes in their circumstances occur in exact proportion to their mental changes. When someone sincerely works to fix their character's flaws and makes quick and noticeable progress, they often go through a series of changes.

The soul attracts what it secretly harbors, loves, and fears. It reaches the heights of its aspirations and falls to the level of its unrefined desires, and circumstances are how the soul receives its due.

Every thought planted in the mind takes root, grows into action, and bears fruit in the form of opportunity and circumstance. Good thoughts bring good fruit; bad thoughts bring bad fruit.

The external world shapes itself to the internal world of thought. Both pleasant and unpleasant conditions ultimately benefit the individual. As a harvester of his own crop, a person learns through both suffering and joy.

By following the desires, aspirations, and thoughts that dominate him—whether pursuing fleeting fantasies or steadfastly following the path of high endeavor—a person ultimately reaches their fulfillment in the outer conditions of their life. Everywhere, the laws of growth and adjustment apply.

A person does not end up in poverty or jail because of fate or circumstance but by following lowly thoughts and desires. Similarly, a pure-minded person does not suddenly commit a crime due to external forces; the criminal thought was nurtured in their heart long before, and opportunity revealed its power. Circumstance does not make the man; it reveals him to himself. One cannot fall into vice without vicious inclinations or rise into virtue without nurturing virtuous aspirations. As the lord of thought, a person makes himself, shaping his environment and destiny. Even at birth, the soul attracts the conditions that reflect its purity and impurity, strength and weakness.

People do not attract what they want but what they are. Their whims and ambitions are thwarted, but their innermost thoughts and desires are fulfilled, whether good or bad. The "divinity that shapes our ends" is within us; it is our very self. Only a person can chain themselves. Thought and action are the jailers of fate, imprisoning us when base and liberating us when noble. A person does not receive what they wish and pray for, but what they earn. Their wishes and prayers are fulfilled only when they align with their thoughts and actions.

In light of this truth, what does it mean to "fight against circumstances"? It means continually opposing an external effect while nurturing and maintaining its cause in one's heart. This cause may be a conscious vice or an unconscious weakness, but it hinders progress and calls for remedy.

People want to improve their circumstances but are unwilling to improve themselves, so they remain stuck. A person who does not shy away from self-sacrifice will always achieve their goals. This applies to both earthly and heavenly pursuits. Even someone who wants to become wealthy must be willing to make personal sacrifices to succeed. How much more must one do to achieve a balanced and strong life?

Consider a man who is desperately poor. He wants to improve his surroundings and comfort but shirks his work and thinks he is justified in deceiving his employer due to low wages. Such a man does not understand the basic principles of prosperity and is not only unable to rise out of poverty but attracts deeper misery by indulging in lazy and deceptive thoughts.

Or consider a wealthy man who suffers from a persistent disease caused by gluttony. He is willing to spend large sums to cure it but won't give up his excessive desires. He wants to enjoy rich food and good health, but he is unfit for health because he hasn't learned the basics of a healthy life.

Then there is the employer who cuts wages to increase profits, not realizing he is setting himself up for failure. When he faces bankruptcy in both reputation and wealth, he blames circumstances, not knowing he is the sole author of his condition.

These examples illustrate that a person often unconsciously creates their circumstances. While aiming for a good outcome, they undermine their success by nurturing thoughts and desires that don't align with their goals. Readers can trace the action of thought in their minds and lives and see how external circumstances cannot serve as the sole basis for reasoning.

Circumstances are complex, thought is deeply rooted, and the conditions of happiness vary greatly among individuals. A man's entire soul condition, though it may be known to himself, cannot be judged by another based solely on his external life. A man may be honest in some areas yet suffer privations; a man may be dishonest in some areas yet acquire wealth. The conclusion that one fails due to honesty and the other succeeds due to dishonesty results from superficial judgment, assuming the dishonest man is entirely corrupt and the honest man is entirely virtuous. Deeper knowledge and experience show such judgments to be false. The dishonest man may have virtues the other lacks, and the honest man may have vices the other is free from. The honest man reaps the rewards of his good thoughts and actions and suffers from his vices. The dishonest man similarly experiences his own suffering and happiness.

It's comforting to human vanity to believe one suffers due to virtue, but until a man removes every bitter and impure thought from his mind and cleanses his soul of sin, he cannot declare that his suffering is due to his good qualities. Before reaching supreme perfection, he will find the Great Law of Justice operating in his mind and life, which does not give good for evil or evil for good. With this knowledge, he will look back on his past ignorance and blindness and know that his life is and always has been justly ordered and that all his past experiences, good and bad, were the fair outcomes of his evolving self.

Good thoughts and actions never produce bad results, and bad thoughts and actions never produce good results. Just as corn cannot produce anything but corn and nettles nothing but nettles, this law is understood in the natural world. Still, few understand it in the mental and moral world, though it operates just as consistently there.

Suffering always results from wrong thoughts. It indicates that an individual is out of harmony with themselves and the law of their being. The sole purpose of suffering is to purify and remove all that is useless and impure. Suffering ceases for the pure. There is no reason to burn gold once the impurities have been removed, and a perfectly pure and enlightened being cannot suffer.

The circumstances a man encounters with suffering result from his own mental disharmony. The circumstances a man encounters with blessedness result from his own mental harmony. Blessedness, not material possessions, measures right thought; wretchedness, not a lack of material possessions, measures wrong thought. A man may be cursed and rich, or blessed and poor. Blessedness and riches only come together when riches are rightly and wisely used. A poor man only falls into wretchedness when he sees his situation as an unjust burden.

Poverty and indulgence are the two extremes of wretchedness, both equally unnatural and the result of mental disorder. A man is only rightly conditioned when he is happy, healthy, and prosperous, and happiness, health, and prosperity result from harmoniously aligning his inner self with his surroundings.

A person begins to truly live when they stop complaining and blaming others and start searching for the hidden justice that governs their life. As they align their mind with this justice, they stop blaming others for their condition and build themselves up with strong and noble thoughts. They stop fighting against circumstances and begin to use them to progress faster and discover their inner powers and possibilities.

Law, not chaos, is the dominant principle in the universe; justice, not injustice, is the soul of life; and righteousness, not corruption, is the force behind the spiritual governance of the world. This means that by aligning himself with righteousness, a man will find that the universe aligns with him. As he changes his thoughts towards things and people, things and people will change towards him.

The truth of this is in every person, allowing for easy investigation through introspection and self-analysis. Let a person radically change their thoughts, and they will be amazed at the rapid transformation it brings to their material conditions. People think thoughts can be kept secret, but they can't; thoughts quickly crystallize into habits, which solidify into circumstances. Bestial thoughts lead to habits of drunkenness and sensuality, which result in poverty and disease. Impure thoughts lead to habits of confusion and distraction, resulting in adverse circumstances. Fearful, doubtful, and indecisive thoughts lead to weak habits, resulting in failure and dependence. Lazy thoughts lead to habits of uncleanliness and dishonesty, resulting in poverty. Hateful and critical thoughts lead to habits of accusation and violence, resulting in injury and persecution. Selfish thoughts lead to self-seeking habits, resulting in distressing circumstances. Conversely, beautiful thoughts lead to habits of grace and kindness, resulting in pleasant circumstances. Pure thoughts lead to habits of self-control, resulting in peace. Courageous and self-reliant thoughts lead to successful and free circumstances. Energetic thoughts lead to habits of cleanliness and industry, resulting in pleasant circumstances. Gentle and forgiving thoughts lead to protective circumstances. Loving and selfless thoughts lead to self-forgetfulness habits, resulting in prosperity and true riches.

A particular train of thought, whether good or bad, will inevitably produce results on character and circumstances. While a person cannot directly choose their circumstances, they can choose their thoughts and, by doing so, indirectly shape their circumstances.

Nature helps everyone fulfill the thoughts they most encourage, and opportunities arise that will quickly bring good and evil thoughts to the surface.

Let a person abandon sinful thoughts, and the world will soften towards them and be ready to help. Let them discard weak thoughts, and opportunities will arise to aid their strong resolves. Let them nurture good thoughts, and no hard fate will bind them to wretchedness and shame. The world is your kaleidoscope, and its ever-changing patterns are the carefully adjusted pictures of your thoughts.

"So You will be what you will to be;
Let failure find its false content
In that poor word, 'environment,'
But spirit scorns it, and is free.
"It masters time, it conquers space;
It cowes that boastful trickster, Chance,
And bids the tyrant Circumstance
Uncrown, and fill a servant's place.
"The human Will, that force unseen,
The offspring of a deathless Soul,
Can hew a way to any goal,
Though walls of granite intervene.
"Be not impatient in delays
But wait as one who understands;
When spirit rises and commands
The gods are ready to obey."

Chapter 3

Effect of Thought on Health and the Body

The body serves the mind. It follows what the mind thinks, whether those thoughts are intentionally chosen or come automatically. When the mind is filled with negative or unlawful thoughts, the body quickly falls into sickness and decay. On the other hand, when the mind is full of happy and beautiful thoughts, the body becomes youthful and healthy.

Just like circumstances, disease and health are rooted in thought. Sickly thoughts show up in a sickly body. Fearful thoughts can kill a person as quickly as a bullet, and they are constantly affecting thousands of people, even if not as suddenly. Those who fear disease are the ones who often get it. Anxiety weakens the entire body and makes it susceptible to disease, while impure thoughts, even if not acted upon physically, will eventually harm the nervous system.

Strong, pure, and happy thoughts build up the body with strength and grace. The body is sensitive and responds to the thoughts it receives, and habitual thoughts will have their effects, whether good or bad.

People will continue to have impure and unhealthy bodies as long as they have unclean thoughts. A clean heart leads to a clean life and a healthy body. A polluted mind leads to a corrupt life and an unhealthy body. Thought is the source of action, life, and expression; make the source pure, and everything will be pure.

Changing one's diet won't help if a person doesn't change their thoughts. When a person purifies their thoughts, they no longer desire unhealthy food.

Pure thoughts lead to clean habits. A so-called saint who does not wash is not a saint. A person who strengthens and purifies their thoughts does not need to worry about harmful germs.

To protect your body, guard your mind. To renew your body, beautify your mind. Thoughts of malice, envy, disappointment, and despair rob the body of its health and beauty. A sour face is not an accident; it is created by sour thoughts. Wrinkles are caused by foolishness, passion, and pride.

I know a woman who is ninety-six with the bright, innocent face of a young girl. I know a man who is much younger, yet his face is distorted by passion and discontent. The difference is that the woman has a sweet and sunny disposition, while the man has been consumed by negative emotions.

Just as you cannot have a sweet and healthy home without letting in air and sunshine, you cannot have a strong body and a bright, happy face without letting thoughts of joy, goodwill, and calmness into your mind.

On the faces of the elderly, some wrinkles are made by sympathy, others by pure thought, and others by passion. Who cannot tell the difference? For those who have lived righteously, old age is calm, peaceful, and gently mellowed, like a setting sun. I recently saw a philosopher on his deathbed. He was not old, except in years. He died as sweetly and peacefully as he lived.

Cheerful thoughts are the best medicine for curing the body's ills, and goodwill is the best comfort for dispelling grief and sorrow. Living with thoughts of ill will, cynicism, suspicion, and envy is like being in a prison you've built yourself. But thinking well of others, being cheerful, and finding the good in everyone—such unselfish thoughts are like the gates to heaven. Living each day with thoughts of peace toward all creatures will bring peace to the person who has them.

Chapter 4
Thought and Purpose

Until thought is linked with purpose, there can be no intelligent accomplishment. Most people let their thoughts drift aimlessly through life. Aimlessness is a vice, and anyone who wants to avoid catastrophe and destruction must not let it continue.

Those who lack a central purpose in their lives are easily overwhelmed by worries, fears, troubles, and self-pity, all of which are signs of weakness. These lead to failure, unhappiness, and loss just as surely as deliberately planned sins, though by a different path, because weakness cannot survive in a universe where power is constantly growing.

A person should form a clear purpose in their heart and work towards achieving it. This purpose should become the center of their thoughts. It could be a spiritual ideal or a worldly goal, depending on their nature at the time, but whatever it is, they should consistently focus their mental energy on the goal they have set. This purpose should be their highest priority, and they should dedicate themselves to reaching it, not letting their thoughts wander off into temporary fancies, desires, and imaginings. This is the key to self-control and true concentration of thought. Even if they fail repeatedly to achieve their purpose (as they inevitably will until they overcome their weaknesses), the strength of character they gain will be a true measure of their success. This will become a new starting point for future power and triumph.

Those who are not ready to grasp a great purpose should focus their thoughts on performing their duties flawlessly, no matter how unimportant their tasks may seem. Only in this way can they gather and focus their thoughts, develop resolution and energy, and once this is achieved, there is nothing that cannot be accomplished.

Even the weakest soul, knowing its own weaknesses and believing the truth that strength can only be developed through effort and practice, will begin to exert itself. By adding effort to effort, patience to patience, and strength to strength, it will never stop growing and will eventually become divinely strong.

Just as a physically weak person can become strong through careful and patient training, so can a person with weak thoughts make them strong by practicing right thinking.

To get rid of aimlessness and weakness and to start thinking with purpose is to join the ranks of those strong individuals who only see failure as one of the paths to achievement, who make every condition serve them, and who think strongly, attempt fearlessly, and accomplish masterfully.

Once a person has conceived a purpose, they should mentally map out a direct path to its achievement, without looking to the right or the left. Doubts and fears should be strictly avoided; they are disruptive elements that break up the straight line of effort, making it crooked, ineffective, and useless. Thoughts of doubt and fear have never accomplished anything and never will. They always lead to failure. Purpose, energy, and the power to act disappear when doubt and fear creep in.

The will to act comes from knowing that we can act. Doubt and fear are the greatest enemies of knowledge, and anyone who encourages them or fails to eliminate them hinders themselves at every step.

A person who has conquered doubt and fear has conquered failure. Every thought they have is connected to power, and they face all difficulties bravely and overcome them wisely. Their purposes are planted at the right time, and they bloom and produce fruit, which does not fall prematurely to the ground.

Thought that is fearlessly linked to purpose becomes a creative force: anyone who knows this is ready to become something higher and stronger than a mere bundle of wavering thoughts and fluctuating sensations; anyone who does this has become the conscious and intelligent wielder of their mental powers.

Chapter 5
The Thought-Factor in Achievement

Everything a person achieves or fails to achieve is the direct result of their own thoughts. In a universe that is justly ordered, where any loss of balance would mean total destruction, individual responsibility must be absolute. A person's weaknesses and strengths, purity and impurity, are their own, not someone else's. They are created by themselves, not by others, and can only be changed by themselves, never by another person. Their condition is also their own, not someone else's. Their suffering and happiness come from within. As they think, so they are; as they continue to think, so they remain.

A strong person cannot help a weaker one unless that weaker person is willing to be helped, and even then, the weak person must become strong on their own; they must develop the strength they admire in another through their own efforts. No one but themselves can change their condition.

People have often thought and said, "Many people are slaves because one is an oppressor; let's hate the oppressor." However, there is now a growing tendency among some to reverse this judgment and say, "One person is an oppressor because many are slaves; let's despise the slaves."

The truth is that both oppressor and slave are cooperating in ignorance, and while they seem to harm each other, they are actually harming themselves. Perfect Knowledge understands the law at work in the weakness of the oppressed and the misused power of the oppressor; perfect Love, seeing the suffering that both states bring, condemns neither; perfect Compassion embraces both oppressor and oppressed.

Anyone who has conquered weakness and let go of all selfish thoughts belongs to neither oppressor nor oppressed. They are free.

A person can only rise, conquer, and achieve by lifting up their thoughts. They can only remain weak, miserable, and abject by refusing to lift their thoughts.

Before a person can achieve anything, even in worldly matters, they must raise their thoughts above base animal indulgence. To succeed, they may not need to give up all animality and selfishness, but they must at least sacrifice some of it. A person whose main focus is base indulgence cannot think clearly or plan methodically; they cannot find and develop their latent resources and will fail in any endeavor. Without beginning to control their thoughts, they are not ready to control affairs or take on serious responsibilities. They are not fit to act independently and stand alone. But they are limited only by the thoughts they choose.

There can be no progress, no achievement without sacrifice, and a person's worldly success will be proportional to how much they sacrifice their confused animal thoughts and focus their mind on developing their plans, strengthening their resolve, and becoming more self-reliant. The higher they lift their thoughts, the more manly, upright, and righteous they become, and the greater their success, the more blessed and enduring their achievements will be.

The universe does not favor the greedy, the dishonest, and the vicious, although it may sometimes appear to do so on the surface; it helps the honest, the generous, and the virtuous. All the great Teachers throughout history have declared this in various ways, and to prove and know it, a person has only to persist in making themselves more and more virtuous by raising their thoughts.

Intellectual achievements result from thought dedicated to the pursuit of knowledge or the beautiful and true in life and nature. Such achievements may sometimes be associated with vanity and ambition, but they are not caused by those traits; they naturally result from long and arduous effort and pure and unselfish thoughts.

Spiritual achievements are the culmination of holy aspirations. A person who constantly thinks noble and lofty thoughts and focuses on all that is pure and unselfish will, as surely as the sun reaches its peak and the moon becomes full, become wise and noble in character and rise to a position of influence and blessedness.

Achievement, of any kind, is the crown of effort and the diadem of thought. With self-control, resolution, purity, righteousness, and well-directed thought, a person rises; with animality, indolence, impurity, corruption, and confused thoughts, a person falls.

A person may rise to great success in the world and even reach high spiritual levels, but they can also fall back into weakness and misery by allowing arrogant, selfish, and corrupt thoughts to take over.

Victories achieved through right thinking can only be maintained with vigilance. Many people give up when success seems assured and quickly fall back into failure.

All achievements, whether in business, intellectual pursuits, or spiritual growth, result from well-directed thought, are governed by the same law, and follow the same method; the only difference is in the goal.

Someone who wants to achieve little must sacrifice little; someone who wants to achieve much must sacrifice much; someone who wants to reach great heights must make great sacrifices.

Chapter 6
Visions and Ideals

Dreamers are the saviors of the world. Just as the visible world is supported by the invisible, so people, through all their struggles, sins, and mundane tasks, are nourished by the beautiful visions of their solitary dreamers. Humanity cannot forget its dreamers or let their ideals fade away; it lives through them, recognizing them as the realities that it will one day see and know.

Composers, sculptors, painters, poets, prophets, sages—these are the creators of the future world, the architects of heaven. The world is beautiful because they have lived; without them, working humanity would perish.

Anyone who holds onto a beautiful vision, a lofty ideal in their heart, will one day realize it. Columbus had a vision of another world, and he discovered it. Copernicus imagined a universe full of worlds, and he revealed it. Buddha envisioned a spiritual world of pure beauty and perfect peace, and he entered it.

Cherish your visions; cherish your ideals; cherish the music that stirs in your heart, the beauty that forms in your mind, the loveliness that wraps around your purest thoughts. From them will grow all delightful conditions, all heavenly environments. If you stay true to them, your world will be built from them.

To desire is to obtain; to aspire is to achieve. Should man's basest desires be fully satisfied while his purest aspirations starve? This is not the Law: such a situation can never exist. "Ask and receive."

Dream big dreams, and as you dream, so shall you become. Your Vision is the promise of what you shall one day be; your Ideal is the prophecy of what you shall finally reveal.

The greatest achievement was once a dream. The oak sleeps in the acorn; the bird waits in the egg; and in the highest vision of the soul, an awakening angel stirs. Dreams are the seeds of reality.

Your circumstances may be unfavorable, but they will not remain so if you see an Ideal and strive to reach it. You cannot change within and remain unchanged without. Here is a young man struggling with poverty and labor; confined to long hours in an unhealthy workshop; uneducated and lacking refinement. But he dreams of better things: intelligence, refinement, grace, and beauty. He mentally builds an ideal life; the vision of greater freedom and opportunity fills him. Unrest drives him to action, and he uses his spare time and resources, however small, to develop his latent powers. Soon, his mind changes so much that the workshop can no longer contain him. It becomes so out of tune with his mentality that it falls away like an old garment, and as new opportunities match his expanding abilities, he leaves it forever. Years later, this young man becomes a mature leader. He masters certain mental forces, wielding worldwide influence and nearly unmatched power. He holds great responsibilities, speaks, and changes lives. People hang on his words and reshape their characters. He becomes the central, luminous figure around which countless destinies revolve. He has realized his youthful Vision. He has become one with his Ideal.

And you, young reader, will realize the Vision of your heart, whether it is base or beautiful, or a mix of both, because you will always gravitate towards what you secretly love most. You will receive the exact results of your thoughts; you will earn exactly what you deserve. Whatever your current environment, you will fall, remain, or rise with your thoughts, Vision, and Ideal. You will become as small as your strongest desire or as great as your highest aspiration. In the beautiful words of Stanton Kirkham Davis, "You may be keeping accounts, and soon you will walk out of the door that seemed to be the barrier to your ideals, and find yourself before an audience—the pen still behind your ear, the ink stains on your fingers, and there and then you will pour out the torrent of your inspiration. You may be driving sheep, and you will wander into the city, wide-eyed; you will follow the spirit into the master's studio, and after a while, he will say, 'I have nothing more to teach you.' Now you have become the master, who dreamed of great things while driving sheep. You will set down the saw and the plane to take on the regeneration of the world."

The thoughtless, ignorant, and lazy see only the apparent effects and not the things themselves. They talk of luck, fortune, and chance. Seeing someone grow rich, they say, "How lucky he is!" Observing someone become intellectual, they exclaim, "How fortunate he is!" Noticing the saintly character and influence of another, they remark, "How chance favors him!" They don't see the trials, failures, and struggles these people have voluntarily faced to gain their experience; they don't know the sacrifices made, the undaunted efforts, and the faith exercised to overcome the seemingly impossible and realize their heart's Vision. They don't know the darkness and heartaches; they only see the light and joy and call it "luck." They don't see the long, arduous journey but only the pleasant goal and call it "good fortune." They don't understand the process, only the result, and call it chance.

In all human affairs, there are efforts and results, and the strength of the effort measures the result. Chance does not exist. Gifts, powers, and material, intellectual, and spiritual possessions are the fruits of effort; they are thoughts completed, goals achieved, and visions realized.

The Vision you glorify in your mind, the Ideal you hold in your heart—this you will build your life upon; this you will become.

Chapter 7
Serenity

Calmness of mind is one of the beautiful jewels of wisdom. It is the result of long and patient effort in self-control. Its presence indicates matured experience and a deeper knowledge of the laws and operations of thought.

A person becomes calm as they understand themselves as a being shaped by thought. This knowledge requires understanding others as being shaped by thought, too. As someone gains the right understanding and sees more clearly the connections of things through cause and effect, they stop fussing, fuming, worrying, and grieving, and instead remain poised, steadfast, and serene.

The calm person, having learned to control themselves, knows how to adapt to others. Others, in turn, respect their spiritual strength and feel they can learn from and rely on them. The more tranquil a person becomes, the greater their success, influence, and power for good. Even a regular businessperson will find their business prospering as they develop greater self-control and calmness, because people always prefer to deal with someone whose demeanor is steady and balanced.

The strong, calm person is always loved and respected. They are like a shade-giving tree in a thirsty land or a sheltering rock in a storm. Who doesn't love a calm heart and a sweet-tempered, balanced life? It doesn't matter whether it rains or shines, or what changes come to those with these blessings, for they are always sweet, serene, and calm. That exquisite balance of character, which we call serenity, is the final lesson of growth, the fruit of the soul. It is as precious as wisdom and more desirable than gold—yes, even fine gold. How insignificant mere money-seeking looks compared to a serene life—a life that lives in the ocean of Truth, beneath the waves, beyond the reach of tempests, in Eternal Calm!

How many people do we know who sour their lives, ruin all that is sweet and beautiful with explosive tempers, destroy their balance of character, and create bad blood! It is a question whether the majority of people do not ruin their lives and mar their happiness by lack of self-control. How few people do we meet in life who are well-balanced, who have that exquisite poise that is the hallmark of a developed character!

Yes, humanity surges with uncontrolled passion, is tumultuous with ungoverned grief, and is blown about by anxiety and doubt. Only the wise person, only one whose thoughts are controlled and purified, makes the winds and storms of the soul obey them.

Storm-tossed souls, wherever you may be, under whatever conditions you may live, know this: in the ocean of life, the isles of blessedness are smiling, and the sunny shore of your ideal awaits your arrival. Keep your hand firmly on the helm of thought. In the vessel of your soul lies the commanding Master; He only sleeps—awaken Him. Self-control is strength; right thought is mastery; calmness is power. Say to your heart, "Peace, be still!"

Self Reliance

Ralph Waldo Emerson

Self Reliance

"Don't look outside yourself for answers."

"Man is his own guide, and the soul that can live honestly and perfectly commands all light, influence, and fate. Nothing comes too early or too late for him. Our actions are like angels, good or bad, our constant companions.

Throw the child onto the rocks, feed him with the she-wolf's milk; if he grows up with the hawk and the fox, power and speed will be his hands and feet."

~ Ralph Waldo Emmerson

Recently, I read some original poems by a well-known painter. The soul always finds something meaningful in such lines, no matter the topic. The feeling they bring is often more important than any single idea in them. Believing in your own thoughts and trusting that what feels true to you deep down is true for everyone—that is genius. Speak your hidden beliefs, and they can become universal truths; eventually, our deepest thoughts return to us like a final judgment.

The voice of our mind is familiar to each of us. We admire people like Moses, Plato, and Milton because they ignored other people's ideas and books. They didn't repeat what others said; they spoke what they truly thought. We need to learn to recognize the spark of insight that comes from within us, even more than the brilliance of poets and philosophers. But we often push away our thoughts just because they're ours. In every great work, we see our own dismissed ideas coming back to us with a grand, powerful feeling. Great art teaches us to hold onto our first impressions, especially when everyone else disagrees. Otherwise, someday, a stranger will say what we've always felt, and we'll be embarrassed to agree with them.

There comes a time in everyone's life when they see that jealousy is foolish, and copying others is like losing your true self. We have to accept ourselves, with all our strengths and weaknesses, as the share we've been given in life. Although the world is full of good things, nothing worthwhile will come to us unless we work hard on the part we're given to care for. The power inside each of us is unique, and only we know what we can do, but even we don't fully know until we try. Certain faces, people, or events make a deep impression on us, while others do not. This memory isn't random but part of a larger harmony. Our eyes are placed where they are to catch a certain light. We only express part of who we are and feel ashamed of the special idea that each of us represents. If we share our thoughts honestly, we can trust they will lead to good results, but God doesn't show His work through cowards. A person feels truly happy and at peace when they put their heart into their work and do their best; otherwise, they find no rest. Their creativity leaves them, and they find no support or inspiration.

Trust yourself: everyone feels the strength that comes from self-confidence. Accept the place that has been given to you by divine guidance, the society of your time, and the flow of events. Great people have always done this, trusting in the spirit of their time, feeling that the most trustworthy thing is what's in their hearts, guiding their hands and filling their being. We must embrace this same great destiny, not as children or weaklings hiding in a safe corner, nor as cowards running from change, but as guides, helpers, and redeemers, following the will of God and pushing forward against chaos and darkness.

Nature gives us wonderful examples of this truth in the faces and actions of children, infants, and even animals! Their minds aren't divided or uncertain; they don't doubt a feeling just because their calculations disagree with it. Their minds are whole, their eyes bold, and when we look at their faces, we feel disarmed. Infants don't adjust to anyone; all people adjust to them, so often one baby will make four or five adults play and babble. God has given youth, puberty, and adulthood their own charm, making them desirable and kind, and their needs undeniable if they stand on their own. Don't think that a young person has no power because they can't speak to you and me. Listen! In the next room, their voice is clear and strong. It seems they know how to talk to their peers. Whether shy or bold, they'll know how to make us adults unnecessary.

Boys who are sure of their next meal carry themselves with the free spirit of human nature. A boy in the living room is like an audience in a theater: independent, not responsible, observing people and events as they happen. He judges them fairly and quickly, like boys do, as good, bad, interesting, silly, eloquent, or annoying. He never worries about consequences or personal interests; he gives an honest, independent opinion. You must seek his favor; he doesn't need yours. But adults are like prisoners, trapped by their own awareness. Once they speak or act successfully, they become tied to it, watched by the kindness or anger of many, whose opinions now matter to them. There's no escaping this. Oh, if only they could go back to being neutral! Whoever can stay free from all ties and, after seeing, can see again with the same innocent, unbiased, and fearless spirit, will always be a force. They would speak on all matters passing by, and their words would be seen as essential rather than personal, creating awe among people.

These are the voices we hear when we are alone, but they vanish when we join society. Everywhere, society works against each person's individuality. Society is like a shared company where people agree to give up their freedom and growth in exchange for the comfort of their basic needs. The main virtue it demands is conformity. Society doesn't value reality and creativity but only follows names and customs.

To truly be yourself, you must reject conformity. To reach greatness, don't let so-called "goodness" hold you back; instead, question if it's truly good. The only thing that should be sacred to you is the integrity of your mind. Be true to yourself, and the world will support you. I remember an answer I gave when I was young to a respected advisor who always pressed me with the old doctrines of the church. When I said, "Why should I care about the sacredness of traditions if I live completely from within?" my friend warned, "But these impulses might come from below, not above." I replied, "They don't feel that way to me; but if I'm a child of the Devil, then I'll live from the Devil." No law is sacred to me except the law of my own nature. Good and bad are only labels that can be easily applied to anything; the only right is what agrees with my nature, and the only wrong is what goes against it. A person should carry themselves as though everything else is temporary and fleeting, except for themselves. I am ashamed of how easily we bow to titles and names, to large organizations and outdated systems. Every polite, well-spoken person influences me more than they should. I should stand firm and speak bluntly, expressing the full truth at all times. If spite and pride hide behind kindness, should that go unnoticed? If an angry fanatic claims the noble cause of Abolition and comes to me with his latest news from overseas, why shouldn't I say to him: "Go love your own child; love your neighbor; be kind and modest; show that goodness; and stop hiding your harsh, selfish ambition behind this false concern for people far away. Your distant love is just hidden spite at home." Such a statement might sound rough and unrefined, but truth is more appealing than fake love. Your goodness must have some strength in it, or it is worthless. When love becomes weak and whiny, then hatred must be taught as a balance. I avoid even my father, mother, wife, and brother when my true calling summons me. I would write on my doorpost: Whim. I hope it's more than whim in the end, but we can't spend time explaining. Don't expect me to justify why I choose certain company or avoid others. And don't, as a good man did today, tell me about my duty to place every poor person in a better situation. Are they my poor? I tell you, foolish philanthropist, I begrudge the dollar, the dime, the cent I give to people who aren't connected to me and to whom I am not connected. There is a group of people I'm spiritually linked to; for them, I would go to jail if needed. But as for your random charities, college for the foolish, meeting houses for showy purposes, alms to drunkards, and endless Relief Societies—though I sometimes give the dollar out of shame, it's a wicked dollar that I'll one day have the courage to withhold.

Virtues are seen as exceptions, not the standard. People do what is considered a good action, like a brave deed or act of charity, as if paying a fine for failing to show up regularly for a parade. Their good deeds are done as a way to apologize or make up for living in the world, just as sick and insane people pay high fees. Their virtues are simply penances. I don't want to make up for anything; I just want to live. My life is for itself, not for show. I prefer it to be simple and real, not flashy or unstable. I want it to be steady and pleasant, without needing special handling. I ask for proof that you are genuine, and I reject appeals from someone to their actions. I know, for myself, that it makes no difference whether I perform or avoid actions that others see as excellent. I cannot agree to pay for a right that I naturally possess. Small and limited as my talents may be, I exist and don't need extra evidence for my own assurance or the assurance of others.

What I must do is all that matters to me, not what others think I should do. This rule, as tough in practical life as in intellectual life, might be the sole difference between greatness and smallness. It's harder because you'll always find people who think they know your duty better than you do. It's easy to live by the world's opinion; it's easy, in solitude, to live by our own; but the great person is one who, in the middle of a crowd, keeps the independence of solitude with complete peace.

The problem with following customs that feel lifeless to you is that it drains your energy. It wastes your time and muddles who you really are. If you support a church that's lost its spirit, contribute to an empty Bible society, vote with a big political party either for or against the government, or set your table like a bland host, then under all these acts, I struggle to see the real you. So much energy is pulled away from your true life. But if you do your own work, I will see you. Do your work, and you'll strengthen yourself. A person should realize that conformity is like playing a game of blindman's bluff. If I know your group, I already know your argument. I hear a preacher choose one of his church's institutions as his sermon topic. Don't I know right away that he won't say anything new or genuine? Don't I know that, despite the show of questioning, he won't actually question the institution's foundation? I know he's committed to seeing only one side—the accepted side, not as a true individual, but as a parish minister. He's like a lawyer arguing his client's case, and his show of impartiality is the weakest pretense. Most people have tied blindfolds over their eyes and bound themselves to some shared opinion. This conformity doesn't just make them false in a few points; it makes them false in everything. Every truth they tell is slightly off. Their two is not really two, their four not quite four; so every word they say frustrates us, and we don't even know where to begin to correct them. Meanwhile, nature isn't slow to dress us in the uniform of the group we align with. We end up taking on one style of face and body, slowly forming a subtle, foolish look. There's a particular humiliation that never fails to show itself in history; I mean "the foolish face of praise," the forced smile we put on when we're stuck in conversation that doesn't interest us. Our muscles, moved not by true feeling but by stubborn will, tense up on our faces in an unpleasant way.

For nonconformity, the world punishes you with its disapproval. So, a person must learn how to handle sour looks. Strangers might glare at you in public, or friends might look at you oddly in their living rooms. If their scorn came from genuine conviction like yours, you might go home feeling sad; but the sour looks of the crowd, like their cheerful ones, are usually shallow and change with the wind or the latest news. Even so, the discontent of the crowd can feel more intimidating than the anger of officials or scholars. It's easy for a strong person who understands the world to bear the scorn of the educated classes. Their anger is usually restrained and careful, as they are timid and vulnerable themselves. But when their controlled rage mixes with the anger of the masses, when the ignorant and the poor are stirred up, and when the raw brute force at society's bottom starts to growl and scowl, it takes great courage and deep faith to view it as a small matter.

Another fear that stops us from trusting ourselves is our need for consistency—our respect for our past words or actions, because others have no other way to judge us but by our past, and we hesitate to let them down.

But why constantly look over your shoulder? Why drag around this memory, worried you might contradict something you once said in public? If you do contradict yourself, so what? It seems wise to rely on memory as little as possible, even in acts of memory itself, to bring the past into the present for judgment and live fully in the new day. In your philosophy, you may have denied personality to God, yet if your soul feels drawn to Him, surrender to it with all your heart, even if it means picturing God with form and color. Leave behind your theory, like Joseph left his coat in the hand of the harlot, and flee.

A foolish consistency is the worry of small minds, admired by small-minded politicians, philosophers, and ministers. Consistency means nothing to a great soul. You might as well worry about shadows on the wall. Say what you think now in strong words, and tomorrow, say what you think tomorrow in equally strong words, even if it contradicts everything you said today. "Oh, you'll be misunderstood," some might say. But is it really so bad to be misunderstood? Pythagoras was misunderstood, as were Socrates, Jesus, Luther, Copernicus, Galileo, Newton, and every pure, wise spirit that ever lived. To be great is to be misunderstood.

I believe no one can act against their true nature. All their desires and whims are bound by the law of who they are, just as the peaks and valleys of mountains are minor compared to the curve of the Earth. It doesn't matter how you measure or analyze them. Character is like a pattern; read it forward, backward, or across, and it still reads the same. In this simple, humble life in the woods that God has allowed me, let me record my honest thoughts each day without looking ahead or back. I am sure they will form a harmonious pattern, even if I don't try to make it so or even see it happening. My book should smell of pine trees and echo with the sounds of insects. The swallow outside my window should weave the thread or straw he carries in his beak into my work as well. We are seen for what we are. Character teaches more than our intentions. People think they show their virtue or vice only through obvious actions, not realizing that virtue or vice radiates from them every moment.

There will be harmony in any variety of actions as long as they are honest and natural at the moment. For a single person, actions will be in harmony, even if they seem different. These differences fade when viewed from a higher perspective. One purpose unites them all. The path of the best ship is a zigzag line of many turns. Seen from afar, the line appears straight along its general direction. Your true actions will explain themselves and your other true actions. Conformity explains nothing. Act as an individual, and your past individual actions will justify you now. Greatness looks to the future. If I am firm enough today to do right and ignore opinions, then I must have done enough right before to defend myself now. No matter what happens, do the right thing now. Always disregard appearances, and you'll always be able to. Character builds up power over time. Every day of past virtue strengthens today. What fills the imagination with the greatness of heroes from the senate and battlefield? The awareness of a series of great days and past victories. These cast a united light on the one acting now. He is accompanied by an invisible host of angels. That's what gives power to Chatham's voice, dignity to Washington's stance, and vision to Adams's gaze. Honor is sacred because it isn't fleeting. It always represents ancient virtue. We admire it today because it isn't just for today. We love and honor it because it isn't meant to trap us for our love and honor, but is self-reliant and self-made, with a pure, noble lineage, even when it appears in a young person.

I hope we have seen the last of conformity and consistency in these times. Let these words be mocked from now on. Instead of a dinner gong, let us hear the call of a Spartan flute. Let's stop bowing and apologizing. A great person is coming to dine at my house. I don't want to please him; I want him to want to please me. I will stand here for humanity, and while I'd make it kind, I would also make it true. Let us stand up to the smooth mediocrity and shallow contentment of our time, and throw in the face of custom, trade, and duty the fact that is the essence of all history: that there is a great responsible Thinker and Actor working wherever a person works; a true person belongs to no time or place but stands at the center of all things. Where he is, there is nature. He measures you, all people, and all events. Most people in society remind us of others or something else. But character, reality, reminds you of nothing else; it is above all of creation. A person should be so substantial that circumstances mean nothing to them. Every true person is a cause, a nation, and an era, needing boundless spaces, people, and time to fully realize their purpose— future generations seem to follow them like a procession of loyal followers. When a Caesar is born, we get a Roman Empire for ages. When Christ is born, millions of minds grow and attach themselves to his genius, confusing him with human virtue and potential. An institution is the shadow of one person, as Monasticism is the shadow of Antony the hermit; the Reformation, of Luther; Quakerism, of Fox; Methodism, of Wesley; Abolition, of Clarkson. Milton called Scipio "the height of Rome," and all of history can be understood as the biography of a few strong and devoted individuals.

Let a person understand their own worth and keep everything else in its rightful place, under their feet. Let them not sneak around or act like a beggar, an outsider, or an unwanted guest in a world made for them. Yet the person on the street, finding nothing in themselves that feels equal to the force that built a towering structure or sculpted a marble statue, feels small when looking at these. A palace, a statue, a rare book—all have a distant, intimidating look, like a fine carriage that seems to ask, "Who are you, Sir?" But these things all belong to him, waiting for his attention, asking his abilities to awaken and take possession. The painting waits for my opinion; it doesn't command me. I am the one who judges its value. The popular story of a drunken man found on the street, taken to a duke's house, cleaned, dressed, laid in the duke's bed, and then treated with full ceremony like the duke, being assured he'd been out of his mind, owes its charm to its symbolism of humanity's condition. We, too, are in the world like this drunk, stumbling, but sometimes we wake up, think clearly, and realize our true nobility.

Our reading is humble and often sycophantic. Our imagination tricks us when we read history. Kingdoms, power, and wealth seem grander than the daily lives of ordinary John and Edward in their small homes, but the essence of life is the same for both; the total sum is the same. Why all this reverence for figures like Alfred, Scanderbeg, and Gustavus? Suppose they were virtuous; did they use up all the virtue there is? Your actions today, as a private individual, carry as much weight as the public, celebrated deeds of kings. When private people act with their own views and vision, the glory will shift from the actions of kings to those of common people.

The world has been taught by its kings, who have captured the imaginations of nations. This grand symbol—the king—taught people to respect each other. The deep loyalty with which people have let the king, the noble, or the wealthy walk among them by law, creating their own scale of value, overturning other scales, paying with honor instead of money, and embodying the law in their person, was a symbol by which they hinted, even if dimly, at their own awareness of personal rights and dignity—the rights of every person.

The attraction that original action holds over us becomes clear when we explore the reason for self-trust. Who is the Trustee? What is this original Self, on which universal reliance can be based? What is the essence of that unmeasurable, science-defying light—without angles, without elements—that shines beauty even into trivial or flawed actions if they carry a trace of independence? This search leads us to the source of it all: the force known as Spontaneity or Instinct, the essence of genius, virtue, and life. This fundamental wisdom is called Intuition, while all other teachings are just instructions. In this deep, final power—beyond which nothing else can be analyzed—all things find their common origin. For that sense of existence, which in calm hours rises mysteriously in the soul, is not separate from things, space, light, time, or humanity, but one with them, evidently arising from the same source as their life and existence. We first share in the life by which all things exist, then see them as forms in nature, forgetting that we share in their cause. Here lies the source of thought and action. Here are the lungs of the inspiration that grants humanity wisdom and cannot be denied without irreverence. We lie in the embrace of a vast intelligence, which makes us receivers of its truth and vessels of its actions. When we recognize justice or truth, we aren't doing anything by our own power but allowing a channel for its light to pass through. If we ask where this comes from, if we seek to analyze the soul that causes it, philosophy fails us. All we can affirm is its presence or absence. Each person distinguishes between their mind's voluntary actions and its involuntary perceptions, knowing that perfect faith belongs to these involuntary perceptions. They may make mistakes in expressing them, but they know these things to be as undeniable as day and night. My purposeful actions and achievements are mere wanderings—yet the smallest native feeling, the slightest natural emotion, demands my respect and attention. Thoughtless people easily dismiss perceptions as if they were opinions or random choices, because they don't understand the difference between perception and idea. They assume that I choose to see this or that. But perception is not a whim; it is bound by fate. If I see a trait, my children will see it after me, and eventually, everyone will, even if no one else has noticed it yet. For my perception of it is as real as the sun.

The soul's relationship to the divine spirit is so pure that it is profane to add anything else to it. When God speaks, it must be that He communicates everything, not just one thing; He fills the world with His voice, radiating light, nature, time, and souls from the center of present thought, renewing and recreating all. Whenever a mind is simple and receives divine wisdom, old things pass away—means, teachers, texts, temples fall; it lives now, absorbing past and future into the present moment. All things are made sacred by their connection to it—one thing as much as another. Everything is reduced to its core by its cause, and in the universal miracle, small, specific miracles vanish. Therefore, if someone claims to understand and speak of God but points you back to the language of an ancient, decaying nation in another world, do not believe them. Is the acorn superior to the oak, its fullness and completion? Is the parent better than the child into whom they have poured their mature being? Why, then, this reverence for the past? The ages conspire against the clarity and authority of the soul. Time and space are merely colors produced by the eye, but the soul is light itself; where it is, it is day; where it was, it is night; and history is nothing but an intrusion and a harm if it serves as anything more than a cheerful story of my own existence and growth.

Humanity is timid and apologetic; no longer bold, we don't dare to say, "I think" or "I am," instead quoting some saint or wise figure. We feel embarrassed before a blade of grass or a blooming rose. The roses outside my window don't refer to roses of the past or better roses somewhere else; they are simply what they are, existing with God in the present. Time means nothing to them. Each rose is perfect in every moment of its life. Before a leaf-bud bursts, its whole life is already active; when fully open, it has nothing more; when only a root without leaves, it has nothing less. Its nature is fulfilled, and it fulfills nature in every stage. But humanity delays, or dwells on memories, unable to live in the present. Instead, we look backward with regret or ignore the riches around us while trying to catch a glimpse of the future. We cannot be happy and strong until we live with nature in the present, above time.

This should be easy to understand. Yet even the strongest minds often won't hear God unless He speaks through the words of David, Jeremiah, or Paul. Someday, we won't value a few texts or certain lives so highly. We are like children repeating by memory the sentences of elders and teachers, and later, of the influential figures we meet—carefully recalling their exact words. But as we grow to see things as those people did, we understand their thoughts and are ready to let the words go. At any time, we can speak equally well when needed. If we live truthfully, we'll see truthfully. It's as easy for a strong person to be strong as it is for a weak person to be weak. When we gain new insights, we will gladly clear away old memories as if they were clutter.

When someone lives with God, their voice becomes as gentle as the sound of a stream or the rustling of corn.

And now, the highest truth on this subject remains unspoken; it probably can't be said, as all speech is just a distant echo of intuition. The thought, as best as I can express it now, is this: When goodness is near you and you have life within yourself, it doesn't arrive through any familiar path; you won't trace anyone else's footsteps; you won't see any face or hear any name—the way, the thought, the goodness will be entirely fresh and original. It excludes all examples and past experiences. You move away from humanity, not toward it. All people who have ever lived are its forgotten messengers. Both fear and hope fall beneath it. Even hope feels small in comparison. In moments of vision, there's nothing that can be called gratitude, nor exactly joy. The soul, raised above passion, perceives identity and eternal causation, sees the self-existence of Truth and Right, and settles peacefully in knowing that everything is going well. Vast distances in nature—the Atlantic Ocean, the South Sea—or long stretches of time—years, centuries—become meaningless. What I think and feel is the same force underlying all previous stages of life and experience, just as it underlies what I now call life, and what is called death.

Life itself is valuable, not just having lived. Power fades the moment we rest; it exists in the shift from past to new states, in the leap over boundaries, in aiming toward a goal. This single truth disturbs the world: the soul is always becoming; this process endlessly devalues the past, turns all wealth to poverty, all reputation to insignificance, and equalizes saints and rogues alike, brushing aside both Jesus and Judas. Why then speak of self-reliance? As long as the soul is present, there is power—not a passive confidence, but active force. Talking about "reliance" is just a weak, external way of speaking. It's better to speak of that which relies because it acts and exists. Whoever has more obedience to principle than I do will naturally hold authority over me, even without lifting a finger. I must orbit around them, drawn by the pull of spirits. We think we're just using rhetoric when we speak of high virtue. We don't yet understand that virtue is

Height, and that any person or group, open and attuned to principles, will inevitably overpower and surpass all cities, nations, kings, wealthy people, poets, who lack that openness.

This is the ultimate realization we reach on every subject: everything resolves into the ever-blessed One. Self-existence is an attribute of the Supreme Cause, marking the measure of good by its degree of presence in all lesser forms. Everything that is real holds its reality through its virtue. Commerce, farming, hunting, whaling, war, eloquence, personal influence—all these reflect its presence and imperfect action, and so they earn my respect. I see the same law working in nature for preservation and growth. Power is, in nature, the essential measure of right. Nature allows nothing to stay in her realm that cannot support itself. The formation and balance of a planet, the tree bending back from a fierce wind, the life force within every animal and plant—all demonstrate a self-sufficient, and thus self-relying, soul.

So everything converges: let us not wander; let us stay close to the source. Let us stun and awe the crowd of people, books, and institutions that intrude by a simple declaration of divine truth. Tell the intruders to remove their shoes, for God is here within us. Let our simplicity judge them, and our commitment to our own law show the poverty of nature and fortune when compared to our own inner riches.

But we have become a mob. People no longer revere each other, nor are they drawn to stay at home to connect with their internal depths; instead, they go out to beg for a mere cup of water from others. We must go alone. I prefer the quiet church before the service starts to any sermon. How distant, how cool, how pure people seem, each surrounded by a sacred space! So let us always sit. Why should I take on the flaws of my friends, family, or children just because we share a home or blood? All people are my kin, and I am kin to all. But for that, I won't adopt their impatience or foolishness, nor will I feel ashamed for it. However, your solitude must not be mechanical but spiritual; it must be uplifted. Sometimes, the whole world seems to conspire to load you with petty concerns. Friends, clients, children, sickness, fear, need, charity—all knock at once, saying, "Come out to us." But keep your state; don't join their confusion. The power others have to disturb us is one we give them through weak curiosity. No one can come close to me except through my own actions. "What we love, we have, but through desire, we deprive ourselves of love."

If we can't immediately rise to the sanctities of obedience and faith, then let us at least resist temptations; let us declare a state of battle and awaken Thor and Woden—courage and determination—in our Saxon hearts. In our calm times, this is done by speaking the truth. End false hospitality and affection. Stop living to fulfill the expectations of these deceived and deceiving people we associate with. Say to them, "O father, O mother, O wife, O brother, O friend, I have lived with you by appearances until now. From now on, I belong to truth." Let it be known that henceforth, I obey no law lesser than the eternal law. I will not make promises, only stand nearby. I will aim to support my parents, provide for my family, and be the faithful husband of one wife, but I must fulfill these relationships in a fresh, unprecedented way. I defy your customs. I must be myself. I can no longer break myself for anyone. If you can love me for who I am, we will be happier. If not, I will still work to deserve your respect. I won't hide my preferences or dislikes. I will trust that what is deep is sacred, doing openly under the sun and moon what satisfies my heart and inner calling. If you are noble, I will love you; if not, I will neither harm you nor deceive myself with false attention. If you are true but not in the same truth as I, stay with your companions; I will seek mine. I do this not selfishly, but sincerely and truthfully. It is in the interest of you, me, and everyone, after living in untruths for so long, to live in truth. Does this sound harsh today? Soon you will love what your nature and mine require, and if we follow truth, it will lead us safely in the end.

But in doing this, you may cause your friends pain. Yes, but I cannot sell my freedom and strength just to protect their feelings. Besides, everyone has moments of reason when they look into the realm of absolute truth; then they will justify my actions and may even do the same themselves.

The masses believe that rejecting popular standards means rejecting all standards, mere lawlessness, and that a bold sensualist uses philosophy's name to excuse his wrongs. But the law of conscience remains. There are two places where we must account for ourselves, and we will confess in one or the other. You may fulfill your obligations by clearing yourself according to the direct or indirect way. Consider whether you have met your duties to your father, mother, cousin, neighbor, town, cat, and dog; whether any of these can find fault with you. But I may also ignore this indirect standard and absolve myself. I have my own stern obligations, my own complete inner circle. It denies the name of duty to many tasks that are usually thought of as duties. But if I can meet its demands, it lets me disregard the common code. If anyone thinks this inner law is easy, let them try obeying it for a single day.

Indeed, it requires something godlike in a person to throw off society's ordinary motives and dare to trust themselves as their own guide. Let their heart be high, their will firm, their vision clear, so that they can sincerely be their own doctrine, their own society, and their own law, where a simple purpose feels as binding as iron to others.

Anyone looking at the current state of what we call society can see the need for these ethics. Humanity's strength and spirit seem to be drained out, leaving us fearful, complaining, and timid. We're afraid of truth, fate, death, and each other. Our age doesn't produce great, complete individuals. We need people who can renew life and society, yet most are unable to meet even their own needs, harboring ambition far beyond their abilities, while constantly asking for support. Our way of life is poor, our arts, trades, marriages, and religion are chosen not by us, but by society. We are mere parlor soldiers. We avoid the tough battles of life, where true strength is born.

If young people fail in their first attempts, they lose hope. If a young merchant fails, they say he's ruined. If the brightest mind graduates from one of our colleges but doesn't secure a position in a city within a year, friends and even they themselves feel justified in feeling defeated and resigned. But a sturdy young man from New Hampshire or Vermont, who tries every profession in turn—driving a team, farming, selling goods, teaching, preaching, editing a paper, entering Congress, buying land, and so on, year after year, always landing on his feet like a cat—is worth a hundred of these city-bred ornaments. He moves through his days with pride, not embarrassed that he hasn't "studied a profession," because he isn't postponing his life; he's already living it. He has not one chance, but a hundred. Let a Stoic come forward to reveal humanity's potential and tell people that they are not weak, clinging vines, but can and must stand on their own; that with self-trust, new abilities will emerge; that each person is a living word, meant to uplift nations, that they should be ashamed of our pity, and that once they act from within, throwing away rules, books, idols, and traditions, we pity them no longer, but admire and respect them. Such a teacher would restore life's splendor to humanity and make their name beloved in history.

It's clear that greater self-reliance would bring about a revolution in all of life's roles and relationships—in people's religion, education, work, ways of living, associations, property, and even their philosophies.

What prayers people indulge in! What they call a holy act is neither brave nor strong. Prayer turns outward, asking for some external addition or foreign virtue, losing itself in endless complexities of the natural and supernatural, mediatorial, and miraculous. Prayer that begs for a specific benefit—anything less than all goodness—is flawed. True prayer is contemplating life's facts from the highest viewpoint. It is the monologue of a watching, rejoicing soul. It is the spirit of God announcing His works as good. But using prayer as a way to get a private benefit is mean and dishonest. It assumes dualism, not the unity of nature and consciousness. When a person is truly one with God, they will no longer beg. They will then see prayer in every action. The farmer's prayer is in kneeling to weed his field; the rower's prayer is in each pull of the oar. These are true prayers heard by nature, even if they are for simple purposes. In Fletcher's *Bonduca*, Caratach, when advised to seek guidance from the god Audate, replies,—

"His hidden meaning lies in our efforts; our courage is our best god."

Another type of false prayer is regret. Discontent reflects a lack of self-reliance; it is a weakness of will. Regret calamities if you can help those who suffer; if not, focus on your work, and already the harm begins to mend. Our sympathy is just as flawed. We approach those who mourn senselessly and sit down to cry with them, instead of offering truth and health like a shock of energy that would reconnect them to reason. The secret of good fortune is joy in our own hands. The self-reliant person is always welcome among both gods and people. For him, every door opens: all tongues greet him, all honors are given, and all eyes follow him with admiration. We love him because he does not need our love. We carefully and humbly celebrate him because he stayed true to himself and disregarded our disapproval. The gods love him because people resented him. "To the persevering mortal," said Zoroaster, "the blessed Immortals are swift."

Just as people's prayers show weakness of will, so do their beliefs show weakness of mind. They echo the foolish words of the Israelites, "Let not God speak to us, lest we die. Speak thou, any man, and we will obey." Everywhere I am prevented from meeting God in my brother because he has closed his own temple doors, repeating only what he learned from his brother's or his ancestors' God. Every original mind brings a new perspective. If it proves a mind of rare energy and depth—a Locke, a Lavoisier, a Hutton, a Bentham, a Fourier—it imposes its classification on others, creating a new system. The greater the depth of thought and the number of insights it reaches, the more satisfaction it brings to those who learn from it. This satisfaction is most evident in religious creeds and doctrines, classifications created by some powerful mind interpreting basic truths about duty and humanity's relationship to the Highest. Such are

Calvinism, Quakerism, and Swedenborgianism. The learner finds joy in fitting everything into the new language, like a girl who has just learned botany, discovering a new world of plants and seasons. For a time, the learner feels empowered by studying the mind of their master. But in all unbalanced minds, the classification becomes an idol, seen as the goal rather than a limited tool, so that the system's walls appear to merge with the universe itself; the stars seem hung on the arch their teacher built. They cannot imagine how outsiders could see anything else—"You must have somehow stolen this light from us." They do not yet realize that untamed, uncontainable light will enter any home, even their own. Let them chirp for a while and call the light their own. If they are honest and work well, their tidy enclosure will soon prove too narrow and low; it will crack, lean, rot, and fade, while the immortal light, forever young and joyful, will shine with endless colors across the universe, as it did on the first morning.

The obsession with travel, with places like Italy, England, and Egypt as its idols, still captivates educated Americans, likely because they lack a true sense of self. The people who made England, Italy, or Greece legendary in our minds did so by staying rooted in one place, like an anchor of the earth. In moments of strength, we understand that duty is where we belong. The soul is not meant to wander; the wise person stays home, and even when duty or necessity calls them to other lands, they still carry home within them. They show, by their demeanor, that they travel as someone in control, not as a mere visitor or servant.

I have no problem with going around the world for art, study, or kindness, as long as the person remains grounded and isn't looking for something beyond what they already know. Someone who travels for fun or to find something they're missing only moves further away from themselves, growing old even in youth among things that are already old. In Thebes, in Palmyra, their will and mind become as ancient and worn-out as the ruins they see. They bring ruins to ruins.

Traveling is an illusion. Our first trips show us how indifferent places are to us. At home, I imagine being overwhelmed by beauty in Naples, in Rome, leaving behind my sadness. I pack my things, say goodbye to my friends, set out, and finally arrive in Naples, only to face the same unchanging truth: the same self, still the same, the one I tried to escape. I visit the Vatican and the grand palaces. I pretend to be thrilled by the sights and the ideas they inspire, but deep down, I am not. My burden, my giant, follows me wherever I go.

The urge to travel points to a deeper restlessness of the mind. Our intellect tends to wander, and our education encourages this restlessness. Our minds roam even when our bodies stay at home. We imitate, and isn't imitation just mental travel? Our homes show foreign influences; our shelves hold decorations from distant lands; our views, tastes, and skills lean toward what's far away and long ago. The soul inspired art wherever it blossomed. Artists found their models in their own minds, applying their thoughts to the task at hand. Why must we copy the Doric or Gothic style? Beauty, practicality, depth of thought, and expression are just as available to us as to anyone else, and if the American artist works with hope and dedication, taking into account the climate, the land, the hours of sunlight, the needs of the people, and the form of government, they will create a building that fits all of these, satisfying both taste and feeling.

Rely on yourself; never imitate. Your unique talent comes with the power of a lifetime's growth, but when you adopt someone else's skills, you only gain a temporary, limited ability. What each of us does best, only our Creator can teach us. No one knows what that is, nor can know, until it's shown. Who could have taught Shakespeare? Who could have guided Franklin, or Washington, or Bacon, or Newton? Every great person is unique. What made Scipio special was exactly what he couldn't borrow. Shakespeare won't be created by studying Shakespeare. Do the work assigned to you, and you can dream and strive as much as you wish. There is a bold and noble expression meant for you, different from the mighty chisel of Phidias, the bricks of the Egyptians, the pen of Moses, or Dante, yet distinct from all of these. The soul, rich and expressive with its many voices, won't repeat itself; but if you listen to what these ancient voices say, you can respond in that same spirit, for listening and speaking are two sides of the same nature. Stay true to your simple, honorable place, follow your heart, and you will create a new world.

Just as our religion, education, and art look outward, so does our social nature. Everyone takes pride in society's progress, yet no one personally improves.

Society never truly moves forward. It loses on one side as quickly as it gains on the other. It constantly changes; it can be barbaric, civilized, Christian, wealthy, scientific—but change is not the same as improvement. With every gain, something is lost. Society acquires new skills but loses old instincts. Compare the well-dressed, literate, thoughtful American with a watch, pencil, and bank notes in his pocket to the naked New Zealander, whose possessions are a club, a spear, a mat, and a shared piece of a shelter. But if you compare their health, you'll see that the modern man has lost his original strength. An honest traveler would notice that a deep wound on the native would heal in days, like soft pitch, while the same injury would kill the modern man.

The modern person has made a coach but lost the use of his feet. He relies on crutches but lacks the support of his own muscles. He has an expensive Geneva watch but can't tell time by the sun. He trusts a nautical almanac from Greenwich to give him information, yet he doesn't recognize a single star in the sky. He knows nothing of the solstice or the equinox, and the entire brilliant calendar of the year is empty in his mind. His notebooks weaken his memory; his libraries overwhelm his wisdom; the insurance office actually leads to more accidents. We might even wonder if machinery doesn't hold us back, if we've lost strength through comfort, the energy of untamed virtue through organized Christianity. For in ancient times, every Stoic truly lived as a Stoic; but in Christian society, where is the Christian?

There is no more variation in moral character than in height or size. No greater people exist today than in the past. There is a certain equality between the great individuals of early times and those of today; not even all the science, art, religion, and philosophy of the nineteenth century can create greater people than the heroes of Plutarch, who lived twenty-four centuries ago. Human progress is not bound to time. Phocion, Socrates, Anaxagoras, and Diogenes were remarkable individuals, but they left no group in their likeness. A person who belongs in their class would not be called by their name but would be entirely their own, becoming a founder of their own group in time. The arts and inventions of each age are like costumes; they don't make people stronger. The harm of advanced machinery may even outweigh its benefits. Hudson and Bering performed remarkable feats in simple fishing boats, surprising Parry and Franklin, whose equipment used the full resources of science and art. With just a simple opera glass, Galileo discovered more wonders in the sky than anyone else. Columbus found the New World in a small, open boat. It's strange to see how tools and machines that were once celebrated gradually fall out of use and decay. The true genius returns to the basics of humanity. We once thought improvements in warfare were among the triumphs of science, yet Napoleon conquered Europe with little more than camps and sheer courage, shedding unnecessary aids. The Emperor believed, as Las Casas reports, that a perfect army would be impossible "without getting rid of weapons, supply depots, and transport, until soldiers, like the Romans, received grain, ground it by hand, and baked bread themselves."

Society is like a wave. The wave moves forward, but the water making it up does not. The same particle doesn't rise from the valley to the crest. Its unity is just an illusion. Today's people of a nation will die within a year, and their experiences vanish with them.

In this way, reliance on property—including governments that protect it—comes from a lack of self-reliance. People have focused on possessions for so long that they have come to view religious, educational, and civil institutions as guardians of property, fearing attacks on them as attacks on property itself. They measure worth by what they have, not by what they are. But a person who cultivates themselves grows ashamed of mere property, finding worth in their own nature. They especially dislike what is accidental—inherited, given as a gift, or even wrongly gained; then they feel it's not truly theirs, just something lying there because no revolution or thief has taken it yet. What a person really is always draws what they need, a living possession beyond the reach of governments, mobs, revolutions, fires, storms, or bankruptcies, constantly renewing wherever they are. "Your share in life," said Caliph Ali, "will come to you, so stop seeking it." Our dependence on foreign goods leads to a blind respect for numbers. Political parties gather in conventions; the larger the crowd, and with each new announcement, "The delegation from Essex! The Democrats from New Hampshire! The Whigs of Maine!" the young patriot feels encouraged by the support of a thousand eyes and hands. Likewise, reformers gather conventions, taking votes and making decisions as a crowd. But that is not the way, friends! The divine presence will enter and reside within you only by the opposite approach. Only as a person lets go of outside support and stands alone do I see them grow strong and successful. Each new follower weakens them. Isn't one person worth more than a town? Expect nothing from others, and while everything around you changes, you, the one firm pillar, will support all that surrounds you. One who knows their inner strength, who weakens from searching for good outside themselves, who throws themselves without hesitation onto their own thoughts, immediately finds balance, stands tall, controls their actions, and works wonders; just as a person standing on their own two feet is stronger than one trying to balance on their head.

Therefore, make use of all that's called Fortune. Most people take chances with her, gaining and losing as her wheel spins. But consider those gains as undeserved, and instead rely on Cause and Effect, the laws of God. Work and achieve in line with your Will, and you chain the wheel of Chance, freeing yourself from its spins. A political victory, a raise in rent, someone recovering from illness, the return of a friend, or any other fortunate event lifts your spirits, and you think good times are on the way. Don't believe it. Nothing can bring you peace but yourself. Nothing can bring you peace but the victory of your own principles.

On the Shortness of Life

Seneca

On The Shortness of Life

A person is indeed truly lazy and careless, my dear Lucilius, if he only remembers a friend when he sees a place that reminds him of that friend. But sometimes, familiar places bring back a feeling of loss that we've kept hidden inside. They don't just bring back dead memories but wake them up from where they've been sleeping, like how seeing a lost friend's favorite slave, cloak, or house can renew the sadness, even if time has made it softer.

Now, look at Campania, especially Naples and your beloved Pompeii. When I saw them, they made me miss you a lot. I can picture you clearly in my mind, like I'm about to say goodbye to you. I see you trying hard to hold back your tears but not being able to stop the emotions that rise up just when you try to control them. It feels like I lost you just a moment ago because, when we use our memory, everything feels like it happened just a short while ago.

It seems like just a moment ago that I was a young boy sitting in the philosopher Sotion's school, just a moment ago that I started working as a lawyer, just a moment ago that I lost the desire to practice law, and just a moment ago that I lost the ability to do it. Time flies incredibly fast, especially when we look back at it. When we're focused on what's happening now, we don't notice how fast time is passing because it moves so gently and quickly.

Do you wonder why? All the time that has passed is in the same place; it all looks the same to us, like it's all mixed together. Everything slips into the same emptiness. Also, something that is so short can't have long periods within it. The time we spend living is just a tiny point, or even smaller than a point. But this tiny bit of time, short as it is, nature has tricked us into thinking it's longer than it really is. She has divided it into parts like infancy, childhood, youth, the gradual slope from youth to old age, and old age itself is yet another part. How many steps there are for such a short climb!

It feels like just a moment ago that I saw you off on your journey, and yet this "moment ago" makes up a good part of our existence. This existence is so brief that we should remember it will soon end altogether. In other years, time didn't seem to go by so quickly; now, it seems to fly by faster than I can believe, maybe because I feel that the end is getting closer, or maybe because I've started to notice and count my losses.

For this reason, I'm even more upset that some people spend most of this short time on things that don't matter—time that, no matter how carefully we protect it, isn't enough even for the important things. Cicero said that even if he had twice as many days to live, he wouldn't have time to read the lyric poets. You could say the same thing about people who study complicated arguments, but they are foolish in a sadder way. The lyric poets admit that they are writing for fun, but these people think they're doing something serious.

I'm not saying you shouldn't look at these complex arguments, but you should only glance at them, like saying a quick hello at the door, just to avoid being tricked into thinking they're really valuable. Why stress yourself out and lose weight over some problem that it's smarter to ignore than to solve? When a soldier is relaxed and traveling at his own pace, he can stop to look at small things along the way, but when the enemy is close behind and the order is given to speed up, he has to throw away everything he picked up during peaceful times.

I don't have time to figure out the tricky details of words or to show off how clever I am with them. Look at the enemy gathering, the gates locked tight, and weapons ready for battle. I need a strong heart to listen to this noise of battle all around me without flinching.

Everyone would rightly think I was crazy if, while the older men and women were piling up rocks for the walls, and the young men in armor inside the gates were waiting or even asking for the order to attack, and the enemy's spears were shaking our gates, and the ground was trembling with mines and tunnels, I sat there doing nothing, asking silly questions like, "What you haven't lost, you still have. But you haven't lost any horns. So, you must have horns," or other nonsense like that.

And yet, you might think I'm just as crazy if I spend my energy on that kind of thing, because even now, I'm under siege. But in the first case, the danger would only be from the outside, with a wall between me and the enemy; but now, the danger of death is right here with me. I don't have time for such foolishness; I have a big task ahead of me. What should I do? Death is close behind me, and life is slipping away.

Teach me something to help me face these troubles. Help me stop trying to run away from death, and help me stop letting life slip through my fingers.

Give me the courage to face hardships; make me calm in the face of what I can't avoid. Help me make the most of the short time I have. Show me that the value of life doesn't depend on how long it is, but on how well I use it. Also, show me that it's possible, or even common, for someone who has lived a long life to have actually lived very little. Tell me when I lie down to sleep, "You might not wake up again!" And when I wake up, "You might not go to sleep again!" Tell me when I leave my house, "You might not come back!" And when I come back, "You might not leave again!"

You're wrong if you think that there's only a thin line between life and death on a sea voyage. No, that line is just as thin everywhere. It's just that we don't always see death so close by, but he's always just as near.

Take away these shadowy fears, and then it will be easier for you to teach me the lessons I'm ready to learn. When we were born, nature made us capable of learning, and she gave us reason, not perfect, but capable of being perfected.

Teach me about justice, duty, self-discipline, and the two types of purity—one that keeps us from harming others and one that keeps us true to ourselves. If you don't lead me down the wrong paths, I'll reach my goal more easily. As the tragic poet says: "The language of truth is simple." So we shouldn't make that language complicated; nothing is less suitable for a person with great goals than tricky cleverness. Farewell.

The End

Thank You for Reading

Dear Reader,

We hope this timeless classic has sparked your imagination and enriched your literary journey. Now that you've turned the final page, we want to share a vision for the future of reading—one where every classic you've ever wanted to explore is at your fingertips, in a format that best suits your life.

We'd like to invite you to gain immediate, unlimited digital & audiobook access to hundreds of the most treasured literary classics ever written—along with the option to secure deluxe paperback, hardcover & box set editions at printing cost. Together, we can spark a new global literary renaissance alongside our small, independent publishing house called "The Library of Alexandria."

Thousands of years ago, the Library of Alexandria stood as a beacon of knowledge—until it was lost to history. We aim to reignite that spirit of preservation and discovery right now, in the modern age— only this time, it's accessible to all, in every language and every format.

Picture a world where every timeless classic, novel, poem, or philosophical treatise is not only available to read but also updated for today's readers—modernized, translated into any language or dialect, and ready to enjoy in any format you choose, whether that is in an eBook, audiobook, paperback, or deluxe hardcover & box set version a printing cost.

By joining our movement to rebuild the modern Library of Alexandria, you become part of an unprecedented mission to offer:

- **Unlimited Audiobook & eBook Access to the Greatest Classics of All Time**

  Instantly explore thousands of legendary works, from Plato and Shakespeare to Jane Austen and Leo Tolstoy. All are instantly ready to read or listen to, giving you a complete literary universe at your fingertips.

- **Paperback & Deluxe Editions at Printing Costs:**

Purchase any title in a paperback, deluxe hardbound, or deluxe boxset edition at printing costs, shipped right to your doorstep. Curate your personal library of Alexandria with editions worthy of display—crafted to last, designed to captivate, and delivered straight to your door.

- **Modern translations for Contemporary Readers in all languages and dialects**

Discover a vast selection of classics reimagined in clear, current language—no more struggling with outdated phrases or obscure references. Next to the original versions, we aim to offer translations in as many languages and dialects as possible.

As we continue our translation efforts and add new languages, readers everywhere can connect with these works as if they were written today. By bridging linguistic divides, you're contributing to ensuring that these timeless stories become more meaningful, accessible, and inspiring for people across the globe.

- **Your Personal Library of Alexandria:**

Over the months and years, you'll curate a unique physical archive of classics—each volume a testament to your taste, curiosity, and love of knowledge. It's not just about owning books—it's about curating a cultural legacy you'll cherish and pass down for generations to come.

- **Join a Global Literary Renaissance:**

Your support fuels an ongoing mission: allowing us to reinvest in offering deluxe print editions (including special boxsets) at their true cost, broaden the range of available formats and translations, and extend the reach of these works to new audiences worldwide. By joining today, you're not just preserving a legacy of masterpieces; you set in motion a powerful wave of literary accessibility.

We are more than a publisher—we're a movement, and we can't do it alone. Your support lets us scale our mission, preserving and reimagining history's greatest works for tomorrow's readers.

Become a Torchbearer of knowledge.

Thank you for picking up this book and allowing us into your literary journey. As you turn the pages, know that you're part of something larger: a global effort to keep these stories alive, share their wisdom across borders and generations, and spark a true cultural revival for the modern era.

If this resonates with you—please consider taking the next step by visiting:

www.libraryofalexandria.com

With gratitude and a shared love of knowledge,

The Modern Library of Alexandria Team

Visit:

www.libraryofalexandria.com

Or scan the code below:

www.ingramcontent.com/pod-product-compliance
Lightning Source LLC
Chambersburg PA
CBHW011652010726
47499CB00010B/3232